SHADOW OF PASSION

"If you wish to go, Brianna, I will not stand in your way." Seth's words were certain. If he cared for Brianna at all, she thought, he would have insisted that she stay.

"You don't care, do you?" Brianna asked, fury growing within her.

"I did not say that, Brianna. I said I would not stand in your way," he corrected, his hand reaching out to caress her cheek. And then he lowered his head to seek her tempting lips with his own. And all at once, Brianna's anger was replaced with yearning. When Seth's strong arms encircled Brianna, a soft moan escaped her lips. All of her solemn vows to keep Seth at a safe distance and to refuse his caresses vanished among the night's shadows, and she found herself wanting Seth. But more than that, she wanted him to desire *her,* to possess her—if only for this night.

ROMANCE
From the Civil War to the Wild West

REBEL PLEASURE (1672, $3.95)
by Mary Martin
Union agent Jason Woods knew Christina was a brazen flirt, but his dangerous mission had no room for a clinging vixen. Then he caressed every luscious contour of her body and realized he could never go too far with this confederate tigress.

SAVAGE TORMENT (1739, $3.95)
by Cassie Edwards
Judith should have been afraid of the red-skinned warrior, but those fears turned to desire as her blue eyes travelled upward to meet his. She had found her destiny—bound by his forbidden kiss.

FORBIDDEN EMBRACE (1639, $3.95)
by Cassie Edwards
She was a Yankee nurse, and he was a Confederate soldier; yet it felt so right to be in each other's arms. Today Wesley would savor Serena's sweetness because tomorrow he had to be gone with only the memory of their FORBIDDEN EMBRACE.

PASSION'S VIXEN (1759, $3.95)
by Carol Finch
When Melissa ran away into the mountains, her father paid the handsome woodsman, Zack Beaugener, to find her. Succumbing to her captor's caresses, she prayed he would not betray her love.

WILDFIRE (1737, $3.95)
by Carol Finch
If it meant following him all the way across the wilderness, Alexa had to satisfy the sensual agony Keane ignited in her soul. He was a devilish rogue who brought her to WILD-FIRE.

Available wherever paperbacks are sold, or order direct from the Publisher. Send cover price plus 50¢ per copy for mailing and handling to Zebra Books, Dept. 0105, 475 Park Avenue South, New York, N.Y. 10016. DO NOT SEND CASH.

Endless Passion

BY
CAROL FINCH

ZEBRA BOOKS
KENSINGTON PUBLISHING CORP.

ZEBRA BOOKS

are published by

KENSINGTON PUBLISHING CORP.
475 Park Avenue South
New York, N.Y. 10016

Fourth printing: July 1986

Printed in the United States of America

To my husband, Ed

Love is not standing apart, gazing at each other, but rather walking together, hand in hand, facing new horizons.

Bristol, England
1784

Chapter One

A look of boredom tugging at her exquisite features, Brianna Talbert sat quietly beside William Fairchild. Brianna's golden eyes had glazed over as she put her mind to some pleasant thought that would help her endure the presence of her gentleman companion. William continued to brag about his management of his father's shipping company, and Brianna had closed her ears and mind to all that he had said since they had left the theater.

"What do you think of the idea, Brianna?" Fairchild questioned as he glanced sideways at her.

His inquisition filtered into her thoughts when she noticed the slight inflection in his otherwise monotonous voice. She gazed absently from the carriage window to the fair-haired man who awaited her reply. Her dark brows arched faintly, but her expression still held a hint of disinterest.

Fairchild cast her a disappointed frown. "You didn't hear a word I said, did you?"

"Nay, William, not a word. Now please take me home. I'm not feeling well at all," she muttered as she squirmed restlessly on the seat.

In truth she was sick of keeping Fairchild's company. She had done so only at her father's stern request. Lord Gerald Talbert had insisted that she accept another of William's offers to escort her out for the evening. Although Brianna had enjoyed the play, the time she spent alone with William was agony, pure and simple.

For his part, William could stand no more of his monkish behavior; he was aching for Brianna. All of his chatter had been his attempt to take his mind from the bewitching beauty who sat beside him. Suddenly, before Brianna knew what he was about, William clutched her to him. His lips swooped down on hers, bruising her mouth with his eagerness. With an indignant shriek, Brianna shoved him away, soundly slapped his face, and climbed from the carriage. She dashed across the street while William stumbled from the coach in his haste to pursue her.

Squinting into the darkness, she ran along the cobblestones, hearing William's footsteps behind her. When she spied two coaches waiting on the opposite side of the street, she scrambled inside the one closest to her and curled up in the corner on the floor, gasping for breath.

Seth grabbed for his pistol before taking time to appraise the petite bundle of silk and petticoats that had invaded his coach. A curious smile grazed his lips as he watched the lass put her index finger to her lips, requesting his silence. Seth tucked the flintlock in his coat and eased back in his seat, casually crossing his arms on his chest while he surveyed his uninvited guest.

William hurried past the carriage and then walked back to glance inside. A large figure of a man dressed in a black topcoat stared back at him.

"Excuse me, sir. Did you happen to see a young woman run past here?" he questioned, producing a polite smile.

Brianna did not move a muscle, her eyes silently pleading with the raven-haired gentleman who sat above her.

"I heard someone run past my carriage, but I could

10

not swear that it was a woman. I was too preoccupied in thought to notice." Seth's rich, husky voice was laced with indifference. He produced a cheroot from his vest pocket and dismissed the nobleman by glancing out the opposite window.

William heaved a despairing sigh as his eyes swept the crowded boardwalk. It seemed Brianna had vanished into thin air. He had not handled himself well at all, but she was so damned tempting that he had been unable to contain himself. Each time they had been together, Brianna had shown no more than mild interest in him. He had become impatient with portraying the gentleman. He had yearned to kiss her soft lips while she had become more stand-offish and aloof when they were alone. Each time he tried to display his affection, she would accept no more than a fleeting good-night kiss.

Brianna's reputation was often the topic of conversation among the men at the club. None had ever been able to get anywhere with the tempting beauty with eyes the color of the sun and hair the color of midnight. With her wealth and stunning looks, she was one of the most sought after young women in Bristol. Yet she had never shown much interest in any of the long line of suitors who requested audiences with her. Brianna was wary of them all, and William had been elated when she had accepted his marriage proposal two months earlier. He had become the envy of many of his friends who were left to wonder what qualities he possessed that had caught the interest of Brianna Talbert.

With a hopeless shrug, William stepped back into his coach and slammed the door behind him. One mistake with Brianna had cost him a fortune and had dashed all of his arousing thoughts. There would be no apology for his behavior. He was well aware that when Brianna cast one of her beaux aside, he could never redeem himself. The saucy lass would snub him as she had all of the others who had fallen from her good graces. He didn't have a snowball's chance in hell of making amends. It was over, and he had lost.

Brianna breathed a relieved sigh that sent her full breasts pressing against the restraining bodice of her blue silk gown. Seth swallowed air as he gazed down at the dark beauty who was huddled on the floor. He was mesmerized by the mysterious woman who had intruded into his carriage and his thoughts.

Attempting to mask his lusty gaze, he lit his cigar, illuminating the exquisite face of the lass who edged up on the seat beside him. Her features were flawless, her complexion so soft and creamy that it begged to be touched. She was like a goddess who had appeared in the night, a gem wrapped in a package of silk. Another arousing thought skipped across his mind, wondering what else lay beneath the layers of petticoats.

"And just what was that all about?" Seth inquired as his emerald eyes made another deliberate sweep of her figure.

Brianna eyed him warily, reminded of a wolf who waited for the opportune moment to spring on his prey. Her hand moved toward the door latch, in case she found it necessary to make another hasty departure.

"That man was no gentleman. I decided to escape before I was abused," she explained, hoping to imply that she did not expect the same behavior from the stranger with whom she now shared a coach.

A low rumble erupted from Seth's massive chest as he regarded Brianna with mild amusement. "If you are not woman enough to keep company with your eager, hot-blooded swain, perhaps you should have stayed at home," he suggested, his tone carrying a hint of mockery.

Her eyes flared indignantly as she sliced Seth a cold

glare. "I am quite capable of taking care of myself. If men weren't such love-starved creatures I wouldn't be forced to flee from them."

Seth puffed on his cheroot, seemingly indifferent to her harsh generalization. "And I suppose that you expect me to believe that you did nothing to encourage him." He sent her a side-long glance as the smoke curled around his head like a misty halo.

"Men do not have to be encouraged. They have only one thing on their narrow minds. If a woman even looks at a man, he is quick to fantasize that the innocent glance was an invitation to take privileges with her," Brianna defended, her chin tilting to a proud angle. "I see no reason why I should have to take the blame for being mauled."

His eyes made a critical sweep of Brianna's shapely form and then slowly returned to her face. "If you do not wish to spur a man's interest, don't tempt and entice him. I suggest that the next time you venture out among us heathens you take care to wear a high-collared gown that does not display every alluring curve and swell you possess. The daring gown of silk that you are wearing now, plays havoc with the imagination." His eyes lingered on her breasts before sliding to her waist, making Brianna feel as though she was not wearing a stitch of clothes. "Perhaps you are one of those vixens who enjoys taunting her suitors and thrives on protesting that she has been unjustly abused," Seth concluded with an insulting smirk.

Brianna gasped at his remark. "I escaped from one lecherous fop to find myself in the company of the most inconsiderate, callous, annoying excuse for a man that I have yet to meet. You, sir, are another example of the masculine sex! You could never be described as a gentleman."

Before flinging open the door, Brianna shot him a

reproachful glare, making certain the rake could read the disgust in her eyes. His arm snaked out to grab her, detaining her from her escape.

"And you, little Miss High-and-Mighty, should be home in bed, tucked safely away. I cannot imagine why your beau would even attempt to steal a kiss or a caress from such a fire-breathing witch. The poor man must have had bats in his belfry. No sane man would want to come near you." His harsh tone slashed across Brianna's pride like a sharp-edged saber.

Damn him! Who did he think he was? God himself? What right did he have to sit in judgment of her behavior? He didn't even know her! When she squirmed for release, Seth's grip tightened, refusing to allow her to flee. Smoldering amber eyes locked with the icy green pools that sent a chill down her spine. The fist of her right hand doubled up and then landed squarely on his jaw.

Seth, who never saw the coming attack and would never have believed it even if he had seen it, was soundly jarred by the well-aimed blow. Before the stars had faded from his blurred vision, the golden-eyed hellcat was gone. Seth sat alone in the darkness, just as he had before the wench had clambered into his coach to interrupt his silent reverie.

As he rubbed his throbbing cheek, a faint smile caught one corner of his mouth. At first he had deemed her to be a dark angel who could catch and hold a man spellbound. But nay, she was no angel, he thought to himself. She was a witch who could fight like a sailor. If he had received a blow like that for merely spurring her anger, he could well imagine what type of assault the wench would launch if a man was foolish enough to try to capture her in his arms. Seth had had his share of women, but never had he met the likes of this hot-tempered spitfire.

As he stepped from his coach a chuckle escaped his lips and floated through the darkness. At least Lenora would be awaiting him with open arms instead of a doubled fist, he mused as he took the steps two at a time to reach Lenora's apartment.

He was met with a willing smile from the woman who wore a sheer gown that left little to the imagination. Although his senses were filled with the tempting sight and the sweet fragrance of Lenora, another woman kept creeping into his thoughts, bringing a hint of a smile to his lips.

Chapter Two

"Grant!" Gerald Talbert beamed happily as his son came through the front door of the mansion. His smile quickly faded as he noted Grant's sober countenance.

"Hello, Father," he murmured in quiet greeting as he hung his hat on the hall tree and heaved a melancholy sigh.

Gerald followed Grant into the sitting room and requested that one of the servants bring them tea. As Grant sank down on the sofa, his spirits plunged with him. What a fool he had been! Caroline had used him, played with his emotions, pitted him against the Duke of Bourdoin to gain what she had wanted from the very beginning. She had never really cared for him. It was only a ploy to make the duke take note and become jealous. That conniving little bitch! She had laughed in his face while she flaunted her huge diamond engagement ring before him. Never again would he fall prey to any wench. He would never trust another woman ever again. From now on he would be in command, using each and every one of them for his own purposes. His heart would never be a part of any bargain. *Damn that woman! Damn the whole lot of them!*

"I've signed on as a crewman with the *Mesmer*," Grant stated flatly.

Gerald's jaw sagged in bewilderment. "Why the devil would you do that?" he gasped. Grant's announcement had come from out of the blue and Gerald had not been prepared for it.

"I need to get away for a while, to do some thinking. I'm tired of the life your wealth offers. I want to fend for myself." They were lame excuses. The truth was Grant didn't want to walk on the same ground that Caroline had trod, even if she was still in London. The greater the distance between them, the happier he'd be.

"But why?" A perplexed frown furrowed Gerald's brow. "What has happened to cause you to make such a rash decision?"

A long, strained moment passed while the servant set the tea tray in front of them, allowing Grant to gather his thoughts before making his reply.

"Caroline and I will not be married. I have decided to see the world before I settle down. I need time to get my bearings. I'll only be gone about six months," Grant assured him calmly, although his insides were twisting and churning with anger and frustration.

Gerald dropped his head and frowned thoughtfully. Grant was twenty-six years old and capable of managing his own life. Perhaps he was right. Maybe he did need to fend for himself. Gerald hated to see him go, but he knew that his son was in need of some soul-searching.

"Very well, Grant," he conceded quietly. "I won't try to persuade you to stay. I can see that you have made your decision. You have a good mind for business. You always have. I hope you will be ready to take control of the factory when you return. Our interests are wide-spread and I have no desire to continue running myself ragged between here and London. When you return, I hope you will consider relieving me of managing the factory."

Grant glanced at his father and then averted his gaze. At the moment he never wanted to set foot in London again. Perhaps when he returned to England he would have put the events of the last few days in proper perspective and could face Caroline without wanting to strangle her for her deceitfulness.

"We can discuss that when I return," Grant replied wearily. "I'm going to my room for a bath. I made the trip back from London in half the time it took me to travel there." He rose to full stature and walked to the door before bidding his father a quiet good night.

Gerald listened to the footsteps fade and then heaved a heavy sigh. Grant had suffered a great deal at Caroline's expense. She had led him on a merry chase and had gotten the best of him; Grant needed to regain his confidence after dallying with that pretentious twit. Gerald had never thought Caroline to be sincere; now his suspicions were confirmed. She was a social climber who could never be content until she had married the wealthiest man in England. Gerald had never cared for the wench, but nothing he had said had persuaded Grant to keep his distance from her.

As Gerald sat sipping his tea, he heard the door open and close. He glanced up to see Brianna, with shoes in hand, tiptoeing down the hall. "Brianna, come here," Gerald called to his daughter.

Brianna's back stiffened and she swallowed with a gulp. Her father sounded impatient. She was in no mood to be interrogated, but it seemed she could not bypass his questions. When she entered the sitting room, Gerald motioned for her to sit down beside him, which she did reluctantly.

"Where is William? Why didn't he come inside with you tonight?" he questioned, his eyes narrowing suspiciously.

"William will no longer be escorting me home," Brianna murmured as she settled her silk skirts about her, purposely avoiding Gerald's probing stare.

Gerald moaned miserably. This was the fourth

broken engagement in the past two years. Brianna was as fickle and flighty as the wind. No man could catch and hold her interest for any length of time.

"Brianna, this is becoming monotonous. I am beginning to think that your sole intention is to drive me mad. Our door has been worn thin by the steady rapping of your suitors. If that constant tapping were not enough to render me senseless, your continual dismissal of would-be husbands is. Is there no man who pleases you?"

A deliciously mischievous smile curved her mouth upward, her amber eyes radiating with that sparkle that had melted many a man's heart. "Would you have me settle for second best?" she quipped, raising a perfectly arched brow. "I have yet to find a man who compares to you and Grant. To find such perfection in a man who does not bear the name of Talbert takes a great deal of time and patience."

Gerald scoffed at her attempt to soft-soap him. "There is not a man in all of England who could meet your standards, my dear. There is no knight in shining armor to carry you away on his white stallion." He snorted caustically. "You have always prided yourself on being an equal to men. Now none of them is good enough for you. You grew up trying to compete with Grant. You could never be content until you could ride as well as he could, handle a pistol with the same accuracy, outplay him at cards, and only God knows what else you sweet-talked him into teaching you while my back was turned. I have failed in my attempt to raise the genteel lady that your mother would have expected you to be. I have only added to your problem by allowing you more schooling than most women need. I openly admit that I have contributed to turning you into a misfit and have spoiled you beyond repair." Gerald's eyes seemed to bore into her like tiny, penetrating barbs that were meant to prick her pride.

Brianna regarded him bemusedly, wondering why he was lashing out at her. In the past, when she had turned away some gentleman, he had only shown mild irritation. This time he was attacking her personality, blaming her for not finding a suitable husband.

She attempted to shrug off his rebuke with her usual manner of teasing. "Why are you so upset? If I were to find a husband I wouldn't be living here with you. Are you trying to get rid of me? Papa, I am wounded to the quick by your insults."

Gerald's breath came out in a rush. The hell she was, he mused. "Don't evade the point, Brianna. You know damned well I'm not trying to shuffle you out from under my feet. You are twenty-one years old. Most women your age are already married and have a houseful of children. You cannot even light on any one man who interests you, much less wed one. Sometimes I could swear that when the devil was passing out orneriness and impatience, you managed to get in line twice," he accused, giving her a meaningful glance.

Brianna placed a fleeting kiss on her father's cheek and stood up in front of him. "You are just afraid that I'll be an old maid and that you'll be shunned by your friends," she mocked, displaying that devilish smile that Gerald had come to know all too well. "Now I must get my beauty rest or I will be unable to find a respectable husband. I'll be a shriveled-up old witch and you will have to provide my future husband with a healthy sum to take me off your hands."

The fragrance of jasmine encircled Gerald's senses as Brianna left the room, leaving him muttering to himself. Grant was sailing away and Brianna was fluttering about, breaking engagements, keeping tongues wagging, and irritating him with her denial of her need to take a husband. If only Anna could have lived to help

20

him manage the children. Children? Gerald snorted disgustedly. If they were children he would have thrashed them both and confined them to their rooms until they had come to their senses.

What was he to do with Brianna? He had approved of every one of her short-lived engagements, but Brianna had cast them all aside for one petty reason or another. Gerald unwillingly smiled to himself when he recalled her excuse for discarding her first fiancé. She had claimed that she could not abide the way Robert grinned. She had said if she had to go through life watching his lopsided grins that she would go stark, raving mad.

"Oh, Brianna," Gerald breathed despairingly, "with your stubbornness you will never find the perfect man for whom you search, and all of your antics are wearing my patience thin."

Brianna crawled into bed, smiling to herself. She was finally free of William. She had granted him every opportunity to prove himself worthy of her love, but he had failed miserably. Nothing about him excited her or intrigued her to spend more time than necessary with him. Perhaps her father was right. Maybe she was looking for a prince who only existed in fairy tales. And yet, she would rather live at home with Gerald and Grant than to be married to some fumbling dandy whose embrace made her shiver with revulsion.

Most men were womanizers, she thought cynically, except for Grant and Gerald. Her father had a tendency to lose his temper occasionally, but she knew what to expect from him since she had inherited that very trait. And Grant . . . Brianna breathed a weak sigh. He was everything she would like to be and the man she wished she could find.

She frowned to herself as her thoughts turned to the

other men she knew. None of them was interested in whether she had a head for business, could discuss politics, or could carry on an intellectual conversation. William was a prime example. He always bored her with his monotone voice, nearly wrenching his own arm patting himself on the back, always bragging about his abilities. Each time she dared to speak, he patronized her with one of his indulgent smiles that made her cringe. Well, she was not some empty-headed twit who could only bat her eyes and compliment her gentlemen companions! No man alive could master or outwit her! Not even that dark-haired rogue whom she had met when she had escaped from William.

An impish grin caught one corner of her mouth as she rubbed the knuckles of her right hand. The look of surprise and disbelief that had filled his green eyes when she had punched him in the jaw would always bring a self-satisfied smile to her lips. Little Miss High-and-Mighty indeed! At least she wasn't a pompous ass like that rake. He was probably the worst womanizer on the face of God's green earth. How dare him accuse her of deliberately taunting a man to molest her!

The tapping on her door roused Brianna from her pensive musings and she frowned at being disturbed. Her father had probably been sitting downstairs, thinking of more comments to make about her behavior and had decided to march upstairs to blow off steam while the thoughts were fresh on his mind. *Let him blow,* she muttered under her breath. He would have his say tonight and then she would charm him tomorrow, just as she always did. Life would be back to normal after he had aired his grievances.

"Come in," she called as she propped herself up on her elbow, allowing her long raven hair to spill over her shoulder like a black cape.

As Grant strolled into the room, Brianna bounded

out of bed and flew into his arms, squealing in delight. "I didn't know you were home. When did you return? Papa didn't even mention it to me," she breathed, hugging him close.

Grant's face regained some of its lost color as he gazed down at his sister who was squeezing him in two with her tight embrace. She was petite, but she was a fiery bundle of spirit. Why couldn't he find someone like Brianna, one who could keep him content for the rest of his days? Well, maybe not exactly like Brianna, he thought to himself, giving the idea a bit more consideration. Brianna was hot-tempered, far too clever and competitive, and as daring as a she-cat. That's what she had always reminded him of, he mused as a broad smile surfaced on his lips. She was like a feisty black panther. Her coal black hair glistened with a mysterious luster as if it were constantly bathed in moonlight. Her eyes could flicker like crackling amber flames that could ignite into a raging forest fire. She was too much woman for any normal man to control, although many had tried.

Grant had gone back downstairs after his bath to await Brianna's return, but after overhearing part of the conversation between Gerald and Brianna, he decided to greet his sister later. And Gerald was correct. If he knew all that Grant had taught Brianna, he would have put the blame for turning Brianna into an uncontrollable misfit on Grant's shoulders. Brianna and Grant had always been close, always discussing politics, the family business, and any other subject she chose when they were together. He had even allowed her to ride in his breeches and shirts that she had saved and stashed out of Gerald's sight. Each time Gerald left the country estate to travel to London, Brianna would coax Grant into some escapade, and he could never refuse her. If Gerald could have seen Brianna racing against the wind at breakneck speeds, her hair flying wildly about her as she thundered away on her spirited black stallion that no one dared to ride, Gerald would have been furious. Grant would have been thrashed within an inch of his life and, as usual, Brianna would have charmed Gerald out of her punishment.

Perhaps he was to blame for the way Brianna behaved, but they had enjoyed an adventurous childhood. He would never relinquish one of the memories. He had even permitted Brianna to tag along with him and his friends. He had taught her how to defend herself with her hands as well as with a pistol and knife. She had wrestled and fought with the best of them and had dished out one or two black eyes to the unruly group when they tried to overstep their bounds. It was little wonder that Brianna had such a reputation. Stories about her were passed by word of mouth. All of his childhood friends were grown men and they could tell some lively tales about Brianna. And yet, he couldn't condemn them for it. He was guilty of relating a few himself. When he was at the pub and the liquor began to talk he could keep an audience spellbound with his anecdotes.

He was going to miss Brianna more than he wanted to admit. She had lifted his spirits with her impish grins and devilish ideas that could fill the hours of what might have been a dull day. Although Brianna had become a beautiful young woman, she had a bit of the devil in her soul. She was prone to allow the demon to have his way with her occasionally. Well, more often than naught, Grant mused as another smile traced his lips. But that was what made Brianna so fascinating— her thirst for adventure, her desire to take all that life could offer, and her unpredictable behavior. She was enticing, mysterious, and elusive. That was the reason so many men flocked to her door. She was the lovely temptress whom all would love to claim, but whom none could ever hold. She was the unattainable star to wish upon and admire from afar. Grant could not name one man in their social circle who could control her untamed spirit. Aye, leaving her behind would be difficult, he thought as he hugged her close and then led her to the bed to ease down beside her.

"I just came home this evening," he explained, "but I'm leaving early in the morning. I wanted to see you before I go."

Brianna's eyes lost part of their golden flame. "But, Grant, you just came home. I haven't seen you in over a month. We haven't had a chance to spend any time together," she breathed disappointedly as she gazed up into his handsome face.

"I know, Brianna." Grant wrapped his arm about her shoulders and nodded in agreement. "But there is something I must do. I need time to think and escape from Father's protective wings. I signed on with the *Mesmer* to sail to the colonies. I have to report to the ship tomorrow. We set sail at the end of the week."

"Sail to America? But you'll be gone forever!" she groaned in dismay. "Grant, please don't go. I don't want you to leave." Her tone seemed to crack and waver as she nuzzled her head against his shoulder.

"Caroline played me for a fool, using me as a stepping-stone to acquire the Duke of Bourdoin and all of his inexhaustible wealth. She had her sights set only on money. I suppose she thought the Duke was the only man who could afford her expensive tastes," he grumbled bitterly.

"Why, that conniving wench! I'd like to clamp my fingers around her skinny throat," Brianna hissed spitefully as her golden eyes flared in outrage. How could that woman have treated Grant so cruelly? He was everything a woman could ever desire. How dare that bitch use her brother with no concern for his feelings!

"'Twas my own fault," Grant admitted sullenly as he studied the thick carpet beneath his feet. "I think I knew it right from the very beginning, but I was so fascinated by her beauty that I pretended not to know what really motivated her." He paused a long moment and slowly lifted his brown eyes to meet Brianna's sympathetic gaze. "That's really why I'm going away. I want to put the past behind me and seek out a new adventure that will rid my mind of Caroline."

Brianna huddled within Grant's protective arms, knowing in her heart that a change of scenery would help him deal with the pain he was suffering, but distressed that she would not have him here to share her innermost thoughts. He had always been a dear friend as well as a brother. The idea of no longer being able to talk away their problems as they had in the past left an unexplainable ache in the pit of her stomach. It was as if he were uprooting the depths of her soul.

"I want you to promise me that you'll stay out of trouble," Grant insisted as he cupped her chin and gazed into her vibrant, golden eyes that were shimmering with the slightest hint of tears. "I won't be around to rescue you from the near-catastrophes in which you have always managed to entangle yourself."

"Then perhaps you shouldn't go." A mischievous grin curved the corners of her mouth as she leaned back in his arms. "I seem to attract trouble with little effort. I always count on you to save me."

Grant chuckled and gave her a loving squeeze. "Aye, dear sister," he agreed. "I am convinced that your middle name is trouble. But now you're all grown up. If you can get yourself into mischief, you better learn to squirm out of it. If you don't, Father will wash his hands of you and toss you out on your ear."

26

"I have the feeling you were eavesdropping tonight," she accused, her eyes narrowing suspiciously.

"Indeed I was." Grant cast her a subtle wink and then grinned. "But I would not have had to overhear that conversation to make my prediction. Father intends to see you married to some well-deserving nobleman. Every man whom he has approved has never stood a chance with you. I've often wondered if you have turned them away just to spite him. He is bound and determined to see you married, but he doesn't have the patience of Job."

"But what am I to do?" Brianna questioned with an exasperated sigh. "I cannot condemn myself to a life of misery just because Papa wants me married. I would much rather be an old spinster than suffer a dull existence with someone like William Fairchild. God forbid!" She wrinkled her nose at the distasteful thought. "I have tried to find a man whom Papa would be proud to call his son-in-law, but love and marriage should go hand in hand. I could never profess to love a man like William Fairchild. If I did, I would be living a lie. He is much too dull and stuffy and would never approve of my behavior if we were married. I have no intention of changing my ways. With him, I would feel as though I had been chained to a stone post."

"I think Father has relinquished any hope of your finding a man you could love. Now he is concentrating solely upon marriage." Grant cast her a glance that held a hint of accusation. "I'm not at all sure you will fall in love."

"Et tu, Brute?" Brianna's delicate brow arched in mild amusement.

"Nay, not Brutus, dear sister. I would never sell you out." Grant grinned as he flicked the tip of her upturned nose. "But you had better watch your step with Father or you may find yourself wed to some undeserving man whom he has selected for you. The swain may have nothing more to offer than his distinguished name. Perhaps he will be some hideous creature whose sight repulses you," he teased.

"Papa would never do any such thing to me," Brianna scoffed, quickly shrugging away the ridiculous thought. "He may growl and snarl at me like a vicious dog when he loses his temper, but he is as harmless as a pup."

"Even a playful pup can inflict a painful bite. You would do well to remember that. You have managed to charm him out of his boots these last few years, but one of these days he will become immune to your wily ways. Between his short-fused patience and your inflammable temper, all hell will break loose one day," he warned, his meaningful glance meeting her unconcerned stare. Grant placed an affectionate kiss on her cheek and eased from the bed. "Remember what I said, Brianna."

She climbed beneath the quilts, her reckless chuckle filling the room. "I can handle Papa," she assured him saucily. "You just take care of yourself and return home as quickly as you can or I shall never forgive you for leaving me here at home alone while you are traipsing halfway across the world, viewing new horizons." Her bottom lip jutted out in an exaggerated pout as she crossed her arms beneath her breasts and cast her brother a look of feigned annoyance.

Grant glanced back over his shoulder at the golden-eyed enchantress who was bathed in the soft lantern light. Why couldn't Caroline have been more like Brianna? Somewhere there had to be a woman who could hold a candle to his lively sister—one with her spirit and beauty, but perhaps a little less mischievousness. One who could offer her love without using a man for her own purposes.

"Good night, Brianna," Grant whispered fondly as he closed the door, wishing that his search for Brianna's double would be short and successful.

Brianna squirmed in her bed, seeking a comfortable position and heaved a disappointed sigh. Without Grant close at hand she was certain to be miserable. He had always helped her soothe Sir Gerald's ruffled feathers when she had bristled him with one of her pranks. She and her father would most likely be at each other's throats if Grant was not around to referee their bouts.

Chapter Three

Grant's departure quickly placed Brianna and Gerald in sour moods, and Brianna had succumbed to tears as she watched Grant step into the carriage and disappear down the cobblestoned street. Two gentlemen arrived to call upon Brianna during her quiet breakfast with her father. Gerald overheard the rude manner in which his daughter had turned her suitors away and he had come to the end of his patience with her before the day had hardly begun.

"Brianna, must you always display such detestable manners when a gentleman asks for an audience?" Gerald chided gruffly as he shook out his napkin for the third time, tossed it in his lap, and stabbed at his fried eggs, causing them to weep all over his plate. "'Tis a wonder to me that men even dare to call upon you at all!"

"I have just sat down to my morning meal and have not even had the opportunity to collect my thoughts. Already I am forced to greet some dandy whose overly charming smile leaves me slightly nauseous. And if that were not enough, I must listen to you criticize my behavior. Is there no peace to be found within these stone walls?" she muttered as she shot her father an icy glare and overzealously carved the slice of ham that was cold and dry from all of the interruptions. "Perhaps I should take up residence at Newgate with the other outcasts of society. At least I would not be sub-

30

jected to this constant ridicule since I would be sharing a cell with the other misfits of England." Her sarcastic tone made her father's brows furrow in irritation.

"Enough!" Gerald snapped with a finality that would have silenced anyone but his daring daughter.

"Enough? Nay, I think not! You chastised me last night for disposing of dear, dull William and for discrediting the name of Talbert. This morning you insist upon harrassing me because I am not in the mood for a ride in the park with some beady-eyed bloke who reminds me of a slimy snake that has slithered up on my doorstep." Brianna laid down her fork and leaned forward, her gaze boring into her father. "I am going to stay in this house and torture you the rest of your days. You are not shuffling me off to the first man who raps on my door and looks at me with hungry eyes!"

"I will see you wed to a proper gentleman if it's the last thing I do!" Gerald thundered back at her.

When Brianna bolted from her chair and dashed from the room, Gerald growled under his breath. The next thing he knew she would probably resort to wearing men's clothes, just to prove that none of them were better than she was. While Gerald sat at the table, considering the trials that lay ahead of him, his worst fears materialized before his eyes.

"What in the name of heaven do you think you're doing?" he gasped. His astounded gaze flickered down his daughter who stood in the entryway wearing black kid boots, form fitting black breeches, and a white linen shirt.

"I'm going riding in the park on my black stallion. And, by the way, I have been riding him for the last few years without your permission. If anyone dares to stop me, I'll shout at the top of my lungs that I'm Gerald Talbert's daughter. The tongues of Bristol will be wagging a new tale," Brianna threatened, her golden eyes blazing with defiance. "If I am as wicked as you seem to think, then by damned, I'm going to behave like the unruly misfit you have claimed me to be!"

Before Gerald could find his voice to reply, the front door slammed and Brianna was gone.

"Grant, come back home and do something with your sister!" Gerald pleaded. Lord, it was going to be a long six months without Grant to talk some sense into Brianna. That ornery wench was already driving him mad.

When Brianna stalked into the barn, the groomsmen watched her saddle her steed and lead him outside. They had never seen her dressed so outrageously and could not imagine that she intended to ride the flighty stallion. The steed was practically unmanageable and the stable boys always argued about who would have to feed and care for the devil stallion that disliked humans. As Brianna swung onto the steed's back, Thor sidestepped nervously. His wild eyes darted about as he tossed his head. When she dug her boot heels into his ribs, Thor lunged forward, his nostrils flaring as he galloped away. The groomsmen gathered at the stable door, expecting to see Brianna tossed from the steed's back as if she were nothing more than a feed sack. To their amazement, she held on, urging him to a faster pace.

Her heart raced with a surge of freedom. She was liberated at last, no more pretentions of concealing her true nature and spirit. She was as good as any man. From now on she would tell them what she thought of their double standards. After the story of her morning ride had made it through the grapevine with its usual prefabricated twists, her gentlemen callers would realize that she would never conform to their standards.

"The devil take them all!" she mused aloud as the wind whipped past her face, carrying her words through the air like a hushed curse.

Seth had just stepped from his carriage and was about to assist Lenora out when he heard the thundering of hooves behind him. As he glanced over his shoulder he saw the huge stallion that glistened in the sunlight. Upon his back was a woman dressed in breeches, her ebony hair billowing about her like the cape that might have been worn by Satan himself. Her eyes were like fire, matching and reflecting the sunbeams that sprayed about her.

Seth stepped back against the carriage as the steed approached. His quick movement alarmed Thor. The stallion reared, pawing the air with his powerful hooves. Brianna had expected Thor to be flighty since he was not accustomed to being ridden in the city. As he came up on his hind legs, she held her seat, casting the gentleman an annoyed glance for startling her horse.

Vibrant green eyes locked with the fiery pools of gold. It took only an instant for them to recognize each other, bringing frowns to their faces.

When Thor came down on all four legs, Seth's hand jerked out to grasp the reins, trying to hold the frantic stallion in place. Thor had only one mistress and had never been fond of men. Snorting at the restraining grasp on his reins, Thor tossed his head and pranced a tight circle. Brianna brought the quirt down on the back of Seth's hand, forcing him to release the reins. Seth stepped back, glaring at the witch who had not only whipped his hand, but who had sent his senses reeling with a blow to the jaw.

"Out of my way, you dolt!" she snapped, raising her

33

quirt again as she stared down her nose at Seth.

His eyes were as cold as the Arctic waters, his irritation obvious. Brianna could easily read his thoughts and laughed wickedly, undaunted by his glare. When she nudged Thor, he bolted across the square, sending the pigeons to their wings to keep from being trampled beneath his hooves.

Seth reached up to lift Lenora from the carriage, but his gaze followed the flight of the steed and the vixen upon his back.

"Who was that?" Lenora asked as she wrapped a possessive hand around Seth's arm and watched the young woman thunder across the park at breakneck speed.

A hint of a smile tugged at Seth's mouth as he watched the wench circle the stone benches at the far end of the square. "That, my dear, is a witch if ever I've seen one," he chuckled.

Lenora's brows furrowed skeptically as she glanced at Seth. Then she turned her attention to the woman who was galloping toward them, her sable mane flying out behind her, her eyes filled with mischief. Aye, she was a witch, Lenora muttered under her breath. It was none other than Brianna Talbert, the temptress who left a path of broken hearts behind her wherever she went. Lenora's eyes narrowed as she backed against the carriage to keep from being crushed by the stallion.

Seth boldly stood his ground and tipped his hat, his smile hinting at amused mockery. As Brianna galloped past him she leaned away from the steed to snatch the hat from Seth's fingertips. Lenora gasped and covered her mouth, certain that Brianna was about to topple from her precarious perch to be stomped to death by her own wild stallion.

As Brianna scooted back into the saddle she waved

34

the silk hat in the air and grinned wickedly as she glanced back at Seth who stood mesmerized by her reckless ride. She pulled the top hat down around her ears to keep it from flying off and then nudged Thor through the trees that lined the edge of the park. Her laughter floated back to Seth, leaving him intrigued and motionless as he stared after her.

Lenora's face reddened in irritation. Quickly grasping Seth's arm, Lenora urged him to the carriage. "I've changed my mind. I don't wish to take a stroll this morning," she said stiffly.

As Seth assisted her into the coach, a merry twinkle filled his eyes. It seemed the sea had its sirens and England had claim to at least one witch, a beautiful, uninhibited creature who could captivate a man and hold him spellbound.

"Have you ever seen that wench before?" he questioned as he seated himself beside Lenora.

His tone was too curious to please Lenora. "Nay," she lied. Not only did she not want Seth to discover the woman's name from her, but she had no intention of him questioning anyone else in the park. "Whoever she is, she is no proper lady. I don't care to discuss her further. The wench has managed to disrupt what might have been a pleasant morning stroll." She settled her pink silk skirts about her and frowned in annoyance.

As the coach lurched forward, Seth chuckled to himself. Lenora was right: The wench was no lady. He turned his hand to see the bright red streak that lay across his knuckles. First, it had been a blow to his jaw. Now he had suffered a welt on the back of his hand. If he ever came across that wicked witch again, he would bind and gag her, retrieve his stolen hat, and stake her out in the sun for the vultures to feast upon. What a bundle of trouble that vixen was! His smile faded as he glanced out the window, unconsciously searching for her among the trees. Seth chided himself for giving her a second thought. Her image kept coming at him from all directions. Her eyes were like fire, her hair as black as night. There was something about her that amused and fascinated him, making her impossible to forget.

Chapter Four

Andrew Donnovan glanced up from where he sat at his desk when he saw his grandson stroll past the door of the study. "Quentin, I want a word with you!" he demanded gruffly as he looked over the top of his spectacles to send his grandson a stern glance.

Quentin flinched at the sound of his own name. His grandfather could make it sound like a curse at times. Quentin would have been satisfied if Andrew would never utter his name at all since he had never been fond of it himself. As Quentin ambled into the study, Andrew motioned for him to take a seat and then cast the young rake an accusing frown. It was obvious to Quentin that he had already been tried and hung for some unpardonable crime before Andrew had even voiced his grievances.

"There is a matter that we must discuss. I think you know exactly what it is although you're looking at me with that innocently unconcerned expression of yours." Andrew propped his forearms on the desk and impatiently drummed his fingers when Quentin made no comment. "Well, have you made your decision?"

A faint smile curved one side of Quentin's mouth as he lazily bent his gaze toward the gray-haired old man who had become even more cantankerous over the last ten years. Mild amusement was hinted in his tone as he replied, "I have not yet found one to my liking even though I have searched these cobbled streets with a careful eye." Quentin was met with the reaction he had come to expect when they hit upon this touchy subject.

Andrew's fist slammed against the walnut desk. The sound echoed across the tiled floor like a sudden crack of thunder. "I have had enough of your mockery, Quentin! If you cannot find a woman to wed this time, I will see to this business myself!" His tone was razor-sharp, but his thick-skinned grandson did not bat an eye.

"An excellent idea, Grandfather," Quentin said blandly. He eased back in his seat and clasped his hands beneath his chin, thoughtfully studying Andrew. "Since you are so intent on tying me to some noble wench, you should choose your granddaughter-in-law. You seem to have a greater need of her than I do. It will save me a good deal of time if I don't have to pick out one that might please you and Grandmother."

Andrew's eyes narrowed into hard, angry slits. "'Tis by your choice that I care for this matter. You will find no complaint with the woman I choose, even if she looks like the back end of a horse!" he snapped as he wagged a stubby finger at his apparently indifferent grandson. "'Tis not enough that we chose opposite sides during the revolution with the colonies. And then you insisted upon making your home with those heathens and savages. Now you are making light of our family tradition. You are thirty-two years old and have no son to carry on the name of Donnovan, nor have you taken me seriously the last five years when I have sought to discuss this matter with you. 'Tis time you were wed, and I intend to see that you are."

Inhaling a deep breath, Andrew plunged on while Quentin sat calmly in front of him, undaunted by the tirade of threats and insults. "You will marry into the English nobility or you will be banished from our family. You know that the name Donnovan has opened many doors for you in your fur and tobacco trading here in Bristol and London as well. But if you don't take this marriage business seriously, then by God, those doors will slam right in your face. Do you understand me, Quentin? I have had enough of your foolishness."

Quentin admired the old scoundrel who was ranting and raving like a madman, but he wasn't concerned by his threat. Quentin had made his own fortune in the colonies and only continued to trade with the British as an opportunity to visit his grandparents. Even if Andrew tried to do as he threatened, he would not see Quentin wed before he left for America. Let him search, Quentin thought as he suppressed the wry smile that tried to force its way to his lips.

"Very well, Grandfather," he conceded, nodding slightly. "If you can find me a suitable wife who meets all of your requirements, I will marry her, just as you wish."

A smile split Andrew's wrinkled face. Quentin didn't think he could be trapped, but somehow he would find a wife for his rakish grandson.

Quentin rose from his chair and leaned his hands on the edge of the desk, his smile matching Andrew's in radiance. "Grandfather, if you can find some noble wench whom you would dare to tie to my coattails, whom you, free of conscience, would condemn to a life of suffering with me as her husband, then you have my blessing."

He was a dashing devil, Andrew mused. Quentin could be ornery, staunchly independent, and yet, he was a likable sort. Although Andrew had lost his temper time and time again, he loved his grandson dearly. He would see to it that Quentin was married into a notable family.

"Thank you, my boy." He nodded and then winked

at Quentin. "You may silently laugh and call me a silly old fool, but you might be surprised at my ability to find you a suitable wife."

As Quentin drew himself up to full stature, he shook his head. "I have never doubted your resourcefulness. Go ahead with your plans. I hope you can forgive me if I cannot stay to see the fruits of your efforts. I have an important appointment this afternoon." Quentin bowed, spun on his heels, and swaggered to the door.

"Blonde or brunette?" Andrew questioned as he cast his grandson a knowing glance.

Quentin threw a smile over his shoulder. "Redhead," he replied before he disappeared from view, his reckless chuckle floating back into the study.

"Enjoy your freedom now," Andrew called after him. "Before long you will have a wife, and your wandering life will be over."

When he heard the front door slam, Andrew hopelessly shook his head. His grandson had been in England for a fortnight and had probably bedded a different wench every day since his arrival. Quentin had no difficulty turning women's heads with his striking good looks.

A thoughtful frown furrowed Andrew's brows as he rested his face in his hands and stared off into space. Where was he going to find a woman who would agree to wed Quentin on such short notice? She must be from a good family. Andrew would take no bawdyhouse harlot for a granddaughter. His mind raced over several names, but he quickly discarded them all. What father would permit his daughter to be rushed into marriage, especially to a man with Quentin's notorious reputation with women.

"Your lordship, Mr. Talbert is here to see you," Bascom announced, drawing Andrew from his silent reverie.

Lord Donnovan glanced up and nodded to his servant. "Send him in."

Gerald Talbert strolled forward, extending his arm. Andrew smiled as he shook his hand and then offered his business associate a seat in the chair Quentin had vacated several minutes earlier.

"How are you, Andrew?" Gerald asked absently, his mind preoccupied with troublesome thoughts.

Andrew's blue eyes narrowed in bemusement as he watched Talbert sink down in his chair. "I'm quite well, Gerald, but you look a bit distressed. Is anything wrong?"

"'Tis nothing. Let's see to our business and I will be on my way," Gerald insisted.

Lord Donnovan extracted the documents from his desk drawer and offered them to Talbert. After an hour of voicing and exchanging opinions of their venture, Andrew could stand no more of Gerald's nervous fidgeting. The man simply could not sit still. Donnovan's curiosity had finally gotten the best of him.

"What the devil is troubling you, man? Your anxiety has even got me squirming in my seat," he snorted, frowning at Gerald.

Talbert was up pacing the floor in an instant while Andrew's eyes followed his strides as he stalked the length of the study.

"'Tis my son and daughter." His breath came out in a rush as he raised his arms and then let them drop at his side in a gesture of futility. "I am at my wit's end with both of them. Grant has left home for six months. He says he needs to become his own man and Brianna . . ." Gerald raked his hands through his hair and turned to face Andrew. "Brianna will have the whole damned town's ears burning after the news of her latest escapade has made its rounds. That woman has become completely unmanageable!"

Andrew frowned at Gerald's distressed expression. He had seen Brianna on several occasions and had heard of her antics. The lass was a little spitfire. She was beautiful, charming, but obviously an impulsive bundle of spirit. "What has Brianna done this time?"

Gerald snorted disgustedly and began pacing the floor again. "Last night she discarded her fourth fiancé in two years. This morning after I reprimanded her for turning away two suitors in her rude manner, she vowed that she would never marry and that she would behave as outlandishly as she wished. Not thirty minutes after she returned from her wild ride through the park, Lady Wilburton was at the door relating the entire incident of how Brianna had ridden through the square on that black stallion, scaring the wits out of everyone who was caught in her path. The widow kept raving about how I should keep a tight rein on Brianna before someone drags me away and locks me up for not being able to control her," he explained bitterly. "Grant was the only one who could talk sense into Brianna. Now he's gone and Brianna intends to drive me mad. She can find no man to please her and I wouldn't pit any man in England against that little firebrand now that she has decided to spite me." His gaze dropped to the floor as he let his breath out in a rush. "I hate to admit it, but I can do nothing with her, short of tying her to her bedpost and locking the doors and windows to keep her from her shenanigans." Gerald plopped back in his chair, exhausted by his frantic confession.

A mysterious gleam sparkled in Andrew's eyes, drawing a curious glance from Talbert. "Quentin is back in England. I think we can both solve our problems with a simple contract," Andrew said as he pulled some parchment from the drawer and took quill in hand. "You have saved me from a long, harrowing search."

Andrew's grandson was as notorious as Brianna. Gerald had often heard the old man rave about controlling Quentin. Since Gerald had listened to Andrew grumble about Quentin, he had not hesitated to air his griefs in front of Andrew. But what did Donnovan mean by his remark? Was Andrew thinking of committing both of them to an asylum or just their parents and grandparents?

"What do you propose to do?" he questioned, eyeing Andrew skeptically. "What are you searching for?"

"We can both save ourselves a good deal of trouble," Andrew replied with a nonchalant shrug. "We will write up a contract joining your daughter and my grandson in marriage. We can rid ourselves of our biggest headaches. If ever there were two better matched misfits, I can't think of whom they might be. While Quentin and Brianna are trying to outdo each other with their shenanigans, we will sit back and watch from the ringside instead of being in the middle of the fray for a change. By God, they deserve each other." Andrew leaned back in his chair, grinning wickedly. "And who knows, they may even come to find that marriage isn't such a distasteful existence after all."

"I don't think I could convince Brianna to go along with this odd arrangement, and I have my doubts that Quentin would ever agree since you have not been able to tie him down in the last five years. I have no idea what reaction you could expect from Quentin, but I would not be surprised if Brianna threw another of her tantrums like she did this morning," Gerald muttered with a hopeless shake of his head.

"Quentin will do exactly as I tell him because he has

given me his word this very afternoon that if I found a woman whom I would dare to tie to his coattails, then he would marry her just as I wish." Andrew chuckled heartily. He couldn't wait to see the look on his grandson's face when he was informed that he was finally trapped into marriage, and by his own words. "Quentin will have his match with Brianna and she will finally meet a man who can put her in line, if indeed there is one. All you must do is tell your daughter that she is going to be married to a man of your choosing. She will do exactly as you command or you will lead her to the altar with her hands tied in front of her. You are still her father and she must obey your wishes. Well, what do you say? Do we have an agreement?"

Talbert thoughtfully rubbed his chin. The idea was insane—and very appealing—but he could well imagine the reaction he would receive from Brianna when she learned that her father had signed a contract of marriage, binding her to a man she had never even met. The fires of hell could not hold a candle to the flames that would ignite in her fiery amber eyes. Sweet merciful heavens! She would be furious.

"I don't know, Andrew," he muttered hesitantly. "I think the two of them should meet before we decide to follow through with this."

"There is no time. Quentin leaves soon. We must act quickly. The marriage must be tomorrow and she must be prepared to set sail the following day."

"Set sail? Then I would lose both my son and daughter!" Gerald gasped as he sat straight up in his chair. "I can't do it, Andrew."

Donnovan eyed him levelly. "Perhaps she can remain here in England while Quentin is away," he suggested. "Brianna and Quentin would probably prefer that arrangement, but we will have solved our problems. Quentin will have a wife from a notable family and Brianna's behavior will be no reflection on you. She will be a married woman and her husband will be forced to handle her."

Gerald slumped back in his chair and heaved a pensive sigh. What Andrew proposed was tempting, but there was still the matter of convincing Brianna to agree to the arrangement.

"Lord Donnovan! Did you hear about Brianna Talbert's antics in the park this morning? They say she was dressed in breeches, riding on a black stallion that looked like the devil himself. She even snatched the hat right off of—" Bascom quickly swallowed his words and came to an abrupt halt when Lord Talbert peered around the side of the large, high-backed chair that had concealed him from the servant's view. The color drained from Bascom's face as he ducked his head in apology. "Begging your pardon, Lord Talbert. I thought you had left the house. I didn't mean to be spreading stories about—"

"That is quite enough!" Andrew snapped, motioning for the servant to take his leave.

Gerald studied Bascom's retreating back and rolled his eyes as he turned back to Andrew. No doubt the tale was all over town by now. "Give me the damned quill. I'm ready to sign that agreement. Brianna is about to receive her just reward for this last bit of mischief."

Chapter Five

When Andrew heard the front door open and close, a victorious smile parted his lips. He spied the tall, muscular frame of his grandson pass the door of the sitting room and called for Quentin to join him. Quentin came slowly toward his grandfather, eyeing him warily.

"You look like the crafty weasel that has just feasted upon a whole henhouseful of chickens." Quentin smirked as he eased down beside his grandfather, casting him another suspicious glance.

"I look that way because I have accomplished a most difficult task in one short afternoon. 'Tis rather astonishing what a man can do in a matter of minutes when he puts his mind to it," Andrew replied before leisurely sipping his tea. He peered at Quentin from over the rim of his cup. The twinkle in his blue eyes made his grandson frown bemusedly.

"And what miracle have you performed that has left you with that self-satisfied smile? Have you finally managed to buy up all of England?" Quentin questioned disinterestedly as he reached for a cream-filled tart that sat on the tray in front of him. He was preoccupied with another matter. The subject he and his grandfather had discussed earlier was the farthest thing from his mind at the moment.

"You don't seem very impressed with my accomplishment. If I had managed to stamp the Donnovan crest all over England, it appears that you would not be awe-struck by it." Andrew sat down his teacup and winked subtly at Quentin. "If I were you, I would show a bit more interest in this conversation."

Quentin sighed impatiently and rolled his eyes. "Why don't you just tell me about your afternoon and dispense with the prattle," he suggested as he bit into the custard pastry and leaned casually back against the sofa to prop up his feet.

"Very well," Andrew nodded slightly. He was going to delight in seeing Quentin's expression. "I signed a marriage contract this afternoon with a well-to-do gentleman who has agreed to supply you with a wife. After we join them for dinner this evening, you and the young lady will be married in a short ceremony tomorrow afternoon," he stated nonchalantly, his eyes resting on his grandson, awaiting his reaction.

Quentin sucked in his breath, lodging a bite of tart in his throat, and he sputtered and choked attempting to breathe while he met his grandfather's steady gaze.

Andrew reached over to unsympathetically pat Quentin on the shoulder while a taunting smile parted his lips. He adjusted his wire-rimmed spectacles and carefully observed the look of dismay that Quentin could not mask.

"You didn't think I could perform such a difficult task in such a short time, did you, m'boy?" he said smugly. "Well, it seems you have underestimated me. You have been trapped by your own pledge. You cannot squirm out of it because you have given your word. The word of a Donnovan is as good as a signed agreement that has been witnessed by an entire regiment of soldiers and God himself." His blue eyes narrowed meaningfully as he watched Quentin reach for a cup of tea to wash down the pastry that had nearly strangled him.

"And just what does my bride-to-be look like? I do hope I can at least stand the sight of her." Quentin replied as he leisurely bent his gaze to his grandfather, masking his disappointment.

Andrew appraised his grandson curiously. He expected Quentin to begin making excuses, but he simply sat there, seemingly unconcerned that he had been outfoxed for the first time in years. "She is quite unusual," he began with a sly smile. "You might say that the lass is in a class all by herself. The wench could barely waddle through our front door. She has one green eye and one lovely blue one, about the color of mine, I believe," he added with a smirk. "A distinct hooked nose, and the finest set of fangs that I have ever laid eyes on," he teased wickedly, arching a gray brow as he sent Quentin a sidelong glance.

Quentin eased back in his seat after returning his cup to the silver tray, and then casually laid his arm across the back of the sofa. "And what color of hair does this distorted excuse for a woman have, or does she have any?" he questioned, allowing the old codger to play his spiteful game.

"Long, stringy black strands that intermingle with drab gray. As you might have guessed she rather resembles a witch and some have occasionally claimed her to be." Andrew chuckled to himself as he remembered the last thing Gerald had said before he had left the house. Lady Wilburton had claimed that Brianna was possessed by evil spirits and Gerald had agreed with her remark. He had cautioned Andrew on what he might come to expect with Brianna as his granddaughter-in-law. "Her father even offered to pay me a handsome sum to take the wench off his hands. I was his last resort. If I didn't agree to take her in, he was considering stuffing her in a sack, provided he could obtain one large enough to hold her, and have her tossed into the river to end his misery and hers as well."

Quentin chuckled in amusement. "And you decided to play the good Samaritan in order to save a damsel from such a horrible plight. Now I know why you have accepted the proposal for me. You think that by tying such dead weight to my coattails that you have hobbled me for life," he smirked, delighting in his grandfather's mischievous bantering. It was good to see such sparkle in the old man's eyes.

"Don't look so smug, Quentin," Andrew warned playfully. "Even if the wench were as ghastly as I have described, I would still expect you to marry her since you have given me your word."

Breathing a relieved sigh, Quentin glanced at Andrew, picked up his teacup, and raised it in toast to the sly gent who had somehow managed to do exactly as he had threatened. Quentin wasn't the least bit concerned about the contract. All he would have to do was spend the evening with the wench, take her for a stroll in the moonlight, offer her a pouch of coins to refuse the marriage contract, and find her a place to hide out for a couple of days. Then he would be on his way to the colonies. Andrew would be upset, but he would not be able to blame his grandson if the wench left them standing at the altar. Quentin suppressed the smile that attempted to force its way to his lips. Let Andrew think that he had bested his grandson. It was good for his ego.

"What time are we joining the bride-to-be for dinner?"

"Eight o'clock, and you better be on your best behavior. I want none of your deceitful tricks. Don't think you can make some amorous pass at the wench and infuriate her so that she will refuse to wed you. It won't work. This time you will act the perfect gentleman and by tomorrow night you will finally have a

49

wife. And let me tell you, Quentin, you deserve just exactly what you will receive by wedding the wench I have selected for you," he assured Quentin with a deliciously wicked grin.

Quentin regarded his grandfather skeptically. Perhaps the wench looked almost as bad as Andrew had described. How could a seventy-year-old man be a good judge of beauty when his spectacles were as thick as ice cubes. Lord have mercy, he muttered under his breath. Mayhaps the wench would be set on winning herself a wealthy husband and couldn't be bribed. Then what the hell would he do? It seemed that his only other alternative was to marry her and make his visits to England less frequently than he had in the past, leaving the wench behind. It appeared that Andrew had finally managed to entrap him. But if there was a way to wiggle out of this distressing situation, Quentin was determined to find it. He hadn't managed to escape from such dire circumstances in the past without gaining a little knowledge of cunning.

Brianna seated herself in the stuffed chair across from her father and bravely squared her shoulders, knowing full well what was in store for her. Gerald was going to lash out at her again for her unforgivable antics. He would find some method of punishment that she would tolerate only to pacify him until he had cooled down. She had been terribly upset about Grant's leaving home that morning and had spoken disrespectfully to her father. And then she had totally humiliated him by thundering through the park dressed in breeches. There was naught else for her to do in this instance but to beg for mercy, take the punishment, and promise never to behave so badly again. Brianna would spend the following week catering to his every wish, being escorted about town by any gentleman who met with Gerald's approval. When she had her father wrapped around her finger once again she would return to her old ways until the next time he called her upon the carpet.

"Brianna, I have come to a very important decision this afternoon and you will obey my wishes in this matter. I will hear no argument from you," Talbert insisted in a firm tone as he peered at his docile daughter who in no way resembled the wild heathen who had fled from the house earlier in the day. "I suppose I should have taken matters in my own hands long ago. Having made my decision, I feel better than I have in the last two years," he added with a relieved sigh.

Brianna arched a curious brow. *Get to the point, Father,* she thought impatiently. But she did not utter a word. She had said too much already. It was time to listen, not annoy him further.

"Lord Andrew Donnovan and his grandson, Quentin, are joining us for supper tonight. I want you to dress in your finest gown to meet our guests. I expect you to be the most gracious hostess and the most charming young lady that you can possibly be when they arrive. As a matter of fact, I intend that your somewhat tainted halo be glowing radiantly when you descend the stairs. I would also suggest that you polish it while you're preparing yourself for the evening." He paused for Brianna to nod her consent. Begrudgingly, she did. "Tomorrow afternoon the Donnovans will return so that you and Quentin can be married in a simple ceremony here in our home."

The words he had spoken so softly seemed to roar in her ears. The color immediately drained from her cheeks. "A marriage ceremony?" she repeated incredulously, stunned by what she thought he had said. Surely she had heard him incorrectly. Gerald Talbert would not do such a thing to his only daughter, no matter how far she had stepped out of line. Would he? God, how could he?

Gerald nodded affirmatively. "You are going through with this marriage just as surely as you are sitting before me, Brianna. I told you that I would hear no argument and I meant it. You have forced my hand. I have put my signature on the marriage contract. I'm certain that you will be pleased to learn that your husband-to-be only visits England on occasion. That will make it easy for the both of you. You will become a married woman and will no longer be pestered by the ruttish boors who insist upon annoying you with the eloquent lines of flattery that you detest," Gerald mocked dryly. "After tomorrow you will be able to ride Thor in the park without wearing a stitch of clothing if that is your wish. Lady Wilburton will not be bending my ear, repeating scandalous gossip because you will be a Donnovan. You will not pose a threat to the good name of Talbert. It will be the Donnovans who must suffer the fate that has plagued me for the past few years."

Brianna's eyes widened in disbelief. "Papa, you cannot mean what you're saying! This is much too rash a punishment. Perhaps I have behaved badly, but—"

"*Perhaps?*" Gerald cut her short, casting her a reproachful glare. "You, Brianna, have behaved abominably. Once and for all you will pay for your scandalous escapades. In the past, you have breezed by with only mild punishment. I'm sure you were planning to soft-soap me for a week or two, as you have a tendency to do, until I had forgotten about your mischief. This time you will receive your just reward. Maybe in the future you will think twice before you behave like some uncivilized heathen. You must learn to consider the repercussions of your actions. As Quentin Donnovan's wife, you will answer to him. If his reputation permits his wife the same privileges that he allows himself, you might slip by unreprimanded for your mischievousness." Gerald displayed a satisfied grin as he watched Brianna swallow the lump that had suddenly collected in her throat. "And then again, Quentin may demand that you honor the name of Donnovan. Whatever the case, the two of you deserve each other. At last I am free of your ornery pranks."

Talbert was surprised that Brianna had not thrown one of her tantrums. But then, he had caught her off guard. She had no time to gather her thoughts. Taking advantage of her silence, he continued, casting her a stern glance, "Now I want you to march upstairs and tend to your appearance before our guests arrive. When you return, I expect you to be on your best behavior. Do we understand each other?" Gerald's brow arched slightly as he eased back in his chair. He pulled his pipe from his pocket and tapped the ashes in the tray before looking to Brianna.

"Perfectly." Brianna rose from her chair, her thoughts spinning in chaotic confusion. She stalked toward the door and then paused to glance back at her father. "Very well, Papa. It seems that I am left with very little choice in this matter."

"You are indeed correct. I have made my decision," he assured her as he lit his pipe and gazed at her through a cloud of smoke. "You will comply with my wishes without complaint."

There it was, that fiery blaze in her golden eyes, assuring Gerald that she was silently raging like a forest fire. He inwardly cringed as Brianna shot him a murderous glare. As she ascended the stairs, the weight of her father's words settled about her like a heavy yoke that had been strapped on her shoulders. Grant had warned her that something like this might happen if she pushed Gerald too far. Brianna wanted to erase the entire day and begin again. If she could have known what Gerald had intended to do, she would have attempted to control her temper and would never have acted so irrationally. With a hopeless shrug, Brianna picked up the front of her skirt and took the rest of the steps two at a time in her haste to seek refuge in her room.

If only Grant were here! He could plead her cause and free her from this horrible mess. Marry her off to a man she had never even seen and who had his own scandalous reputation? Indeed! Gerald had taken leave of his senses. If he thought for one minute that she was going to be led to slaughter like a timid lamb, he had sorely misjudged her! She was not about to spend the rest of her life with a man she didn't love. That was the main reason she had refused matrimony. She had not fallen head over heels for any of the dandies who had taken her in their arms. Most of them had left her cold and unimpressed by their embraces. Never had she heard bells; never had a man taken her breath away and left her heart fluttering wildly. Somewhere there had to be a handsome prince whom she was destined to meet; one that commanded her admiration without asking for it, one who could outwit her and outride her, and yet one who was capable of tenderness and compassion. Somewhere there was a man who could win her love without making an effort to gain her attention. She was not about to give up her search for the man of her dreams. Brianna was much too stubborn and proud to agree to this ridiculous contract without a fight. In a week, perhaps two, Gerald would regret signing his only daughter's life away. He would come crawling on his knees to beg forgiveness for his addle-witted arrangements.

Brianna slammed the door of her room and stomped her foot in outrage. Shining halo? She snorted disgustedly. There would be no angelic smile pursing her lips tonight. Perhaps she deserved to be forced into such a predicament after what she had done. But, by damned, she would fight her father's decision. When Quentin Donnovan arrived for dinner, he would not meet a China doll who smiled coyly and batted her eyes! Bah! Be on her best behavior? Nay! Not Brianna!

Hastily stripping from her velvet gown, she tossed it in a crumpled heap on the bed and watched as it slipped to the floor. Brianna muttered a string of curses over her distressing situation. Quentin Donnovan was probably old enough to pass as her father; he probably had a lame leg that he dragged along with the support of a cane. He was incapable of finding his own bride and had to resort to a contract to gain what he desired. Brianna shivered in revulsion as she pictured the ugly, distorted face of the monstrous creature who was to be her husband.

"Damn it," she muttered under her breath. How did she always manage to embroil herself in such formidable situations? Something Grant had said to her the previous evening skitted across her mind. He had assured her that if she could get herself into trouble then she was clever enough to squirm out of it. Her mind raced with frantic urgency. After a long moment, a deliciously wicked smile curved her lips. Brianna chuckled quietly. Aye, there was a way, and she had found it.

Quentin assisted his grandfather from the coach and kept a strong supporting arm on the old man's elbow. He rapped lightly on the door, calmly awaiting his fate. Out of the corner of his eye, Andrew appraised his grandson's confident manner. It had squelched the thrill of victory when Quentin had not floundered like a fly caught in a black widow's web. The sly rogue must have something up his sleeve or he would not have been behaving so indifferently.

Andrew's brows narrowed suspiciously. "I don't know what devious scheme you have in mind to free you from this contract, but let me warn you that I will be watching you like a hawk tonight."

Quentin chuckled at his grandfather's threatening frown. "You have already accused me of wrongdoing. I have not even set foot in the house, much less met my intended bride. Grandfather, I am wounded to the quick by your unwarranted suspicions," he mocked, a lopsided grin tugging at the corner of his mouth.

"Just remember what I said, Quentin. I'll be watching your every move. If you attempt to take this on the lam, I will call you out!" He wagged an accusing finger in his grandson's face. "I am not about to let you weasel out of this marriage, not this time."

"Put your fears to rest, sir. You have trapped me and I concede," Quentin murmured just as the door was opened by the butler, who ushered them inside.

Lord Talbert strolled forward, producing a broad smile as he extended his hand to Andrew and then to Quentin. The younger Donnovan was strikingly handsome. It was little wonder that his reputation with women was the subject of many conversations. Brianna and Quentin would make a perfect couple, he thought as he appraised the expensive black velvet garments that Quentin wore. How Andrew had convinced his grandson to follow through with the arrangement, Gerald would never know. But here he was, prepared to meet his intended bride. Brianna might be irritated with the contract now, but once she laid eyes on the dashing rogue she might change her tune. She just might be fascinated by Quentin Donnovan. Gerald chuckled to himself as he led his guests into the study for a glass of brandy. It would serve Brianna right to fall hopelessly in love with the man he had chosen for her.

As the three gentlemen stepped into the library, Quentin came to an abrupt halt when he spied the large portrait of the dark-haired beauty with mysterious golden eyes that hung above the fireplace. The look of surprise and disbelief that spread across Quentin's face was quickly noted by his grandfather.

"So now you know that my description of Brianna could not have been further from the truth," Andrew snickered. "She is even lovelier in the flesh than she is on canvas."

Quentin continued to study the bewitching portrait, his brows furrowing in a thoughtful frown. "Now 'tis my turn to be suspicious," he mused aloud.

Andrew and Gerald stared curiously at him, unable to comprehend the meaning of his quiet statement. Quentin turned slowly to face them, focusing his attention on Gerald. "Just when will I meet my intended bride? I'm most anxious to make her acquaintance since we will be man and wife in less than twenty-four hours," he snorted, sarcasm dripping from his rich voice.

"She is upstairs and will be down soon," Gerald assured him as he offered the Donnovans a seat on the sofa.

After waiting fifteen minutes, Gerald decided to call Brianna, allowing himself the opportunity of making a last word of warning. It was not like her to be late, especially when he had instructed her to be on her best behavior. "I'll see if I can hurry Brianna along. She has kept us waiting long enough. Will you excuse me a moment?"

When Talbert left the room, Quentin glanced over his shoulder to re-examine the portrait. A sly smile crept to his lips while his eyes made careful appraisal of the delicate features and hint of mischievousness that had been captured on canvas. So this was Brianna Talbert—the high-spirited wench who left a trail of broken hearts behind her and made wild rides through the park. Quentin chuckled in amusement. Brianna was as much of a rogue as he was. If all that he had heard about her was true, she didn't give a fig for anyone's opinion and did just as she pleased. Andrew would indeed have his revenge if he managed to tie his grandson to this spirited wench. If he thought Brianna could get the best of Quentin, then Andrew was in for a surprise. Quentin swished his brandy around in his glass, a ghost of a smile grazing his lips. This wench may be a little termagant, but he could manage her if he must—if he could find no escape. Quentin had vowed never to take a wife after what had happened in the colonies. If Andrew had known about the incident, he would have been incensed, but Quentin had never mentioned it to him and never intended to do so.

Gerald appeared in the doorway, his face drained of color, a letter in his trembling hand. "She's gone," he breathed weakly.

"What?" Andrew gasped, his brows furrowing over his angry blue eyes.

Quentin gazed up at Gerald, who came forward to hand him the note. Talbert promptly chugged his drink in his haste to pour himself another tall glass of brandy. Quentin opened the letter and a hint of a smile played on his lips while he read.

Papa,
Since you have made your decision, you have forced me to make one of my own. I am leaving home and I do not intend to return until you have had time to reconsider your rash actions. I will not marry a man you have

selected under any circumstances.

It will serve no purpose to search for me. I will take great care not to be found. Do enjoy your evening with the Donnovans and give them my apology.

As ever,
Brianna

A broad smile forced its way across Quentin's face as he handed the paper to his grandfather. "At least you cannot claim that I was the one who foiled your well-laid plans."

Andrew grumbled disgustedly as he read Brianna's note. "Damn!"

Quentin reached over to return the unsympathetic pat that Andrew had bestowed on him earlier that day. "Don't take it so hard. It seemed that you had me trapped, but you failed to consider my cunning ex-bride-to-be. I must admit that I'm rather surprised you didn't request that Gerald tie Brianna to the staircase until we arrived," he taunted as he arched a mocking brow and allowed his gaze to slide to the portrait on the wall.

Andrew snatched his grandson's hand away from his shoulder and shot him an annoyed glower. Then he turned cold blue eyes to Gerald who was pouring himself his third drink. "I should have tended to that myself, but I thought Gerald could handle his own daughter. Apparently she is every bit as troublesome as Talbert has claimed," Donnovan muttered. Damn that little vixen! She had ruined his plans. Andrew was thoroughly disgusted with Gerald for not keeping an eye on Brianna.

The servant tapped lightly on the door to call the men to dinner. Quentin was the only one of the three who had any appetite for the delicious meal that

59

awaited them. He bantered lightly throughout dinner, but the other men ate in silence, each lost to their own troublesome thoughts.

When the Donnovans stepped onto the front porch, Gerald apologized for the fourth time. As Quentin ushered Andrew into the coach and waved good-bye, Andrew heaved a disappointed sigh. His spirits plunged, his shoulders slumping in defeat. If he wasn't certain that Quentin had no way of contacting Brianna to suggest an escape, he would have accused his grandson of just that. But Andrew had not allowed Quentin out of his sight long enough for him to leave the house or even send a note to the wench. Andrew had lost again. He had failed to see Quentin married before he sailed back to the colonies.

Although Quentin had breathed a sigh of relief, he had to admit that he would have enjoyed meeting Brianna after all he had heard about her. Ah, well, it was better this way. Brianna had solved his problem. Wherever she was, Quentin had no doubt that she could manage to take care of herself. This was yet another of her pranks that would set tongues wagging when the story got out. Quentin silently thanked the wench for making her hasty escape. He was still free, and Andrew could not blame him for what had happened.

Chapter Six

Brianna made her way to Sabrina Rutledge's home and quickly scaled the lattice that was covered with green ivy. When she had struggled up to the terrace door, she saw Sabrina sitting at the dressing table, brushing her golden hair and daydreaming while she gazed into the mirror. Brianna tapped on the door and Sabrina gasped when she saw the dark silhouette among the shadows.

Quickly scrambling from her chair, Sabrina backed toward the door, expecting a thief to come rushing in to attack her. She could not even find her voice to scream for help, for which Brianna silently thanked her as she moved closer to the glass. When the intruder made no attempt to gain forceful entrance, Sabrina took a reluctant step forward, squinting her eyes to make out the petite form who waited impatiently outside. Brianna tapped again and Sabrina edged toward the door until she finally recognized Brianna.

"For heaven's sake, what are you trying to do, scare the life out of me? Why are you dressed like that? What are you doing out alone at night?" Once Sabrina found her tongue, she assaulted Brianna with a tirade of questions. She ushered her friend inside and quickly locked the door behind them.

Brianna sank down on the edge of the bed. As she tossed her pouch on the floor she breathed a despairing sigh and raised her gaze to meet a pair of pale blue eyes that were alive with curiosity.

"Well, what is going on?" Sabrina said impatiently as she rested her hands on her hips. "Are you off to a late-night costume ball, or are you merely charading as a boy to add another escapade to your long list of antics?" A mischievous smile curved one corner of her mouth as she peered at Brianna.

Casting her a disgruntled frown, Brianna shook her head negatively. She was in one hell of a scrape and she did not find the situation amusing. "Nay, Sabrina. 'Tis nothing as harmless as one of my pranks. I'm running away from home."

"Why? Did your father find that your reckless ride through the park was more than he could tolerate? Did he toss you out?" she queried, snickering playfully.

"You know about that?" Brianna peered into Sabrina's shimmering eyes, watching as she nodded affirmatively.

"Who doesn't?" she replied with a careless shrug. "Your timing was terrible, Brianna. There was a whole pack of gossiping mongrels in the park when you thundered across the square, riding Thor, cackling like a demented witch, and swiping top hats from men's heads. Why, you were positively wicked. And to think that I dare to call you my friend." A taunting smile grazed her lips as she eased down beside Brianna. "Your father has probably disowned you. I should refuse to be seen in your company. My own reputation will be ruined because of my association with you."

Brianna groaned and plopped back on the bed to stare up at the ceiling. Perhaps that was why her father had taken such drastic actions. The widow Wilburton had probably risked breaking her own neck in her haste to dash to the Talbert mansion to relate the story to Gerald. That meddlesome old woman had chased her father for years, attempting to get him to show interest in her. When he didn't, she resorted to bending his ear with tales of Brianna's escapades. After that woman related a story, it was so laced with fabrication that it was hardly recognizable. She was always wedging her nose in Brianna's affairs, delighting each time Brianna had given her some gossip to take to Gerald.

Brianna rolled to her side and propped herself up on one elbow, glancing at Sabrina who was still grinning at her. Sabrina obviously approved of her antics even if she had teased her unmercifully. But, of course, she would, Brianna mused thoughtfully. Of all the well-bred ladies in Bristol, Sabrina was the only one with spunk. The rest of the lot were content to sit in the parlor with their stitchery and assume the role of the fairer sex—lovely and fragile, but submissive and obedient. No one could ever claim Brianna to be among that subservient group, but she had paid dearly for her nonconformity. Sabrina had been more discreet. She could flutter back and forth between the fragile flower and the wild weed. Suddenly Brianna was envious of Sabrina's cleverness and found herself wishing that she hadn't acted rashly.

"Papa intended to marry me off tomorrow. The rogue has a reputation that would put mine to shame. I had to leave home before the dandy arrived to take supper with us tonight," she explained bitterly.

The playfulness vanished from Sabrina's face. "You really must have angered Lord Talbert this time, Brianna. I cannot belive he would do such a thing to you!"

"Believe it," Brianna snorted derisively. "For that is what he did. He means to wash his hands of me once and for all. I cannot go home until he has had time to recover from my last bit of mischief and my escape."

"What are you going to do?" A concerned frown gathered on her brow.

"I have to find Grant and tell him what has happened. Papa will probably go to him and Grant will be distressed if he doesn't know I'm all right. I'll tell my brother that I'm going to stay at the country estate. He will undoubtedly give the information to Papa," Brianna explained.

Sabrina's concerned frown deepened, her eyes mirroring her confusion. "But your father will come after you. Then what are you going to do? Return and marry this man?"

"I won't be at the estate," she stated simply.

Sabrina's breath came out in a rush. "Then where will you be? You can't stay here. Your father will search me out before too long and question me and my family."

"I'll be sailing to the colonies with Grant."

"Grant is going to America? But why?" The disappointment in Sabrina's voice caused Brianna to arch a wondering brow.

So Grant was the man Sabrina had secretly admired, Brianna mused as a sly smile crept to her lips. Sabrina had always carried a torch for some unidentified man, but she would never tell Brianna his name. And Brianna would have bet her life, although it wasn't worth much at the moment, that it was none other than Grant Talbert.

After explaining what had happened between Caroline and Grant, Brianna told Sabrina what Grant planned to do. If Brianna couldn't find the man of her dreams, perhaps she might be able to help Sabrina capture the one who had caught her eye.

As Brianna and Sabrina climbed into bed, Brianna's mind was busily devising a plan to elude her father and reintroduce Sabrina and Grant. Although she had finally made her decision, she had difficulty falling asleep. She was about to embark on a new life, one of adventure, one that she had never even imagined. The thought of what lay ahead of her, the problems she might face, made her toss and turn restlessly. It was the early hours before dawn when she drifted into slumber.

The following morning, Brianna instructed Sabrina to collect some servant's clothing and bring it back to the room. Although Sabrina regarded her suspiciously, she did as Brianna requested. She returned a few minutes later with a gray muslin gown, a plain white apron, and a cap. After Brianna explained what she intended to do, she climbed down from the terrace and changed into the maid's garments. When Sabrina arrived with the coach, they made their way to the wharf.

When they arrived, they hurried from the carriage to seek the whereabouts of Grant Talbert. Sabrina explained to the first mate of the *Mesmer* that she had come to say farewell to one of the crew. Derrick Sayer summoned Talbert and left the three of them alone. Grant peered curiously at Sabrina and the dark-haired lady's maid who kept her head ducked to keep from gazing at her brother.

"What are you up to now, Brianna?" Grant questioned, a skeptical frown causing his brows to furrow above his brown eyes.

She slowly raised her gaze to meet his inquisitive regard. "Papa signed a marriage contract and was planning to hold the wedding this afternoon. I took refuge at Sabrina's house. I'm planning to leave for the country estate before Papa catches up with me," she explained hastily, her alert eyes sweeping the deck of the schooner.

"So you finally pushed him too far, didn't you?" he

accused with an I-told-you-so grin that made Brianna wince uncomfortably. "What did you do now, dear sister?"

Brianna shrugged nonchalantly. "I went riding in the park yesterday morning after Papa and I had a small argument."

Sabrina chuckled out loud and rolled her eyes in disbelief. Brianna had given the truth, but that was the grossest understatement she had ever heard. "She was riding Thor and was dressed in your old clothes, Grant. And I doubt that any argument in which Brianna is involved could be considered insignificant."

Grant arched a heavy brow as Sabrina provided the necessary details and then he rested his gaze on his suddenly innocent-looking spitfire of a sister before throwing back his head and laughing heartily. "And I can guess the rest," he remarked between chortles. "The tongues were wagging all about town. Father washed his hands of you and decided to put an end to your shenanigans once and for all. Really, Brianna," he chided with a hopeless shake of his head. "You are going to have to gain control of that fiery temper of yours before you get burned."

"It would seem so, but 'tis too late to undo the damage that has already been done," she breathed in exasperation.

"And just what is the name of the poor gent who was almost condemned to be your husband?"

"Quentin Donnovan," Brianna answered bitterly, annoyed with Grant's teasing comment.

Grant chuckled again. "Quentin Donnovan? Did you know that he is—" he began.

"Oh, my God, there's Papa!" Brianna gasped as she glanced around Grant's broad shoulders to see the Talbert's carriage rumbling along the street.

Brianna grabbed the front of her skirt and dashed

across the deck to scramble down the plank before her father caught sight of her. Scurrying along the pier in the opposite direction of the approaching carriage, Brianna gulped fearfully, praying that Gerald had not recognized her. Sabrina and Grant stared after the fleeing lass and then forced a faint smile when Gerald stepped from the carriage to wave to them.

While Brianna continued to run along the wharf, a coach pulled up beside her, and she glanced up to see the raven hair and the vivid green eyes of the same rogue whom she had met on two other occasions. Quickly flinging open the door, she scrambled inside the coach and leaned her head back against the seat to catch her breath while her heart pounded frantically beneath her breasts.

As Seth regarded her with an amused smile, he drew a cigar from his pocket. "Do you mind if I smoke?" he questioned in the rich voice that carried its usual self-assurance.

Brianna cast him a disinterested glance before cautiously peering out the window and then quickly drew away. "You have my permission to do whatever you wish so long as you don't tell anyone that I'm here."

Seth chuckled and cocked a heavy brow. "I must say you are the most mysterious little witch I have ever come across. First you appear out of the darkness clothed in an elegant gown of silk and plant your fist in my face. Then you come thundering through the park on a demon stallion, nearly trample me to death, strike me with your quirt, and steal my hat. And now here you are dressed as a lady's maid and climb into my carriage without being invited. I'm beginning to wonder if I've become a tormented man, and I can think of no reason why I should deserve such a fate."

Brianna produced an impish grin and moved to the opposite side of the coach to sit directly across from

Seth. "I must admit that I have had a rather busy week," she declared saucily.

When Seth leaned his head out of the window to instruct the coachman to proceed down the street, he noticed the dark-haired gentleman who strolled toward the young couple on the deck of the schooner. His brows furrowed thoughtfully as he surveyed the scene, but when he turned back to Brianna, his expression did not reveal his curiosity.

Brianna breathed a restricted sigh of relief and pulled the cap from her head, allowing the long mass of ebony curls to tumble about her shoulders in disarray. Combing her fingers through her hair, she attempted to organize the thick strands in a fashionable order. As the carriage lurched forward she gazed into the vibrant green eyes of the ruggedly handsome rogue who was studying her as carefully as she was appraising him. In the other two brief encounters she had not had the opportunity to notice much about him.

The swain was dressed in a brown velvet suit, and as he lit his cheroot, Brianna slowly regarded his muscular frame. He was strikingly attractive with his tailor-made clothes that emphasized his broad shoulders and masculine thighs. The shiny raven hair that framed his face lay recklessly across his forehead, and his sparkling emerald eyes were rimmed with long black lashes. A certain confidence was revealed by his nonchalant smile and the distinct lines around his mouth, and Brianna could almost feel the strength and self-assurance that radiated from him. The sun had bronzed his dashing features and the forces of nature seemed to have eroded and hardened the lines and creases on his forehead, around his eyes, and down the sides of his mouth. His dark brows were heavy and thick, as if to protect his vibrant eyes from harsh weather. Her gaze was quickly drawn to the deep pools of green which appeared to be fathomless lakes that revealed nothing more than an alert awareness of all that moved around him. Brianna could read nothing in them, except perhaps a cool indifference. As she continued to study him, he smiled slightly and she came to the immediate conclusion that the expression was not a show of pleasure or politeness, but rather a taunting display, as if he could read her thoughts and was amused by them. His self-confidence and aloofness made her bristle as his gaze seemed to touch every inch of her flesh, carefully calculating what lay beneath the servant's garb. He was a rogue by all descriptions and there was no hint of gentleness in his features or his manner. It was apparent that he thought himself to be better than she was. She could sense it, and another twinge of irritation seemed to strike an exposed nerve, causing Brianna to squirm nervously in her seat. And yet when she met his eyes again, there was something in them that intrigued her, some strange force that compelled her to meet his unwavering gaze. A curiosity seemed to swim about her mind, drawing questions about his identity, his name, and the type of work that afforded his expensive clothes.

It seemed that he had accurately read her thoughts as if they were mirrored in her golden eyes.

"The name is Seth. And what may I ask is yours, my dear?" he inquired glibly, never allowing his gaze to waver from her lovely face.

Brianna was startled by his words. It seemed she must carefully mask her thoughts or he would know what she was thinking without her having to utter a word. Resuming her casual air, Brianna replied, "My name is Sabrina." She was not about to tell him who she was since she was not certain she could trust the handsome stranger or if she even cared to try. He might turn on her if he knew her identity. "'Tis the second time you have saved me from disaster, Seth," she continued with a grateful smile. "I suppose I should apologize for behaving so badly."

"Aye, that you should, my dear," Seth agreed with a light chuckle as a sly grin parted his full lips. "I'm not accustomed to being punched in the jaw or being run down by women on spirited steeds. I don't suppose you would attempt to explain why you have acted so strangely each time we chance to meet?" he questioned as he arched a dark brow and puffed on his cigar.

"Nay, I suppose I wouldn't." Along with her flippant reply came that mischievous smile that made her golden eyes flicker in the same manner that Seth had noticed in the park.

"I thought not." He shrugged indifferently and settled himself in his seat, seemingly unconcerned that she did not intend to go into detail.

"'Tis a long story and it would serve no useful purpose to discuss it. Besides, I have to work this out myself," she added as she glanced out the carriage window, purposely avoiding his gaze.

"Who better to help you than a total stranger, my dear?"

Brianna cocked her head and eyed him skeptically as her gaze slid the full length of his virile form. And for some strange reason she had a change of heart. Perhaps she could use his assistance. After Sabrina was left standing on the schooner, Gerald would probably assume that she knew about Brianna. She did not dare return to the Rutledge's to seek refuge. Gerald would probably be waiting for her.

A long moment of silence passed between them before she spoke. "Perhaps you are right," she said thoughtfully. "But how do I know that I can trust you? All I know about you is that your name is Seth." His eyes narrowed suspiciously as she studied his handsome face.

"How do I know that your name is really Sabrina and that I won't end up with a knife in my back for my efforts to aid a damsel in distress?" Seth countered with a mocking smile. "So far all I have gotten from you is a sore jaw, a welt on the back of my hand, and I have been robbed of my hat. It seems to me that *I* am the one who should be leery of you, Sabrina."

"Then why would you offer to help me?"

"Perhaps I'm a glutton for punishment or maybe 'tis just that you have piqued my curiosity," he replied as he flicked the ashes of his cigar out of the window and slowly returned his probing gaze to the dark-haired beauty across from him.

"Very well then, I will tell you," Brianna replied with a firm nod. "I am in need of a place to stay for the rest of the day so that I may leave town in the morning. My father is looking for me because he has decided to marry me to some frivolous dandy, and I refused to go through with it."

Seth's dark brows furrowed slightly as he listened to the young woman's bitter words. "Why does he think you should be married?"

"Because he has come to the conclusion that I am an incurable misfit and he no longer wishes to be responsible for my peculiar antics," she muttered disgustedly as she straightened the apron on her lap.

"You are, aren't you?" Seth quipped as a taunting smile tugged at the corners of his mouth, making his emerald eyes glisten in amusement.

A deliciously mischievous grin spread across Brianna's delicate features as she slowly raised her face to meet his steady gaze. "How could I possibly hope to convince you otherwise after you have witnessed one or two of the incidents that brought my father to the limits of patience?"

71

"You couldn't," Seth assured her with a smirk. "And just who is this fop that your father expects you to marry? Is he the one that you fled from the first night we met?"

"Nay." Brianna hesitated a moment, unsure whether she had revealed much more than she should have already. Perhaps the name of her would-be husband should not be disclosed.

"I don't intend to hold you for ransom and turn you over to your father," Seth insisted impatiently. "I have no need of his money since I will never live long enough to spend all of my own fortune," he added. There was no arrogance in his tone. It was merely a bland statement of fact. "Now what is the man's name?"

"Quentin Donnovan," she grumbled resentfully. "Papa said his reputation was as sordid as mine and that we deserved each other. It seems a rather lame excuse for matrimony, but nevertheless, 'tis the main reason he decided that I should marry Donnovan."

Seth chuckled heartily. "Donnovan is an infamous rake and I must agree with your father," he added between chuckles. "The two of you probably deserve each other, but it would be one hellish marriage which neither of you could possibly survive. Such a perfect match would be an open invitation for trouble."

Brianna shot him an annoyed frown. "Perhaps my actions merit such a miserable fate, but I'll be damned if I'm going through with a marriage to a man I don't even know and have no desire to ever meet."

"I can't blame you for that, Sabrina," Seth conceded with a wry smile. "I would imagine Quentin Donnovan shares the same opinion."

"Do you know him well?" Brianna questioned curiously. "What is he like? Is he as notorious as my father claims?"

Seth nodded affirmatively. "I know the chap quite

well. And I must admit, although I like him, all that has been said about him is true, or close enough to be repeated as fact."

"Although I have never seen him, I imagined him to be a shriveled-up old lech with an unappealing face." Brianna chuckled as the image of Donnovan that she had conjured up the previous night came to mind. "I do hope he isn't as hideous as I thought him to be."

Seth shrugged nonchalantly. "I am a better judge of women than men," he confessed soberly, "but I wouldn't describe him as ugly. I think of him as rather distinguished-looking. And with his wealth, I'm sure women have a tendency to overlook some of his obvious faults. Money and titles have a mystical way of concealing many character flaws."

The sudden seriousness in his tone caused Brianna's brows to arch curiously. Somewhere in that comment was a hint of bitterness, but Brianna wasn't sure if Seth was envious of Quentin or of something that had happened in his past.

"If what you say is true, perhaps I should have at least met Lord Donnovan. He may not have been as horrible as I had imagined."

"I think you chose the best course of action, Sabrina. Why invite trouble when you could easily avoid it?"

"Then you are willing to help me and you won't tell my father or Donnovan where I am?" Brianna turned pleading, amber eyes to the handsome gentleman who was slowly gaining her trust.

With a reassuring nod, Seth smiled down into Brianna's perfect face. "You can stay at my flat for the rest of the day and then you can be on your way. If you need supplies or money, I will gladly furnish you with them," he offered graciously.

A relieved smile parted her lips and she raised up from her seat, intending to place a grateful kiss to his bronzed cheek, but the carriage came to an abrupt halt and she found herself sprawled in Seth's lap. With an embarrassed shriek she attempted to squirm from his arms but they had quickly become bands of steel that held her securely in place.

Cupping her chin, Seth raised her face and slowly lowered his raven head, seeking her lips in a strangely gentle kiss that caught her completely off guard. There was no rough urgency, none of the devouring insistence that she had suffered with William Fairchild, only a tender, warm display that Brianna had never imagined this handsome stranger was capable of showing. It was in direct contrast to his rugged appearance.

When Seth slowly pulled away from the embrace, his green eyes seemed to entrance her and hold her captive in their colorful depths, rippling with emerald waves that carried her from reality's shore. Easily lifting Brianna from his lap, he placed her beside him on the padded seat and reached into his pocket to hand her the key.

"My room is the first door on the right at the top of the stairs. I will return about twelve o'clock and we'll dine together at the inn," he stated in a husky voice.

Brianna continued to stare up at him in confusion while his eyes seemed to focus on her lips and for a moment she thought he was about to kiss her again. Nodding mutely, Brianna started to rise, but she found herself effortlessly swept from the carriage by Seth's strong arms and placed on the street. Brianna stared after him as he climbed back into the coach and leaned his raven head from the window. The sun seemed to glisten about his dark, thick hair and Brianna stood speechless as her eyes moved over his bronzed face, memorizing each line of the distinct features that captivated her.

"Your secret is safe with me, Sabrina," Seth assured

her with a faint smile as the carriage lurched forward and rumbled down the cobblestones in a hasty departure.

A reckless chuckle filled the coach as Seth leaned back in his seat and grinned wickedly. Sabrina? Nay, that was Brianna Talbert, he mused with a disbelieving shake of his head. Lenora had attempted to keep him from discovering the name of the wild witch, but he had' come by the information quite by accident. What a deliciously charming lass, although she was a bit high-spirited, he thought to himself. Perhaps her father was right. Brianna and Quentin might deserve each other, but a marriage between two such reckless individuals could only mean devastation and destruction. Seth could just picture the two of them matching wits and coming to blows at the end of each heated argument. And there would be disagreements, plenty of them, and sooner or later they would manage to destroy each other. It would most certainly be a disastrous marriage, he decided with a firm nod. Brianna was like a free flying eagle that soared gracefully across a cloudless sky. The mere sight of her was enough to take a man's breath away, but if he ever captured her, he would be assaulted by long, sharp claws that could rip his flesh to bloody shreds. She was a wild creature who must be free to survive, and Quentin was too much like her. Even though he might be able to win her untamed heart if he handled her with kid gloves, that was not his way. Women came to him much too easily for him to waste his time trying to domesticate that little vixen.

Seth sighed as he crossed his arms on his chest and stared thoughtfully at the cushioned seat across from him where Brianna had been sitting. Nay, he would not turn her over to her father or Donnovan, but he was curious where the wench planned to seek asylum. It seemed she was destined for trouble. Bundles of spirits like her usually were. But Brianna was just gathering steam; before she was through, she would most likely meet with some sort of catastrophe in which she would carelessly embroil herself. Aye, the lovely witch would be stewing in her kettle one fine day and Seth would not be around to put out the fire. He was not about to become entangled with that adorable misfit. He would allow himself the pleasure of her company for the day, keep her out of mischief, send her on her way, and that would be the end of it. Quentin didn't need her and Seth certainly had no desire to keep her for any length of time. He chuckled again as his thoughts took him back to the night she had ducked into his carriage to escape from her over-zealous beau, and then her image changed as he recalled Brianna thundering across the grass on the back of that black stallion while she laughed wickedly and leaned from her steed to swipe his hat from his hands.

Suddenly, his lips were tingling as he remembered the feel of her soft lips pressed timidly against his. She had been set to refuse him, but he had instantly sensed that Brianna had unwillingly responded to his embrace. Seth had expected to have his face soundly slapped, but she had only stared at him in confusion, not truly understanding his action or her own reaction.

A slow smile surfaced on his lips. He would allow himself to enjoy her charms for the day. What could it hurt? Lenora would be annoyed that he had not called upon her, but he had grown tired of the wench. She was much too predictable and he could easily maneuver her, whereas Brianna offered an interesting challenge. The dark-haired beauty with the glistening golden eyes had managed to capture his thoughts and he intended to sample the lovely witch's passions before they parted.

Chapter Seven

After Brianna had found Seth's apartment, she walked back to collect the belongings that she had stashed behind Sabrina's house. Since the carriage had not returned, she did not seek out Sabrina. There would be no farewell to be said to her, but Brianna was certain that Sabrina would understand. When she returned, Brianna would apologize for not going back to see her, but she was afraid to take a chance of being seen by the Rutledges. When Brianna was safely back inside Seth's room, she changed into a pale yellow gown and combed the tangles from her long ebony hair, making herself presentable once again.

While carefully appraising her reflection in the mirror, a warm memory tugged at her thoughts. She had experienced a strange tingle when Seth had kissed her, but he had not seemed the least bit affected by their sudden embrace. His green eyes had not flickered with desire as had William's or most of her other suitors, for that matter. Perhaps he did not find her attractive, or perhaps he was in love with the wench who had hung onto him like a clinging vine when Brianna had seen them in the park. This was ridiculous, she chided herself as she attempted to fasten the stays on the back of her gown. Seth meant nothing to her and she would probably never see him again after tonight. What did she care that he was not interested in her?

After hearing the click of the door, she glanced over

her shoulder to see Seth's large, sturdy frame fill the entrance. She smiled slightly and tried to finish fastening the dress, but the mere appearance of the handsome rake turned all of her fingers to useless thumbs. As Seth ambled toward her, a taunting grin seemed to settle in the defined lines and creases of his bronzed face and his vibrant green eyes began to sparkle with devilment. There it was again, Brianna mused thoughtfully. He had the look of confidence while at the same time he seemed to guess what disturbed her.

"May I help?" he questioned softly.

Before Brianna could reply, her hands were brushed away and Seth took up the chore, adeptly lacing the stays while his knuckles gently caressed her skin, sending an unwanted wave of excitement rippling down her spine. When he had finished his task, Brianna quickly stepped away, carefully averting her gaze from the dashing rogue.

Seth cocked a wondering brow at her odd behavior. "It seems that 'tis I who should be cautiously edging away from you," he began as a mocking smile surfaced on his lips. "You are the one who has inflicted pain on me. I have yet to make any attempt to assault you."

Brianna shot him a quick glance that was neither hateful nor pleasant, merely an acknowledgment that she was not alone in the room. "Even though you have agreed to help me, I still do not trust you completely, sir," she retorted glibly. "You are a man and my past experiences have made me wary."

"I must conclude from that remark that being of the male persuasion is similar to being infected by plague," Seth replied with a derisive snort as he turned to pour a basin of water to wash his hands.

Brianna's tone was cool and aloof when she spoke to him. "Only an addle-witted fool would put her complete trust in a wolf who dresses in lamb's wool."

Seth shrugged indifferently and dried his hands before turning to face Brianna. "My dear lady, not every man is enamored of your beauty and charms, and I have no intention of falling into the category that labels me as one of your fumbling dandies who cannot resist you," he stated placidly. "You are not woman enough to satisfy a man like me, nor Quentin Donnovan for that matter. There are those in the male species who like their women warm and willing and do not seek to master wild creatures, such as the likes of you who do not possess an ounce of passion. Beauty is an attractive wrapper for a package, but it is what is found beneath the pretty paper that holds a man spellbound for any length of time. You, dear Sabrina, are the tinsel and foil of an empty package," he added with an intimidating smirk.

Brianna's golden eyes were immediately blazing like a forest fire as she turned on the arrogant rogue who dared to speak to her as no man had. With her hands on her hips, her feet widespread, and her delicate features alive with indignation she took a bold step toward Seth. "Does the fact that I do not peddle my wares on the street corner like a common trollop make me less passionate? Does the fact that I do not wish to be a man's mistress before I am his wife imply that I have no desires?" she said caustically and then hurried on allowing Seth no time to reply, for she was intent on answering her own questions. "Nay, my arrogant rogue, it only means that I have yet to find a man who has tempted me beyond my will to resist and that I have not found a man who has earned my love and respect," she assured him as her chin tilted defiantly. "If a man beds every wench who catches his eyes, he is a man among men, a dashing rake who is admired and envied by his friends, but if a woman lays with every man who

79

intrigues her, she is deemed a whore. And if she does not yield to the rogue whose only intention is tasting her passions, then she is frigid, unfeeling, an ice-maiden," she bellowed, her face flushed with anger. "I do not intend to be classified in either category. The fact is I know what I want and I have yet to find it!"

Seth studied the hot-tempered witch while mild amusement twinkled in his emerald eyes. It had been difficult to keep his mind on her words while her full, creamy breasts were heaving against the yellow silk, temptingly drawing his gaze from her lovely face to her alluring bodice. What was it she had said? He didn't dare ask her to repeat it for he would only confirm her cynical opinion of men. Finally he hit upon the train of thought and followed in her tracks.

"I seriously doubt that there is any room for someone else on your lofty pedestal and I don't imagine that you have ever really allowed yourself to know a man well enough to decide if you could ever love him. Your kind usually don't. And even if you could ever find such a man," Seth added in a skeptical tone, "how can you be certain that you will want to be his wife *and* his mistress?" The same intimidating sparkle alighted his eyes as it had a few minutes earlier, and Brianna bristled angrily when she noticed its return.

She was quickly losing patience with Seth. He had already called her a passionless wench who was too conceited to ever find the man of her dreams. And if that were not humiliating in itself, he was implying that she could never satisfy the man she loved. Brianna was not about to be bested by this rake! Damn him!

As her brows arched tauntingly, Brianna slowly appraised Seth's muscular stature. "You have done nothing but criticize me, but what about you? Do you consider yourself to be a man who can satisfy a woman? Do you enjoy humiliating other people to hide your own inferior qualities? Is there something magnetically attractive about you that women cannot resist?" Brianna's eyes mocked him as she turned up her dainty nose. "I do hope that you are not foolish enough to think that *all* women would come willingly to your arms. If you do, you are even more arrogant than I first realized."

Seth was well aware of her ploy and grinned wickedly, displaying even white teeth. "I have never had to force myself on any wench, but then, I have always kept company with women, not innocent little girls who do not know the meaning of love or passion—until now, that is." He smirked as his eyes roamed over her in the same aloof manner with which Brianna had just surveyed him.

"I am more woman than you could ever handle!" she insisted smugly.

Regarding Brianna skeptically, Seth released a derisive snort as his piercing gaze raked her shapely form once again. "I don't have time to play games with children. If and when you grow up, come around and we'll continue this discussion on a higher intellectual level."

"I know exactly what we are talking about and I am *not* a child. I am a woman!" Brianna stormed furiously at him.

Seth chuckled heartily and slowly shook his head, denying her self-righteous claim. "I kissed you in the carriage this morning, my dear Sabrina, and there was nothing that compelled me to continue the embrace," he reminded her with a mocking grin.

Crimson red began to work its way up her neck until her amber eyes were spewing the fire of blazing torches. She reacted just as she had the first time she had met Seth, but this time he was prepared for her attack and grabbed her doubled fist in mid-air. A victorious smile parted his lips as he peered haughtily into her enraged face.

"Another display of childishness," he taunted wickedly. "Admit it, my dear. You have a lovely body, but your beauty is only skin deep. You are all show. You can fight like a wildcat and set tongues wagging with your daring pranks, but when a man takes you in his arms, he walks away unaffected and has no reason to return."

"You think not?" she hissed as she jerked her hand from his grasp.

"I speak from experience. You are a witch with a heart of ice," he jeered insultingly.

Brianna was not about to back down to this damned rogue. Although she would have preferred to slit his despicable throat, she decided to put him in his proper place with a little feminine finesse. A provocative smile curved her soft lips as she stepped closer, pressing full length against his sturdy frame while her arms slid gingerly over his broad shoulders. "Then teach me the way to arouse a man. I intend to be both a mistress and a wife to the man I marry one day," she purred softly as her golden eyes silently pleaded with him. "I would not dare make such a bold request to a lesser man, only to a master among the apprentices who have attempted to make me feel the kindling of desire."

Her firm breasts seemed to bore into his muscular chest and the light touch of her thighs against his made Seth's heartbeat quicken. He had her exactly where he wanted her, he mused haughtily as he lowered his head to capture the tempting lips that parted in invitation to his embrace.

Brianna accepted his encircling arms and melted against him, offering herself to the conceited rogue as she had never done with any other man. His kiss began as a slow, unhurried caress, but as his breath quickened, his tongue played at her lips and began to explore her mouth. Against her determined will, Brianna felt herself responding to him. His arms tightened about her, molding their bodies together as his hands lowered to press her hips against his muscular thighs. She inwardly flinched at his intimate touch, but she did not pull away. Not yet! But when she did, she would have her sweet revenge for his cruel, biting remarks.

A passionate spark jumped between them and Brianna could stand no more. His kisses were demanding, urgent, insistent, and his hands seemed to burn a searing path across her quivering flesh. Her heart was running away with itself and Brianna willfully summoned her composure as she slowly withdrew and leaned back in his encircling arms to gaze into the captivating green eyes that had begun to sparkle with unmistakable desire. Brianna produced a pretentious smile, slightly aloof, tritely innocent, and yet a mite mischievous.

"Shall we go to dinner, Seth? I missed breakfast and I must admit that I'm famished," she stated saucily as she removed his hands from her waist and sauntered toward the door. "Are you coming?"

Seth was furious, knowing that he had been outmaneuvered by the cunning witch. The bulge in his tight breeches was obvious and Brianna made certain that he saw where her eyes had strayed, silently assuring him that she was well aware of how she had affected him. Damn that vixen! Although he was inwardly fuming, Seth attempted to mask his irritation, displaying a shallow smile that never reached his eyes as he ambled toward her.

"Whatever you wish, my dear," he remarked tightly.

Brianna flashed him a satanic grin as she curled her hand in the crook of his arm. "Now I know what makes men like you so agreeable."

Seth returned the rakish grin and closed the door behind them. Suppressing the urge to clamp his fingers around her dainty neck, he chuckled lightly. "You have convinced me that you are a tempting witch, but I'm sure half of the men in Bristol are aware of that, Sabrina. You still have not proven yourself worthy of lengthy involvements so you might as well swallow your smugness. It should curb your appetite. You still have not persuaded me that you are a woman, and I doubt that you ever will."

"I need not convince you," Brianna replied smoothly. "Only the man who wins my love—my future husband." She glanced quickly at him, casting him a subtle wink.

As Seth and Brianna descended the stairs, many pairs of eyes lingered on the striking couple. Seth resentfully noted the appreciative gazes that roamed over Brianna's perfect figure, only irritating him further, especially since she was aware of the attention she was receiving.

"By the time you find your imaginary hero, you will be too old to satisfy him," he insulted through his charming smile, lazily bending his gaze to Brianna.

For the benefit of those who watched them, Brianna returned his smile, squelching the urge to slap the arrogant expression from his face. "Perhaps that is true, sir," she conceded, her honeyed tone belying the oncoming gibe. "But at least my epitaph will not be as pitiful as the one that will stand over you for eternity."

Seth cocked a curious brow, his eyes sliding back to Brianna.

"At the bottom of this deep, dark hole,
Is what remains of this tortured soul.
He loved too many, once too often.
But now he sleeps alone in his coffin."

When Seth chuckled at her retaliation, Brianna chimed in with him. No matter how much he had annoyed her earlier, she still owed him a great deal. Without his help she could not escape from an unwanted marriage. She could forgive his arrogance and insults since he had graciously offered to aid her.

While they dined, Brianna noticed how often the eyes of other women came to rest on Seth. A certain sense of pride warmed her heart, knowing that she was the one who had his attention. Quickly routing such foolish thoughts from her head, she tried to ignore the strange feeling. He meant nothing to her. They were merely acquaintances. What did she care that Seth was being openly admired by other women?

When Seth escorted Brianna back to his room, he hesitated at the door, wondering whether to take his leave before he found himself wanting more than just stimulating conversation. As Brianna raised questioning eyes that could capture and hold him spellbound he quickly made his decision. Seth stepped into the room and locked the door behind him. He would prefer to fence words with Brianna than to return to Lenora. This room held a challenge while Lenora's room held only the conquered.

"What shall we do with our time?" Brianna queried innocently as she strolled across the room. "I dare not show my face on the street until after dark."

"I should think you would be more concerned about being seen in the company of a man and being escorted back to his room unchaperoned," Seth mocked dryly as he shrugged off his brown jacket and tossed it on the edge of the bed, realizing that was the one place that it wouldn't be in the way. He seriously doubted that they would be using it—at least not now.

Her shoulder lifted in a disinterested shrug. "My reputation is already ruined. What difference does it make now? It is of little importance to me what others think."

How very true, he mused as he eased down in a chair beside the table. Brianna had a point. After all she had done, one more incident only added bulk to her long list of iniquities. He watched Brianna retrieve a deck of cards from her pouch as she sank down on the chair across from him. Arching a dubious brow, he studied her as she shuffled the cards and dealt him a hand. Oddly, he was not surprised that Brianna might be a cardsharp along with the rest of her unusual talents.

"What game are we playing?" he inquired as he reached for his cards.

"I shall let you name it, sir. I play them all." A saucy smile crept to her lips as her gaze momentarily slid to Seth.

After she had won the first hand of piquet, she scooped the coins to her side of the table, grinning smugly. Defeating Seth was pure delight. The cocky rake was forced to swallow a little pride.

"Who taught you to play cards?" Seth questioned as he shuffled the deck, keeping her busy talking while he dealt.

"My brother. He taught me almost everything I know. Grant is the only man I trust. The rest of you are a dangerous lot," she added, casting Seth an accusing glance.

"So he is the one who must take the blame for molding your odd personality." Seth smirked as he collected his cards and quickly surveyed his hand.

"You would do well to take a few lessons from him," she suggested as she flashed him a mocking smile.

Seth released a derisive snort. "I think perhaps I shall limp along on my own meager abilities. Thank you just the same, Sabrina."

After two hours, Brianna frowned disgustedly at the

neat stack of winnings on his side of the table. Now she had no funds for her trip and had no opportunity to collect a few pounds before leaving. With a disappointed sigh, she pushed away from the table and impatiently paced the floor, wondering how to occupy her time before she sneaked aboard the schooner.

"Are you admitting defeat?" Seth queried as he leaned back in his seat and lit his cheroot.

Brianna shot him an annoyed frown. "It seems I must since I am without funds to continue. I'm sure you don't want to play if you have nothing to gain."

A sly smile hovered on his lips as he critically assessed Brianna. "You are worth a small sum, I suppose. We could play for other stakes."

Brianna immediately acquainted him with her look of contempt. "I have lost my money to you. I have no intention of forfeiting anything else."

"I thought you had more spunk than that, Sabrina. You gambled and lost. If you don't wish to accept my offer to play for something other than gold coins, then don't pout," he mocked as he blew several smoke rings into the air and glanced sideways at her.

"I have nothing left for my trip and no way to obtain money before I leave. Do you expect me to be happy about losing?" she questioned, her voice rising testily.

Seth pushed the coins to the far side of the table. "Take my winnings, my dear. Defeating you was victory in itself. The money is not the valued prize. As I told you before, I am in no need of funds or a daughter's ransom."

Brianna's jaw sagged as she peered in bewilderment at Seth. Was he offering her the money with no strings attached? Him? The arrogant rogue? A cynical frown knitted her brow. *There must be a catch,* she mused. What must she forfeit for the coins?

"You won it in a fair game. Why would you relinquish your winnings?"

Seth gave his head a denying shake. "Nay, Sabrina. I cheated you," he confessed, a wry grin catching one side of his mouth.

"Cheated me?" she repeated incredulously.

Seth had expected her to explode in anger, but a slow smile spread across her lips.

"Show me how you did it," she requested as she slid into the chair, her eyes dancing with anticipation.

Seth chortled amusedly and then explained how he had discreetly marked the cards while she had been discussing her brother. Brianna clasped her hands in delight and then practiced what he had taught her. As Seth watched her deal him another hand, he hopelessly shook his head. This was insane! He could be entangled in Lenora's embrace, tasting her passions, satisfying his desires. And yet here he sat with a most delectable young woman, teaching her to cheat at cards, as if the wench did not possess enough sordid traits.

What mysterious spell had she weaved about him? She had intrigued him the first night she had clambered into his coach. She had delighted him with her reckless ride through the park, and she continued to amuse him with her quick wit and feisty temperament. Brianna was beautiful, high-spirited, but damned sure no lady, he decided, silently chuckling to himself. Ladies did not go around stuffing their fists in men's faces, riding demon stallions that were barely manageable by men, parading in breeches, or learning the knack of cheating at cards. But he was here with this vixen who defied conformity. The distressing truth was that he was thoroughly enjoying himself. Perhaps he was the odd one instead of Brianna, he thought to himself. What the hell, he muttered under his breath. He could go to Lenora later if he was unable to maneuver Brianna into his bed. But for now . . .

A light rapping at the door brought puzzled frowns from Seth and Brianna. "Who is it?" Seth questioned as he rose.

"Lenora. I thought something might have happened to you since you didn't come by my apartment," came the impatient voice from the hall.

A deliciously wicked grin settled on Brianna's face as she watched Seth scowl disgustedly. Scrambling to her feet, Brianna scooped the cards and coins onto her lap and hurried to hide beneath the bed.

When Seth glanced back over his shoulder to speak to Brianna, she was nowhere to be seen. A wry smile crept to his lips as he opened the door to meet Lenora's disdainful glare.

"Why didn't you come to call?" she snapped as she brushed past him and swept into the room.

"I do have other obligations," he reminded her glibly.

Lenora gave him a cold glance and flounced down on the edge of the bed while Brianna suppressed a giggle.

"What duties were so pressing that you could not inform me that we had to cancel our afternoon together?" she inquired, her tone sharply accusing.

"Business," he stated simply.

"Then why are you still in your room?" she cross-examined.

"My associate is to meet me here in a few minutes," Seth explained as he extracted his watch from his pocket to check the time. It was a bald-faced lie, but he was certain she would rather hear it than the truth.

Lenora breathed a despairing sigh as she folded her hands in her lap. "Will you come by to see me this evening?"

"Of course," Seth assured her as he drew her to her feet and into his embrace. "I'll call for you later." When he placed a kiss to her eager lips, he had second thoughts about ushering her out the door. But he had already given the lie and did not dare to expose himself.

"You better go before my associate arrives. I'll see you tonight," he whispered when he had willfully dragged his lips from hers.

Her arms drew him closer to plant another passionate kiss to his lips, but Seth resisted the temptation. "Later, Lenora," he murmured, his gaze promising that she would not regret the wait.

Breathing a weak sigh, Lenora dropped her arms to her sides and allowed Seth to escort her to the door. Reaching up on tiptoe, she placed a farewell kiss on his cheek. "Until later then. . . ."

Seth propped his arms against the door casing and watched Lenora gracefully descend the stairs. When she was out of sight, his eyes strayed over his shoulder to see Brianna's dark head appear from the far side of the bed. She propped her elbows on the edge of the bed, resting her chin on her hands.

"Business?" she taunted. "My, but those lies slip so easily from your lips that it leaves one to wonder just what type of profession supports a man like you."

After closing the door with his boot heel, he sauntered back to the table, chewing leisurely on his cigar. "Bring the cards, Sabrina. I believe it's your deal."

Brianna pulled a face at him as she dumped the coins and cards in front of him. "I'm so sorry I kept you from willing arms this afternoon." Her voice lacked sympathy. "That was such a touching scene. I wish I could have viewed it instead of only listening from my hiding place."

Seth snorted caustically as he separated the coins and cards. "When a gentleman offers to aid a damsel in distress, he often finds that he must disregard his pleasure to see to his moral duties."

Brianna took her seat to shuffle the cards. Another mischievous smile made her amber eyes sparkle. "But fortunately for you, Lenora has agreed to wait until dark. I'm sure you will not be disappointed."

"I'm sure I won't," Seth agreed, returning her smile.

Brianna dealt the cards and eased back in her chair to study her hand, smothering the twinge of jealousy that invaded her thoughts. Why did she care that Seth and Lenora were lovers? It was none of her concern. She was just not accustomed to having a man discuss his amorous intentions for another woman while he was in her presence, she told herself. He had pricked her pride and she was not accustomed to it. Forcefully dismissing her jealous thoughts, she concentrated on her cards, her consolation coming from winning back her money.

Seth retrieved his timepiece and stared at it in disbelief. Damn! It was seven o'clock and he had several matters to attend. Tossing his cards on the table, he arose from his chair and walked around to draw Brianna up beside him.

"I'll take you to dinner and then I must go."

Brianna was disappointed. She had enjoyed his company more than she wanted to admit. For the first time in her life she found herself regretting to leave a gentleman's company. Usually she was bored to tears with the men of her social circle. But Seth was fascinating, secretive, and undeniably handsome. He knew what she was like and had accepted her the way she was, making no attempt to change her into something she had no desire to be.

Her lashes caressed her cheeks as her gaze fell to the floor, drawing Seth's attention to her bewitching features. "I think I will regret seeing you go, Seth," she murmured as she toyed with the buttons of his shirt. Then she chuckled lightly. "'Tis strange, but true. I know little about you, except your name. And yet, oddly, 'tis enough."

Reaching beneath her chin, Seth raised her face to see those mystifying pools of amber that could smolder like heated lava or ripple with tenderness. He lowered his head to taste her honeyed lips, unable to resist the temptation. The luring fragrance that hovered about her invaded his senses and he drew a ragged breath.

Although she had timidly returned his embrace, Seth felt desire raging in his loins. He wanted her. God, how he needed to feel her satiny flesh molded to his. His arms tightened about her, drawing her to the hard wall of his chest until logic tapped him on the shoulder. Reluctantly he withdrew. He could not afford to become involved with this bewitching young woman. For once in his life, he denied himself and his passions.

"We'd better go," he whispered huskily, urging her to the door.

Her flesh tingled from his touch. Her lips trembled from his ardent kiss. What was wrong with her? Why had she responded so easily to this rogue? Had she taken leave of her senses? What would she have done if he hadn't ended the embrace when he did? She was afraid to answer her own questions. Nodding slightly, Brianna silently agreed with him. They had better leave this lair before she found herself losing control. As she glanced up at Seth there was a hint of mockery glistening in his eyes and Brianna began to feel a mite foolish. He did not appear shaken by their embrace. To Seth, it probably meant nothing, no more than the unconscious batting of an eye. He had kissed more women in his lifetime than she even wanted to imagine.

He probably considered a kiss to be merely that—a simple, impulsive response that had very little effect on him. Brianna tried to stop her somersaulting heart, determined to feel no more than Seth had, but it was no easy task.

As they sat taking their meal, Brianna gazed into his unreadable emerald eyes, thoughtfully studying their depths. "Have you ever been in love?" she questioned, surprising him and herself with her inquiry.

"That's a personal question," Seth snapped more harshly than he intended. Then he permitted a hint of a smile to curve one side of his mouth. "We are strangers, remember? 'Tis a topic only to be discussed by close friends, not brief acquaintances, my dear."

Her lips parted in a wry grin as she regarded him critically. "Although you have refused to answer, you have made your reply. I can tell by your remark that you have been and the experience was not a pleasant one."

His shoulder lifted in a noncommittal shrug. "You will not pry information from me by intimidation, Sabrina. I have no desire to discuss the subject," he added with a hint of finality in his voice that only challenged and piqued Brianna's curiosity.

"Lenora?" she questioned as she cocked her head to the side to study Seth from a new angle. "Nay, I think not. Someone else I would imagine. Did she play you for the fool? Leave you with a broken heart while she pursued another man who caught her eye?" Her delicate brow arched mockingly.

The reply was on his lips, ready to take flight, but Seth swallowed his words. "If you've finished your meal, I'll escort you back to the room before I go," he offered, stiffly, his mouth thinning into a controlled smile that revealed nothing more than a slight change of expression.

Brianna silently taunted him as she rose from her chair and Seth inwardly flinched as he glanced down at her. The self-satisfied grin that played on the soft curve of her lips was annoying, but he vowed not to let this vixen creep beneath his skin. The wench had an uncanny way of testing his patience. He could never let his guard down with her. She was far too clever, dangerously so. He had to respect her cunning although it galled him to do it.

When the door closed behind them, Brianna ambled to the bureau, pulled the pins from her hair, and began brushing her ebony tresses. She waited, expecting Seth to say good-bye and be on his way to Lenora's.

Raking her shapely form with his gaze, Seth stood mesmerized by her innocent movements. The lustrous strands formed a cape that tumbled to her trim waist. Brianna was so damned tempting! She was like a wild rose, a soft, delicate flower whose fragrance was intoxicating and whose velvety skin begged to be caressed. A man would reach out to touch her, seeing only the outward beauty of such a desirable flower. Only too late would he discover the thorny stem. Before he knew what had happened, he would be pricked by her sharp defense.

"Look, but do not dare to touch," he mused as he silently watched Brianna. He was held suspended in a trancelike fantasy, aroused by what he could imagine awaited him, excited by the challenge of conquering this enchanting temptress. She was what dreams were made of. Brianna was an alluring witch who could draw men to her charms, but once they were within her clutches, she would rake their flesh with her long claws, poisoning their blood with the unquenchable need that paralyzed them, leaving them helpless and frustrated.

94

But then what man could know the dangers that awaited him? Who could see beneath that soft, creamy skin to perceive the deceitful sorceress who waited to capture and torture her prey?

Seth grumbled to himself as his eyes touched what his hands ached to caress. He knew exactly what awaited him, perhaps more so than the other fools who had attempted to draw her into their arms. And yet, he was tempted to toss caution to the wind, disregarding his own convincing arguments against such idiocy. His body seemed to be moving involuntarily toward Brianna, defying rationality. Damn that witch! Damn the appointment. To hell with the prickly thorns and sharp claws. Nothing worth taking was won without peril. As he walked toward the tempting maid whose skin glowed in a honey hue against the lantern light he knew he had lost the battle of mind over body.

Brianna watched him approach, seeing his reflection in the mirror. She smiled ruefully. "I wish to thank you for your assistance, Seth. I am indebted to you." Gazing down at the ivory-handled brush in her hand, she continued to speak without meeting those captivating green eyes that could entrance her, especially now that she was feeling envious of Lenora. "I won't be here when you return. I'm leaving tonight to find asylum elsewhere," she murmured.

"In the darkness?" his breath caressed the curve of her neck as he stepped up behind her.

She raised her eyes to meet his steady gaze in the mirror. A ghost of a smile hovered on her lips, her voice raspy as she spoke: "That shouldn't surprise you. You have referred to me as a witch more often than naught. Do you find it odd that I would prefer to travel in the cloak of darkness?"

A deep chuckle came from his massive chest as his

eyes roamed boldly over her reflection. "Nay, I suppose I shouldn't be shocked by anything you do, witch," he teased, his tone husky.

A long moment of silence passed between them before Seth reached around Brianna to snuff out the lantern. He placed light, feathery kisses on the hollow of her neck. Brianna closed her eyes and leaned back against the hard wall of his chest, reveling in the tenderness he displayed. Was this someone else who was responding to this handsome rogue? Was this Brianna Talbert?—the woman who had never been aroused by a man's touch? Why was she so vulnerable when he was close to her? She knew nothing about him, except his name. He had made no attempt to reveal anything of his past or the business that supported his expensive tastes. Was he a wandering gambler who made his living by cheating other men out of their fortunes?

As his arms tightened about her waist his skillful hands moved to her breasts, roaming over her flesh, burning every inch of skin that he touched. A gasp of alarm burst from her lips. A wild shiver of delight trickled down her spine. His bold advances were making her heart run away with itself and her thoughts were reeling in chaotic confusion.

Sensing her fright, Seth slowly turned her in his arms. His mouth covered hers in a kiss that was gentle, yet demanding. The feel of her body pressed intimately to his ignited a wildfire that began to burn out of control. He couldn't release her, not now. He had spent the entire afternoon trying to ignore his desire for her, formulating excuses as to why he should keep his distance. Now his body had disregarded restraint and was yielding to the temptation, yearning to know the passion that this enchanting woman possessed.

His kiss carried enough heat to melt the moon, and

Brianna could not remain indifferent to the devastating effect of it. Her skin tingled each time he touched her, igniting a flame that refused to be smothered. This was madness. What strange emotion had encompassed her? Why wasn't she squirming for release, lashing out at him in indignation and rage? The darkness began to circle about her, distorting her reasoning, drawing from her strength. She was painfully aware of the musky fragrance that hovered around her and the warm, arousing sensations that trickled through her veins.

When his nimble fingers worked the stays of her gown, she felt the dress being pulled away, leaving her thin chemise as meager protection from his hungry gaze. Seth lowered his head to trace a path of searing kisses down her neck to the fullness of her breast. A soft moan escaped his lips as his mouth captured the rosy peak.

Brianna was jolted by an indescribable need that demanded satisfaction, a need that she never realized existed until that moment. He had awakened a sleeping passion that nurtured a willing response. But as the seed of desire began to grow and spread across her flesh it triggered the protective device that defied raw emotions. Her eyes fluttered open as logic sparked her senses like a bolt of lightning.

She could not yield to this rogue! He sought only to appease his lust and he could do so with any trollop. It made little difference to him whom he held in his arms. Brianna would not become his conquered prize!

Cautiously reaching behind her on the bureau, she groped for the handle of the pitcher and grasped it in her hand. As she circled her arm back toward Seth, the porcelain found its intended mark and cracked against the back of his head. Seth groaned as the world suddenly turned a darker shade of black. He tumbled over the edge of consciousness into a deep silent abyss.

As Seth crumbled to the floor in a lifeless heap, Brianna grinned devilishly at him. "I warned you, my handsome rogue. So now you see that I *am* too much woman for you to handle. You'll have to search out someone who does not know how to defend herself."

Brianna stepped over the unconscious form that lay at her feet and then shed her chemise to don her breeches and shirt. With her long hair twisted beneath a cap, Brianna gathered her belongings and started toward the door. A deliciously wicked thought came to her and she hurried back to the bureau to write a note. She pulled a coin from her pouch and crouched down beside Seth to place the letter and money in his hand. A reckless chuckle floated in the dark room as Brianna opened the door and fled down the stairs to disappear from the inn.

As she scurried down the boardwalk, she ran head-long into two men who had just stepped out of the alleyway. One of the men grabbed her arm and yanked her around to face his angry scowl.

"Watch where you're going, brat," he snapped as he handed the confiscated loot to his companion.

"Sorry, sir," she replied, carefully ducking her head. "Me ma's sick and I was in a hurry to get home. I'm sorry," she apologized again, keeping her voice low and muffled.

"Let the lad go," came the other man's voice. "'E didn't mean no 'arm."

The firm grasp on Brianna's forearm eased slightly. The moment she was free, she darted across the street and fled into the darkness, breathing a sigh of relief. If only she could get on board the schooner, she would be safe. A fearful shudder raced down her spine when she realized what might have happened had she confronted those scoundrels.

Brianna made her way along the wharf until she found the *Mesmer* and then she crept on deck. Her gaze carefully swept her surroundings as she moved toward the steps that led to the hull. When she heard muffled voices and footsteps behind her she began to wonder if the two men had followed her. Brianna quickened her pace to seek refuge in the bowels of the ship.

Chapter Eight

With an agonizing groan, Seth propped himself up on one wobbly elbow, glanced around the dark room that swam before his eyes, and fought the powerful undercurrent that again tried to draw him into its recesses. What the hell had happened? Shaking his head, Seth tried to clear his muddled thoughts. He was watching Brianna, they were talking, he took her in his arms . . .

"Damn that witch!" he cursed spitefully as his mind stumbled onto the incident that had left him with a splitting headache. He glanced down to see the pale yellow gown that lay beside him and he cursed her image again.

As Seth struggled to his feet he grasped the dress in his clenched fist, wishing that little bitch was still within the confines of the gown. But no, the amber-eyed sorceress had flown from her human form, leaving her clothes behind when she spirited off into the night to consort with the other demons that roamed the earth during the witching hour. God, what a fool he had been!

Seth tossed the yellow gown on the bed and turned back to the basin to wash his face and tend to the knot on his head. Unfortunately, the only water was that which had been used earlier and the pitcher lay on the floor in a thousand pieces.

"Damn it," he muttered furiously. That witch was

nothing but trouble and he was only too happy to be rid of her. He had burned with desire for her delectable body, but he could appease himself with any woman. He didn't need that little bundle of mischief. Lenora was what any man would want. She was soft, yielding, rarely demanding, and she did not dare ask him for more than he could offer for the moment. But Brianna, as lovely and tempting as she was, would never submit without a fight. Again she had gotten the best of him. The silent acknowledgment of the fact made Seth's blood boil, coursing his veins like simmering lava.

It was a shame Brianna hadn't been forced to marry Donnovan. Quentin could have subdued the wench one way or another. Seth smirked scornfully as he folded the gown and chemise and tucked them in with his belongings, wishing he had dumped that ornery witch on Andrew Donnovan's doorstep.

When he turned to leave, he spied the note and coin lying on the floor. His brows furrowed thoughtfully as he picked them up.

My dearest Seth,

Seth gritted his teeth at the mockery in the endearment.

> I'm sure that you have cursed me for showing my gratitude in such a disrespectful manner, but then what did you expect? The coin is your good luck charm. When you receive a talisman from a witch, it will protect you from all other dark demons. Guard it carefully and you will never again be haunted by evil spirits. . . .

Seth rolled his eyes toward the ceiling, muttering to himself as he tucked the coin in his pocket. He was not

101

a superstitious man, but after his experience with Brianna, he was beginning to think that a little caution might need to be observed. Aye, Donnovan should have married that little witch and confined her to her quarters for all eternity.

As Seth stalked from the room he felt as though a pair of mystical golden eyes hovered above him, taunting him, and tempting him with their lingering presence. Brianna had refused to allow him peace even when she had vanished in the night. Her inviting lips had tasted like honey, instantly addicting him to their sweetness. He had been unable to draw away from the pleasure her kisses aroused. Her velvety skin begged for his touch and the subtle fragrance of jasmine still clung to him, filling his senses with the intoxicating memory of her presence.

Donnovan would have tasted that wench's passions even if he had to take her by force. He would have mastered that vixen, given time. Brianna could not have withstood his advances. Sooner or later she would have yielded to the stronger force. Brianna did indeed deserve to marry a man like Donnovan. The more he thought about it, the more he became convinced that her father was right. *Damn that witch!*

As Seth stepped onto the street, he glanced about him, squinting in the darkness, hoping to catch sight of Brianna even though he knew she wouldn't be there. He had allowed the deceptive wench to escape, and never again would he have the opportunity to kiss those sensuous lips, to hold her shapely body against his, or to gaze into that bewitching face that always hinted at mischievousness.

Why was he regretting that she had fled? That was what he had intended when he had come to her aid, wasn't it? Well, wasn't it? Seth muttered under his breath when the answer didn't come immediately. But then, what difference did it make? She was out of his life now and that was the end of it. Any more of her brutal assaults might have rendered him senseless and he was lucky to escape with his injured ego.

When Grant escorted Sabrina back to her home late that evening, a strange loneliness crept over him. He had found this lovely lass too late. If he could have shirked his duties aboard the schooner, he would have, but he felt obliged to follow through with his commitment.

As Grant took Sabrina in his arms, her lips parted, eagerly awaiting his kiss. The entire day had been a dream come true for her. Grant hadn't taken his eyes off of her. Each time he touched her she melted like butter. *Why must it end so quickly?* she mused ruefully.

"Will you wait for me to return?" Grant whispered against her lips.

"Do you even have to ask?" She leaned back in the circle of his arms to gaze into the warm brown eyes that watched her intently.

There was an open honesty in her expression. Sabrina was everything Caroline wasn't. For the first time in his life Grant realized that searching for the perfect woman was a waste of time. She had been right under his nose. He clutched her close, nestling her head against his shoulder.

"I won't forget you, Sabrina. This day will be on my mind until I return," he assured her before his lips captured hers.

As he stepped away, a mischievous smile curved her mouth upward. "You won't forget me, Grant Talbert. I have waited much too long to see this dream come true."

Grant's brows furrowed thoughtfully. Her smile

reminded him of Brianna's when she had some devilment brewing. With a light chuckle he blew Sabrina a kiss and ambled down the path.

Sabrina watched him disappear into the swaying shadows and then slipped into the house. Every moment of the day she had spent with Grant came back to her in vivid memories, and she had Brianna to thank for her dream coming true. Brianna . . . With all that had happened, Sabrina had forgotten about her unfortunate friend. Ah, well, Brianna had always been able to fend for herself. There was no need to worry about her. Sabrina quickly turned her thoughts back to Grant as she strolled into her bedchamber and stripped from her gown. That mysterious smile continued to hover on her lips as she walked out to the terrace where Brianna had been the previous night.

When Quentin sauntered through the front door, Andrew was descending the stairs. An annoyed frown knitted his brows when he spied his grandson.

"Where the hell have you been?" he snapped. "Your grandmother has been overwrought with worry. Have you no sense of decency left in you? It seems you have lived too long with those colonial heathens and savages."

Quentin heaved a tired sigh, hung his coat and hat on the coatrack, and then turned to meet Andrew's condemning scowl. "I was unavoidably detained with last minute details. I'm sorry," he muttered in explanation as he met his grandfather at the bottom of the steps.

"I don't want to hear your lame excuses, Quentin. You have kept your grandmother and me waiting over an hour while you were out with only God knows whom!" Andrew snorted disgustedly. "I deeply regret that I was not able to arrange the marriage between you and Brianna Talbert. You would have been far too busy trying to keep that little termagant in line. There would not be time for your carousing until all hours of the night! If it were she whom you had kept waiting, you would now be out on the streets searching for *her* because she would have stomped out of the house to pursue her own mischief."

A wry smile traced Quentin's lips as he studied Andrew's reddened face. "You made a valiant effort to tie me down, but it seems you should have kept a watchful eye on Miss Talbert instead of me. Has she turned up yet?" he asked, as he went into the study to pour himself a brandy.

"Nay. Gerald came by this afternoon to inform me that Brianna had gone to their country estate and that he was going after her," he grumbled. "He also said that he had had a change of heart. He wouldn't go through with the arrangement even if he caught up with her in time to bring her back."

"Oh?" Quentin arched a brow as he leisurely turned his gaze to Andrew. "Did he decide that I was not worthy of wedding his precious daughter?"

"He was certain that you were just what she needed to tame her wild spirit, but his conscience wouldn't allow him to force Brianna into a marriage to a man she had never met." Andrew took the glass from Quentin's hand and sipped freely, forcing his grandson to pour himself another brandy.

"Can you blame him?" Quentin cast his grandfather a quick, sidelong glance as he reached for the snifter of liquor. "I must admit I have more respect for the man now that I know he is not as uncaring for his daughter's feelings as I had first suspected. I would have been disappointed in Talbert if he had followed through with the contract."

Andrew released a disdainful snort. "Are you insinuating that your opinion of me has slipped a notch since

I was bound and determined to see you wed to this wench, sight unseen?"

Quentin chuckled as he raised his glass in toast to the spry old man. "I have the utmost respect for you, sir. I realize that you had my best interests at heart, although your methods were a bit unscrupulous."

Andrew's breath came out in a rush as he peered at his handsome grandson. "I am an old man, Quentin, and I have lost my only son. You are all I have left. If I tend to dote over you as if you were still a young lad, 'tis because your grandmother and I are so very fond of you. We want to see you married to a woman from a distinguished English family and watch your children grow. Perhaps when you reach our age you will understand what I'm trying to say."

Humbly bowing his head, Quentin averted his eyes from Andrew's steady gaze. "And I never seem to live up to your expectations as a Donnovan, do I?"

"Do not misunderstand me, Quentin. I am proud of your accomplishments. You are a man of convictions and you must always do what is best for you." He fondly patted his grandson's shoulder and then strolled over to the window. A rueful smile touched his lips as he gazed out into the darkness. "I did want you to marry Brianna. You have never met anyone like her. Brianna possesses a rare beauty that far exceeds any that you could name. And her spirit . . ." Andrew grinned as his gaze swung back to Quentin. "She would have led you on a merry chase, m'boy. You would have grumbled about being saddled with such a lively bundle and you would have had one hell of a time controlling her. But Brianna is just the challenge you need. In time I think you would have found it to be a delightful chase that you would never have regretted accepting."

Andrew shrugged disappointedly as he moved back

to Quentin. "I would have been a happy man if you had married Brianna, but it is your loss. Her thirst for adventure would have made the two of you an equal match. Now some fortunate gentleman will take your place one day and you will only admire her from afar."

Quentin studied the old man's sad smile. How could he be so certain that Brianna was the one woman who could make his grandson change his ways? What mysterious quality had Andrew seen in her that had convinced him to contract a hasty wedding. "Perhaps another time, Grandfather," he murmured as he swished the brandy around in his glass and then took a small sip.

"Perhaps . . ." The word hung in the air as Andrew set down his glass and gestured toward the parlor. "Shall we join your grandmother? She is most anxious to see you."

"I'll be along in a minute," Quentin replied as he strolled to the window and drew back the velvet drapes. If his time had not been limited, maybe he would have journeyed to the Talbert estate to see Brianna, just to satisfy Andrew. He owed his grandfather that much. But he was committed to his duties, and business came first. Perhaps if he had married, Andrew would have been content and there would have been fewer arguments between them. Heaving a heavy sigh, Quentin let the curtains drop back in place and followed after Andrew. When he returned to Bristol he would seek out Brianna and take the matter up with her. They could both profit by the marriage arrangement if they could come to terms. He could continue to come and go as he pleased and Brianna could do whatever met her whim, seeing her vagabond husband occasionally. Aye, he would discuss the matter with Miss Talbert on his return trip. Well, he would consider it anyway. . . .

Brianna found a small niche in the hull of the ship between the stacked crates, but she wasn't pleased with her accommodations. Although she had made herself a pallet with the bundles of cloth, she expected to see a rat scampering over her at any moment. She shuddered at the thought, but gritted her teeth, determined not to cry out if it did happen.

While Brianna spent a fretful night in the bowels of the ship, the vision of the handsome stranger tugged at her mind. She was tempted to climb from the frightening hole and run back to his protective arms, forgetting her plan to sail to the colonies. Perhaps her father had had time to reconsider his rash decision. Maybe he was ready to apologize for making the ridiculous contract and could forgive her shenanigans. The thought of returning to her own room was more appealing than staying in the musty hull of the ship. Brianna rose to her feet and crept to the door, indecision etching her brow.

When dawn spread its first light on the oaken decks of the *Mesmer,* the captain was at the helm, giving instructions to his crew. With the wind in his face, a small twinge of regret pierced his heart, sweeping his gaze back to the shore that faded in the distance. He had left unfinished business behind and it nagged at his thoughts. Seth hated to admit it, but he could not get Brianna out of his mind. She was a troublesome little misfit, but she had a bewitching way of burrowing into a man's thoughts. He had spent just enough time with her to arouse his interest, but not enough to appease the desire that he was doing his damnedest to forget. If he could have been the one to leave her behind, he could have easily dismissed her. Instead, she had vanished in the night, leaving him with one hell of a headache and a taunting note. It goaded his ego to be outwitted by that vixen. Seth clasped the gold coin that hung on a chain around his neck. A golden talisman, he mused bitterly. It was a painful reminder of those flaming amber eyes that were so mysteriously lovely and yet so hauntingly wicked.

Derrick Sayer had noticed the medallion and had questioned him about it, but Seth had not given his first mate an explanation. The fact that Sayer would find the incident amusing was one reason Seth had avoided explaining. When Seth could relate the story without allowing his voice to tremble with fury, he would answer Sayer's question.

An unwelcomed smile grazed his lips as he peered at the rippling water, seeing Brianna's reflection appear on its surface. If he could have spent a few days with her, he would have grown tired of her. No woman had held his interest for any length of time since his affair with Priscilla. The effect of that relationship had left him cynical. Brianna was only an unanswered challenge. If he had subdued her, taken her to his bed, and left her to return to sea, he would have been more than willing to see the brief encounter end. But nothing had gone according to plan. Seth was certain that any forethought he had in maneuvering that wench was useless. She never knew what she was going to do until the moment was upon her. That little spitfire was unpredictable. Even when he thought he had her in his grasp she had strolled away, standing smugly before him with that damned, mocking smile of hers. And she wore it so well. Brianna was quick-witted and clever—dangerously so. She had played him for a fool more times than he cared to count. It did not sit well to be bested, nor was he accustomed to taking it on the chin or on the back of the head, especially from such a petite young woman.

The vision of Brianna straddling that magnificent black stallion came to mind, convincing him that if he did believe in witches Brianna would be at the top of the list. With her long, ebony hair flying recklessly about her shapely body, her golden eyes dancing, and her laughter crackling in the air, she had presented a bewitching picture. Any man who had seen her would have paid a king's ransom to take her in his arms. But all of them would have regretted ever laying eyes on her, just as he did. Brianna was a fiery bundle of trouble who was headed for disaster. And she would find it, Seth decided with a spiteful smirk. Behind her lay a path of destruction. Unfortunately, he had been another victim who found himself in the wake of her devastating spell.

He raked his fingers through his raven hair, feeling the tender knot on the back of his head. Seth muttered to himself at the reminder of playing the dolt. Aye, Brianna was like a whirlwind and it was impossible not to be swept into her tempest. He should have hauled her to Donnovan's doorstep when he found her on the wharf, but he hadn't, and he had paid dearly for his folly.

Inhaling a deep breath of salty sea air, Seth willed himself to dismiss the thought of Brianna Talbert. They were worlds apart now and it served no purpose to dwell on the past. Brianna had been a lively diversion, but it was over. He would have to learn to accept the fact that somewhere in England there was a woman who had outwitted him.

As Grant worked beside Lucas Patton, he glanced up to see the captain staring pensively out over the sea. A wry smile crept to his lips as he watched Seth amble across the quarterdeck with his hands clasped behind his back. Grant had not yet met the captain since he had been hired by the first mate, but he was anxious to make his acquaintance. Patton's gruff words filtered into Grant's thoughts, and he reluctantly swung his gaze to the burly, stubble-faced seaman who demanded his attention.

"Damn it, man, pay attention when I talk to ye!" Lucas snapped impatiently. "Ye dandies are all alike. Yer too soft to 'andle a schooner. Ye should 'ave stayed ashore and left sailin' to men who kin manage a tub."

Grant resentfully muttered an apology. Although he could barely endure Patton's presence, he didn't dare bring the bloke's wrath down on him. Soon Grant would be able to maneuver the sails by himself and he wouldn't have to suffer the biting remarks. Patience, man, he told himself as he copied Patton's procedure.

Seth poured Derrick a drink and rested questioning green eyes on his blond-haired first mate. "Did you have difficulty filling the two positions on the crew?"

"Nay." Derrick accepted the liquor and eased back in his chair. "I think both men will make good sailors once they learn the ropes."

With a casual nod, Seth eased into his seat and propped a booted foot on the edge of his desk. "I'm sorry I returned too late last night, leaving you to check the ship yourself. I had several matters to attend to."

Derrick lifted a shoulder in a careless shrug. "'Twas a quiet night, Captain. I didn't mind." A sly but envious smile touched his bronzed features as his gaze slid to Seth. "I suppose you found yourself in the arms of some willing wench who refused to release you."

Seth's brows slanted into an annoyed frown, but he attempted to keep the bitterness from creeping into his voice. "I found myself coldcocked and woke up with a throbbing headache."

"What?" Derrick gasped in concern. "Were you robbed?"

"Only of my pride. The little wildcat shattered a pitcher over my head and left me sprawled on the floor of my room," Seth muttered as he swirled his brandy around the rim of his glass and then guzzled it. "I didn't realize nightmares could be so vivid."

Derrick chortled at Seth's sour expression. "Who hit you?"

"'Twas a dark-haired witch who fought as dirty as a sailor. If she hadn't disappeared into the night to consort with the bats and banshees, I would have delighted in wringing her damned neck."

Derrick threw back his head and guffawed. "I should think you would have been relieved that you escaped with your life instead of thirsting for revenge."

The laughter came to an abrupt halt when Seth frowned menacingly. "I should have known better than to relate the story to you," he grumbled as he lifted the medallion in his hand. "That is how I came to have this good luck charm. The witch told me to keep the talisman so I would be spared the visit of other demon spirits. You merely snicker at my misfortune. Tell me, friend, would you have been dismayed if she had managed to crack my skull wide open?"

"But, of course," he assured Seth, biting back a grin. "Until now I was envious that you were ashore and I was left to tend the ship. Your story has me convinced that I was better off where I was. But I do find it ironic that a man who usually leaves his ladies groveling at his feet has been tripped up by a woman."

"Not a woman," Seth scornfully corrected before his eyes took on a faraway look. "A beautiful, desirable, but deceitful witch, the likes of which you cannot begin to imagine."

"Do I detect a hint of remorse?" Derrick taunted as he cocked a brow. "It wouldn't be that you were intrigued by her? Is that why you keep the talisman?"

Seth snorted cynically. "I keep the charm as a reminder of a foolish mistake that I never intend to repeat. I like my women warm and willing. That temptress was neither. I'm glad to be rid of her."

Derrick rose to full stature and placed his glass on the desk. As he strolled to the door he glanced back at his captain. "'Tis fortunate that she fled before you found yourself in love with this mysterious witch."

"I was fascinated with her," he conceded hesitantly. "But in time she would have been purring like a kitten. I would have tired of her. I intended to take her, but I had no thought of keeping her. That is another long story that I will relate one day while we are becalmed. It will help pass the time and I'm sure you will find it equally amusing." Seth cast Derrick a hasty glance, silently dismissing him from the captain's quarters.

"I'm looking forward to it. Perhaps by then you will be willing to admit that the wench occupies your thoughts far more than you would have me believe."

Derrick's reckless chuckle floated back to Seth, causing him to inwardly cringe as the door closed, leaving him alone with his thoughts. Strange, he mused as he spread the chart out in front of him. Why was the one who got away always the one everyone thought would have been a prize worth keeping? Shrugging away all reminders of Brianna, Seth tried to set his mind on the maps. But the wench kept creeping into the corner of his thoughts. What annoyed him the most was that his last night on shore had ended in disaster. It would be an eternity before he could take a woman in his arms. The recollection of his last encounter should have been a pleasant one that would sustain him for the next two months. Instead, it could be aptly described as a nightmare. He had gone to Lenora, but he had found no pleasure in her arms. He had wanted Brianna and Lenora was a poor substitute for the daring beauty who had tempted him and left him discontented. A thoughtful frown clouded his features as he remembered the Indian myth about the wandering spirit that roamed their land; the goddess had taken human form in a woman with eyes the color of the sun and hair as dark as the moonless night. The Tuscarora tribe would see the folly of their beliefs if they had met Brianna, for she had the Devil's ways and a good portion of his luck.

Seth was about to climb into bed when his first mate rapped on the door. When he allowed Derrick to enter, the first mate seemed unduly troubled and yet there was something strange in his smile.

"Well, what is it?" Seth quipped impatiently.

"I found a stowaway in the storeroom, Captain."

Seth growled in irritation. "I thought you checked this ship from bow to stern before we sailed. How is it someone sneaked aboard?"

"I did check," Derrick defended, his voice rising testily. "But, unfortunately, I was left to see to *all* of the duties myself and to ensure that all of the crew returned. Patton and Catlin were drunk and rambling on about some waif trying to steal from them. I had to tuck those two fools in bed like a mother hen. 'Tis often difficult to be two places at once!"

Seth scowled disgustedly. He had no reason to blame Derrick. After all, he should have seen to his own ship, but he had been detained by a frightful witch. "Just put him in the brig and I'll see to him in the morning," he ordered, silently dismissing Derrick.

When Seth started to unfasten his breeches and climb into bed again, he glanced back to see Derrick had not budged from his spot. "Was there something else?"

"I think you should see the stowaway tonight, Captain," Sayer insisted, a subtle smile playing on his lips.

"Tomorrow will be soon enough," Seth replied. "Let the scoundrel spend some time in that dingy hole. He deserves no better for trying to sail with us without paying his way."

"The stowaway is not a he, she's a she," Derrick snickered.

"What?" Seth gasped incredulously as he wheeled to face Derrick.

The first mate nodded affirmatively. "She says her name is Sabrina Rutledge."

"Sabrina," the captain repeated, his green eyes glistening wickedly. Could it be that it was Brianna who had hidden on his ship, still clinging to her assumed name? The thought of seeing her again was making her heart leap with anticipation. Perhaps he would have his revenge after all.

"Shall I bring her in?" Derrick questioned, his mouth curving in a knowing smile.

"Aye." Seth grabbed his shirt and shrugged it over his broad shoulders.

A wicked grin caught the corners of his mouth as he imagined seeing Brianna again. What was she doing on the *Mesmer?* Why would she leave England? Seth hopelessly shook his head. There was no sense wasting time wondering what motivated that unpredictable wench. His mind raced, formulating what he intended to say to her. He would give her an earful, have his revenge with some hideous method of torture, and then he would cast her into the sea. But it wasn't revenge that caused the tingle of excitement that coursed his veins as Brianna's image rose above him. He could still feel her shapely body molded tightly to his, making him ache with a need that had yet to be satiated.

When Derrick escorted the young woman into the captain's quarters, a look of surprise and disappointment flickered in his eyes. The lass was attractive with her flaxen blonde hair and comely figure, but she was not the woman he had hoped to see.

"What are you doing on my schooner, young lady?" Seth snapped as he grabbed her arm and roughly pushed her into his cabin.

Sabrina's eyes darted fearfully from Derrick to Seth. Both men appeared so menacing that she couldn't find her tongue to reply.

"Well, Miss Rutledge, answer me!" Seth bellowed, causing Sabrina to shrink away from the booming voice that bounced off the walls and came at her from all directions.

Her mind fumbled over several excuses since she hesitated to give the scowling captain the truth. "I'm running away from home."

Derrick and Seth exchanged skeptical glances before Derrick summoned the captain for a private conference. "I saw this wench with her lady's maid on the schooner before we sailed. She wanted to talk with one of the new men."

Seth's gaze glided back to the woman, lingering momentarily before he spoke to Sayer. "I'd like to speak to Miss Rutledge alone. Why don't you see what type of accommodations can be arranged for her?"

"But, Captain, we don't have—"

"Derrick," Seth interrupted as he nodded toward the door.

A sly smile crept to his lips as he spun on his heels. "Aye, Captain, whatever you say."

Seth motioned for Sabrina to take a seat while his eyes boldly raked her from head to toe. "Now that we are alone, I want to know the truth. First of all, tell me if your name is really Sabrina."

She frowned bemusedly at his question. "Aye, 'tis Sabrina. I came to see—" She halted abruptly. Once

116

she had found her tongue it seemed to be running away with itself. If she revealed Grant's name it might cause him distress.

"To see whom?" Seth prodded, a dark scowl settling in the craggy lines of his face.

With a fearful gulp, Sabrina raised her gaze to meet his threatening glare, but still she refused to answer. Seth grabbed her by the shoulders and jerked her up in front of him, shaking her soundly as his eyes penetrated her flesh with their fierceness.

"Whom did you come to see?" he growled impatiently. "You better tell me now, young lady, or you'll regret it later."

Sabrina tilted a stubborn chin, regaining her courage. Before she knew what was happening, Seth's mouth captured hers, taking her breath away with his bruising kiss. Sabrina squirmed in panic as his hands worked the stays on the back of her gown. His arms were like steel bands, securely holding her in place.

"Let go of me, you scoundrel!" she shrieked when she dragged her lips away from his.

"Unless you tell me whom you were following, you will not leave my cabin tonight," Seth assured her, a sardonic smile curling his lips. His gaze boldly undressed her and Sabrina could almost believe he could see through her silk gown. "Consider what you will lose to guard your secret, Sabrina."

Seth lowered his head for another ravishing assault when she refused to reply. Sabrina twisted her face away and pushed against the hard wall of his chest in another futile attempt to escape. Her breath lodged in her throat as his kiss deepened, his tongue searching the recesses of her mouth.

"Grant!" she blurted out, unable to keep the silence.

Seth's heavy brows furrowed over his cold, green eyes as he held her at arm's length. "I know no one by that name. Don't play games with me, Sabrina. My patience is short."

"He just signed on for this voyage," she explained as a tear formed in the corner of her eye.

Suddenly she was standing on her own and she stumbled back into the chair while the captain leaned over her, his smoldering gaze burning her with its intensity.

"Why did you follow him? Does he know you're here?"

Sabrina shook her head negatively and shrank away as Seth leaned closer, his face only inches from hers. "He doesn't know."

"And just why are you here?" he prodded, his stern voice making her quiver uncontrollably.

"Because I love Grant, and I didn't want to see him leave without me, not after all the time I've waited for him." Sabrina was on the brink of bursting into tears as Seth scowled down on her.

He slowly rose to full stature and looked down at her. "And what if he doesn't want you here, Miss Rutledge? Then what am I to do with you?" he smirked cruelly.

"But he does!" she insisted as she clenched her fingers around the arms of the chair. "And I will gladly pay my passage. I'll sleep in the storeroom. I don't need special accommodations," she added, gathering more courage.

Seth arched a wondering brow at Sabrina's sudden burst of self-assurance. "Do you know Brianna Talbert?"

His question startled Sabrina, draining her newfound confidence. Her blue eyes narrowed suspiciously as she peered up at the rogue who towered over her. "Why, yes, I have heard of her," she said cautiously. "Do you know her?" Sabrina averted her eyes, nervously toying with the folds of her gown.

"And just how well do you know the wench?" Seth thoughtfully rubbed his stubbled chin, eyeing her as deliberately as she had studied him.

Sabrina bit her lip, giving herself time to think. He was asking too damned many questions and she could read nothing in those icy green pools that watched her like a hawk. "I know who she is," she answered with a noncommittal shrug.

"When I met her, she told me her name was Sabrina." He waited, assessing her reaction.

"Oh?" Sabrina forced a feeble smile. "I wonder why she would say something like that?"

"It does tend to raise one's curiosity, doesn't it?" he said dryly. "I would venture to guess that you know Miss Talbert better than you would have me believe. And just why is that?" He shot her an accusing glance which Sabrina shrugged away all too quickly.

"I'm sorry if I have inconvenienced you, Captain," she began, tactfully dismissing the subject of Brianna. "I don't know what possessed me to stow away. I suppose I was just afraid of losing Grant. I didn't consider the consequences of being caught."

Seth's mouth twisted in a knowing smile. Sabrina was hiding something. He could see it in the pale blue eyes that refused to meet his unwavering gaze. Resting a hip on the edge of the desk, the captain reached over to pull the log book onto his lap and quickly thumbed to the list of the crew. His brows lifted in surprise when he spied Grant's last name and then furrowed as his stern gaze swung back to Sabrina. Laying the book aside, he paced the confines of the cabin, his thoughts sorting through the incidents of the past week.

He would have bet his entire load of cargo that Brianna, who had portrayed Sabrina's lady-in-waiting, had come on board to see her brother before they sailed. Pausing to stare at Sabrina, he critically appraised the lovely blonde who eyed him warily. Watching Sabrina fidget beneath his scrutinizing gaze, he smiled to himself. He was willing to wager double or nothing on his cargo that Brianna was the one who instilled the idea of stowing away into Sabrina's head. That ornery little witch might well be hiding on the schooner after all. A wicked grin pushed its way to his lips as he continued to peer at Sabrina. She was probably full of information, and he would have it all before the night was out.

"Where is Brianna?" he questioned, breaking the silence.

Sabrina flinched as she met his frosty glare. "I believe she went to their country estate to escape from her father."

"Oh?" Seth's brow raised acutely and then returned to its normal arch. "And why was she running away from him?"

Squirming uncomfortably beneath his probing gaze, Sabrina stared out the porthole. "Why are you so interested in Brianna?"

With a nonchalant shrug, Seth eased back against the corner of the desk, crossing his arms on his chest. "I met her while we were docked in Bristol. I was curious to know what became of her. She was quite secretive."

"Her father contracted her into marriage to a man she refused to wed, so she fled," she explained, hoping that if Brianna were discovered, she would not be treated as harshly. And yet, Sabrina wondered whether the captain had a compassionate bone in his body. He towered over her like some dark, avenging god. How could such a sour dispositioned rogue show sympathy? "Brianna was upset about what her father had done and was probably afraid to confide in anyone," she added in Brianna's defense.

"Does Grant know where she is?" Seth opened the box beside him and lit a cigar, his gaze never leaving Sabrina.

Sabrina nervously chewed on her lip. The captain had discovered the relationship between Grant and Brianna. He was prying information from her and Sabrina was having difficulty preventing it. "She wouldn't leave without telling Grant good-bye," she said lamely.

A shallow smile that did not reach Seth's eyes surfaced on his lips. No doubt, Sabrina knew every detail and he was certain that he had drawn the correct conclusion. Brianna was on the *Mesmer*. She had lied about where she was going just as she had lied about her name. Sweet revenge! When he got his hands on that deceitful witch, he would make her beg for mercy and he would allow her none.

"Well, it seems then that Brianna is safe and you are the one in trouble," Seth remarked in an intimidating tone.

"But I can pay for my passage," she insisted. "I'll sleep in the storeroom. You won't even know I'm aboard."

Seth chuckled lightly while regarding her wide, blue eyes. "Very well, Miss Rutledge. I will have Derrick escort you to your meager quarters and we will continue this discussion in the morning. The hour is late and there is another matter which needs my attention before I can retire."

When the captain strolled outside to summon his first mate, Sabrina breathed a sigh of relief. The fact that the captain was curious about Brianna troubled her greatly. Why did he want to know about her? Why had Brianna told him that she was Sabrina? Something was amiss and Sabrina was determined to find Brianna and talk to her before she was forced to meet with the captain again.

Sabrina rose from the chair when Seth gestured to her. Nodding slightly, she brushed past the captain only to be grabbed by the first mate who hastily whisked her away.

"Lock Miss Rutledge in the storeroom for the night," Seth called after them, his wicked chuckle filling the darkness.

Sabrina glanced over her shoulder at the awesome silhouette of the captain who leaned against the door casing. The golden lantern light that sprayed from the cabin outlined his muscular frame, casting an ominous shadow across the deck. *Damn him!* Now what was she to do? If she couldn't find Brianna tonight, then she didn't dare to offer the captain any further information. She didn't trust that scoundrel. Even when he smiled at her, it seemed he was mocking her. And when he had kissed her so brutally, she had feared that she would learn more about him than she cared to know.

"Who is he?" Sabrina questioned as her gaze slid to Derrick and then returned to the sturdy form propped against the door.

The first mate grinned down at her. "My orders were not to divulge any information to the prisoner," he replied as he ushered her down the dark steps that led to the storeroom.

Sabrina muttered to herself as she was shoved into the dark niche and then shuddered involuntarily when she heard the click of the lock. There were rats in the room and she could hear them scampering about. They had caused her to be discovered. She had not been able to contain the cry of anguish when one of those disgusting rodents had scrambled onto her lap. Now she was locked in with them for an eternity. The captain was

122

certainly no gentleman, she mused bitterly. He could have offered to relinquish his quarters to her so she could sleep on a bed instead of on the floor with the rats. Somehow she would get even with that man, she swore as she tucked her skirt tightly about her and huddled in the corner, knowing it would be impossible to sleep. And Lord, what a long night it was!

Chapter Nine

Brianna had made her way to the deck to inhale some fresh air, ridding her senses of the musty stench that clung to her after being confined to the ship during the day. In the peaceful darkness there was only the helmsman with whom to contend and she always positioned herself behind him on the lower deck so that he would not notice her. Breathing a sigh of relief, Brianna sat down cross-legged and pulled the dried beef from her pocket. She had refused to eat when she was in the bowels of the schooner. The rancid odor below deck was enough to nauseate her and the thought of food was repulsive.

They had been at sea three days and this was the night Brianna had chosen to search out Grant, hoping that he could manage to find her another place to stay that would not be so frightfully miserable. A faint smile curved her lips when she imagined the look of surprise on Grant's face. He would be irritated with her for stowing away, but there would be nothing he could do now that they were at sea. His only choice would be to care for her as best he could until they reached the colonies. Brianna hated to deceive her own brother, but if she would have told him what she intended to do, he would have never allowed her to come along.

Seth had been watching for a sign of Brianna and had seen the small shadow dart from the steps to the wall of the quarterdeck. It was just as he had suspected.

The little witch only appeared at night and kept to her hiding place during the day when the crewmen were about. A deliciously wicked grin surfaced on his lips as he tiptoed across the deck and peered around the corner to see the petite lass dressed in breeches, quietly gazing out over the sea. Reaching in his pocket, he drew out a coin and tossed it to the far side of the deck to gain Brianna's attention. Brianna glanced in the direction from which the sound had come and cautiously backed away from it. Seth pounced on her with the quickness of a crouched panther and then covered her mouth before she made any noise. Roughly yanking her to her feet, he grabbed her to him and stalked back to his cabin. With the door locked behind them, Seth shoved Brianna toward the cot and lit the lantern to again see the face of the wench who had haunted his dreams.

As the dim light dissolved the shadows, Brianna gasped in surprise as she gazed into the smoldering green eyes of the handsome rogue she had left behind in Bristol. Seth chuckled satanically as he surveyed Brianna's shabby appearance and bewildered expression. She looked a sight! Her oversized cap was pulled down around her ears, covering her head of ebony hair. Her cheeks were grimy and her baggy clothes were stained and soiled. The beautiful witch now appeared to be a scrawny little ragamuffin. If it had not been for those flaming amber eyes, Seth would have sworn that this pitiful-looking urchin was not Brianna.

"It doesn't appear that your stay on the *Mesmer* has been a pleasant one," he smirked as he sauntered toward Brianna. "You could use a bath and a change of clothes." Seth's lips curled in a sneer, his fiery eyes boldly assessing her.

"What are you doing here?" she asked, infuriated by the arrogant expression on his face.

Seth laughed without humor as he met her defiant glare. "Where else would you expect the captain of a ship to be, except maybe lying unconscious in his room after being brutalized by some heathen." The bitterness that laced his deep voice made Brianna wince uncomfortably.

"How did you know I was here?" she queried, taking a step backward as Seth approached.

Seth lifted the chain on his neck and dangled the coin in front of her. "When there are evil spirits about, this golden talisman sends a deathly chill down my spine and warns me to beware," he retorted caustically, his brows furrowing over the hardened slits of his eyes.

Brianna boldly appraised the dashing captain who towered above her, acutely aware of the strength and rage that emanated from his virile form. His gaping shirt was parted to the waist, exposing the dark hair on his chest. The tight black breeches he wore revealed the bulging muscles of his thighs. His shiny black boots reached to his knees. Brianna came to the quick conclusion that Seth would have made the perfect pirate, especially with that diabolic expression chiseled in his bronzed features. Brianna knew that she should fear him, but she had known a gentler man who lay beneath that sinewy surface. That knowledge aided her in mustering courage. But then she saw the scorching fire that blazed in his emerald eyes and it shattered her confidence. Seth reminded her of a stone mountain—massive, invincible, and unyielding. And yet, the unsettled fury that raged beneath his solid surface alerted her to the fact that he could explode like a volcano. She was sure that she wanted to be nowhere near him when that happened.

An impish grin parted her lips as she met his contemptuous glare, hoping to cool the hellish fires that burned within him. "I'm glad you liked my gift. It seems that it has already served its purpose."

With a derisive snort, Seth yanked her up in front of him while his lean fingers squeezed into the tender flesh of her arms. "It appears that you have deceived me once again, you vicious witch! This golden talisman *attracts* evil spirits instead of *repelling* them!" he thundered into her startled face.

Brianna kicked him soundly on the shin, stuffed her elbow in his belly, and scrambled away as Seth doubled over. But by the time she reached the door he was upon her, a bellow of pure rage resounding about the room like the explosion she had feared and expected.

"Damn you!" he cursed furiously as he grabbed her up off of the floor, carried her to the bunk, and fell on top of her, pinning her arms and legs beneath his heavy frame. "You have played me for the fool for the last time Brianna! From now on I'm going to make you dance like a puppet on a string!" he vowed menacingly as his mouth twisted in a cruel sneer.

Brianna immediately ceased her struggling and gazed up into his angry face, eyeing him quizzically. "How did you know my name?"

"I've known from the beginning who you were," he answered, his tone razor-sharp. "I chose to help you escape from an unwanted marriage and you have repaid me with constant abuse!"

"How could I know for certain that you wouldn't return me to my father?" she defended heatedly. "Would you really expect me to put my faith and confidence in a total stranger?"

Seth snorted disgustedly as he peered into her belligerent golden eyes. "Nay, but I did not expect to be knocked in the head and left unconscious either."

"I'm sorry," Brianna apologized quietly. "I just couldn't take the chance of being found and I was afraid you were going to . . ." Her voice trailed off as she quickly averted her eyes from his probing gaze. She hadn't meant to bring it up, but the words slipped carelessly from her lips before she had time to bite them back.

"Going to what?" he asked, arching a taunting brow.

Her gaze slid back to meet his mocking smile. "Take advantage of me."

"I cannot imagine how a man could take advantage of you, Brianna. You have an uncanny way of having the last word and the last laugh."

"But I have never been alone in a man's room before and it seemed you had no intention of leaving with only a farewell kiss. I doubted that men like you usually do," she added cynically.

"That still does not change the fact that you were the one who took advantage of me, young lady—and I use the term loosely," he retorted sarcastically. "I offered you refuge, paid for your meals, and attempted to befriend you when you were distressed. But did I receive your gratitude? Nay, Brianna. I have received nothing but injuries at your hands. You are a little hellcat! You may appear to be tame and gentle occasionally but you are vicious and dangerous. I made the foolish mistake of taking for granted that you were a lady, but describing you as such is a bald-faced lie! Never again will I trust you. I will treat you as I would any wild, uncivilized beast—with a great deal of caution and suspiciousness."

"You don't understand, Seth," Brianna explained hastily. "I was desperate. I needed your help so I would not be found. My father had sentenced me to a living hell and I was afraid of what awaited me. And when you . . ." Brianna fumbled for the right words to describe what had passed between them without allowing him to know how he had affected her, but she stumbled when the thought of his hot, searing kisses sent a wild quiver across her skin. "Well, I just panicked and reacted the only way I knew how," she muttered lamely.

Seth scoffed down at her. "Perhaps you would have been better off as Donnovan's wife than finding yourself in my clutches now that I have decided to have my revenge for your treachery."

"Nothing you could do could be worse than a marriage to some bungling fop," she insisted as her dirt-smudged chin tilted defiantly.

"You think not? There are tortures worse than death, ones that you probably aren't even aware exist, my naïve little witch. I may even decide to keep you in my cabin and use you to satisfy my desires, if you're worth having," he jeered.

"You said I was not woman enough for you," she reminded him caustically. "Why would you wish to burden yourself with a passionless misfit?"

"'Tis better than no woman at all," Seth countered as his green eyes flickered with a lusty gleam. "Perhaps I will use you to satisfy me for a time. We will be at sea at least six weeks and my men and I are already hungry for a wench. We cannot afford to be particular and I doubt that any of my crew will be concerned whether *you* enjoy the experience, only that *they* do."

Brianna eyed him warily. Would he do such a thing? Hell yes, her mind screamed in hasty reply. She had gotten the best of him once too often and he would abuse her, if only for revenge. What was she to do? "You cannot do that," she insisted.

"And why not? As captain of this ship, my word is law," Seth smirked arrogantly. "If I command that one of the crew is to be flogged, then he shall be. If I decide to toss a stowaway into the sea to feed the sharks, then she will be." His voice lowered into a threatening hiss as he continued, "If I decide to use a woman for the pleasure of every man on board, none will object to that either."

"My brother is on this ship and he will not allow me to be abused!" Brianna's amber eyes sparked fury. "If any man lays a hand on me, Grant will have the scoundrel's head on a platter!"

Seth chuckled wickedly. "Then I can easily alleviate that problem, Brianna," he assured her as his contemptuous gaze locked with hers. "I will merely make your brother the sharks' dinner and he will have no say in the matter."

"You wouldn't dare!"

"Without giving it a second thought," he assured with a stern nod of his raven head. "I have cast more than one man into the sea for a crime that I could not tolerate and I wouldn't hesitate to do the same with your brother. We are not in England, and society's rules do not apply at sea."

"My family is well respected in England. If my brother does not return, my father will see you hang for your demented cruelty." Brianna warned boldly. "You cannot send a man overboard just because he protests an injustice. I will see to it that you are punished if you dare follow through with such a dastardly threat!"

"And what makes you think that you will ever see England again?" Seth asked as his dark brows arched mockingly. "When we are finished with you, your fate may be the same as your brother's, or perhaps I will sell you as a slave to the highest bidder. I will simply tell Lord Talbert that his son perished during a storm at sea. I won't have to answer for you since I seriously doubt that he even knows where you are."

A sense of hopelessness flooded over Brianna as she

lay pinned beneath Seth's solid form, unable to move, incapable of protesting against the unyielding, emerald eyes. "And if I accept my fate, will you promise not to harm my brother?" she queried in a subdued tone.

A sly smile threatened the corners of his mouth as he peered down into Brianna's grimy face, delighting in the supremacy he held over her for once in their brief acquaintance. "You cannot be trusted and I will not give my word. Your actions will determine what I decide to do with you and my judgment will be subject to change in accordance to your deeds."

Damn him! He had an answer for everything and there was no hesitation in any of his replies. She was trapped! "Then I will fight you with my last dying breath," Brianna sneered contemptuously. "You and your crew may seek pleasure at my expense, but I swear you will not enjoy it. If the opportunity presents itself, I will inflict pain and even death on any man who dares to touch me!"

Seth threw back his head and laughed wickedly. "You are such an innocent, Brianna. I could tie you to this bunk and my men could each take their turns with you and you would have no choice but to endure their animal lusts."

Brianna was at her wit's end. It seemed Seth had turned into a dark demon with whom she could not reason. And there was no appealing to his sense of decency—the rogue had none! "I wish I had stayed home to marry that damned fop, Donnovan," she muttered bitterly.

"You would have been much better off," Seth agreed with a dry smile. "But it seems that you have a way of inviting trouble and this time you have most certainly found it."

"Seth, please don't do this to me!" Brianna pleaded

frantically. "I will yield to you if that is what you wish, but I beg you, do not turn me over to your crew. I would rather die than suffer such a degrading assault." Her lips quivered uncontrollably as she gazed up at him, beseeching him to show mercy.

Agilely hopping to his feet, Seth released her. "How do I know that you will not attack me the minute my back is turned? Your past history is evidence of your untrustworthy behavior. I do not intend to meet my death at your hands, witch," he sneered hatefully.

Brianna slowly sat up on the edge of the bed and rubbed her wrists that burned painfully from his fierce grasp. "To save my brother's life and my own as well, I give you my word that I will not attempt to escape from you," she assured him solemnly.

Seth eyed her skeptically. Why should he trust this wench? He should do as he had threatened and be done with her. That was what she deserved, the conniving, deceitful, unscrupulous witch. But then the thought of taking her in his arms without a fight began to tempt him. Perhaps she would cooperate if her brother's life hung in the balance, he mused thoughtfully.

Brianna waited tensely while Seth stood before her in silent reverie, considering what he had to gain and to lose in dealing with her. "Well, do we have an agreement, or am I wasting my breath attempting to reason and bargain with you?" she asked, her tone harsh.

Looking down at her shabby appearance, Seth snorted disgustedly. "Take a look at yourself, Brianna," he suggested. "There is nothing tempting about you, especially now."

She appraised her soiled attire. He was right. She could not even lure a fish onto a hook. "Perhaps a bath and a change of clothes would help," she said blandly as she swept the cap from her head, allowing the long,

132

thick strands of ebony to cascade over her shoulders as she raked her fingers through her hair.

"Perhaps," he agreed brusquely. "But the hour is late and it has been a long day." Quickly closing the distance between them, Seth clamped his hand on her arm, pushed her back to the bunk, and tied her to the cot. "I will consider your proposal and give you my decision after you have had the opportunity to present yourself as a woman instead of a repulsive wretch. I'll find a hammock to serve as my bed."

When Brianna was bound to the cot, Seth stood above her, allowing a satanic smile to curl his lips. "You could have been the wife of a nobleman, living in Bristol with servants at your beck and call, but instead you chose to stow away on the *Mesmer*. 'Tis a pity, Brianna. Now you will suffer for your foolishness," he taunted in an icy tone. "Think on that while you lay strapped to your bed, my dear."

After Seth had stepped outside his cabin, he chuckled vengefully. Seeing Brianna beg for mercy was a priceless moment that helped to heal his injured pride. Revenge was sweet and it left no bitter aftertaste in his mouth. Brianna had deserved the harshness and cruelty he had given. That wench needed to be taught a lesson and he was just the man to master the little witch.

When he returned, Seth worked silently while Brianna watched his every movement. Maybe if she could soften this calloused man she could wrap him around her little finger. She could play the charade of the willing wench if it meant saving Grant's life, and eventually the arrogant captain would let his guard down. If she could only play the game until they arrived in the colonies, she could escape and return to England. She would see this rogue hang for what he threatened

133

to do. With that spiteful thought milling about her mind, Brianna closed her eyes and was about to drift off to sleep when Seth spoke to her from across the room.

"Pleasant dreams, Brianna," he mocked as a deep-throated chuckle filled the silence.

"Go to hell, Captain," she muttered and then bit her lip, remembering she had intended to soft-soap him as she often did her father.

While Seth swayed in his hammock, squirming occasionally to seek a more comfortable position, an unseen smile played on his lips. He would have this little firebrand eating out of the palm of his hand before this voyage was over. Brianna would come willingly to him each time he requested it and when they parted, he would leave her behind with no regrets. Once he had conquered Brianna he would be content to walk away from her. No longer would the thought of the golden-eyed witch come to haunt him. He would be free of her once and for all. He would be the envy of her forlorn suitors who had attempted to take the wench in their arms and discover her charms. No longer would he be among those who yearned for an impossible dream. He would be the one to decide whether this wench was what dreams were made of.

A small flame began to kindle within him as he remembered her velvety flesh pressed against his. He wanted her even after all she had done to him—the pain, the humiliation, the torture of denied passion. Seth heaved a perplexed sigh as another, more disturbing thought crossed his mind. There was Grant Talbert with whom to contend. Sooner or later, Talbert would discover that Brianna was on board this ship and then what was he to do? Seth grumbled under his breath. He would have to deal with Talbert. It was inevitable. Damn, that wench had done it again! She had managed

134

to disrupt his life with her mere presence. What could
have been smooth sailing could very well be the worst
storm he had ever weathered at sea. Perhaps he should
toss her overboard during the night. No one would
know that she had been on the *Mesmer*. There certainly was something to be said for drowning one's
troubles.

Chapter Ten

While Brianna was bathing in the captain's quarters, Seth unlocked Sabrina from the storeroom and brought her up on deck to see Grant. At the sight of Grant, Sabrina shrieked delightedly and dashed into his arms.

Grant's dark eyes widened in surprise. "Sabrina, what are you doing here?" he questioned bewilderedly, his gaze sliding from her to the captain.

"Following you. I didn't want you to forget me," she breathed happily, nuzzling in his protective embrace.

A wide grin spread across Grant's face as he peered into her glistening blue eyes. "You are almost as mischievous as Brianna," he chided, playfully flicking the end of her nose. "I should have known some of her orneriness would have rubbed off on you."

Sabrina glanced back over her shoulder at the captain, knowing full well that he had heard what Grant had said. A sly smile etched Seth's bronzed features as he strolled forward. Sabrina inwardly cringed, wondering what the scoundrel was thinking and how much he knew.

"We have a problem, Talbert. What shall we do with the wench?" Seth's voice barely carried the inflection of a question.

Grant surveyed the rugged captain and pulled Sabrina close. "What choice am I allowed?"

"Only two," Seth replied as he crossed his arms on

his chest and eyed Talbert levelly. "She can remain in the storeroom throughout the voyage or you can keep her in your room and I'll move Lucas to other quarters."

"Can Sabrina and I discuss the matter before I give you an answer?" Grant questioned solemnly.

"Take her with you to your quarters and the two of you can make your decision. I want your answer by tonight. No matter what you decide to do, she will not be allowed on deck after dark. There are those here who would challenge your right to the wench," he warned before he spun on his heels and stalked to his cabin.

When Seth flung open the door, Brianna gasped and sank beneath the bathwater's surface, attempting to shield herself from the probing emerald eyes that raked her hungrily. "Do you mind, Captain!" she protested as her brows furrowed into an annoyed frown. "I want to finish my bath in private. You are intruding!"

"I most certainly do mind!" Seth retorted as he locked the door and sauntered toward her. Lord, but she was lovely. Her creamy skin sparkled with droplets of water and her ebony hair that was piled recklessly upon her head glowed as the sun rays streamed around the edge of the drawn curtains to dance enticingly on them. "'Tis my cabin, Brianna, and I will continue to come and go as I please. You are the intruder and I have been gracious enough to share my quarters with you," he reminded her in a sharp tone.

Her golden eyes spewed with heated sparks as she shot him a contemptuous glower. "There is nothing gracious or noble about you. You are a loathsome scoundrel," she insisted harshly. "If you had any decency, you would at least turn your back so that I would not have to suffer such embarrassment."

Seth shrugged casually, not the least bit intimidated

by her remark. "'Tis a shame that you didn't remain in Bristol to marry Donnovan. Consider all of the humiliation and misfortune you could have avoided. Now you find yourself in the company of a scoundrel. What a pity," he mocked unsympathetically.

"I would have married Lord Donnovan in a minute if I had known that I would have to choose between him and you!" she sneered as she raked his sturdy form with a look of disgust.

"Would you really?" Seemingly undaunted by her insult, Seth cocked a wondering brow and returned her bold appraisal. "I thought you said your intended husband was nothing but a bungling fop and that you were repulsed by the idea of marrying the chap."

"'Tis better than being in the company of a cruel, callous scoundrel," she assured him in a vicious hiss.

"Nay, 'tis all the same, Brianna. 'Tis all the same," he chuckled amusedly as he strolled over to the desk to reach for a cheroot.

As he lit his cigar and puffed on it, the smoke curled lazily around his dark head and Brianna muttered a curse to the emerald-eyed demon who continued to observe her with his leering gaze. Instead of seeing him hang for his wickedness, she would find a way to slit his miserable throat herself. Hanging would bring an end to him much too quickly. She would gain more satisfaction if he suffered at her hands.

A long moment of silence passed between them while Brianna's fiery eyes pierced him with their intensity. Seth drank in the delicious sight that intoxicated his mind with lusty thoughts until the knock at the door drew his attention from the appetizing wench.

"Captain Donnovan, the helmsman would like a word with you," came the timid voice of Kenton Marsh, a young seaman who was making his first voyage on the *Mesmer*.

138

"Captain Donnovan?" Brianna repeated incredulously. The color drained from her cheeks. "Donnovan . . ." The word was no more than a hushed whisper as she raised wide, disbelieving eyes to Seth.

A deliciously wicked grin curved the corners of his mouth upward and the fathomless emerald pools rippled with amusement. Seth swaggered toward Brianna and bowed mockingly. "Aye, m'lady," he assured her with a throaty chuckle. "Captain Seth . . . Quentin . . . Donnovan . . . at your service." Noting the rash of unanswered questions that flashed through her eyes, Seth attempted to explain, thoroughly delighted that for once the wench was speechless. "My grandfather has always insisted on calling me Quentin. In the past five generations of our family, the first child has always been a male—hence the name Quentin Donnovan. In the colonies I am known only as Seth and 'tis the name I prefer. Now, Miss Talbert, would you still care to marry Lord Donnovan without a second thought?" he taunted as he arched a heavy brow.

When Brianna finally found her tongue, she growled and flashed him a murderous glare. "Never in a million years!"

Seth sauntered toward the door and paused to glance back at the lovely little witch who was stewing in her kettle. "The feeling is mutual, Brianna. Why the hell do you think I was so eager to help you escape from your father? I had no desire to be burdened with such troublesome baggage for the rest of my days."

As the soaked sponge came flying across the room, Seth ducked away from its path, snickering all the while. He watched as it splashed against the door and then dropped to the floor to leave a puddle by his feet. He laughed heartily as his gaze returned to the enraged wench who sank into the water to cool her fuming temper.

When Seth had left the room, Brianna scrambled from the tub. "Why, that unscrupulous, deceitful, arrogant . . . Oh!" she grumbled furiously. "If he thinks for one minute that I will come willingly to him now, he is daft!" Brianna quickly dried herself as her thoughts filled with revenge. She would tempt him, taunt him, entice him, and then slit his miserable throat. There was no need to wait until they reached the colonies! He may think he had her under control, but he would most certainly be in for one hell of a surprise! But then harsh reality invaded her spiteful thoughts and dampened the fires of revenge. Where would she go when she escaped from him as she had in Bristol? There was no place to run and those who waited outside the cabin may be far worse than the ruthless captain. Damn him! Where was Grant? What had the captain done with her brother? She was cornered and there was naught else to do but accept her fate.

After Seth had talked with the helmsman he climbed down from the quarterdeck to find Grant waiting for him, his brown eyes set in grim determination.

"Captain, may I have a word with you?"

Seth turned to face Grant's stern expression. "Have you made your decision?" he questioned blandly.

"Aye, but it seems that I am plagued with yet another problem. Sabrina told me that my sister had planned to stow away on this ship, and I am well aware that you are the man Brianna was supposed to marry," he stated boldly.

"Oh?" Seth cocked a dark brow as he slowly appraised Talbert. "And I suppose you wish to know my intentions if the wench is found and brought to me."

Grant nodded affirmatively. "Brianna is very difficult to manage and I have already brought you enough

140

trouble. I do not wish to have you at my neck the same way Patton is," he added. "If Brianna is on the *Mesmer*, do you still intend to marry her?"

Seth frowned thoughtfully as he surveyed the young man. He liked Talbert's honesty and straightforwardness. 'Twas a pity that Brianna did not possess some of her brother's noble qualities. Disregarding Grant's question, Seth made his own inquiry. "What do you intend to do with Sabrina?"

"I would request that you marry us," Grant replied as a subtle smile crept to his lips.

"I will not condemn you if you merely wish to keep her with you. 'Tis none of my concern what you do with her so long as she doesn't cause trouble among the crew."

Grant's smile suddenly vanished. Although Donnovan had not answered the previous question outright, he had threaded an underlying meaning into his own question. "I have no intention of making Sabrina my mistress. That way of life no longer interests me. I have known the lass all of my life and now I want her as my wife. Sabrina is from a proper family and I could never face her father again if I compromised her morals, nor would I place my sister in such a position." Grant's eyes narrowed meaningfully as he stared at the captain. "What do you intend to do with Brianna if she is found on this ship?"

Seth was acutely aware of Talbert's insinuation, but he attempted to explain the situation. "The marriage between Brianna and myself was merely an agreement between my grandfather and your father. Brianna and I had nothing to do with it and neither of us wanted to wed."

"I'm aware of the circumstances, but where will Brianna stay if she is on the *Mesmer?*" Grant persisted. "Do you want her with you and your new bride?"

141

Seth quipped as he arched a mocking brow.

Grant's eyes sparkled with amusement. The evasive captain would reveal none of his intentions. "Not particularly, but if there is no other place for her, I will allow her to room with us. . . . Unless you decide to marry her. Under the circumstances, it seems the only proper action to take since the contract has been signed and both families have already agreed."

Seth chuckled at Talbert's attempt to persuade him to comply with his moral duty, but the captain chose to ignore his comment. "Come to my cabin tonight at eight o'clock and I will perform the ceremony."

Grant opened his mouth to make one last plea to Donnovan, but the stern gleam in the captain's emerald eyes told Grant that he was wasting his breath. With a quick nod, Talbert spun on his heels and returned to his quarters.

With a thoughtful frown furrowing his brows, Seth watched Grant stroll away and then glanced toward his own cabin. What the hell was he going to do with that little witch? Grant would not stand for any injustice where his sister was concerned and Seth had no intention of tossing the nobleman into the sea, although Brianna would never know that. Could he and Brianna reason with each other? Would she be willing to discuss the situation like two rational individuals? Brianna rational? There was nothing logical about that fiery wench. She defied all rules and he had discarded all thoughts of reasoning and logic the night he had met her. Would she be waiting with a pistol, intent on disposing of him when he returned, or would she find the situation amusing as she had done when she discovered he had cheated her at cards? Seth shrugged hopelessly. He didn't have the slightest idea what awaited him. There was only one way to find out—

confront the spitfire and bring along his protective armor.

As Seth carefully opened the door, he peered inside to ensure that Brianna wasn't waiting to pounce upon him. Brianna was arranging her hair as Seth stepped into the room and she turned a dazzling smile to him, causing his brows to furrow suspiciously. She stood dressed in his linen shirt, exposing her shapely legs to his eager gaze. Seth sauntered toward her, his eyes roaming over her tempting flesh in a bold caress that touched every inch of her body.

"I'm sorry I am dressed improperly, Captain, but all of my belongings are still in the hull of the ship. 'Twas this or nothing," Brianna explained as a hint of mischievousness flickered in her eyes.

Seth was mesmerized by her bewitching form and it was difficult to concentrate on her words. "I envy my shirt," he breathed quietly.

A provocative smile played on her lips as she stepped in front of him and laid her silky arms about his broad shoulders. Raising her gaze, she silently beckoned him to kiss her. Seth could not resist the temptation, nor was he about to try. She was beautiful. The subtle fragrance that clung to her body seemed to wrap itself around his senses, drawing him hopelessly into her bewitching spell. As his lips touched hers in a gentle caress, Seth drew her against him, feeling her luscious curves and swells beneath his hands while he ached with the overwhelming need of her.

"Seth, when can I see my brother?" she questioned in a raspy whisper that sent a wild tingle sailing down his spine.

"Tonight, if you wish," he offered huskily as he placed searing kisses against the hollow of her neck.

An unseen smile curved the corners of her mouth

upward. That was easy enough, she mused wickedly. She would have the scoundrel groveling at her feet when she was through with him.

"That is, if you behave yourself," he taunted as he pulled far enough away to gaze into her face.

The smile on Brianna's delicate features became an instant frown. That cad! She would love to slap that mocking grin off of his face!

Suddenly his lips were against hers, playing softly on her mouth, subtly commanding her to respond to his skillful embrace. Brianna felt a strange tremor spread through her limbs, igniting a small flame of desire that refused to be ignored. Her heart quickened its pace as his tongue explored the recesses of her mouth and his hands moved slowly down her back to press her hips against him.

"I want you, Brianna," he whispered hoarsely. He knew she was deliberately taunting him to have her way, but this had gone far enough. No more games. The thought of making love to this bewitching goddess had become an obsession since she had escaped him in Bristol.

Her eyes widened in alarm as she gazed into the emerald pools that rippled with unmistakable passion. "Nay, I will not submit to you. You deceived me."

"You were well aware of what you were doing when you dressed in my shirt. You sought to tease me to get what you wanted and now you have. I have compromised by allowing you to see your brother and now, so must you."

"I cannot!" Brianna squirmed for release, but Seth effortlessly held her in place.

"Are you afraid to become a woman?" His intimidating question was followed by a mocking smile. "You tempt a man into your spell, but once he is aroused, you run like a frightened child. When you play with fire, Brianna, oftentimes you find you have been burned."

Brianna's lips quivered nervously as she burrowed her head into the hard wall of his chest, unable to meet his ridiculing gaze. "I have never before been with a man. Is it so hard to understand that I fear the unknown? Why do you think I reacted the way I did when we were alone together in Bristol? I was afraid of myself and you, afraid of what might happen between us."

Seth was caught off guard by her sudden outburst of honesty. In the past, Brianna had fought against him like a wildcat when he purposely insulted her. Now she huddled against him, seeking the comfort of his arms, begging for him to consider her feelings. His heart filled with a strange tenderness that erased the revenge that had driven him to this moment. He had never taken a maiden and had given little thought to patience and care for the woman in his arms, only a desire to fulfill his needs. His women had come willingly, accepting his caresses, urging him to take them to ecstasy, knowing what awaited them. But Brianna was different. She had never tasted passion, knew nothing of love, and had no concept of the pleasures that might await her.

Suddenly Seth released her and turned his back on her. Brianna was making him feel like a loathsome cad. He was giving her the opportunity to do what she usually did—attack him like a she-cat who had been threatened. But now she just stood there, not uttering a word.

"Damn," Seth muttered under his breath. Things had been so simple before Brianna had appeared from the darkness to disrupt his life. Now his grandfather wanted him married to this wench, there were two desirable women on his ship that needed protection, and Brianna's brother was a member of the crew. If he

145

took Brianna to his bed, Talbert would be infuriated. And if he didn't take her, he would be frustrated. Perhaps *he* should be the one cast overboard.

"Seth," Brianna whispered as she moved closely behind him.

Her raspy voice came to him from across a sea of muddled thoughts. He glanced over his shoulder, wishing she would knock him over the head and put him out of his misery. He could deal with the spitfire who came at him with claws bared, but this soft, vulnerable maiden who gazed up at him with those mysterious, amber eyes was unnerving. He had endured her anger, but he was afraid to confront her in this realm. The consequences might be more disastrous than those of the battlefield.

Brianna felt trapped. Seth had described his crewmen as brutal and ruthless. She was afraid to set foot outside the cabin without Seth's protection. He had warned her that the laws of the sea and those of the land did not necessarily coincide. Her only choice was to yield to the captain and beg for mercy to prevent being ravished by the crew or to jeopardize Grant's life.

Heaving a weak sigh, Brianna stepped in front of Seth, her eyes failing to meet his steady gaze. "For once I find that my hands are tied. No matter what I do, I'll lose. I have no wish to be abused, and I could never forgive myself if Grant comes to harm because of my foolish actions." Slowly, she lifted her eyes to his rugged face. "Perhaps I deserve the punishment you have suggested, but if you allow me a choice, I want to know only you." Her lips trembled and her vision clouded as she continued quietly. "If you still want me I won't fight you, but please . . . don't hurt me, Seth."

There was a hint of tears lurking beneath the surface and Seth was painfully aware of their existence. Again, he felt like the scoundrel Brianna had accused him of being. She was offering herself to him, asking only that he be tender. He was bargaining with the woman that many men sought to possess and his body raged with desire. Could he turn his back on this temptation? Could he walk away and put Brianna out of his mind, knowing how much he wanted her?

Confused by his hesitation, she dropped her head, humiliated, embarrassed, at odds with herself. A moment earlier she had felt a strange security when he held her close. A spark of passion had leaped between them. But perhaps he despised her so intensely that his only enjoyment could come from abusing her. Her confidence was shattered. She felt inadequate and self-conscious. He was right. She was like a frightened child, afraid of the unknown.

As she moved away, Seth reached for her, reason overridden by need. "I still want you," he confessed in a husky tone.

Seth folded her in his arms and she nuzzled her head against his sturdy chest, fighting back the tears that threatened to flood her eyes. Her arms involuntarily slid over his shoulders and she raised quivering lips to him, prepared to yield to the inevitable.

He inwardly cringed as he gazed into the amber eyes that were rimmed with tears. She was so damned tempting, so soft and desirable. And those glistening pools of gold drew him into their fathomless depths. A quiet moan escaped him as his lips captured hers. He was drifting on an endless sea, hypnotized by her spell, unable to fight the need that consumed all reasoning. What had she done to him?

The world was spinning out of control as his touch wandered over her firm flesh, memorizing each tempting curve and swell, savoring the feel of her alluring body molded to his.

Brianna closed her eyes as a wild tingle darted down

her spine, freeing her restraints. His caresses roamed daringly beneath her shirt and she could not find the will to stop him. Where was logic? This was madness! She had offered herself to the very man from whom she had attempted to escape. And yet, she was responding to his experienced touch, burning with desire, reveling in the pleasure she had discovered in his arms.

Seth effortlessly lifted her from the floor and carried her to his bed. Brianna nestled against his shoulder, afraid to look at him, afraid to see the ridicule in his gaze. As he stood her beside the bunk, he worked the buttons of her shirt and then drew the meager covering away, his hungry gaze devouring her creamy flesh. He was spellbound as the sunlight curled about her. It was as if he had disrobed a goddess that no mortal before him had dared to love. He had been whisked up from the fires of hell to revel in one glorious moment of heaven. For that instant that knew no time or space, Brianna was his.

Shrugging off his shirt, he carelessly tossed it aside and then encircled her in his arms. As his mouth covered hers in a gentle kiss, his hands roamed over her skin, touching every inch of her body that his eyes had so boldly caressed. Her arms slid gingerly over his shoulders, fanning over the dark furring of his chest as they descended. But when he cupped her breast, touching her so intimately, she gasped and drew away, her gaze glued to the hard wall of his muscled chest.

"Brianna, I won't hurt you. Trust me," he coaxed breathlessly.

Why should she trust him? He had done nothing but deceive her. When she raised her eyes to him she was met by a strange glow in those emerald pools, a glow she had never seen, a silent message that she couldn't decode.

As he drew her to the bunk, she stiffened again when

his hands wandered tauntingly over her abdomen to her thighs. Seth assured her until she began to relax beneath his exploring touch. A wild, budding pleasure coursed her veins, stripping her thoughts. And then he was above her, parting her legs with his muscular hips. Another gasp of alarm escaped her lips when a searing pain shot through her loins. Brianna flinched as he pressed intimately against her.

Tears began to cloud her eyes, trickling down her flushed cheeks. But as he thrust against her tender flesh, he kissed them away. The pain was replaced by a new sensation that she never realized existed. She was gliding like an eagle, circling and spiraling her way above the clouds. Her flesh was warmed as the sun rays danced over her, filling her with exquisite pleasure. Nothing compared to what she was feeling while she was floating above the world of reality, suspended in timeless ecstasy, never wanting the moment to end and unsure she could endure its pleasure. She was living and dying, unable to catch her breath, unconcerned if there was to be a tomorrow. And then she was falling like a weightless feather, carried by a gentle breeze to be placed on earth with the greatest of care. Her strength was drained and she lay motionless, confused by the strange feelings that tore at her heart. Brianna smiled to herself, wondering why she felt such a bond of tenderness for the powerful man who had taken her to new horizons.

Seth rolled beside her and pulled her close, a contented sigh escaping his lips as he gazed into the warm, golden eyes that still glowed with passion's flame. She had surprised and satisfied him with her innocent response. At that moment he found it hard to believe that this was the same hellcat who had spurred his fury.

"Is it always like this?" Brianna questioned huskily as she traced her fingertips across his full lips.

Seth nearly choked on his breath. He had intended to introduce this adorable witch to passion, but he had not planned to discuss it at any length. And of all the women he had taken in his arms, none had made such an inquiry. But then, this was Brianna, not some other woman. And the fact that it had never been like this was disarming. His brows arched curiously as he glanced down into the exquisite face that was framed with a tangled mass of ebony curls.

"And if it was, would you have yielded to me that night in Bristol?"

Brianna giggled as she laid her head back against his shoulder, grinning impishly. "Nay, I think not." She pulled up on his chest, her breasts pressing wantonly against him. "Perhaps, after you make love to me again, I will reconsider my reply."

"Right now?" This wench never ceased to amaze him with her impulsiveness.

Brianna shrugged carelessly. "What better time than the present?"

"My word, woman. At least give me a moment to catch my breath and gather my strength."

"Woman?" Her brow arched tauntingly. "I thought you said I was a passionless child."

"It seems I made a hasty judgment, Brianna. You will make an excellent mistress for your husband," he teased as he flicked the end of her dainty nose.

Brianna suddenly pulled away, finding no amusement in his reckless comment. Harsh reality had invaded her dreamlike existence and the thought of what she had done so willingly stung her conscience. "Perhaps he won't want me at all when he realizes that I was another man's mistress before I became his wife," she muttered dismally.

Seth pressed Brianna to her back and propped himself up on his elbow to peer down at her, but she refused to look at him. Cupping her chin in his hand, he raised her eyes to meet his unwavering gaze. "Then he would not be worth having. Only a fool would deny himself the pleasure you can give."

"And what of you, Captain? If you were to marry would you expect your bride to be a virgin? Would you care that she had discovered passion in the arms of another man, that she willingly responded to him, that she offered herself to him as she had no other? Would it inflame your pride that she had found contentment with someone other than you?"

A thoughtful frown creased his rugged features. He had never considered lovemaking in that respect. Always before, he had sought to appease his desires and bring his women pleasure, but of the woman he would take as his wife? Would he care that she had responded to another man's caress as innocently and as freely as Brianna had to him? There was something unique about his experience with this vixen. Even with Priscilla he had never given a thought to what it could have been, should have been. He had only accepted their relationship for what it was. He had been young and foolish in the beginning, but now he was a man of experience and he had changed. Would he wish to share such an enjoyable moment with his wife, just as he had with Brianna?

His hesitation sent Brianna's spirits plunging. "I can see by your refusal to answer that you would not be satisfied with another man's leavings when it comes to the woman you would take as a wife," she murmured despairingly. "It seems you have a double standard, one set of values for the many women who appease your desires, and an entirely different code of ethics for the one woman you would wed. I expect the same would be true of my future husband, if indeed there will be one, especially now."

151

Brianna attempted to squirm away, but Seth refused to release her. He could think of nothing appropriate to say since she had read his thoughts. Slowly lowering his raven head, he sought her inviting lips in a tender kiss, but she was unresponsive to his embrace. Seth gazed down into her amber eyes, wishing to erase the pain and disillusionment he saw in them.

"The Indians believe that life begins when a man and woman become as one in heart and soul. There is no past from the moment that they share love and soar beyond physical pleasures. Perhaps the red man has discovered the essence of life. You know little of love, Brianna, nothing of pleasing a man except with an innocent response and you have only begun to understand contentment. There is much more to love and passion that you must learn. You must decide for yourself what love really is and perhaps in time you can answer your own question."

Brianna listened to his hushed words, mesmerized by the soothing effect of his tone. A demure smile grazed her lips as she looked deeply into his sea green eyes. There was no use worrying about her future husband. After all, it was as her father had said and Seth had agreed. She sought a man who only existed in her imagination—the bold knight on his magnificent stallion who would take her into a world of fantasy. She must contend with the present and allow the future to take its own course.

"'Tis ironic that the man I refused to marry, sight unseen, would be the very same man who first taught me the meaning of desire."

Seth grinned down at her as he smoothed the tangled strands of ebony from her face, loving the feel of her silky hair in his hands. "And even more ironic that the woman I helped to escape from me is the same one that I cannot seem to leave alone."

"We make an odd pair." Brianna laughed softly as she laid her head back and peered up at the ceiling, as if there were something there that had suddenly drawn her attention. "That which we both tried so desperately to avoid is the very thing that neither of us refused. At least I could not," she added as she glanced sideways at Seth to display a mischievous grin.

Seth chuckled as he observed the devilish gleam in her golden eyes. "Nor could I, my lovely witch, nor can I now."

As Seth captured her mouth in a possessive kiss, she looped her arms about his neck, accepting his embrace, wondering why she was so strangely drawn to the dashing rogue who controlled her life.

"Captain, may I have a word with you?" Derrick called from outside the door.

Seth grumbled under his breath and reluctantly drew away from the tempting wench who had again aroused his passions. "Can it wait?" he called over his shoulder before turning flaming green eyes back to Brianna. His all-consuming gaze spoke of a growing need to appease his desires before the tender moment was destroyed and lost forever.

"Nay, I'm afraid not, Captain," Derrick quickly assured him.

As Seth grabbed for his clothes and hurriedly dressed, Brianna watched him, marveling at the strong, virile man who stood before her. She was intrigued by his rippling muscles that flexed as he moved and the lean contour of his sturdy frame. He towered above her like a mountain carved of solid rock.

Seth muttered under his breath at the interruption and stared at Brianna, savoring the delectable sight. Without a word he wheeled around and stalked from the room, leaving Brianna alone to her thoughts and the lingering vision of the handsome captain who had taught her the meaning of passion.

Derrick arched a curious brow as he gazed at the dark scowl on Seth's face. "What the devil is wrong with you?"

"Nothing," Seth snapped brusquely. "Now what is so damned important?"

A bemused frown spread across Derrick's bronzed features. What could have happened to cast the captain into such a sour mood? With a slight shrug Sayer put the thought from his mind and told the captain about the pouch he had found in the hull of the ship. The information seemed to annoy Seth further and Derrick was completely baffled by his odd behavior. Damn, but he was acting strangely, Derrick mused as he followed the captain's swift, impatient strides across the deck.

Chapter Eleven

While Derrick and Seth stood at the helm a sudden gust of wind seemed to catch the schooner, causing the sails to clap and billow. The mast creaked with the force of the gale, moaning like a banshee. In the wake of the breeze, a calm settled over the *Mesmer* and the low murmur of the crew halted as an eerie silence held them suspended. It seemed Brianna had appeared from nowhere, and all eyes turned to the dark-haired beauty who was dressed in tight breeches and soft, black kid boots that clung to her calves. The white linen shirt was molded against her breasts, revealing each shapely curve and swell that lay so temptingly beneath it. Around her trim waist a crimson sash was tied and the tails of silk tumbled recklessly down her hip as she walked. The crew stood in awe as Brianna focused on the two men on the quarterdeck above her. Her golden eyes flickered with mischievousness, knowing that each man on the ship stood mesmerized by her appearance. Obviously they had not been informed that there was a woman on board, she mused. When Seth had left the cabin unlocked, Brianna had peeked outside to find her pouch sitting by the door and had donned the most comfortable suit of clothes that she owned—her brother's hand-me-downs.

Seth sucked in his breath as he gazed down at Brianna, noting that each man on the schooner was entranced and that the same wicked sparkle rippled in those golden pools just as it had the day Seth had seen Brianna riding through the park on her demon stallion.

"My God," Derrick breathed, enchanted by Brianna's devastating beauty. "Who is that?"

Seth shot him an annoyed glance when he saw the lusty flicker in Derrick's eyes. "Do you believe in witches?"

"I do now." Derrick's gaze never wavered as he slowly and deliberately appraised the mysterious sorceress who sauntered across the quarterdeck toward them. "Where did she come from? That is not the woman I found in the storeroom, but there is something strangely familiar about her."

"Sea witches appear from the black depths," Seth grumbled, wishing he would have remembered to lock the door to his cabin so he could have kept the crew from ravishing the little vixen with their leering gazes. Her appearance was sure to cause trouble.

"I didn't know witches came in such lovely packages," Sayer murmured hoarsely.

Seth scoffed as he viewed Derrick's awestruck expression. "You think not? That is what makes this one so damned dangerous."

Derrick slowly pulled his gaze to the captain as a sly smile crept to his lips. "She's the one, isn't she?" he questioned.

"What one?" Seth quipped as his own eyes betrayed him, roaming hungrily over Brianna's tempting figure.

"The one that got the best of you in Bristol?" Derrick taunted as his smile widened into a knowing grin.

"Aye," Seth assured him resentfully. "Every time I turn around Brianna appears from out of nowhere to haunt me. This is one demon who can cancel the usefulness of this talisman."

"Brianna Talbert?" Derrick's brows shot up in surprise.

Seth nodded affirmatively.

"So this is the woman I've heard so much about in the pubs of Bristol," he mused aloud as his eyes rested on the lovely lass. "From all that I've heard about her, I would say the wench leads a lively existence."

Seth would have agreed, but Brianna was within earshot and he focused his attention on her, sending her a murderous glare.

What happened to the gentleman she had found earlier that morning? she wondered. So they were back to swords and daggers again. Well, if that was the way he wanted it, then she would play his game. Brianna turned to boldly rake the first mate, her gaze slowly appraising his muscular form.

"Brianna, this is Derrick Sayer," Seth muttered in introduction.

Derrick bowed slightly as he placed a light kiss to her wrist. "'Tis a pleasure, m'lady."

Brianna nodded as a faint smile curved her lips. "Thank you, sir."

"Derrick, would you excuse us for a moment?" Seth commanded abruptly. "I would like a private word with the lady."

"If you insist," Sayer replied with a wicked grin to Seth who seemed none too pleased with Brianna's appearance.

"I do," Seth assured him icily.

"Perhaps you could join the captain and me for lunch, Derrick," Brianna suggested, completely ignoring Seth and his black mood.

"I would be most happy to accept your invitation, Brianna." Derrick let his gaze slide over the top of her dark head to meet Seth's annoyed frown. "Captain," he said with a slight nod before taking his leave. He warded off the hearty chuckle by camouflaging it with a cough, but Seth knew very well that Derrick was delighting in the situation.

"What the hell are you doing up on deck and why are you dressed like a damned pirate?" Seth hissed angrily. The rugged lines of his face seemed to turn to stone as he glowered at her. "I didn't give you permission to leave my cabin." He would have been in a fit of rage if Grant had been on deck to see his sister.

"I do not need your permission," Brianna snapped hatefully as she whirled to face him. "I am not your slave, nor a member of your crew, and you will be wasting your breath attempting to give me orders."

"You seem to have forgotten the consequences that await you if you dare disobey me," he reminded her in a razor-sharp tone.

Brianna arched a taunting brow, undaunted by his threat. "The idea is not so frightening as it was earlier, Captain. And the thought of surrendering to someone like Derrick is rather appealing. He is quite handsome," Brianna added as her eyes strayed to the first mate who strolled across the deck below her. "And the rest of the crew do not seem as dangerous as you described."

Seth snorted derisively as a twinge of jealousy hit upon an exposed nerve. The vision of Brianna in Derrick's arms made much too vivid a picture, and he cursed himself for allowing her comment to creep beneath his skin. Clamping his lean fingers about her elbow, he spun Brianna around to squarely face his angry sneer. "Don't cross me, Brianna. If you're looking for trouble I'll damned sure give you more than you can handle."

Brianna's free hand slid lightly against his ribs and Seth stiffened when he felt the point of a dagger prick his side. He had never even seen her pull the knife, and his eyes widened in surprise as he peered into the stormy amber pools.

"Don't threaten me, Captain," she hissed venomously.

"'Tis not a threat, only a promise," he assured her with a determined frown. "Now get back to the cabin."

Brianna moved the blade away and tucked it back in her sash, impatiently waiting for Seth to release her arm. When he finally loosened his grip, Brianna glowered up at him. "Where is my brother?"

"Below deck. He's tied up at the moment," he retorted as a wry smile grazed his lips.

Brianna took his meaning literally and her face colored hotly, enraged that this scoundrel would dare treat Grant so mercilessly. "When can I see him?"

"I told you I would allow you to see him tonight if you behaved yourself," he reminded her in that annoying tone that made the hair on the back of Brianna's neck rise in angry defense.

"You're despicable," she snarled viciously.

"Get back to the cabin!" Although Seth's voice was hushed there was no mistaking the deadly hiss in his tone.

Brianna spun on her heels and stalked away while all eyes again rested on her shapely form. It was a long moment after she had disappeared from sight that the men went back to their tasks.

Seth muttered to himself as he motioned for the helmsman to take the wheel. Damn that wench! It seemed the short truce had ended and the war of wills had begun again. Brianna would have a case of cabin fever and be climbing the walls if he attempted to imprison her in his quarters. If he turned her loose on deck, the men would be unable to keep their minds on their duties. What the hell should he do with her? Seth heaved a perplexed sigh and raked his fingers through his raven hair. If Andrew knew that Brianna had stowed away on the *Mesmer* to allow Seth not a moment's peace, he would have thoroughly delighted at the turn of events. The captain had been treading a narrow line, constantly torn between the overwhelming desire to take Brianna in his arms and the uncontrollable urge to clamp his hands around her lovely neck. He never knew what to expect from Brianna. Each time he attempted to out-guess her she would do something completely unpredictable, thoroughly convincing him that he was wasting his time trying to foretell her behavior. He might as well just sit back and ride the waves, allowing them to carry him where they would.

When Brianna returned to her room she was fuming in outrage. Seth had become an annoying thorn in her side once again, pricking her pride with his biting words and attempting to dictate to her as if he were some oppressive tyrant who ruled her life with an iron hand. Perhaps she had submitted to him in a moment of weakness, but she had no intention of becoming some simpering twit who followed at the captain's heels, taking his commands and insults without argument or complaint. He was not her master and she would not kneel to him! Brianna paced her confining quarters in determined strides. She was not about to spend the entire voyage in the captain's cabin. If she had to work as a member of the crew, then she would do it, but she did not intend to remain in Seth's room, waiting for him to return to keep her company.

After Kenton Marsh brought their noon meal, Brianna set the table and anxiously awaited the entrance of the captain and his first mate. When Derrick strolled into the room, Brianna displayed a blinding smile and purposely avoided meeting Seth's dark scowl. As they dined, Brianna questioned Derrick about any and all subjects that came to mind, completely ignoring Seth. Sayer was delighted by Brianna's undivided attention and the opportunity of taunting Captain Donnovan.

"Tell me, Brianna," Derrick began as a curious smile touched his lips. "Why did you leave Bristol? I cannot imagine why you would wish to sail to the colonies when England has so much to offer a woman of your status."

Brianna chuckled lightly as she set her teacup down, her golden eyes glistening with mischief. "My father attempted to marry me to a most irascible character and I simply refused to wed him. So I left."

Derrick cocked a dubious brow as he surveyed Brianna's amused smile. "Why would your father do that? Didn't he give you any choice in the matter?"

"None whatsoever," she replied with a reckless shrug. "I suppose he had become impatient with my refusal to select a suitable husband or perhaps he was just tired of being held responsible for my behavior. I have a tendency to act impulsively at times and he did not approve of some of my antics."

"Most likely an overabundance of both," Seth interjected as a sour frown settled in the chiseled lines of his face.

After Brianna shot Seth a silencing glare, she turned a courteous smile to Derrick. "I am so interested in learning all about the schooner. I was wondering if perhaps you would acquaint me with the workings of the ship when you have the time."

"I would be delighted, Brianna," Derrick replied quickly. Perhaps the lovely lass had not fallen under Donnovan's spell after all, he mused, greatly encouraged by her attention. Derrick had noticed the hammock that hung in the corner of the cabin and naturally assumed, although it came as a surprise, that Seth had not been able to have his way with Brianna. Why would he need a hammock if he had taken her to his bed?

Seth eased back in his chair and lit his cigar, sending a cloud of smoke curling about his raven head, making him appear to be fumingly angry from the discourse between his first mate and the conniving witch. Although Seth was doing his damnedest to remain unaffected by the apparent fascination between Brianna and Derrick, he was silently boiling like an overheated teakettle.

Derrick cleared his throat and glanced sideways at Seth. "If you would like to share my cabin, I won't mind taking the hammock and giving up my bed."

Although Donnovan cast his first mate an irritated frown, he was not allowed the time to reply because Brianna quickly answered for him.

"Thank you, Derrick. I was afraid I would have to sleep in the hull of the ship once again," she interjected as she wrinkled her nose at the repulsive thought.

After Derrick rose from his chair, he ambled to the corner of the room to unfasten the rope bed. As he strolled past the table he paused to produce a charming smile and bowed slightly in front of Brianna. "I truly enjoyed your company, m'lady. You made our meager sea rations seem like a feast with your mere presence."

Returning his grin, Brianna gazed up into his handsome face. "'Twas indeed a pleasure for me too."

Seth rolled his envy-green eyes in disgust. This overly polite conversation and Derrick's obvious interest in the little witch was wearing his patience thin. It was most fortunate that Derrick was taking his leave or Seth would have rudely ordered him out of the cabin.

When Brianna and Seth were alone, he turned a

chilling glare to the saucy lass. "What game are you playing now?" he asked harshly.

"Game?" she repeated innocently as she placed the dishes back on the tray.

"What other term could better describe that sticky sweet scene with you and Sayer?"

"I find Derrick to be quite charming and it seems that it would improve your foul disposition to take a few lessons in courtesy from him," Brianna suggested with a taunting smirk.

Seth grabbed her arm and glowered down into her defiant face. "I don't remember your finding my behavior too detestable earlier this morning," he reminded her bluntly.

Brianna's temper came to a quick boil as she flung her arm from his grasp as if she had been singed by his touch. "You led me to believe that outside your cabin door awaited a crew of ruthless blackguards who would abuse me mercilessly if I dared to show my face without you as my protector," she accused in a hateful tone.

His dark brows furrowed over his angry green eyes. "Are you suggesting that the only reason you yielded to me was because you sought my protection?"

"Precisely, Captain," she stormed back at him. "If I could have the chance to relive this entire day, I assure you, I would have handled it quite differently!"

Seth quickly pulled her into his strong arms, pressing her enticing body full length against him while his mouth swooped down on hers, silencing the protest that she attempted to force from her lips. Brianna could barely breathe beneath his demanding kiss and she cursed herself when she felt the familiar shiver of desire fly across her skin. The man who had taken her virginity was now attempting to prove his strange power over her again.

163

"Even this morning when I held you like this?" he whispered against her soft lips.

"Especially then," she hissed as she gathered enough determination to resist him. "I lost a great deal at your expense, but I have no intention of repeating my mistake. I seem to make enough and there is no need in duplication."

"And you may find that you have no say in the matter," Seth warned as a cruel smile parted his lips. His hands slid beneath her shirt to capture her full breasts. "If I want you, I'll take you, Brianna. Never doubt that."

"I hate you!" she spat contemptuously as she pushed away from the solid wall of muscled flesh. "If you dare touch me again, I'll scream these walls down around us!"

"No one will come to your aid. They know better than to enter my cabin without my permission."

"My brother will!" Brianna insisted as she frantically squirmed to free herself from his iron grasp.

"Nay, he has problems of his own," Seth assured her with a devilish twinkle in his eyes.

"What have you done to my brother?"

"You'll find out tonight," Seth retorted as he abruptly released her. "Until then I expect you to behave yourself or you will not be permitted to see him at all. Do we understand each other?"

"All too clearly," she muttered resentfully.

"Good." Seth sauntered toward the door and then paused to glance back at Brianna. "There are several of my shirts that need mending, and when you complete that task you can clean this cabin," he suggested with a victorious smile. "Since you are here, you may as well make yourself useful. It should be a new experience for you."

When the door was securely closed and locked

behind him, Seth heard the crash of porcelain against the oaken door and chuckled to himself. Brianna was a little firebrand and what had occurred that morning made no sense at all. It was so out of character for Brianna to yield to anyone. Had she really only submitted to him hoping to save herself from a fate that she considered even worse than death? But she had responded to him, openly, innocently, finding a pleasure that she had not expected, and even admitted to enjoying the passion she had discovered. Why has she returned to that stubborn, fiery witch when he had just begun to find himself yearning for her once again? Seth wanted to feel her soft lips responding to his, to know the contentment of holding her in his arms, but it was obvious that Brianna wanted nothing to do with him. She would again, he vowed determinedly, and Derrick was not about to discover how much he was missing! Let him dream!

When Seth eased open the door that evening, he stepped inside as cautiously as a man entering the cage of a wild beast. His eyes swept the immaculate cabin, noting several of his mended shirts neatly stacked on the desk. His eyes finally came to rest on Brianna who lay curled up asleep in the corner with a book in hand. A faint smile touched his lips as he moved toward her.

After studying her for a long moment, he leaned down to press a light kiss to her lips. Brianna moaned drowsily, her eyes fluttering open. When she realized who was bestowing affection on her, she stiffened and pushed Seth away.

"Isn't it enough that you have made me your servant? Must I become your whore as well?" she snapped, her tone laced with bitterness.

The tender moment was smothered by her harsh words and Seth scowled down at the defiant wench.

Why couldn't she accept his embraces as other women had, willingly, eagerly, without this constant bombardment of insults? By damned, he would have this feisty she-cat purring like a kitten before he was finished with her!

"Temper, temper, Brianna," he mocked, a sly smile settling on his bronzed features. "If you expect to see your brother, I suggest that you treat me with the courtesy and respect that is due a ship's captain. Otherwise, you will not only find yourself my mistress and slave, but my prisoner as well."

Brianna swallowed her pride and wrapped her arms about his shoulders as she forced a smile. "Is this the way you would have me respond to your amorous moods, Captain?"

Seth fell into her trap, reveling in the sweetness of her lips playing softly on his. "Aye, m'lady. 'Tis more to my liking."

When Seth finally dragged his lips away from hers, Brianna displayed a bittersweet smile. "Then this will be my response," she assured him in a sugar-coated voice that camouflaged the underbite. "When hell freezes over!" Her pride was like cream that eventually rises to the top, and she found it impossible to be submissive. "You have done nothing to earn my respect and until you do, I will treat you as I would any other malicious viper!"

Brianna bolted from the bed and spun to face him, her long, ebony hair cascading over her shoulders like the Devil's cape. "You didn't wish to make me your wife. You deliberately deceived me," she stormed at him, her voice rippling with fury. "Yet, you would make me your whore and keep me with you on this damned schooner until we reach the colonies where you can cast me aside for another wench. I would rather die than suffer this despicable arrangement."

Her chin tilted proudly, her eyes flashing their usual defiance.

"You were opposed to the marriage too," Seth reminded her as he rose from the bed and took a bold step forward.

"But I didn't even know who you were," she defended. "At least you had the advantage of knowing what your bride-to-be was like. You could have been some effeminate dandy whose sight repulsed me. How was I to know what was in store for me?"

"And if you had met me that night we came for dinner, would you have agreed to the wedding?" His heavy brow arched in question.

"Nay," she insisted haughtily. "But at least I would have known the kind of scoundrel I had rejected!"

Wry amusement danced in his eyes as he raked Brianna from head to toe. Reasoning with this wench was like debating a stone wall. Both were comparably receptive to change. She was too proud and stubborn to back down to anyone. "And what about now, Brianna? Would you prefer to be my mistress or my wife?"

He had taken the wind from her sails with this abrupt question. Brianna eyed his wry smile with apprehension, but despite her mistrust she answered. "I suppose if I were forced to choose between the two evils, I would rather be your wife. At least I would have my pride. Very little else," she added resentfully, "but 'tis more than I have now."

Seth thoughtfully rubbed his chin as his gaze swept over her, never missing even the smallest detail. "I have a proposition for you to consider." Seth paced the floor in front of her, his hands clasped behind his back. "The marriage contract between our families has been made. If we were to wed, my grandfather and your father would be satisfied with the match."

"But they are not the ones who would be forced to suffer the marriage," Brianna interjected.

He paused, glanced over his shoulder, and then nodded slightly. "True, m'lady," he agreed blandly. "But they did not specify the terms of the agreement. Take a moment to consider what you and I have to gain by the arrangement I would suggest." He turned to face Brianna and her skeptical frown. "If we marry, we will no longer be harrassed by our families. You will have the respect of my crew and my protection while you are on board. When you return to England, your affairs will be your own, not your father's." A mocking smile caught one corner of his mouth as he sauntered back to her. "If you wish to parade the streets of Bristol, wearing not a stitch, the gossips would not be hounding your father for he would not be responsible for your actions. My home is in the colonies and that is where I choose to spend most of my time. We need only see each other when I sail to England. We can manage to play the charade for Andrew and Gerald occasionally. You will be free to do as you please with whomever you please, just as I will."

"But your grandfather might be upset when the news that I have tainted the family name reaches his ears," she countered, eyeing him warily.

Seth chuckled as he reached out to smooth her dark hair over her shoulder. "I have already soiled the Donnovan name. My grandfather would find it amusing that my wife was as frivolous as I am. As a matter of fact, that is the reason he selected you. He considered us to be an equal match. But if the thought concerns you, my dear, you could always take up residence in London," he suggested.

"And what if I should choose to remain in the colonies with my devoted husband and select my lovers from his circle of friends?" she taunted, her mouth lifting in a mischievous smile.

"You would do that just to spite me, wouldn't you?" He smirked.

Her shoulder lifted in a leisurely shrug as she ambled across the room to pull her pouch up on the cot. "But then again, I may not find the colonies to my liking. In that case, I might return to Bristol on the first ship that sails." Brianna laid the dresses on the bunk and smoothed the wrinkles away as she threw Seth a quick glance. "And what of you? What will you gain from such an arrangement?"

Seth studied her shapely backside as she leaned over the bunk, knowing exactly what he would gain on the voyage. He had to will himself to look the other direction so that his thoughts wouldn't be filled with lusty ideas. Damn, but she was tempting baggage, he muttered to himself.

"I will no longer be forced to listen to my grandfather nagging me about taking a wife. I can, at last, live in peace. If I take the woman he chooses for me, then he cannot dare to criticize the marriage or our agreement. And, of course, I can continue to choose my companions as I have done in the past," he added glibly.

"But I intended to marry for love," Brianna murmured as she turned to face Seth's bold appraisal of her. "If we wed, I will be forced to relinquish a dream."

Seth scoffed at Brianna's childish whim. "And that is *all* it is, Brianna," he assured her in a cynical tone. "You have yet to meet a man who can capture your heart. Obviously, there is no such man, since you have had the pick of the crop. There is no knight in shining armor to whisk you away, my dear. Take this marriage for its convenience and choose your own lover later. You can have as many men as you desire for as long as you desire. When you tire of one of them, simply cast him aside and search out another. Since you are as fickle as the wind I doubt that any man will hold your interest for an eternity. Your only love is adventure," he predicted with a wry smile. "Our marriage will allow both of us what we crave most—freedom to search for new horizons. I cannot imagine that such an arrangement couldn't please you, for it might be the *only* thing that does."

Brianna regarded him for a long, silent moment, a thoughtful frown furrowing her brow. Perhaps he was right, she mused. She had yet to find a man whom she could honestly admit to love. Maybe she never would. A marriage to Seth would in no way inhibit her lifestyle. There would be no bonds to tie them together. Her childish dream faded as she raised her eyes to Captain Donnovan. There were no knights except in fairy tales, no ideal love except in fantasies. She was destined to thrive on adventure alone. And if she decided to reconsider this marriage, Grant would come to her rescue. She could agree to anything just to pacify Seth. Later she would decide on the proper course of action.

"Very well, Captain," Brianna began as she met his patient gaze. "We shall have the marriage that neither of us wanted and make it suit our needs. A common name will be all that ties us together. We shall not attempt to interfere in each other's lives."

A broad smile split Seth's face, showing even white teeth. "Agreed, m'lady." He strolled over to Brianna and wrapped his arms about her trim waist. "Shall we seal the agreement with a kiss?"

"I think I would much rather have it written in blood . . . yours," she said flatly. "Although this agreement sounds tempting I wonder if I will regret bargaining with the likes of you. I doubt that this will be the perfect solution to the problem."

"There is no such thing as a perfect solution." A

ghost of a smile hovered on his lips as they brushed over hers. "Solutions always create some other problem elsewhere. I have no doubt that somehow we will regret bargaining with each other. But for now, 'tis the best we can do."

As he drew her full length against him, Brianna vowed to make the most of the situation. When his kiss deepened to explore the recesses of her mouth, a wild tingle skitted across her skin. Somehow, this marriage did not sound so cold and calculated when he held her in his arms, filling her with an erotic need that had just begun to live and breathe. If she couldn't find love, she would settle for passion and protection.

The thoughts began to fade as his hands roamed over her, making her heart somersault in response. A light rap on the door brought an annoyed grumble from Seth. Each time he found Brianna warm and willing in his arms, someone interrupted them.

"What is it?" he snapped gruffly.

There was a pause before Kenton's hesitant voice replied, "Sir, I brought your supper tray."

Seth heaved a disgusted sigh and stalked to the door to accept the tray from the lad who waited outside. "Thank you," he muttered as he grabbed the tray and then slammed the door in Kenton Marsh's face.

Brianna chuckled at Seth's sour frown. He reminded her of a pouting child. "He was just doing his duty, Captain. Do you always treat your crew so rudely?"

"Only when they interrupt something as enjoyable as kissing you," he replied as he set the tray on the table and moved toward Brianna, a rakish grin brimming his lips. "Now, where were we?"

"Finished," Brianna said saucily as she dodged his outstretched arms and walked over to lift the cover from the food.

His arms dropped loosely to his sides as he heaved an

annoyed sigh. The only way to have Brianna to himself was to set the entire crew adrift in the middle of the Atlantic. It was a rather drastic measure, but, at the moment, it sounded appealing.

He couldn't help but wonder why she had agreed to the arrangement. As stubborn as she was, it piqued his curiosity. Was it because of her father and his ultimatum? And what of himself? Why had he made the offer? Was it because of her brother and his grandfather? Or was it because he had discovered a passion in Brianna that she had never offered to another man? Or perhaps it was that she was unlike any other woman he had ever met, just as his grandfather had predicted. She was like an untamed creature that man could not help but admire. She was proud, determined, challenging, and the picture of innocence, an enchanting combination. He had never begged or pleaded for a woman's affection, but Brianna forced him to maneuver her into his arms. To have her come willingly with no other motive than to seek her own needs would be a gratifying reward, Seth decided as a demure smile tugged at one corner of his mouth. He had been fascinated by the golden-eyed beauty since the first moment they met. Now the woman whom every eligible nobleman in Bristol would like to claim as his own would belong to Seth Donnovan. He would take this daring wench and make her his pet for a time.

"When your brother arrives this evening, we will be married," Seth stated as he eased down across from Brianna to take his meal.

Her brows shot up in surprise and then returned to their normal arch. "That will be fine, Captain," she agreed. "I have nothing else planned for the evening."

"You hardly sound like the nervous bride who is about to cross the threshold of wedlock," he mocked dryly.

"If this were the usual marriage I might take it more seriously. Under the circumstances, I see no reason for nervousness."

"I would never consider a marriage to you as an ordinary event, Brianna . . . no matter what the circumstances." His blinding smile caused such a glare that Brianna glanced the other way, refusing to succumb to his charm.

"And I consider myself most fortunate to have found such a marvelous man for a husband," she replied, sarcasm dripping from her lips.

"Your compliment has touched my heart, my love," he countered in the same fashion.

Brianna averted her gaze and stared at her plate. It was obvious that it would take an effort for them to be civil to each other, for neither of them had meant a word they had said. Luckily, they would not need to endure each other's company much longer. When Grant arrived, he would come to her aid. After all, she had only agreed to this ridiculous marriage to avoid further arguments with Seth. She was in no position to clash with him. Soon Grant would come to her rescue as he always did. Clinging to that thought, Brianna began biding her time, knowing her brother would untangle the mess she had made.

Lucas Patton strolled into the cabin and tossed his bag on the bunk as Jed Catlin glanced curiously at him.

"What are ye doin' 'ere?" Jed questioned as he swung his long legs over the edge of his cot and sat up.

"Talbert has a wench to share his quarters. The captain signed me to room with you," Patton explained, a wry grin catching his lips. "It will give us the chance to discuss what we intend to do with the loot when we dock."

"I thought that was all arranged."

"Aye, it was, but I have no desire to share the profit with Gibbons. We are the ones who take all the chances and he wants half of the loot. I think it's time we cut Gibbons out . . . permanently."

Catlin returned the wicked grin. "I think ye may be right."

Chapter Twelve

Sabrina donned her pale blue gown and frantically attempted to rearrange her hair for the third time as she peered into the small hand mirror. If only Brianna could have been there to help her, she thought to herself. But obviously Brianna had changed her mind about following Grant. It was no surprise, Sabrina mused as she pinned a loose curl on top of her head. Brianna was prone to do just exactly the opposite of what she said. Sabrina and Grant had searched every niche on the ship, hoping to find Brianna, but she was nowhere. Perhaps she had decided to flee to the country estate after all. Sabrina refused to think that Brianna had come to harm since she was so capable of taking care of herself.

When Grant opened the door, Sabrina inspected her appearance for the last time. As Grant leaned back against the wall, his glowing eyes made a slow, deliberate appraisal of the honey-haired lass.

"I still find it hard to believe that you have been right under my nose for these last few years and I failed to appreciate your beauty," he breathed in a raspy voice.

A radiant smile spread across Sabrina's face. How she adored Grant! He had been a part of her dreams since she was old enough to recognize the difference between men and women. "Brianna and I were always following at your heels and you were always too pre-occupied with someone else to notice me," she replied with a hint of accusation in her tone.

"But no longer," Grant murmured as he strolled up in front of Sabrina. "I love you, Sabrina." He lowered his head to capture her quivering lips and drew her into his arms.

"And I love you, Grant, more than you will ever know," Sabrina whispered, her voice cracking with the overwhelming emotion.

"You will have an eternity to prove it." Grant placed a light kiss on her upturned nose before leading her to the door, and they walked together down the dark companionway that led to the captain's quarters.

Brianna dressed in her yellow gown after ordering Seth from the room. When she allowed him to re-enter, he propped his feet up on the desk and lit his cigar while watching Brianna nervously pace the floor.

"I thought you said Grant would be here at eight," Brianna muttered as she glanced sideways at Seth. "Where is he?"

"He'll be here, Brianna," Seth calmly assured her. "Don't be so impatient."

Brianna frowned at him and was about to make a snide remark, but when someone rapped on the door she shrieked excitedly and flung it open to leap into her brother's arms.

"Sabrina, what are you doing here?" Brianna gasped as Grant allowed her feet to touch the floor, her amber eyes wide in shock.

Sabrina embraced her friend and hastened to explain. "I followed Grant too. Where have you been hiding? We have searched everywhere for you."

"Various places," Brianna replied evasively as she urged Grant and Sabrina into the cabin, closed the door, and shot Seth a murderous glower. Why hadn't he told her about Sabrina? He knew all along and never even told her and had not bothered to tell Grant and Sabrina that she was on board. What game was he playing?

The disgusted glance that Seth received from both women brought a throaty chuckle from him. It was apparent that Sabrina did not like him and that at the moment, Brianna despised him for being so secretive. *Women,* he mused cynically. *What a troublesome lot.*

"Did the captain tell you that Grant and I were getting married?" Sabrina questioned gaily, her pale blue eyes glistening with happiness.

"Married?" Brianna repeated dumbfoundedly as she turned a quizzical gaze to Grant who nodded affirmatively.

Brianna was elated and disheartened all at the same time. Grant would be much too interested in Sabrina to concern himself with his sister. She could tell by the lovestruck expression in Grant's dark eyes that he truly cared for Sabrina, but she felt as if the ship was sinking and she was securely tied to the mast. Her rescuer was too preoccupied to even notice that she was helplessly trapped.

"Shall we get on with the ceremony?" Seth suggested as he rose to his feet and snuffed out his cigar.

Sabrina nodded anxiously as she moved toward the captain with Grant close at her heels. Brianna remained steadfast until Seth's eyes narrowed sternly and he motioned for her to come stand beside him.

"I'm sure you will be happy to know that Brianna and I will also be married tonight," Seth stated as he glanced slyly at Talbert.

A relieved smile spread across Grant's face. That was the best thing that could happen to Brianna, he thought to himself. The little misfit deserved a man like Donnovan. If he couldn't handle her, no one could.

"Good, I'm glad to hear that you took my

suggestion, Captain." Grant winked at Brianna whose face had suddenly drained of color. "Now I will not have to concern myself with the little termagant. She's your misfortune, Captain."

Brianna quickly cast her brother an angry glare. He was in on this treachery too! He had promised never to sell her out and he had just done so, openly admitting to it.

"Aye," Seth heartily agreed as he grinned at Brianna, "but I shall try to make the best of it."

"Shall we get on with it?" Brianna snapped impatiently.

Sabrina arched a curious brow as she peered at her annoyed friend, but Brianna only shrugged recklessly, making Sabrina less confident that Brianna was completely satisfied with this arrangement. There was no time for Sabrina to consider the situation as Seth's rich voice filled the room, speaking the vows that bound both couples in marriage.

When the short ceremony ended and they had signed the necessary papers, Seth opened a chilled bottle of champagne and filled four glasses.

"'Tis the first time I have viewed both sides of this ceremony," Seth chuckled as he passed out the champagne. "I must say it was a rather unusual experience."

"And one that none of us will quickly forget," Brianna muttered bitterly as she gulped the bubbly brew.

After a toast was made and the glasses were emptied, Grant winked at Seth and drew Sabrina with him toward the door. "I hope you will understand if my wife and I prefer only each other's company this evening."

Seth's green eyes twinkled merrily as he regarded the hot blush on Sabrina's face and the eager smile on Grant's lips. "I will have one of the men bring your breakfast to your room in the morning and you will be

178

excused from your duties for the next two days."

"Thank you, Captain. I appreciate your generosity," Grant replied.

When Seth ushered the Talberts to the door, he glanced back to see Brianna finishing her third glass of champagne. It seemed she was determined to render herself senseless before the evening had ended, and Seth was content to allow his new wife the privilege.

"I need to talk to Derrick," Seth informed her as he leaned back against the casing of the opened door. "I'll see you later."

"Take your time, my dear, deceitful, unscrupulous husband," Brianna sneered contemptuously as she raised her glass in a curse rather than a toast. "I'm not going anywhere. There is nowhere I can go to escape this time. 'Tis too late."

When Seth exited from the room, he found Derrick on the quarterdeck. A lopsided grin tugged at the corner of Seth's mouth as he ambled toward the first mate. Derrick was not going to appreciate hearing that Brianna was now a Donnovan. It was obvious that Sayer had quickly fallen for the witch's charms.

"I do not wish to be disturbed for the rest of the evening unless some emergency arises that you are unable to handle," Seth began casually. "I will be spending a long, uninterrupted evening with my wife."

Derrick's eyes narrowed suspiciously. "You married Brianna? Why would you force her into wedlock?"

"I did not force her. She was in favor of it," he assured him.

"Somehow I find that rather difficult to believe," Derrick replied skeptically. "I didn't think the lady had fallen for you. She had just run away from an unwanted marriage in Bristol. Why would she suddenly decide to marry you?"

Seth arched a taunting brow as he observed the look

of disappointment on Sayer's face. "Just who do you suppose the wench was to marry in the first place?" he remarked as he crossed his arms on his chest.

Derrick grumbled under his breath. Why was Seth always the one who found the prizes? His eyes narrowed once again as another thought disturbed him. "If she refused to marry you in Bristol, why would she suddenly decide to change her mind?"

Seth shrugged leisurely. "Brianna told you herself that she was rather impulsive and unpredictable. She's a woman, and who can know for certain what goes on in that lovely head of hers."

"I suppose I should congratulate you, but I must admit that I envy you and the words don't come easily," Derrick muttered bitterly.

Seth's expression suddenly became serious. "I know, Derrick, and perhaps if it was anyone but Brianna I would have stepped aside and allowed you the opportunity to pursue her."

"And if it was anyone but Brianna, I wouldn't be particularly interested," Sayer assured him soberly. He strolled across the deck and then paused to glance back at the captain. "What about Priscilla?"

Seth shrugged nonchalantly as he met Sayer's curious regard. "What about her?"

"She won't like this and you know it. I hope you can handle both her and Brianna. Otherwise, you may wish you had never met this dark-haired wench who is now your wife." Derrick whirled around and strolled away, confused, envious, and disheartened that the woman who could have replaced the lost love of his own life was now married to Seth.

As Sayer's footsteps faded into silence, Seth heaved a heavy sigh. And now to face Brianna, he mused sullenly. What could he expect from her this time? It was obvious that she had counted upon her brother to rescue her and she was probably furious that the captain had not informed her about the marriage of Grant and Sabrina. Would his own wedding night be a moment to remember or a disaster that he would soon wish to forget? Seth opened the cabin door in his usual, cautious manner, again surprised at the scene that awaited him.

Brianna was leaning back in a chair with her bare feet propped on the edge of the desk, clothed in nothing but one of his shirts, holding the empty champagne bottle in the crook of her arm. The dim lantern light hovered about her, casting a golden glow on her silky skin and on the dark cape of hair that cascaded about her shoulders. Seth held his breath as Brianna glanced up at him through glassy, amber eyes. A sly smile curved the corners of her mouth upward as she slowly appraised him. It seemed the lovely witch had consumed a great deal of the bubbly brew and her fiery temper had mellowed.

"Ah, the good captain has returned from his appointed rounds," Brianna managed over her thick tongue before giggling playfully. "Would you care for a drink, dear husband?" she questioned as she carelessly raised the empty bottle and she giggled giddily once again. "It seems you arrived too late to enjoy the champagne."

Seth chuckled in amusement as he watched Brianna. "It seems you didn't bother to wait until I returned to celebrate our wedding."

Brianna wrinkled her nose distastefully after being reminded of the ceremony. As she peered at Seth, attempting to focus on his sturdy frame, the playfulness vanished from her delicate features. "I was drowning my troubles, Captain, not celebrating," she murmured as she swished the last of the champagne around in the bottom of her glass and then quickly finished off the last of the liquor.

Seth's brows furrowed slightly as he strolled toward Brianna. "I was always under the impression that marriages were a time of gaiety and festivity, not a period of mourning."

Brianna slowly raised her amber eyes to meet Seth's steady gaze, carefully appraising the handsome rogue who towered above her. "If we loved each other as Grant and Sabrina obviously do, perhaps I would be in more festive spirits, but as it is I find little reason for gaiety."

The frown on Seth's rugged features deepened as he gazed down at the tempting witch. "You don't know the meaning of love, Brianna."

Brianna cocked a mocking brow. "And I suppose you do, Captain?" she scoffed. "I would imagine that you have been far too busy appeasing your lusts to know a woman. Oh, I'm sure that you know every inch of her flesh by touch, but you never took the time to understand her and learn much else about her. I would venture to guess that your relationships have been extremely shallow except for that one woman who cast you aside for someone else."

Seth released a derisive snort as he roughly yanked Brianna to her feet. The sudden movement sent the world spinning about her and she fell helplessly against Seth's solid chest, clutching at his shirt sleeves to remain on her feet.

Brianna chuckled giddily as she leaned back to peer up at Seth's annoyed expression. "Is this tub rocking beneath my feet, or am I drunk?" she asked as her eyes flickered with a mischievous sparkle.

The biting remark about Seth's lost love seemed to escape his mind as he wrapped his arms around Brianna's trim waist to keep her from weaving unsteadily. "You're drunk," he assured her as a faint smile threatened his mouth.

182

"I was afraid that was the case. But I must admit that I am thoroughly enjoying the effects of the champagne," she replied as she leaned back in his encircling arms.

Seth returned her delicious grin, easily responding to her reckless mood. "Perhaps not tonight, but tomorrow you will regret it."

Brianna cocked her head to the side as she studied his bronzed face. "Why should I?"

Hopelessly shaking his head, he snickered at the intoxicated beauty. "Liquor has a way of making you later regret consuming an overabundance of it, madam. Mark my words. I speak from experience."

"Perhaps it will be worth it," Brianna retorted flippantly.

As Seth lowered his head, he murmured, "I doubt it."

His lips played softly against hers, arousing a kindling flame of desire in Brianna. She was far too intoxicated to refuse his gentle embrace. All restraints seemed to swim about her before they were carried out with the tide. As Brianna returned his kiss, Seth effortlessly swept her up into his arms and carried her to the bed. After laying her on the bunk, he snuffed out the lantern and returned to her side, shrugging off his clothes before he stretched out beside her. Brianna's hand slid across the dark hair on his chest, sending an exciting tingle skittering across his flesh. As she placed light, feathery kisses against his neck, she snuggled against his sturdy frame, surprising Seth with her recklessness. His heart pounded against his ribs and his hands moved to the buttons of her shirt to seek the alluring swells that lay beneath the soft linen, filling her with an undeniable desire. As his experienced caresses roamed boldly over her quivering skin, Brianna moaned softly, surrendering to the effect of the liquor and the passionate spell that had encompassed her.

Seth pulled the shirt from her shoulders as his eager eyes flickered with a fiery flame. Her body was perfection, he mused as his gaze swept her shapely form that was bathed in the moonlight streaming through the porthole above the bunk. He had arrogantly thought that after he had taken her once his desire for her would die. But it had only made him crave her more, addicting him to the feel of her velvety flesh and the soft scent that filled his senses. He placed hot, searing kisses along the hollow of her neck before his mouth covered the peak of her breast, teasing it to tautness.

A rapturous tingle ignited a blaze that burned uncontrollably within her and Brianna reveled in the heady pleasure that possessed her flesh. "Pretend you love me, Seth," she pleaded breathlessly. "If only for tonight, love me as if you have had no other before me."

Seth raised his head, gazing into the amber pools that glowed with desire. "It seems my golden talisman is useless against you, my enticing witch. I fear I will never be able to refuse you."

Brianna smiled ruefully as she clasped the chain in her hand. "I'm sorry I treated you so badly that night in Bristol. I was afraid of you then," she confessed in a raspy voice.

"And are you now, Brianna?" His fingertips traced her lips, memorizing their gentle curve, aching to have them pressed to his.

"Aye." Her lashes swept down to shield her from his probing gaze. "Afraid that I will be unable to refuse your touch. That I will become one of the many women whom you have held in your arms. I want to feel nothing for you. I want to walk away from this marriage without regret."

"Why deny passion, Brianna? You are my wife. We

have the right to enjoy each other . . . for now."

"But each time you touch me, I know it would make no difference who lay beside you," she muttered bitterly. "You are only satisfying your lust. Each time you gaze at me with desire in your eyes I know you have looked at other women in the same manner. And yet, I have known only you, have responded only to your caresses." Brianna turned away from him, regretting ever bargaining with him.

Seth trailed his hand across her face and then lifted it to his. A crooked smile touched his lips, his eyes caressing her shadowed face. "I have made love to many women," he admitted huskily. "But I have never held a witch in my arms before. And that is what you are, Brianna, a beautiful, alluring witch whom I cannot resist." He lowered his head to capture her mouth in a hungry kiss as his hand slid across her shapely hips. "I desire to hold no other in my arms. And when I make love to you, 'tis only your face that I see before me, compelling me to surrender. You make me forget the world exists."

A passionate flame burst between them, igniting a wild fire that consumed their thoughts and flesh. Seth aroused her to rapturous heights until she pulled him close, wanting him to become a part of her, needing him more than life itself. It didn't matter why or for how long, only that they were one for that timeless moment. As he moved above her, Brianna arched to meet him, reveling in the pleasure that encompassed her. Their souls took flight, gliding above the raging fires that singed their flesh. It was a voyage so far beyond reality that Brianna could have sworn she was dreaming.

As Seth shuddered above her, he gathered her into his arms, his ragged breath tickling her neck. Brianna closed her eyes, wishing she could remain in his loving embrace for an eternity. Her fingertips moved across the hard muscles of his back, marveling in the power that lay beneath her hands. Why must Seth be the one who brought her to the brink of sanity? A tear formed in her eye and then trickled down her cheek as reality invaded her hazy dream.

Perhaps this was her punishment for being a troublesome misfit. For each time she had rejected a man's embrace she must surrender to the one man who would never love her. Perhaps this was to be her own private room in hell. His rakish smile tore at her heart, his fathomless green eyes melted her defenses, and his experienced caresses could make her shiver with delight. She was trapped, and fight as she may, she could not ignore the overwhelming need of him each time he came to her, possessing her as no other had.

When Seth started to move away, Brianna clutched him to her. "Hold me," she pleaded, fighting back the tears that were about to spill down her cheeks.

Seth nuzzled her head against his shoulder. She seemed so small and insecure, unlike the high-spirited wench he had known in the past. "What's wrong, Brianna? Did I hurt you?" His hand brushed across her face, feeling the tears that she could not control.

Brianna muffled a sob. "Just hold me."

"For as long as you wish," he whispered tenderly.

A drowsy smile hovered on his lips as he closed his eyes to see Brianna thundering toward him on her black stallion. And then she changed into the sea nymph who had stilled the wind when she appeared on the deck of his schooner. Then she was offering herself to him, yielding to his passions with a wild abandon. She was so unpredictable that he never knew what to expect from one moment to the next. It was impossible to keep the thought of this golden-eyed enchantress from occupying his mind. He cradled her in his arms, wondering what the morrow would hold, wondering where she would lead him.

Seth kicked the door shut with his boot heel and then sauntered into his cabin and put the breakfast tray on the table.

"I was beginning to wonder if you were going to rouse from the dead," he taunted as Brianna raised heavy eyelids and peered at his overly cheerful smile.

Brianna groaned miserably as she held her head with both hands and struggled up on the edge of the bed. As the sheet fell away, his hawkish gaze devoured her, but she was too nauseated to care.

"I'm not so sure I'm still alive," she managed weakly. Her mouth was as dry as cotton, her head throbbing in rhythm with her pounding heart, her stomach lurching with the waves that tossed the schooner.

"I warned you that you would have hell to pay for drinking so much of that brew, but I suppose a witch can never refuse her poison," he mocked as he strolled over to offer her a steaming cup of tea.

Brianna glowered at him through bloodshot eyes and accepted the cup. "And you could hardly wait until I awoke so you could say I told you so, could you?"

Seth chuckled heartily. "Nay, Brianna. You got exactly what you deserved—a dreadful hangover." After walking back to the table, Seth eased into his chair and removed the cover from the plates. "Come eat, madam. It will make you feel better."

Eyeing him skeptically, Brianna grabbed the discarded shirt she had worn the previous evening and shrugged it on her shoulders. "I'm not sure I will ever be the same again," she muttered as she stood up to find the world spinning furiously about her.

After she had picked lightly at her food, she pushed the plate away and poured another cup of tea. "Your remedy didn't help. Have you another suggestion?"

Seth eased back in his chair and grinned at the disheveled wench who sat across from him. Even though Brianna was as white as the linen shirt she wore, she was just as lovely as she had been when she was dressed in her expensive gown. It was impossible to disguise her natural beauty. To see her at this moment only convinced Seth that she was indeed a witch. How could she be so tempting even when she was at her worst?

"You might like another drink," he suggested flippantly. "Perhaps it would make you forget how miserable you feel."

Brianna moaned at the thought. "I never want to see another glass of champagne."

When Seth finished the last of his tea, he rose from the table and leaned over to place a kiss to her pale lips. "I'll have the tub filled. Perhaps a hot bath will revive you."

Brianna nodded, forcing as much of a smile as she could muster. It was a feeble attempt, but it did manage to bring a little color to her cheeks. "I'm sorry I made such a fool of myself last night," she apologized.

Seth winked down at her, a rakish smile grazing his lips. "I'm not. I enjoyed every minute of it."

A perplexed frown gathered on her brow. Her memory was a hazy disarray of thoughts. "And just what is that supposed to mean?"

"Only that I found you warm and willing in my arms." His emerald eyes seemed to bore through her shirt, boldly caressing her. "You assured me that you will not only make a suitable wife, but a very passionate mistress. No man could wish for more."

Brianna nearly choked on her tea and then sputtered to catch her breath. As Seth reached over to whack her between the shoulder blades, his amused chortle infuriated her even more.

"Leave me be!" she managed between coughs. "'Tis humiliating enough that I acted like some drunken trollop, but I need not be reminded of my folly. I assure you that it will never happen again. I will *not* play your willing strumpet." She scrambled to her feet, spinning to face him as her ebony hair whirled recklessly about her. "If you intend to mock me for finding pleasure in your bed then I will search elsewhere to find someone who can satisfy me just as well without ridiculing me."

Seth's eyes narrowed to hard, green slits. "You are my wife and you will limit your affection *only* to your husband," he commanded sharply. "You'll find yourself far too busy appeasing my desires to search out another man."

Brianna tilted a stubborn chin and met his icy glare. "Part of our agreement was that we were free to choose our own lovers," she reminded him, her tone holding scornful mockery. "As a matter of fact, it was *your* suggestion."

Seth grabbed her arms and shook her soundly, sending her head snapping backwards. "If you dare to take any of my men to your bed, you will both suffer for your folly," he warned through gritted teeth. "When we are on the *Mesmer* there will be no other men to take my place. Is that clear, Brianna?"

"Don't threaten me," she flared. "You made the rules and I intend to follow them to the letter. 'Tis your misfortune that there are no other women available to you on this ship. *You* made the agreement and you can live with it, just as I intend to."

"Since when have you become a conformist?" he quipped with a grim smile that merely tightened his lips. "I thought you defied every code or law that has ever been written."

"I comply with those I can accept," she countered.

Suddenly Seth yanked her to him, his mouth swooping down on hers, devouring her with a rough, demanding kiss that spoke of anger rather than passion. He ripped her shirt away and shoved her toward the bed. As Brianna stumbled back against the edge of the cot, Seth fell upon her, yanking her hair to force her to accept another bruising kiss. She found herself pinned beneath his solid frame, unable to prevent his rough assault. He loosened his breeches and forced her thighs apart with his knee. Her shriek was muffled by another scalding kiss. When he raised his head far enough to stare down at her, Brianna knew for certain that the Devil's eyes were green and that he had risen from the fires of hell to torture her.

"I am your master," he sneered into her alarmed face. "I will take you each time I want you and I want you now!"

Brianna gasped as a searing pain made her stiffen. She was not prepared to accept him and she was too tender to be taken by force. He gave no thought to the pain he was inflicting. Again she cried out and again he silenced her with a devouring kiss that stripped her breath from her lungs. As he thrust against her, his rage transforming into passion, unrestrained tears flowed down Brianna's cheeks. She could not believe this was the same man who had made love to her so tenderly the previous day. He was a beast and she despised him for treating her so brutally.

Seth was consumed by a fiery desire that drove him to the brink of sanity, wanting to prove that he was master of her soul. And yet, his reasoning was lost in a whirlwind that was making the world spin out of control. With one final thrust he covered her body with his, holding her in place with her arms pinned above her head to keep her from clawing at him.

"I hate you!" she choked out, hot tears swimming in her eyes.

Seth rolled away and fastened his breeches while she

curled into a ball, shuddering with sobs of pain and humiliation. When he spied the stains on the sheet, the harsh reality of what he had done came like a hard slap in the face.

Never in his life had he taken a woman as cruelly as he had abused Brianna, his own wife, the woman he had yearned to love in passion's most rapturous moment. Yesterday he had taken her virginity and today he had savagely used her with no concern that he might have injured her. She had just learned the meaning of passion and he had raped her. Yes, damn it, that was what he had done. There was no other word for it. What had come over him? Why had he behaved so ruthlessly? He had destroyed the fragile bond that had just begun to grow between them. Now there was nothing except a burning hatred in those golden eyes that were spilling a sea of tears. As he wheeled away Brianna's words lashed out at him like a whip that had snapped across his back.

"I despise you, Seth Donnovan. I thought you were different, but you are like all the others, animals seeking pleasure in another's pain. If you ever come near me again, if you even dare to touch me, I swear by the wrath of the Devil that I will slit your throat. The sight of you makes my skin crawl. Now get out!" Her voice cracked and trembled with fury as she glowered at him.

When Seth started back toward her, her eyes widened in fear and she pulled the quilts about her like a tight cocoon, cowering in the corner like a wounded beast. Seth stopped in his tracks. The wild look in her eyes would haunt him forever. Without a word, he spun on his heels and left the cabin, hating himself for what he had done.

When the door closed behind him, Brianna muffled an enraged shriek in her pillow and clenched her fists so tightly that her nails bit into the palms of her hands. Her entire body quivered as the lingering vision of Seth came at her from a thousand directions at once. Never again would he come near her, she vowed, cursing him over and over until she fell into an exhausted sleep.

Seth placed himself at the helm, hoping to find some consolation in staring out over the sea, but it was like watching the ocean of tears that he had seen rushing from Brianna's golden eyes. He had destroyed her just as surely as if he had put a knife to her throat. Now she would never accept his embraces without a fight. Seth heaved a despairing sigh and nearly choked on his own humiliation. He could never face her again and he couldn't even meet his own reflection. He never wanted to look in a mirror again; he didn't want to gaze at the fool who had lost his temper and behaved like a crazed beast.

If he thought an apology would have righted the wrong, that Brianna would accept it and forgive him, he would have given one. But Brianna was too stubborn. He knew as well as any other man that it was impossible to return to her good graces and he sadly admitted that she had just cause to despise him as she did.

"Damn," he muttered into the wind. How could he have allowed her to infuriate him? He had always been able to control himself, to remain in command of his senses. But not with Brianna, never with Brianna. She could creep beneath his skin, her words pricking his pride, infecting his temper. He clasped the talisman in his hand, feeling the cold medallion in his palm, reminding him of the icy glace in Brianna's tear-rimmed eyes before he had left her alone in his cabin. But it was no longer his cabin, he thought dismally. He had forfeited his right to his quarters and all within it, especially Brianna.

Chapter Thirteen

Seth collected the belongings that Brianna had stacked outside his cabin and swung the hammock over his shoulder. When he knocked on Derrick's door he was met by the first mate's bemused frown.

"You and Brianna have already had a lover's quarrel," he guessed from the look of things.

Seth pushed his way into the room and tossed his arm load in the corner. "That's right, Derrick, and you will have me as a roommate for the duration of this voyage. Any complaints?" His heavy brow arched, daring Derrick to voice any grievances about having his privacy invaded.

Derrick closed the door and then shrugged nonchalantly. "No complaints, Captain, but if I may be so bold, I think you're making a big mistake walking out on Brianna."

A bitter laugh escaped his lips. "The only mistake I made was marrying that wench in the first place." Cold, green eyes swung to Derrick and fastened on his startled expression. "'Twas my grandfather's contract with Brianna's father that brought this all about. Only out of respect for them have I complied. Brianna and I agreed to make this marriage one that would suit our purposes. We both value our freedom and this arrangement is not binding. We had planned to go our separate ways and I intend to leave it at that." Seth could not bring himself to confide the truth of their separation to

Derrick. The first mate was enamored of her and Seth was certain Derrick would be furious to hear what had happened. Sayer would come to her defense, as if the wench needed assistance, he thought resentfully. Besides, she had a knack for managing quite nicely on her own. Seth was in no mood to come to blows with Derrick, which is exactly what would happen.

Derrick sadly shook his head and then rolled his eyes. "I swear you have taken leave of your senses. No man in his right mind would walk out on Brianna."

"No sane man would dare get within ten feet of her," Seth corrected.

A devilish smile caught Derrick's lips. "I consider myself to be in command of my senses and I don't consider that to be such a dangerous distance."

Seth grabbed the hammock and tied it to the ceiling beams, turning his back on the first mate's taunting grin. "You don't know her as well as I do. If you did, you wouldn't make such a remark."

"Be that as it may, Captain, I would never have quarreled with her in the first place," he assured Seth. "Perhaps if you would have apologized . . ."

"Apologized?" Seth wheeled around, letting the unattached end of the hammock drop to the floor. "One does not apologize to Brianna because she would not accept it," he informed Derrick, his voice rising testily.

Derrick ambled over to pour the captain and himself a drink. Seth looked as if he could use one. "You should have tried," he suggested quietly.

"If I want your advice, I'll ask for it," Seth snapped. He had already lost his patience with Brianna and there was none left for anyone who had the misfortune of crossing his path. He took the glass of brandy, drained it and then shoved it back at his first mate. "Refill it."

His sunbleached brow had a mocking tilt. "Is this a

quarrel that requires two full glasses of brandy, Captain?"

Seth scowled at Derrick and grabbed the brandy. "Nay, this one will take the whole damned bottle."

"Do you want to talk about it? I've always been a good listener," Derrick prodded as he watched Seth tip up the bottle and guzzle it.

The brandy scorched his throat and it took a long moment to catch his breath. "Nay." One word was all he could manage. He focused his full attention on his first mate, the chiseled lines of his face softening as he met his friend's sympathetic smile. "But I would ask that you keep an eye on Brianna until we reach Petersburg."

"With pleasure." His face split in a wide grin.

As Derrick swaggered toward the door, Seth took another swig of brandy, sank down on the chair, and propped his booted foot up on the edge of the cot. "Just don't cross her," Seth muttered, wishing he had followed his own advice. "If you do, I won't be the only one with hell to pay. Then whom would I trust to keep a watchful eye on her?"

The door closed quietly behind Derrick and he stared at it for a moment, wishing he could as easily shut out the painful memory that tormented him.

Brianna mustered a meager smile for Derrick who stood holding her breakfast tray.

"The captain asked me to bring this to you this morning. He had several matters to attend," Derrick explained, his gaze failing to meet hers.

She could tell he was ill at ease, but then they both were. Had Seth told him about their argument and . . . ? Brianna squeezed back the thought of what had happened after that. She wanted to forget, but it seemed impossible. The incident had invaded her dreams as well as her waking hours.

"After you finish your meal, I would be happy to acquaint you with the ship, that is, if you are still interested."

A warm smile spread across her features when Derrick's tender gaze finally met hers. "I'd like that very much. This cabin is much too confining and it . . ." Her voice trailed off. The room held too many memories that hovered like ghosts, waiting to terrorize her. "I have never enjoyed being indoors. I have only tolerated it."

"So I've heard." Derrick could not resist the jibe. When Brianna sent him a curious glance, he continued, "Forgive me, Brianna, but I have heard tales of your escapades in Bristol. I take it that you were not one to spend time dawdling with stitchery."

A slight blush crept to her cheeks as she accepted the tray from the first mate and walked over to the table. "Will you join me?"

"I was hoping you would ask," Derrick admitted as he strolled over to take a seat. "I took the liberty of bringing along an extra plate."

Brianna removed the cover and reached for a cup of tea. "And I was hoping you were in no hurry to leave."

"Well?" Derrick queried before sipping his tea.

Her brow arched as she sank into her chair. "Well what?"

"Are all those stories true?" he persisted.

Brianna chuckled lightly. "Perhaps you should tell me what you've heard before I answer that."

The twinkling in her golden eyes sent Derrick's heart into a forward somersault. She was even more breathtaking when she smiled. He would have been content to spend the morning just sitting and staring at her. He had seen his share of beautiful women, but Brianna was in a league all by herself. Her ebony hair sparkled in the light; her eyes danced with an amber glint that mesmerized him. Her lips were sensuously curved, almost inviting a kiss. How in heaven's name could Seth have walked out on Brianna? The man needed to have his eyes examined if he preferred to spend his time staring at the four walls of the cabin, which he had done a great deal of the previous night. But the captain's folly was Derrick's fortune. He was attracted to this charming young woman like a moth to a flame.

"Derrick?"

Her soft, raspy voice filtered into his pensive musings and he gave her an apologetic smile. "I'm sorry. What did you say?" Before she could respond, their conversation came to him and he nodded thoughtfully. "Ah, yes, the gossip," he reminded himself. "Perhaps I should refrain from repeating it. It might be ill-advised to stir up the past."

"Perhaps you're right," she agreed, her gaze falling to the cup clasped tightly in her hands. Another bewitching smile blossomed as her lashes swept up to meet his probing gaze. "I have said and done many things that seemed appropriate at the time, but were a might impulsive when I took the time to reflect on them."

"For instance, pushing your fiancé into the park fountain when he attempted to embrace you in public?" Derrick queried before he could bite back the words.

Brianna picked up her fork and whittled at the dry ham on her plate. "Nay. The bungling fop deserved the soaking." An impish grin pursed her lips as she sent Derrick a hasty glance. "He needed his passions cooled . . . and quickly."

"And what of the beau who claimed that he fell head over heels for you . . . right out of the carriage when you shoved him away. He was heard to say that you practically ran him down with his own buggy and then left him to walk home." His curiosity got the best of him, and once he began, he couldn't quit until he knew if the hearsay was really truth.

"Aye," she admitted with a sheepish grin. "I'm afraid most of the tales are fact. I do have a bit of a temper."

"I will heed the warning, m'lady." Derrick swallowed his next question. He was as bad as the gossiping hens who delighted in hearing all the sordid details. But he could not help himself. He wanted to know everything about Brianna. She fascinated him.

"I could never place you in the same category with those rogues, Derrick," Brianna reached over to pat his hand. "I doubt that you would give me cause to reveal my temper. You seem very much the gentleman."

Derrick gulped over the lump that had collected in his throat. It was a simple compliment and he knew he would never wish to disappoint her. "Thank you, Brianna. I am pleased that you hold me in such high esteem."

Slowly, she withdrew her hand and came to her feet. "Shall we go on deck? I'm anxious to see the workings of this ship. I know little about them since I have never before had cause to sail," she confessed. "I want you to show me the ropes."

As they walked the deck Derrick explained the purposes of the sails that towered over them. Brianna gasped in alarm as she watched Kenton Marsh release his grasp on the mast and swing over to repair a small tear in the canvas. When she found herself clinging fiercely to Derrick's arm, she moved away and glanced up to see Seth on the quarterdeck, his brooding gaze drilling into her. Brianna met his glare without batting an eye. She spitefully curled her hand in the crook of Derrick's arm. *Let him stand there smoldering,* she thought vindictively. Maybe he would reduce himself to a pile of ashes.

"Will you show me the galley?" she requested, flashing Derrick a smile. "And I would like to see the crewmen's quarters."

"Whatever you wish." Derrick escorted her to the steps and together they descended into the dark companionway. "I thought you would be more interested in staying on deck. The hull of the ship is gloomier than your cabin."

"I had intended to until I saw the captain," she muttered.

Derrick sent her a quick glance. "I suppose I shouldn't ask what happened between you and Seth, but—"

"Nay, you shouldn't," Brianna advised, flinging him a silencing frown. "As you said, 'tis not wise to stir up the past."

He dropped the subject and gestured toward an open door. "Here is one of the sailors' cabins."

Brianna peered inside to find a set of bunks and she was grateful that her cabin was more spacious. She would have gone mad if she were forced to stare up at another bed above her while she was trying to fall asleep. Confining quarters made her uneasy.

"There is very little to see," Derrick remarked with a shrug. "Only four walls and two beds."

Her eyes settled on the grimy hat that lay on one of the bunks, her brows furrowed thoughtfully. There was something familiar about it, but she couldn't recall where she had seen it.

"Is something wrong, Brianna?" Derrick inquired.

Her gaze swung back to the handsome first mate. "Nay." But something was troubling her. Where had she seen that hat?

After Derrick showed her the galley, he took her to his cabin. "As you can see, my title warrants me more comfort than the rooms of the crewmen."

Brianna did not fail to notice the hammock hanging in the corner. "But you have the inconvenience of sharing a room with the captain."

"He really isn't a bad sort," Derrick felt obliged to say. Judging by the angry look in her eyes, he needn't have bothered.

"I'm glad you think so since you have the misfortune of enduring his company." Brianna spun on her heels and walked back outside, barely able to contain her irritation. The very mention of Seth brought back those haunting memories so vividly that she had to squeeze her eyes shut to keep them from spilling tears.

"I should like to return to my cabin, Derrick."

"Perhaps we could take a stroll this evening," he suggested. "There is nothing quite as breathtaking as the sea when the moonlight is dancing on the waves. . . ." A gentle smile surfaced on his lips as he cupped her chin in his hand and lifted her face to his. "Except when it is compared to you. Then the sea becomes a distant second."

"And you are one of a kind." Brianna pushed up on tiptoe to place a light kiss to his tanned cheek. "I will be looking forward to this evening, Derrick. If the men of Bristol were like you, my volatile temper would have remained intact."

Seth swore under his breath and clenched the wheel until his knuckles turned white. Watching Derrick and Brianna was his own private torture. Never again would he witness one of her smiles or feel her moist lips parting in eager response. His eyes shifted out over the sea, but Brianna was still there. The terror he had seen in her eyes when he had raped her made another piercing wound in his soul.

"Sir, shall I take the wheel?" the helmsman questioned as he studied Seth's broad back.

"Nay. I'll see to it myself." Seth's tone was so sharp

that the helmsman took a retreating step.

"I thought perhaps . . ."

"Let me be!" Seth snapped impatiently, casting the man a cold glance before his gaze swung back to the countless whitecaps that spread before him. "I'll call you when I need you."

As the helmsman walked away, Seth muttered under his breath. The haunting memory of the incident with Brianna weighed so heavily on his conscience that he could barely be civil to anyone who attempted to speak to him.

The affair with Brianna was over. He had not intended that they part with bitter feelings, but he couldn't change the past. He had paid his due to his grandfather and to Grant Talbert. That had been his only intent, he told himself. If only he hadn't . . . Seth cursed himself all over again when the vision of Brianna rose before him. Involuntarily, he clasped the talisman that dangled from the chain. It was as cold and hard as the look in Brianna's eyes, a look that would forever remind him of the curse she had placed upon him.

Brianna wrapped her hand around the arm Derrick offered her and drew the shawl tightly around her neck as the cool sea breeze curled about her shoulders.

Derrick was quick to notice her discomfort since he never missed a single movement she made. "Would you prefer a heavier wrap, m'lady?"

"'Tis all I brought with me," Brianna replied, sending him a gracious smile.

"You may use my jacket. It would be warmer."

"This will suffice."

Derrick had already made a mental note not to argue with her, no matter how insignificant the matter, and let the subject drop. As he gestured toward the taffrail,

Brianna's gaze followed his arm.

"Have you ever seen such a magnificent view?" he breathed, his eyes sweeping the silver waves that curled and rolled in the moonlight.

"When I was hiding in the hull of the ship, I sneaked up on deck each night just to sit and gaze at the sea." It had been so simple then, Brianna thought dismally. If she had returned to her father when she had had misgivings about following Grant, she would have bypassed the agony that plagued her now.

Derrick chuckled as his eyes rested on the bewitching face that was bathed in moonbeams. "And that will be another escapade that will be on the tongues of those who frequent the pubs of Bristol," he teased, sending her a subtle wink.

Her shoulder lifted in a disinterested shrug, her thoughts preoccupied. Brianna had spent the day wondering why the hat that she had seen on the bunk kept drawing her curiosity. As she glanced over to see the shadow of a man disappearing behind the outer wall of the quarterdeck it came to her: The night she had fled from Seth, she had run headlong into two surly men; one of them had been wearing such a cap. Brianna felt the color drain from her cheeks. She had an uneasy feeling, knowing that one of those men was somewhere on the ship. They had scared the wits out of her. Perhaps Seth had spoken the truth when he warned her that his crew could be a threat. The thought made her huddle closer to Derrick.

"Are you cold?" he questioned, wrapping a protective arm about her shoulder.

"A little," she admitted, but it wasn't from the evening breeze. She wouldn't want to meet up with either of those men again. Just remembering her confrontation with them sent an eerie shiver down her spine.

The smile that had begun to surface on her lips vanished when she met the longing gaze in Derrick's eyes. She was certain that he intended to kiss her, but he hesitated. Her hand brushed across the rugged lines of his face, indecision etching her brow. She had promised Seth that she would seek comfort with another man whenever it met her whim. Opportunity was knocking and she just stood there, afraid to discover whether or not Derrick's embrace could stir her blood the way Seth's had.

"Derrick!"

Derrick turned in front of Brianna, as if shielding her from Seth's condemning glare. "Captain?"

"Escort the lady back to her cabin and meet me on the quarterdeck," he ordered before spinning on his heels and stalking away.

Brianna breathed a sigh of relief and mustered a smile as Derrick urged her along the deck. They walked in silence until the first mate paused at her door and lifted her hand to press a kiss to her wrist.

"I'm sorry, Brianna. I had hoped our evening would not end so quickly. I dare not keep the captain waiting. He has been breathing fire of late."

"There will be other nights," Brianna managed to say, although she was close to tears. Seeing Seth had spurred another round of unsettled emotions that played havoc with her thoughts.

Brianna managed to maintain her composure until the door was closed behind her. But when she was alone, tears scalded her eyes and slid down her cheeks. How could she despise Seth so intensely each time she saw him and then yearn for his embrace each time she closed the door of her cabin? Brianna wiped away the lingering tears and donned her nightgown, determined to put the dashing captain out of her mind. She had sworn never to let him near her again and that was one promise she must keep, even though it was unbearable living with her decision.

Derrick swung his legs over the cot and peered across the room to see Seth tangled in his hammock. Another round of inaudible mumblings brought Derrick to his feet and across the room to give the captain a sound shaking.

"I cannot afford to lose another night of rest because you talk in your sleep," he muttered sourly.

Seth opened one eye, and that with considerable effort. "You better have good cause for waking me," he said hoarsely, his voice overused from shouting orders all day and carrying on conversations with himself all night.

"Waking *you?*" Derrick released a derisive snort as he stalked back to his cot. "I wish I could have said that."

"What the hell is that supposed to mean?" Seth frowned as he strained to see his first mate's shadow disappear beneath the quilts.

"Every night since you moved in here, you have forced me to listen to your incoherent mumblings." Derrick squirmed on his hard cot, seeking a comfortable position. "You are the one who has been keeping *me* awake, Captain."

"Have I?" Seth's tone registered surprise. He had noticed the raspiness in his voice, but until that moment he was unaware of its cause. After swinging from his hammock, he donned his breeches, and walked across the dark cabin.

"Now what are you doing, walking in your sleep?" Derrick quipped caustically as he fluffed his pillow and wormed his way deeper in the quilts.

"I'm going up on deck for some fresh air," Seth threw over his shoulder before closing the door behind him.

His steps carried him to Brianna's cabin. He paused, staring thoughtfully at the weather-beaten oak. Seth raised his hand to knock, but then his arm fell loosely to his side. Heaving a frustrated sigh, he walked away, not knowing what he intended to say even if Brianna would have granted him entrance.

Brianna held her breath until the footsteps had evaporated into silence. She had been lying awake, as she had almost every night. That same eerie feeling chilled her skin, reminding her of the sensation she had experienced when she had been on deck with Derrick. Her imagination was running away with itself, she decided. She was safe behind the bolted door. Besides, just because she had noticed a hat that was similar to the one belonging to the man who had grabbed her that night in Bristol did not mean that it was the same. And why, if it *were* his, would he be standing outside her door? Brianna chided herself for letting her thoughts wander in that direction in the first place. It was ridiculous. Clinging to that logic, her eyes fluttered shut, but they flew open again when the footsteps returned. Tensely, she waited, watching the door latch turn and the door strain against the lock. And then the footsteps faded again, making it even more difficult to rout those thoughts from her mind.

Seth glanced down from the quarterdeck to see a dark silhouette disappearing into the hull, but he was much too preoccupied to give it thought. He was reliving the incident with Brianna as he had each day and night. God forgive him for what he had done; he couldn't forgive himself.

Determinedly, he turned his thoughts to Priscilla, recalling the color of her hair, the gentle curve of her lips. For more years than he cared to count he had been mesmerized by the sight of her. But there was bitterness attached to that memory and his spirits took a headlong dive into the sea. And from those depths came another bewitching face, one that could sparkle with mischief or glow with the warmth of passion.

"Damn," Seth growled to himself. Women had caused him nothing but trouble. Perhaps he should have become a monk. He could have bypassed a great many problems. His gaze swung back to Brianna's cabin and the memories of their time together fell like an avalanche, the weight so heavy that his shoulders slumped in response. What was done, was done. He had made his bed and now he had to learn to sleep in it . . . alone.

Sabrina opened the door and greeted her sister-in-law with a smile. "Brianna, I was wondering when I would see you."

"I thought I would give you and Grant your privacy. After all, this is your honeymoon." Her glance swept the crackerbox cabin and then circled back to Sabrina. "Such as it is."

Sabrina's expression took on a dreamy-eyed glow as she sank down in the chair across from Brianna. "I'm not complaining. The quarters are small, but I'm content just being with Grant." After a long moment, her thoughts returned to the present and she studied Brianna's sullen face. "Grant tells me that you and the captain had a disagreement and that he has taken up residence elsewhere."

Brianna's gaze dropped to the table like a kite taking a headlong dive without a breeze to sustain it. "Our marriage was no more than a fulfillment of a contract," Brianna explained, hoping to sound indifferent. "We plan to go our separate ways when we reach the colonies. I intend to return to Bristol with you and Grant. The only time it will be necessary for us to pretend to be husband and wife is when Seth comes to

England to trade cargo."

Relief seeped into her features. "I'm certainly glad to hear that. At first I thought you had fallen in love with that deceitful rogue. I had feared that you had not seen through him, but I should have known better than to waste my time worrying about you." A knowing smile pursed her lips. "I suppose you have had the last laugh on your father."

Brianna toyed with the folds in her yellow gown, her gaze failing to meet Sabrina's. It was no laughing matter and she felt no consolation in knowing that she had outwitted her father.

"But then, you wouldn't have had to marry Captain Donnovan," Sabrina continued with a leisurely shrug.

A puzzled frown gathered on Brianna's brow. "What do you mean?"

"That day when you hurried away to avoid confronting your father on the *Mesmer,* he admitted that he wouldn't follow through with the contract. He had given the matter some thought and had decided against forcing you to marry," she continued. When Brianna flung her an accusing glance, Sabrina hastened to defend herself. "You didn't come back to the house that night and I had no opportunity to tell you of his change of heart."

Brianna would have been happier if she had been spared that knowledge. If she had returned to her father, she would have saved herself a great deal of misery. But no, she had stumbled blindly ahead, finding herself deeper in quicksand. God, if only she could turn back the hands of time and relive the past few weeks.

"That Captain Donnovan nearly scared the wits out of me when he found me aboard his schooner." Sabrina shuddered, remembering how he had turned her every way but loose. Donnovan was an expert at maneuvering people. Thank goodness Brianna had been clever enough to use the situation to her advantage, Sabrina thought to herself. "He knew your entire story and played me for the fool, trying to pry information from me. And then he threw me back into that dreadful niche to room with the rats." Her nose wrinkled distastefully before her expression mellowed in afterthought. "But then I suppose I must thank him for delivering me to Grant."

"He *was* devious," Brianna agreed. "But . . ."

Sabrina rushed on without allowing Brianna to finish. "The sooner you're away from him, the better. I don't trust him. He always looks at me with that sly grin, as if he can read my mind. It makes me uneasy."

Brianna had experienced that same feeling, only to discover later that it had indeed been true. When Brianna glanced back at Sabrina, she was being regarded all too closely.

"If you are so glad to be rid of that blackguard, why do you seem so melancholy? Your eyes have lost that mischievous gleam, Brianna," she pointed out. "I thought you would be sitting on top of the world."

Brianna mustered a cheerful smile and all it lacked was sincerity. "I am," she confirmed. "Perhaps 'tis just that sea air doesn't agree with me."

Sabrina eyed her skeptically. "I think 'tis more than that. A change of climate never concerned you before."

Her shoulder lifted in a careless shrug. "I find little to occupy my time." Her excuse did not satisfy Sabrina who knew her better than most.

A mocking smile slid across Sabrina's lips, her blue eyes holding a hint of a dare. "That was always when you devised some prank to ease the boredom," she recalled. "I'm beginning to think you actually regret having had a disagreement with that cad you claim as your husband."

Brianna scoffed disgustedly, "He is as annoying as a thorn in the side. I intend to avoid Seth until I set foot on solid ground and then I will be rid of him."

"Good." Sabrina said with a nod. "If you keep your distance from him I will not be forced to be civil to him."

Although Sabrina continued to chatter on about her dealings with Seth, Brianna lost track of the conversation. She was too preoccupied, trying to sort through her emotions, wondering how she truly felt about the man who was her husband. When Grant entered the cabin, Brianna made her excuses and left the two of them alone, especially since they couldn't take their eyes off each other.

Why couldn't she have found such happiness? Brianna mused bitterly as she slipped her nightgown over her head. She would just have to amuse herself as Sabrina suggested. After all, this marriage was made to allow her limitless freedom. Why wasn't she enjoying it?

Chapter Fourteen

Brianna tucked her shirt in the waistband of her breeches, fastened her sash, and strolled outside to inhale a breath of fresh air. She had been giving Sabrina's suggestion a great deal of thought. Her cabin fever had made her restless and she was craving adventure, something to rid her of depressing thoughts. Her gaze lifted to watch Kenton making his way down the mast. A thoughtful smile touched her lips and then broadened. The young man seemed to delight in checking and repairing the canvas, teetering on the ropes like an acrobat. Brianna walked toward Kenton as he hopped to the deck.

"Good morning, m'lady," Kenton greeted when Brianna graced him with a smile.

"I've been watching you maneuver on the sails. Is it frightening?" Brianna questioned.

If Kenton would have known her well, he would have been wary of that golden gleam in her eyes. Kenton, being a young man only a few years older than Brianna, was too captivated to realize that he was being baited. "Nay. Once you grow accustomed to the height, there ain't nothing to it. I could spend the day climbing around up there and never tire of the view." He was bragging a bit. The first day that the captain had given him the duty, Kenton had nearly lost his breakfast when he looked down to see the crew who appeared no more than a crowd of midgets below him. "It's like flying," he continued. "The wind is in your face, the sails are your wings, and you can touch the sky."

Her lashes swept up, carefully studying one of the three towering masts. "Then I should like to see for myself," she said matter-of-factly.

As Kenton's eyes bulged from their sockets Brianna heard a gasp behind her. She turned a curious gaze to Derrick to see his face sagging in shock.

"Brianna, that is no place for you. You could break your neck with one careless move."

A wry smile crept to her lips as she turned squarely to face the first mate. "I wanted to learn the ropes of this ship," she reminded him. "What better way than to climb up on them?" Her eyes swung back to Kenton whose jaw also seemed to be lacking a hinge. "Will you show me the way?"

Kenton shifted his attention to the first mate who was adamantly shaking his head. "M'lady, I don't think . . ."

"Well then, I suppose I must go by myself," she insisted, her chin tilting to a determined angle.

"Brianna," Derrick had barely breathed her name before she headed for the mast. "Damn it, go with her, Marsh," he ordered hurriedly. If he couldn't stop her, at least Marsh could offer his advice.

Brianna was a quarter of the way up when Kenton called up to her. "Tuck in your sash, m'lady. It might trip you up."

After she had clamped herself around the pole she used her free hand to do as Kenton had suggested. When he had scurried up behind her, he pointed to the right.

"Grab hold of the rope and pull yourself up on the bottom of the sail," he instructed and then paused a moment, heaving a heavy sigh. "Are you sure you want to go through with this? I'm afraid I was bragging a bit much. The first time I climbed up here it scared my wits out of me."

Her eyes sparkled like the sun itself, excitement pulsating through her veins. "I'm quite sure. I won't be satisfied until I know what a bird experiences when he's soaring," she replied as she looked down to him.

Derrick's heart skipped a beat when Brianna leaned out to grasp the rope and then swung over to catch her boot heel on the bottom of the sail. "Be careful!" He couldn't help but offer advice. If anything happened to her, he would never forgive himself. He should have refused to let her make the climb, but then how could he have stopped her? Only by brute force, he quickly decided. Damn, that woman was too daring for her own good. Now he was absolutely certain that all he had heard about Brianna was true, even the escapades he hadn't bothered to mention.

Seth had just completed his entry in the log and rose to stretch his stiff body. His lack of sleep was leaving him tired. Sitting and standing for long periods of time were becoming an effort. Heaving a weary sigh, he rubbed his forehead, hoping to ease the dull ache in his head. As he strolled to the deck, he frowned curiously at the crowd that had gathered, their eyes turned skyward. His frown deepened as he followed their gazes and then he swallowed his breath. There was no mistaking the shapely form wrapped in breeches and a shirt, swaying to and fro on the towering mast above him. Anger and fear whipped through him as he stalked toward his crew, forcing his way to Derrick.

"What the sweet loving hell is she doing up there?" He grabbed Derrick's arm and spun him to face the dark scowl that cut through Seth's features.

"Learning the ropes," he explained, his eyes straying back over his shoulder to watch Brianna pull herself up to the tallest sail.

"Damn it, Derrick! How could you allow her to go up there?" Seth's voice wavered with fury, his eyes blazing fire.

"How could I stop her?" Derrick countered when he finally dragged his eyes off of Brianna. He focused his attention on the captain for only a split-second before his gaze circled back to Brianna.

Seth's breath came out in a rush, unable to come up with a retort. How indeed did anyone stop Brianna when she made up her mind to pursue a whim?

A shadow fell over the schooner and Seth was certain it was a sign of forthcoming doom. He glanced up to see the brewing storm clouds swallowing the sun. An uneasy feeling trickled down his spine. If a breeze preceded the thunderstorm, Brianna could be swept from her precarious perch and tossed into the sea. His gaze made fast work of searching the crew to find Grant Talbert watching his sister, a wry smile playing on his lips.

"Talbert, tell her to come down from there," Seth barked impatiently as he shoved bodies from his path to reach Brianna's brother.

Grant chuckled at the concern etched on the captain's face. "She's been climbing trees as tall as the mast since she was but a child. Have no fear, Captain. Brianna is as agile as a cat."

Seth could not share Grant's confidence. He had seen too many men lose their footing and plunge into the sea. Had the entire crew gone mad? Had no one attempted to stop that vixen?

"I don't give a damn if she can fly!" Seth thundered back at him, surprising Grant with his forcefulness. "I want her down!" When a gust of wind made the mast creak and groan, Seth swore under his breath and turned his attention to the young sailor who was cautiously following Brianna. "Marsh, bring her down this instant or you'll find yourself served to the sharks for supper!"

Seth's words wafted their way up to Brianna and she glanced down to see the angry glower stamped on the captain's face, but she didn't care. It was as Kenton had said. She was soaring like an eagle, winging her way toward a new horizon. If anyone ever invented a machine that would sail among the clouds she would be willing to try it. Already, she felt she could touch the sky and her soul cried out for more, wanting to spiral higher, to touch the clouds.

"M'lady? 'Tis the captain." Kenton's face was as white as the sails. He had taken the captain at his word and didn't relish being fed to the sharks. The very idea made him light-headed. He had suggested that Brianna be content where she was, but she had climbed even higher. How could he talk her down to the deck when he couldn't even keep up with her?

Seth's temper reached the end of its fuse when Brianna didn't budge from her lofty perch. Her reckless laughter filtered down to him, enraging him further. He should have tossed her into the sea the first night he discovered that she was on board. He could have saved himself a geat deal of trouble, he thought bitterly. Her middle name wasn't trouble. It was disaster!

After shimmying up the mast, Seth swung to the sail, following the route Brianna had taken. By damned, the rest of those fools might stand on deck watching her, but he was bringing her down and from now on she would remain on deck even if he found it necessary to wrap an anchor around her ankle. Damn that wench!

When Seth was within ten feet of her another gust of wind strained against the sails, causing the schooner to lurch and pitch. Brianna was caught off guard, her attention on the man dressed in black and whose vengeful look could have matched the devil himself. At that moment, Brianna could have sworn Satan had nothing on Seth. If looks could kill, she would have been burned and buried. And she had seen that look before—the moment he had brutally taken her. Never could she have claimed to fear a man until she met Seth. He above all others had taught her the meaning of the word. Her thoughts were rambling and she hadn't realized that she was about to fall until her fingers were abruptly pried loose from the beam. Her booted foot slid from the narrow pole that steadied the bottom of the sail and she shrieked in alarm as she lost her balance.

Seth made a futile attempt to reach for her, knowing he would grasp nothing but air. Instinctively, he closed his eyes, picturing her fall, waiting for the thud as her mangled body bounced on the deck. And then he heard the simultaneous gasp from the sailors below him. After a long moment he braved opening one eye and looked down. Somehow Brianna had managed to grasp the dangling rope, and hand over hand, she had made her way to the bottom of the sail and then to the mast in the middle of the schooner. How she had grasped the wind-blown rope was a feat Seth never expected to have explained. The lady indeed had the devil's luck, Seth concluded.

Brianna scurried down the mast to find that her legs were as wobbly as a newborn foal's. Before they collapsed beneath her, Derrick wrapped a supporting arm around her waist.

"Are you all right?" he breathed hoarsely. It was all he could do to force out the words since he had swallowed his tongue when she slipped from her perch.

She nodded, producing a reassuring smile. "Aye. I am now."

She had barely finished her sentence when Seth's

lean fingers bit into her arm. He whisked her across the deck to her cabin, shoved her inside, and slammed the door behind them. Brianna took a retreating step when she met Seth's murderous glare. He wasn't satisfied that she had nearly killed herself. He intended to see that the deed was done by his own hand.

"Do you know how close you came to meeting your maker?" A cruel sneer thinned his lips, making him appear even more satanic. "And I am referring to the devil, madam." His tone was heavily laden with sarcasm as he stalked toward her. "If you even entertain the idea of attempting that feat again, I'll lock you in this cabin and you won't set foot on deck until we reach Petersburg," he threatened, his fiery green eyes drilling into her.

His broad chest was heaving with every angry breath he took, and Brianna was certain that this was Satan, or at least his identical twin. His eyes narrowed on her again, his features slashed with contempt.

Her chin tilted to a proud angle, her gaze sparking defiance. "'Tis an empty threat, Captain." She fired the words at him, her courage gaining momentum. "These four walls won't hold me if I decide to escape." She flung her arm toward the door. "Now get out of my cabin. You and I have nothing more to say to each other!"

"I'm not leaving until I have your word that you won't attempt that prank again," he persisted, not budging an inch.

"I will promise you nothing." Her chin tilted a notch higher.

Seth heaved a defeated sigh and dropped his head to study the floor. "Isn't it enough that my conscience bears the burden of what happened between us? A few moments ago I was sure I would also be forced to assume another burden, one that would torture me far

216

beyond eternity. Don't you realize how close you came to killing yourself? Was the thrill of adventure worth the price you almost paid?" His gaze slowly rose to meet her bewitching face, one that he had never expected to see again when she had lost her balance. "No matter what has come between us, I want nothing to happen to you, Brianna."

His tone was so soft and sincere that Brianna could only stare at him. She fought the urge to run into his arms, to be encircled in his embrace. The memory of what they had once shared came at her from all directions and her resistance slipped a notch. Her gaze flickered down his sturdy frame, wishing to find something to criticize, but there was nothing. He made the words *handsome* and *virile* seem insufficient when it came to describing him.

Seth moved a step closer, the faintest hint of a smile finding its way to one corner of his mouth. "I admire your daring, but, madam, you scared the hell out of me."

His hand moved toward her face, wanting to reach out to touch her. It hovered there for a long moment before he remembered the curse that she had made the last time they were alone together. His arm dropped to his side. Without another word he spun on his heels and walked toward the door. He paused a moment and glanced back over his shoulder. The thoughts seemed to evaporate before he could put them into words. There was much he wanted to say, but he could find no place to begin.

Brianna stared after him, her emotions in turmoil, wanting to call him back, wishing she could erase the past and transport herself back to the time when they were not at odds. Once they had responded easily to each other. The day she had spent with him in Bristol had been a playful interlude, one that left her feeling more comfortable with him than with any man she had ever met. He had accepted her for what she was without dictating to her. But now that had all changed, and yet she could not help but remember the way they once were. . . . Brianna heaved a sigh. If only she could have captured that time and held it forever.

Seth met the anxious faces of his crew, but he offered no more than a carefully blank stare. "Secure the ship," he ordered briskly, gesturing to the west. "A storm is brewing and I have no intention of being caught unprepared."

His command sent the crew scattering to obey, each of them wondering how Brianna had fared with the captain. There had been a cold gleam in his eyes when he had dragged Brianna to her cabin. A pin could have dropped on the deck of the ship and it would have sounded like ten pounds of iron. They had all listened with eager ears, but their curiosity had not been appeased. No one but the captain and Brianna knew what had been said behind the closed door.

Within a few minutes the schooner was prepared and Seth stood at the helm, watching and awaiting the inevitable. Most of the crew had gone below deck to take their meal and Seth stood alone until he felt a presence behind him, just as surely as someone had called out his name. When he ventured a glance, he saw Brianna, dressed in a blue silk gown, her face to the wind, her gaze fixed on the approaching storm.

Seth stood mesmerized. She was like a goddess, her complexion flawless, her stature poised and erect, her soft lips pursed in thought. Again, he felt the need to touch her, to take her in his arms and beg forgiveness, but the words constricted in his throat. Her eyes swung to him for a fleeting moment and then returned to the churning clouds that towered toward the heavens. And then silently she walked away, leaving him to wonder what thoughts were wandering through her mind.

Seth shook his head, trying to shatter the spell. There was much that demanded his attention and he had no time to dwell on Brianna. She occupied his thoughts too much as it was. After tying the wheel to ensure that they remained on course, Seth climbed down the ladder, and walked to his room to find Derrick taking his meal.

"How long before it hits?" Derrick questioned.

Seth's shoulder lifted in a shrug. "An hour, perhaps two."

Derrick nodded, silently agreeing with the captain. After he watched Seth down his second glass of brandy, a disapproving frown knitted his brow.

"I should think you would want to keep your wits about you when we meet rough waters."

"Do you presume to tell me how to manage my life and my ship?" His dark brow arched in challenge as he sliced his first mate a cold glare. "Perhaps you do not cherish your *present* position as first mate of the *Mesmer.*"

Derrick chuckled, undaunted by the threat. "I have swabbed a few decks in my time, Captain. If I find myself demoted, I suppose I can handle a mop again."

After inhaling a deep breath, Seth guzzled his third drink and reached for the botle again. "It seems that my threats fall on deaf ears. I'm beginning to wonder if I'm deluding myself to think that *I* am captain of this ship," he mused aloud.

A long moment of silence passed while Seth swirled his drink around the edge of his glass.

"What did you do to her?" Derrick questioned, point blank.

Planting himself in the nearby chair, Seth cast his first mate a sidelong glance. "Nothing."

219

"Well then, what did you say to her?" he prodded. "You know damned well that the entire crew and I are dying of curiosity."

"I said nothing that made an impression on her. The wench is stubborn," Seth explained as he propped his feet on the edge of the cot and stared at the opposite wall.

"Aye. So I've noticed," Derrick agreed. He studied the floor and slowly shook his head. "I thought I had seen the last of Brianna when she lost her footing."

Seth lit a cigar and drew heavily upon it. Derrick had voiced his very thoughts. After swishing his drink around once again, he finished the last of it, hoping that the liquor would numb him completely. He wanted to feel nothing. He had been through hell and back during the Revolution, but he had experienced his first bout with fear when he thought Brianna was destined to meet her death. Perhaps a few more drinks and he could forget that feeling that had gripped him earlier. It wasn't one to which he was accustomed and the aftereffect was just as unsettling.

Time ticked by at a snail's pace and finally Seth rose to his feet and weaved toward the door. The ship was strangely quiet. He had expected it to be pitching and rolling. As he stepped onto the deck, relief spread across his craggy features. The storm had veered north and the wind had shifted to follow its course. He could have sworn that he and his crew were in for a long, sleepless night.

A thoughtful frown plowed his brow. He had rarely misjudged storms at sea. There was always a feeling in his bones when the sea was uneasy. Besides, the moon had been pale, encircled with a hazy ring that also encompassed two dim stars. He had seen the sign two days earlier. That was a sailor's warning that a storm could be expected in forty-eight hours. Rarely had those signs proved incorrect. But then, nothing had gone according to plan since they had set sail, he thought sourly.

"Shall I take the wheel, sir?" the helmsman cautiously questioned the captain. Donnovan had been in such a black mood the past few days that the helmsman felt as though he were walking on eggs. He could have been decapitated for asking an innocent question.

"Aye," Seth replied without casting him a glance.

When Seth opened the cabin door, Derrick had just shed his breeches and climbed into bed. "I think I'll catch a few winks before the storm hits."

"It bypassed us," Seth said blandly.

Derrick's sunbleached brow arched acutely. "I do believe that is the first time I've known you to be wrong. Could it be that you're losing your touch?" he taunted, sending the captain a crooked smile.

Seth eased into his hammock. After snuffing out the lantern that hung in the corner, he folded his hands behind his head and stared thoughtfully at the ceiling. "It would seem so." His voice was so quiet that Derrick had to strain his ears to catch his words.

Dressed in her breeches and shirt, Brianna strolled along the deck and then smiled to herself when she saw a group of three men gathered around a wooden barrel playing cards. Among them sat Geoffrey McGowan, a crusty old sailor who was as windy as a thunderstorm, but a very likable sort. Brianna had heard bits and pieces of his stories and she found them fascinating. He had spent his life at sea since he was but a young lad, experiencing adventures that could fill volumes if he decided to write them down. Any remark could remind him of a story. Every ship needed a man like him, Brianna decided. When the days became dull, Mc-

Gowan could keep the crew mesmerized with some wild tale. He could weave such entertaining yarns that he held everyone spellbound for hours on end. He was a master with the spoken word, and no doubt his stories would outlive him.

With a hopeful smile Brianna paused beside the three men. "May I join your game?"

McGowan grabbed a nearby barrel and slid it up beside him, gesturing for her to sit down. "A pretty face is always welcome among this motley crew. Haven't seen any mermaids on this voyage, probably because they knew better than try to compete with your beauty, lass."

His complimenting grin lacked several teeth, but it was no less pleasant. McGowan's skin was weather-beaten and as tough as cowhide. A salt-and-pepper beard lined his jaws and wrapped around his square chin and it always seemed to be in need of a trim. But he wasn't the type of man who gave much thought to his appearance. Brianna discreetly raked him once again, her gaze settling on the bushy brows that hung above a pair of coal black eyes. Their depths were intriguing. He reminded her of the old man of the sea. Without hesitation, she straddled the barrel that served as her chair and picked up the cards he had dealt her. Sharing the game and a little conversation with him was better than remaining within the four dreary walls of her cabin.

"What game are we playing?" Brianna questioned as she studied her cards.

"The very one that Blackbeard, scourge of the Spanish Main, used to play when he was becalmed at sea," McGowan informed her as he rearranged his cards. "You'll catch on after the first hand. The stakes go higher with each deal, until there is but one of us left to claim the treasure." There was a merry twinkle in his eye as he bent his gaze to Brianna. "'Course, there is no treasure aboard this ship. We play only for pride."

"Did you know him?" Brianna's eyes were wide with curiosity, like a small child. She watched the old sailor with a bit of awe in her expression.

McGowan chuckled heartily. "Nay, lass. I may look to be as old as father time, but 'twas my grandfather who met the fiendish pirate, Edward Teach, who well earned the dreaded name of Blackbeard. When my grandfather refused to relinquish the ring my grandmother had given him, the pirate retrieved it from him . . . finger and all."

Brianna shivered at the thought. "He must have been a horrible man."

As McGowan stroked his beard, he nodded affirmatively. "Aye, that he was. Some say he was the devil incarnate. No giant of a man could be compared to the likes of Blackbeard. He had unbelievable strength, equaled to at least three good men. 'Twas his long full beard that helped earn the name that was feared by all. It was braided with jewels he confiscated from his captives and hung on his gold belt buckle. My grandfather said there was a halo of smoke curling about his head, giving him an even more frightening appearance. And to put fear in the hearts of those who confronted him, he drank a flaming brew, guzzling it, fire and all. Women feared him, as well they should. He was ruthless when it came to having his way with them. Lord, the stories I could tell you about that." He shook his head and flung Brianna a hasty glance. "But they ain't tales to be wagging in front of a lady."

Another shudder engulfed Brianna as she pictured the man McGowan described, but he didn't leave it at that. By the time he had finished, Brianna was certain she would see the scoundrel in her nightmares.

"Over his shoulder he carried three holsters with

loaded pistols. And on his head, covering his unkempt, raven hair was a fur cap. There was always a wild, demented look in his bloodshot eyes, as I have heard it told. And that menacing grin on his lips . . ." McGowan thoughtfully studied his hand and then his gaze lifted to stare at the hazy sky. "I've heard it said that he was as harsh with his own crew as he was with his prisoners. They say he shot his closest friend just to prove to the rest of his men that he had rightfully earned his reputation. He had no intention of letting them forget who he was. Rather drastic measures to prove the point, if you ask me," he muttered. "It ain't no wonder why he was the most grizzly pirate to have sailed the Spanish Main. Why, it even took five shots and twenty knife wounds to kill him."

McGowan leaned close to Brianna's ear, as if to tell her the rest in confidence. "After he died, his headless body returned to the den where his crew made their home. And to this day Teach's Hole is still haunted by the ghost, searching for its head." He tossed the ace of spades on top of the barrel and then collected all the cards to reshuffle. "I know I don't want to be nowhere around that cove when that ghost comes back in the dark of the moon."

There was a long silence after he finished and Brianna winced as a shadow fell across her. When she found the courage to glance behind her, she expected to see that very specter grinning maliciously at her. Instead, she met Seth's steady gaze and the wry smile that hovered on one corner of his mouth.

"Is McGowan filling your head with more of his fantastic tales?" he mocked dryly.

"Ain't no tale, Captain. 'Tis fact," McGowan assured him, his gaze quietly sober.

Seth graced him with a patronizing smile and eased down on the vacated barrel when one of the sailors offered him the seat. "Deal the cards, McGowan." His level gaze focused on the scraggly seaman. "And *not* from the bottom of the deck as you have a tendency to do."

Brianna was growing increasingly uncomfortable after hearing McGowan's stories and watching Seth stare her down. She was always tense when he was near, the memories of the past playing havoc with her thoughts. It was all she could do to keep up with the game, especially one that was unfamiliar to her. After an hour there were only the two of them left in the game. Brianna carefully watched Seth, hoping his expression would alert her to the strength of the cards in his hand. She wanted to defeat him, to prove, if only to herself, that she was his match with wits.

"Your play, m'lady," Seth reminded her, his eyes revealing nothing of his thoughts.

He knew as well as she did that they were playing for their honor. A crowd had collected about them, watching to see which one would win "Blackbeard's treasure." Although no money would change hands, the game was no less important. Seth could see the determination in those golden eyes. A wry smile touched his lips as Brianna cautiously laid her card down and gazed quizzically at him. There was only one card that could defeat him. His eyes met hers for a long, silent moment and then he rose to his feet and worked the kink from his back.

"The treasure belongs to the lady," he announced with a conceding bow before he turned and walked away.

After the crowd had dispersed, Brianna reached for the card that lay face down. The ace of spades. A thoughtful frown furrowed her brow as she collected and neatly stacked all of the cards.

Brianna strolled across the quarterdeck and solemnly

peered at the captain's broad back. "Why did you let the crew think that I had won?" she questioned pointedly.

Seth cast her a quick glance, crossed his arms over his chest, and then stared out at the sea. "I owed you one," he said simply. And then he shrugged. "Besides, my men need something to gossip about. You've already dazzled them with your daring. Why not mystify them with your wits?" He chuckled lightly as he bent his gaze to the shapely form whose garb reminded him of a lady pirate, a very believable role, Seth thought to himself. "By the time we reach port, the tale will be taller than you are."

Brianna took a bold step forward, raising a proud chin. "I have no interest in being regarded in the same manner as Blackbeard."

Seth arched a curious brow. "Is that what McGowan was telling you about?"

"Aye. The pirate seems to be as notorious as the good captain of the *Mesmer*," she retorted, her gaze giving him the once over, twice.

The gibe was like a knife in his back. Seth knew she was referring to the pirate's cruel abuse of women. He had heard the full account of the stories that were not fit for a lady's ears.

"Perhaps I have my moments of madness," he agreed, a tight smile thinning his lips. "But usually they are provoked. Blackbeard is said to have taken and discarded at least thirteen wives. As you well know, I have claimed but one."

He slowly turned to face her, his virile frame too close for Brianna not to feel the heat that radiated from him. The smell of musk infiltrated her senses and she could not seem to catch her breath. His dark head moved toward hers until they were only inches apart and Brianna had to force herself to swallow over the

226

lump that collected in her throat. After all she had suffered at his hands, he still had some strange power over her, some animal attraction that she couldn't ignore. Brianna was sure he intended to kiss her and involuntarily, her lips parted in invitation.

Suddenly, he withdrew, his gaze looking past her. "I think perhaps you should go to your cabin," he suggested, his breath slightly ragged. "Derrick will be bringing your supper tray."

Brianna turned her back on him and bit back a tear of confused emotion. If she didn't keep her distance from him, she would have to swallow her pride. All he would have had to do was reach out to her and she would have accepted his encircling arms. But she had vowed never to let him touch her. They had made a bargain and it had been fulfilled. They owed each other nothing more.

Chapter Fifteen

Brianna spent the following weeks in monotony. The days had begun to blend together and she found little to occupy her. Derrick had attempted to cheer her with his light bantering, but she was unreceptive to his humor. Occasionally, he would take her in his arms and she would accept his tender kisses without feeling more than a fond affection for him. Brianna found herself yearning to know the gentle man who had made love to her on her wedding night. But she still could not completely forgive him for what he had done, nor could she bring herself to try to make amends and begin again.

There seemed to be no solution, only an endless wait until they reached the colonies to go their separate ways. Seth had made it a point to keep his distance from her and she had offered no more than a slight nod of greeting when they passed each other on deck. What was there about this man that drew her to him?

As Brianna stood at the taffrail, she heard the shuffled footsteps she had come to know belonged to McGowan. She turned slightly to bless him with a welcoming smile.

"Have you nothing more entertaining to occupy your time, m'lady?" he questioned, his heavy brows arching tauntingly.

Her shoulder lifted in a leisurely shrug as her eyes swung back to the sea that was slowly being suffocated with fog.

"This night reminds me of the time when I was sailing aboard the *Jupiter*," he recalled as he rested his elbows on the rail, his eyes taking on a faraway look that Brianna had often seen in them. "'Twas the blackest of nights, it was. And then from the stillness, I heard the sailor on lookout scream in terror, 'Ship ho! Look astern!' And lo and behold, there she be, a ship in full sail, thrice the size of our tub. It was coming straight at us. The captain wheeled hard at the helm, knowing we didn't have a prayer, but giving it his dying effort."

Brianna was clutching at the rail, her knuckles white as she waited anxiously for McGowan to continue, but he paused, lit his pipe, and then directed her attention to the hovering fog. Brianna would have been on the edge of her seat, if indeed she had one to sit on. McGowan had captured her interest and only waited for her to insist that he continue.

"Well, then what happened?" she prodded, as he knew she would.

"Their vessel veered slightly, just as we did, but the collision was inevitable. We waited, but we heard no splintering of wood, nor did a sea of water wash against us to make our schooner pitch and roll." McGowan took a long draw on his pipe and let the smoke encircle his head. "The vessel slid by us as if it was floating above the water and there was nothing but dead silence. I stared at her, not believing my own eyes. The sails were set and the ropes were tight, but there was no one to man them." His breath came out slowly and then he inhaled more of the damp night air. "'Twas a ghost ship. I wouldn't be a bit surprised to see another one on a night such as this." His gaze swung back to Brianna's bewildered expression and he smiled a bit tauntingly. "'Tis a bad omen to have a woman on board. Perhaps the fact that we carry two of them will attract a ship like I have described."

As McGowan ambled away, Brianna tried to collect her composure. He had been filling her with legends and superstitions for more than a week. Trying to discard her fretful thoughts, she hurried along the deck and took the steps two at a time to reach her brother's cabin. When the door opened for her, she smiled in relief, making her brother frown curiously.

"Are you all right?" he questioned as he wrapped his arm about her waist and ushered her to the table that awaited them. "You look as if you had seen a ghost."

"I'm fine," she assured him as she sank down into her chair.

Sabrina had set an appealing table, considering what she had to work with, but Brianna had lost her appetite. McGowan's stories always had that unsettling affect on her and Brianna decided she was a glutton for punishment. Each time he began spinning his yarn she was caught up and couldn't be satisfied until she heard it through to the bitter end.

"Brianna?" Sabrina frowned at her daydreaming sister-in-law.

"I'm sorry. I wasn't listening," Brianna apologized, displaying a guilty smile.

"Apparently," she scoffed as Grant pulled out her chair and offered her a seat across from Brianna. "I swear, the way you have been behaving lately, it makes one wonder . . ." Sabrina halted in mid-sentence. She had not intended to bring up the captain's name, even though she suspected that was foremost in Brianna's mind.

Brianna had guessed the conversation was to be directed toward Seth. The subject cropped up each time she and Sabrina were together. It seemed Sabrina was trying to incorporate her dislike for Seth into

Brianna's thinking, as if it wasn't already there, and with good reason.

"I was thinking of what Geoffrey McGowan told me while I was on deck," Brianna explained as she smoothed the napkin on her lap.

Grant rolled his eyes and frowned in annoyance. "I wish you would stay away from that bag of wind, Brianna. Before you know it you'll be seeing and hearing things that aren't there," he predicted in the tone of a well-meaning but lecturing brother.

"I find his stories fascinating," she defended as she picked up her fork and cast her brother a silencing frown. "I have very little to do with my time and his tales can while away the hours."

"You wouldn't be so lonely if you would—"

"Grant!" Sabrina cut him short. She had been trying to keep Brianna from returning to the captain and Grant thought that the marriage deserved a chance. It was the only sore spot in their otherwise blissful relationship. "I'd much rather hear what McGowan told her," she insisted, her chin tilting stubbornly.

After Brianna had repeated the story, Sabrina was left wishing she had chosen another subject. Ghost ships and bad omens made her as uneasy as they made Brianna, and yet there was something intriguing about them.

Grant crossed his arms on his chest and eyed his sister curiously. "And I suppose you believe all that rubbish about ships being manned by a crew of ghosts."

Her shoulder lifted in a noncommittal shrug as she sipped her tea. "It makes for interesting stories. And who knows, perhaps there are such vessels looming about."

Grant chuckled at her evasiveness. "Be that as it may, Brianna, I think you should keep your distance from McGowan. The man has a vivid imagination and you possess enough of your own."

Brianna sat quietly as she watched Grant and Sabrina smile affectionately at each other. She could tell that they wanted to be alone. Perhaps she and Seth could have shared that same bond of contentment if she had not lost her temper with him. It continued to baffle her that, after all that had happened, she could still yearn for his touch. Brianna was beginning to wonder if Grant may have been right. McGowan's influence on her was only adding confusion to her thoughts. She was even beginning to think that she and Seth could have found happiness. Why couldn't she understand her own mind and her own desires as she once had? Nothing was making sense, and all this thoughtful contemplation was beginning to bring on a headache. After making her excuses, Brianna walked down the dark companionway and strolled along the deck. She paused to gaze out over the sea. The fog was beginning to lift and pale moonlight splattered over the curling waves.

If only she could straddle her black stallion and ride against the wind, perhaps she could put the past behind her and begin to find more meaning for her life. She was enduring a meager existence of fantastic stories and lonely, sleepless nights. The confinement of the ship and the torment of her experience with Seth was playing havoc with her sanity. How long would it be before she started seeing mermaids appearing from the depths?

"Troubled thoughts, Brianna?" came a soft voice from behind her.

Brianna smiled fondly as she glanced back at Grant. "Aye. I'm beginning to think there are no other kinds."

"You aren't happy, are you? I can see it in your eyes.

They have lost that mischievous sparkle," he pointed out.

Forcing a shallow smile, she tried to make light of her trials. "I have managed to make a mess of things as usual."

"I'm sorry." Grant placed a light kiss to her forehead and wrapped his arms around her waist as he followed her gaze out over the water. "I have been little help to you of late. I have been so preoccupied with my duties and with Sabrina that I haven't given much thought to anything else. I suppose you feel that I have abandoned you."

With a careless shrug, Brianna lifted her gaze to his warm brown eyes. "You once told me that if I was old enough to get myself into trouble that I should be able to work out my own problems. You have your own life to live and I must learn to manage on my own. I know you won't always be there to help me untangle every mess I make." A knowing smile traced her lips. "I really didn't expect to see you up here. I was under the impression that you and Sabrina wanted to be alone tonight."

A sheepish grin caught one corner of his mouth. "I'll admit 'twas difficult to leave Sabrina alone, but I thought perhaps you needed someone to talk to. I have watched you try to amuse yourself with hanging from the sails and listening to McGowan, but I think it's a shallow existence for you," he speculated. "I was hoping this marriage would work out for you, Brianna. Of all the men I can name, the captain could well have been your equal match. And I felt that there was very little choice in the matter when I discovered that you had sneaked aboard the *Mesmer*. The contract had been made and I was afraid for you to remain on board without being married to the captain. You needed his protection. I have often heard of women being used when men are too long at sea." Grant sent his sister a meaningful glance. "I could not think of having you exposed to such trials. Marrying Captain Donnovan seemed the logical answer." His gaze dropped to his feet and he paused a long moment before meeting her eyes. "I had a private conversation with the captain when I learned that you were here. I was very direct in voicing my opinion of the situation and I practically insisted that Donnovan do the honorable thing," he confessed with a despairing sigh. "I feel responsible for your plight."

"'Tis not your fault, Grant." Brianna laid her head against his shoulder and fought back the tears that began to cloud her vision.

"Can't you and Donnovan resolve your differences? Surely it cannot be—"

"Nay," Brianna insisted hastily. "And don't ask me to relate the incident that put us at odds. I cannot discuss it."

Grant slowly shook his head. Brianna was too stubborn for her own good. "Very well. I won't question you about it, but I think you should give some serious thought to what you're doing. You are making yourself miserable. If you would give this arrangement half a chance, you might find it isn't so bad. I've seen the way Donnovan looks at you from afar. Neither of you seem to be content with this separation. Donnovan is your husband and you cannot walk away from him each time the two of you quarrel and refuse to see him again as you have done with your suitors in the past. You must give and take and learn to control that fiery temper of yours."

"I don't need your lectures, Grant." Brianna stepped away, feeling betrayed by her own brother and his insistence that she make amends. "This is not a marriage based on love and devotion. Seth and I have not found the bliss that you and Sabrina share. Do not expect us to behave as you do. If you were married to that scoundrel, perhaps you wouldn't be able to follow your own advice."

Grant chuckled lightly. "We'll never know about that, dear sister, but I suggest that you give some serious thought to what I've said. With a little patience and understanding from both of you, you may be able to find a little happiness." He pressed a fond kiss to her forehead. "Good night, Brianna. Give it some thought. After all, 'tis your life that you're ruining because of stubborn pride."

When Grant had left her to her thoughts, Brianna returned her gaze to the ocean and heaved a heavy sigh. If Grant only knew what had flung them apart, perhaps he would be more sympathetic, but she couldn't tell him. Maybe her hesitation came because she knew that her biting words had evoked Seth's rage. She had been miserable that morning and she had spoken spitefully, intentionally provoking him for taunting her about consuming the champagne. It was rather ridiculous now that she thought of it. She had enjoyed his caresses and was content to share passion with only him for a time. Why had she behaved so cruelly? She was no better than he was. She sought to hurt him with words since she was unable to physically injure him. Brianna shrugged hopelessly. What difference did it make now? It was over and done. He could have apologized and she might have attempted to do the same, but Seth had never been close enough to her to speak.

Suddenly, a callused hand clamped over her mouth and Brianna felt herself being pulled against a man's broad chest. Panic filled her as she was dragged toward the steps that led to the hull of the ship. She was helpless to defend herself against the mysterious man who held her. The smell of perspiration and liquor filled her senses, repulsing her with the stench that hovered about her. Although Brianna struggled and kicked with all of her strength, she could not escape from his iron grasp.

Once they were in the dark companionway she heard the creak of a door. When it closed behind them, she felt her gown being ripped away. Writhing frantically, Brianna squirmed to keep from having the large, harsh hand pressed against her breasts. A wicked chuckle filled the small room and Brianna cringed in fear. As the seaman pulled at her gown, his hand slid roughly across her mouth and she bit into his fingers, causing him to growl in pain. Brianna pushed his hand away and screamed at the top of her lungs before his fist caught her in the jaw. She stumbled back, hitting her head against the wall. A moan escaped her lips as she slumped forward and fell in an unconscious heap on the floor of the storeroom. Her blood-curdling shriek echoed about the room, following at the heels of the sailor who fled before he was discovered and flogged for what he had intended to do.

Seth stepped into Derrick's cabin and unconsciously reached for the bottle of brandy, hastily pouring himself a drink. The first mate's brows furrowed disapprovingly as he watched the captain down the liquor and reach for a refill.

"You've been hitting the bottle overly much lately. I doubt that the stock will last until we reach port," he speculated, his frown remaining intact until Seth had caught a glimpse of it.

"Are you keeping a record of how much whiskey I've consumed?" Seth asked sarcastically and then leveled Derrick a glance from over the rim of his glass.

"If I had written a note in every empty bottle I've had

236

to throw overboard, I may well have had sufficient pages for an entire book," Derrick countered, his tone as caustic as the captain's.

Seth snorted derisively and parked himself in the chair. "Save your motherly lectures for Marsh," he suggested before sipping freely on his drink. "Perhaps he'll be polite enough to listen to all of your advice, but I'm not interested."

Derrick heaved a futile sigh. The captain was using liquor as a crutch, but it didn't steady his step. Instead, Donnovan was beginning to acquire a weave in his walk. It was not difficult to guess the reason for his overindulgence.

"Why don't you just march right up to your cabin door and work out whatever differences you have with Brianna?" Derrick suggested. "It has to be better than all this sulking."

Seth's cold green eyes swung to his first mate, his jaw twitching in annoyance. "Why don't you mind your own business?"

Derrick shrugged off the rebuke and gave a hard rub to the toe of the boot he was polishing. "As I recall, *you* requested that I make Brianna my business."

And so he had, Seth muttered sourly. Most of the crew had befriended her. They all doted over her as if she were the Queen of England and they were her devoted servants.

After chugging the last of his drink, Seth rose and looked down at Sayer. "I'll be back when you have learned to keep a tight rein on your tongue." His tone was razor sharp, but it seemed to do little damage to the thick-skinned seaman.

"And you won't be particularly welcome until you learn to control your lust for liquor," he countered, a mocking smile lifting the corners of his mouth upward.

Seth whipped open the door and stalked out, only to

find that his footsteps had delivered him to Brianna's door. As he raised his hand to rap upon it he heard a muffled shriek from below deck. A cold shiver raced down his spine and he hurried to the steps, taking them two at a time in his haste to learn its cause. He peered down the shadowed companionway and then his gaze focused on the storeroom door that stood ajar. When he had lit the lantern, Brianna's bruised face appeared among the shadows and Seth's breath lodged in his throat as he knelt beside her.

"Oh, God." His guilt-ridden voice was no more than a pained whisper. If he hadn't treated her so cruelly, she would still be under his protection. Damn, this was all his fault.

Seth scooped her lifeless body up in his arms and swiftly carried her to the cabin. After cleansing her face with a wet cloth, he eased back and stared at the still form on the bed. Why had he been so damned stubborn? Why hadn't he kept a closer eye on this little bundle of trouble? Because he was so ashamed of himself that he could barely even face his own reflection in the mirror! Even if he kept his distance he could have watched her come and go, assuring that nothing like this would happen.

When Brianna finally roused, she realized that she had been stripped of her clothes and lay on her own bed. As her eyes fluttered open she shrank away from the dark form that hovered over her. When she realized that the glowing emerald eyes belonged to the captain, her tension evaporated.

"Are you all right, Brianna?" Seth questioned as he drew closer, a concerned frown etching his brow.

His hushed whisper settled her nerves and she nodded slightly as she inspected her swollen jaw with her fingertips. "I think so," she murmured, her voice lacking confidence.

"Did you see who attacked you?"

"Nay. It was too dark. I couldn't see his face." A shiver of revulsion skitted across her skin, as she remembered the feel of his callused hands intimately caressing her body.

Seth tucked the blankets closely about her and then smoothed the tangled tendrils away from her face. Brianna jerked away from his touch, her eyes widening in alarm. Seth withdrew his hand and frowned to himself.

"Brianna, I . . ." His words collapsed before they reached his lips.

With a discouraged sigh, he rose from the edge of the bunk, poured her a cup of tea and then brought it back to her, offering it to her along with a sympathetic smile. "Here, drink this."

After she had propped herself up on an elbow, she accepted the tea and took a cautious sip of the steaming brew. "Did you find me?" she questioned quietly, staring into the contents of her cup.

"Aye. I heard you scream. When I found you in the storeroom there was no one in the companionway," he answered as he took the cup and set it on the night stand.

Brianna breathed a weak sigh of relief. It would have been most embarrassing if one of the crew had discovered her. "I'm glad it was you instead of someone else, my gown was . . ." Her voice trailed off into an inaudible murmur. She averted her eyes from his rugged face and choked back a sob. "I thought the members of the crew had become my friends, but I suppose a smile can often be a disguise." When she finally raised her gaze to him a tear escaped from the corner of her eye and trickled down her cheek. "Like a fool, I had no fear for my safety." Muffling a sniff, she gestured toward the teacup which Seth brought to her as he eased down beside her.

"I'm sorry, Brianna," Seth apologized in a hushed voice. "If I hadn't acted like an ass, we would still be sharing this cabin and no one would have dared to attack you because I would never have allowed you out of my sight."

Brianna shrugged casually. "'Tis not your fault. My brother always said my middle name was trouble and that I seem to attract it," she added, laughing at her own misery. "If I hadn't been daydreaming, he wouldn't have been able to sneak up on me. My thoughts were a million miles away and I wasn't even aware that anyone else was on deck."

Seth frowned in confusion. "You were on deck when you were attacked?"

Brianna nodded affirmatively. "I was leaning against the rail and he came up behind me, clamped his hand over my mouth, and dragged me down the steps."

"From now on I want someone to accompany you when you are taking a stroll at night," he commanded sternly.

"Don't worry," Brianna assured him. "I have no intention of making that mistake again. The experience was horrifying."

A faint smile surfaced on Seth's handsome face as he gazed down at Brianna's bruised cheek. "Good, madam. I'll expect you to keep that promise although I wish I could convince you to break the one you made the last time we were together."

Brianna's eyes narrowed after being reminded of that day. It was her fault, she mused sullenly. She had angered him. But pride kept the words from touching her lips. As Brianna pulled the quilts closely about her and glanced away, Seth heaved a discouraged sigh and rose from the edge of the bed. Brianna would not accept his apology.

"Turn out the lantern," Brianna ordered softly.

As Seth strolled across the room, Brianna studied him carefully. There was no hope for it, she thought to herself. She still wanted him, no matter what he had done. To hell with pride. Why should she be miserable during this voyage when she could enjoy the feel of his strong arms about her? When the room was dark, she watched Seth's muscular form moving toward the door. Tossing the quilts aside, Brianna rose from the bed and moved quietly behind him.

"Where are you going, Captain?" she questioned demurely.

When Seth turned back to her quiet voice, his breath caught in his throat while his emerald eyes feasted on the tempting form that glowed in the scant moonlight that filtered across the cabin. Fighting the urge to take her in his arms, Seth clenched his fists at his side.

"I'm going to Derrick's room to bed," he answered stiffly. Was this the form of torture that the enticing witch had planned for him? Would she allow him to view that which he craved and never permit him to caress the creamy flesh of her perfect body?

Brianna stepped closer and gingerly wrapped her arms about his neck. She reached up on tiptoe to place a light, tempting kiss on his lips. "This is your cabin," she reminded him in a seductive whisper. "If one of us must go, it should be me, and I don't relish the idea of going out alone again after such a frightening experience. And I'm not dressed properly." A faint smile touched her lips.

Seth pulled her arms from his shoulders and stepped away. If he tarried a moment longer, he would devour this tempting morsel. They would be right back where they had started a month ago. "Good night, Brianna," he murmured as he started for the door.

Brianna fumbled in the darkness for the dagger that hung on the peg by the door. After pulling the knife from its sheath, Brianna laid the silver blade against his chest as she moved in front of him. "You are not going anywhere until I have had my revenge," she assured him in a deadly hiss. "Take off your shirt."

Seth's green eyes widened in surprise. So it was revenge that she had in mind for him. It was another of her taunting games. "Do you intend to cut my heart from my chest?"

Although Seth was certain that he could have easily taken the knife from her hand, he allowed her to hold him hostage, knowing that whatever punishment she had in mind was no more than he deserved. He had been plagued with guilt since he had brutally ravished her.

A deliciously wicked smile curved her lips as she gazed up at his dark face. "Nay, m'lord Captain," she retorted saucily. "'Tis not what I plan to cut out, 'tis what I will cut off if you don't shed your shirt, and quickly!"

He obeyed her command as a wry smile crept to her lips. She was a vixen, a witch. God how he loved to see that mischievous sparkle in her eyes once again. It had been an eternity since he had been close enough to her to see those amber pools sparkle with deviltry.

Brianna reached over to unfasten his breeches with her free hand, leaving the point of the stiletto against the dark hair on his chest. "Take off your boots and trousers, Captain," she ordered.

When Seth stood stark naked before her, Brianna pushed him back toward the bunk as another impish grin played on her lips.

When Seth eased down on the edge of the bed, he raised a curious brow. "And now what do you have in mind, madam? Is your intention to render me useless to any woman?"

Brianna pressed her palm to his chest, forcing him to stretch out on the bunk while she crouched beside him. Lightly scraping the blade against his throat, she released a wicked chuckle. Seth was reminded of the wild, spirited witch that had intrigued him in Bristol.

"Do you recall the vow I made to you?" she queried softly.

"Aye, every word of it," he assured her. "And I have not touched you."

"I've decided to change the wording to suit my own purposes," she replied as she ran her fingers through his raven hair. "If you *don't* touch me, I'll put an end to you."

A low rumble came from his massive chest as he raised his hand to grasp the knife and toss it aside. "You need not threaten me, Brianna." A rakish smile parted his lips as his hand slid across her hip, loving the feel of her satiny flesh beneath his fingertips. It had been agony sleeping alone after knowing Brianna. "There was no excuse for what I did to you. I behaved like a scoundrel, but I swear that I will never treat you cruelly again." His voice wavered slightly as his green eyes locked with those glowing pools of gold.

"Then show me how gentle you can be," she murmured against his mouth. "But please don't make me regret my decision. This is the first time in my life that I have allowed a man a second chance. You are my husband and I was partly to blame for what happened."

Seth drew her down beside him, his fingers tracing the delicate lines of her face before pressing a light kiss to her lips. As his experienced hands caressed her flesh, his kiss deepened to explore her mouth. He gently aroused the desire that had been smothered by pride and fear. Brianna responded to his touch, reveling in the warm, budding pleasure that spread through her veins. His fingers teased the peaks of her breasts before his mouth covered the full mounds. A moan of surrender floated from her lips as all inhibitions took flight, setting her adrift. As his wandering caress trailed across her abdomen a wild sensation shook the roots of her sanity, sending the world careening about her. Gasping for breath, Brianna was carried out with the rapturous tide. She tried to draw him closer, but Seth put his hand over hers, guiding it to him, teaching her how to caress and arouse him.

He was lost to her innocent fondling and could no longer deny his need to be a part of her. Each night he had spent alone had been torture, tossing and turning, aching with desire. He had recalled the feel of her skin beneath his hands, the taste of her kisses, the sweet fragrance that was so much a part of her. It all came back to him as it had each night, but now it was over-whelming. He could not get close enough to the flame that warmed him inside and out.

Seth lifted himself above her, willing himself to be gentle. And then they were moving together, striving for unattainable depths of intimacy, caught in the swirling pleasures they had found in each other's arms. Seth pulled her to him, nuzzling his head on her shoulder, as the current of emotions swept him beneath reality's surface. They were drowning in passion's sea, afraid to let go, never wanting to leave each other's arms.

Brianna heaved a weary sigh, certain that he had taken her soul, only to return it once again. But she wasn't the same. That intangible part of her had dis-covered the true meaning of love.

Seth brushed the tangled tresses away from her face and smiled tenderly. "Do you regret changing your mind, Brianna?"

She smiled faintly as she leaned against his sturdy

shoulder. "Nay, Captain. My only regret is that I have wasted an entire month when I could have been sleeping in your arms," she confessed as her index finger wandered across his cheek to trace his lips.

"Brianna," Seth began quietly as he folded her hand in his and gazed into the warm pools of gold that glowed with their mysterious hue. "I . . ."

She pressed her hand to his lips, silencing his words. "Too much has been said and we have wasted a month. 'Tis not the time for talking," she informed him, her mouth curving into a seductive smile.

Seth drew away only far enough to gaze into her shadowed face and then cocked a dubious brow when he noted her expression. "Is there no way to appease the desires of this witch?" he mused aloud. "You leave me to wonder if any mortal man can keep you content. I pity the many who might try."

Brianna giggled giddily, her eyes sparkling like priceless gold nuggets, alerting Seth that she had not lost even an ounce of mischievousness. "Nay, my handsome captain, I fear not." She pressed a lingering kiss to his lips, tempting and taunting him.

Playfully pushing her away, Seth's eyes widened in feigned surprise. "Madam, if I am not allowed to sleep, how can you expect me to chart the proper course? I'll have us sailing in circles."

Her bare shoulder lifted in a careless shrug as her finger made a slow descent to the dark furring on his chest, drawing invisible circles. "It makes little difference to me where we go, and I'm in no particular hurry."

His soft chortle tickled her senses. "And if I do not comply, I suppose I risk the fear of having a frightful witch cast a spell on my schooner," he predicted, his eyes dancing in amusement.

"Aye, m'lord Captain. I had considered it," she

assured him saucily.

His face split in a most agreeable smile. "Then 'tis up to the captain to save this ship from disaster, but, mind you, 'tis only that I feel it my duty to protect the *Mesmer* and all those who sail upon it."

Her delicate brow arched as she flashed him a skeptical glance. "Your duty, Captain?"

Seth propped himself up on an elbow, meeting her level gaze. "Nay, Brianna," he corrected, his voice raspy. "My desire. . . ."

His mouth covered hers in a strangely tender kiss, unhurried, but nonetheless affecting. Brianna melted in his arms with such abandon that she amazed herself. She whispered her need for him without reluctance, understanding at last the reason she was drawn to this handsome rogue. 'Twas love that brought agony to her heart when they were apart and 'twas love that brought ecstasy to her soul when he held her in his arms. And yet the realization was not a happy one. She could never profess to love Seth, for he did not come to her in search of love, only to fulfill desire.

Her quiet words of need lifted a burden from his shoulders. After what he had done to her, he dared not hope for even forgiveness. And yet he was allowed a second chance. And she wanted him just as he had yearned for her. It was enough. At the moment it was all that mattered.

Another timeless moment of passion consumed them, taking them from reality's shore. With her strength spent Brianna closed her eyes, letting drowsiness overtake her.

Seth smiled faintly as he looked down at her. His emotions were in a turmoil. For the past month he had cursed himself for what he had done, but holding Brianna brought another kind of torture to haunt his thoughts. Each time he touched her, he imagined how she would respond to other men. Would she surrender willingly, enjoying the pleasures of other lovers? Would this tempting vixen seek out someone else the moment they stepped ashore? He had often seen Derrick drawing Brianna into his arms and Seth had been stung with jealousy. Only he had possessed her, tasted her passions, taught her to satisfy his needs. Could he release her to run into the arms of another man? The questions came quickly, but the answers were difficult to produce. She was only a woman, he kept telling himself. Once she was out of sight, she would be out of his mind as well. After all, Brianna had brought him nothing but trouble since the first time he had laid eyes on her. There were pleasures to be found elsewhere, ones that had no strings attached. He would be preoccupied with business when he reached the colonies and he would not concern himself with Brianna.

It was only that she was convenient at the moment. He had obeyed Andrew's wishes and had fulfilled an obligation to Grant. They had made an agreement and he would live by it without regretting it.

Seth inhaled a deep breath and then let it out in a rush as he stared at her exquisite face that was partially hidden by the shadows. Somehow his arguments did not sound so convincing when he held Brianna in his arms. He had no desire to let her go, and yet he could not bring himself to ask her to stay. Would she decide to sail for England immediately? Would his feelings for this mystical witch change when he saw Priscilla? He had not given her much thought since Brianna came into his life, keeping the days whirling in her unpredictable tempest. Shaking away his rambling thoughts, Seth wrapped a possessive arm about Brianna's waist and curled his legs behind hers, molding them together.

The sudden movement and the fact that Brianna was

accustomed to sleeping alone, brought her from the depths of drowsiness. As she turned toward Seth, his kiss brought a smile to her lips.

"Love me," she whispered as she wrapped her arms around his neck and pressed against the hard wall of his muscled chest.

His desire rose at the mere sound of her raspy voice and the feel of her enticing body pressed to his. As his mouth captured hers, Seth cast aside his earlier thoughts that Brianna was just an ordinary woman who could easily be replaced. Nay, he mused as his hands roamed over her pliant flesh. No ordinary woman could hold such power over him. Brianna was indeed a witch. It came as no surprise that any man who had fallen beneath her spell was unable to resist her, wishing to possess her as only he had. As passion's wildfire encompassed him, burning all thoughts from his mind, he came to her whispering words of need and desire.

Seth stiffened abruptly at the sound of the creaking door. Damn, he had neglected to lock it!

"Who is it?" he snapped gruffly.

The dim moonlight streamed along the edge of the partially opened door and then faded at the sound of Seth's voice. Seth fumbled in the darkness for his breeches while Brianna clutched the sheet around her to follow after him. When Seth yanked open the door he was met with silence.

"Lock the door behind me," he commanded as he shoved Brianna back inside and climbed to the deck to talk to the helmsman.

Brianna nervously lit the lantern, her hands trembling at the realization that whoever had attacked her might have had his way with her this time if Seth hadn't been with her. She impatiently paced the floor until Seth rapped on the door.

"Dirkson says he didn't hear or see anyone," he explained with an uneasy sigh as he met Brianna's wide-eyed gaze. "From now on, I don't want you to go out after dark unless I accompany you."

Brianna gulped fearfully, secured the door, and then retrieved the discarded dagger.

Seth arched a skeptical brow as he watched Brianna stash the knife under her pillow. "I hope you don't panic and use that thing on me by mistake," he smirked as he rested his hands on his hips, smiling grimly at the goddess who was still cloaked in a sheet.

"I don't panic," Brianna assured him flatly as she rearranged the disheveled bed. "I can handle a knife as well as you can."

Seth chuckled arrogantly as he leaned back against the door and crossed his arms over his broad chest. "I could have taken that dagger away from you with very little effort tonight, madam. You are not as proficient as you think."

The smug grin on his lips was an open invitation for a challenge, one which Brianna did not waste an instant accepting. Retrieving the stiletto, she tested the edge with her fingertip, finding it razor sharp. "You could have taken it *only* if I would have allowed you to do so, Captain."

With a quick flick of her wrist she wheeled around and hurled the dagger across the cabin. Seth flinched as the knife quivered in the door facing, only inches away from the sheath that hung by a leather strap. Slowly, his gaze swung from the knife to the deliciously wicked gleam in Brianna's eyes. If he ever had misgivings about Brianna's competency with blades, they were severed by the toss of her knife.

After squirming beneath the quilts, she glanced at the bewildered captain. "If you wish for the dagger to remain in its sheath, you'll have to put it there yourself, sir. That is as close as I could come without damaging the case. And please snuff out the lantern. It's been a long night and I have had little sleep," she added as she fluffed the pillow and presented her back to him.

Seth pulled the dagger from the wall, turned out the light, and joined Brianna in bed. After tucking the knife beneath the pillow, he placed a fleeting kiss on the curve of her neck.

"Keep your weapon, witch," he conceded, his tone lacking arrogance. He had been properly put in his place, nearly nailed to the wall. "You have convinced me that you are capable of defending yourself unless you are caught completely off guard. And by the way, who taught you to use that damned thing so expertly?" he questioned curiously.

"Grant, of course. I continued to practice until I had mastered it," she replied blandly.

Seth propped himself on his elbow and muttered under his breath, "Is there anything that brother of yours failed to teach you?"

Brianna giggled as she squirmed to face Seth. "Only one thing, Captain," she whispered provocatively. "And for that I found it necessary to seek out the most proficient instructor."

A lopsided grin tugged at the corner of his mouth as he glanced down into her face. "I thought you said you were ready for sleep," he reminded her.

"I've changed my mind."

Seth cursed himself a thousand times as his arms involuntarily encircled her. And then he cursed himself a thousand times more when his lips melted against hers. She could bend him to her will with the slightest caress or faintest smile. His mind kept telling him to keep his distance, but his body was paying no attention. And then they were scaling the mountain of ecstasy to touch the stars. Seth drew a ragged breath as

250

he cradled Brianna in his arms, knowing he had been to heaven and realizing that he would make the climb again, each time he was given the opportunity.

And yet, in time, he knew he would tire of this vixen, just as he had all the others in the past. It was his way. He intended to follow a wandering star. Seth heaved a contented sigh as he let drowsiness overtake him. But for now, he would allow Brianna to amuse him. She was only a temporary pleasure that he would one day replace.

Chapter Sixteen

Brianna's mood lightened throughout the following weeks and she began to enjoy life once again. There were no more attempts made by the man who had seized her in the darkness. Her days were spent on deck, often beside Seth who stood at the helm, guiding the *Mesmer* westward.

Seth was well aware that all eyes followed Brianna each time she appeared. He could easily read the minds of those who cast her discreet glances. Seth could visualize each and every one of them attempting to drag Brianna away to abuse her. He was suspicious of them all and never allowed Brianna to visit Grant and Sabrina unless he personally escorted her to their cabin.

As Brianna strolled across the deck to inhale a breath of fresh air, she met Derrick who was prepared to offer no more than a nod of greeting. Since Seth had returned to his own cabin, Derrick had become more stand-offish. Brianna had missed his company and had invited him to dine with them on several occasions, but Derrick always had an excuse not to take a meal with them.

Brianna attempted to draw him from his shell with a smile. "Hello, Derrick."

"Brianna," he said with a slight nod as he walked on past her.

"Have I done something to annoy you?" she questioned before he was out of earshot.

Slowly, he turned to face her, a faint smile grazing his lips. "Nay, of course not." He tried to sound cheerful, but his tone was flat.

Her delicate brow arched and she regarded him for a long moment. "You don't sound very convincing."

"I thought perhaps you no longer needed my company since you and Seth have made amends." Although he had interceded, trying to bring Seth and Brianna back together, he was having an attack of self-pity. His days and nights had been pleasureful until the captain returned to claim his wife. Now he endured a meager existence, biding his time until they reached Petersburg.

"Nothing could be further from the truth," she insisted. "I have always counted you as a dear friend. My feelings haven't changed."

"Thank you, Brianna. That means a great deal to me," he replied quietly.

A mischievous grin spread across her face, causing Derrick to frown warily. He had seen that look before. It made him uneasy.

"I don't know what you're thinking, but I know you well enough to realize that that look could mean trouble."

Her reckless laughter eased his blue mood. "I was just wondering if perhaps you needed to view the world from a new angle. Maybe that would lift your spirits."

When she tugged on his arm, urging him to follow her, Derrick set his feet, refusing to budge until he knew where she intended to lead him. "What are you up to, Brianna?"

Her gaze lifted to the sails. "Let's climb to the lookout," she suggested.

His brows furrowed disapprovingly. "I think not. I would venture to guess that the captain would have my head if I allowed you to try that again. And I would imagine that if I agreed to join you that I would be hanging from the mast . . . with a rope around my neck."

Brianna heaved a resigned sigh. "Very well then, would you agree to a stroll around the deck?"

When she flashed him a blinding smile, Derrick wilted. It was impossible to refuse her. "To that I will agree, m'lady."

"How long have you been sailing, Derrick?" she questioned curiously as they walked together.

"Since the Revolution," he replied as his gaze swung to her for a moment, trying not to dwell overly long on her bewitching face. She was too much of a temptation and he had no intention of being caught gawking, especially since the captain had become so protective of his wife.

"And have you always been with Seth?"

"Only the last few years."

Brianna was having difficulty making conversation. Derrick would offer no more than an answer to her question.

Derrick stopped abruptly and glanced up to see Kenton Marsh freeing the tallest sail.

"The captain must be anxious to reach shore," he mused aloud. When Brianna peered curiously at him, he hastened to explain as he gestured skyward. "That triangular sail high above the others is the moonraker. Donnovan is making the most of the breeze."

Now it was Brianna's turn to become pensive. Was Seth anxious to be rid of her once they docked? Brianna was afraid she knew the answer. He wanted their marriage of convenience to serve its purpose. She would be returning to England and he would have the freedom he desired.

"Look, Brianna." Derrick directed her attention to

the west. "Those puffy clouds are a sign that land is not too far away. I suppose you will be eager to set foot on solid ground again," he predicted. "But I must warn you, the colonies are a far cry from England." He winked playfully at Brianna's thoughtful expression. "I'm sure you've heard that this land is overrun with savages and thieves, the outcasts of England's noble society."

Brianna nodded affirmatively. "I'm afraid the colonies have a rather bad reputation."

Derrick chortled lightly. "Perhaps you should form your own opinion after you have given my homeland a fair chance," he advised. "You may find that you have a great deal in common with us."

Amusement glistened in her eyes as she glanced at Derrick when she caught his insinuation. "You would dare to label me as an outcast?" she challenged.

Derrick flicked the end of her upturned nose, a wide grin splitting his face. "Nay, m'lady. I am not certain that a word has been invented to aptly describe you," he teased.

When she put out her chin in an exaggerated pout, he chuckled at her childish expression. "My dear Brianna, that was not meant as an insult. Wonders of this world only come in numbers of one and you, m'lady"— Derrick bowed before her, pressing a kiss to her wrist— "are one of a kind."

Brianna's lighthearted laughter warmed Derrick inside and out. "I shall miss you, Derrick. You have a charm that I shall never forget."

Derrick's gaze became suddenly sober. "Nor will I forget you, Brianna."

When land was sighted on the horizon, a shout of cheer resounded among the crew, and Brianna scrambled up the ladder to join Seth at the helm. Dressed in breeches and a shirt, she stood gazing at a new world that slowly began to grow in size. As she glanced at Seth, she saw his emerald eyes fill with pride as he surveyed the distant shore. A sudden pang of sadness seemed to constrict her breath as she followed his gaze over the white-capped water. Never once had they discussed their future. Seth had made love to her while murmuring words of need and desire, but never once had he professed to love her. What was she to do when they reached the colonies? Her delicate brows furrowed thoughtfully as she stared at the coastline.

As Seth glanced down, prepared to speak to Brianna, his words lodged in his throat. The gentle breeze seemed to lift the shining cloak of ebony from her shoulders, as if invisible hands were smoothing the dark tresses away from her bewitching face. Her amber eyes reflected the sun's sparkle and her chin tilted upward, as if courageously prepared to meet whatever lay ahead of her. Her shapely form was cautiously poised at the helm and Seth felt the urge to take her in his possessive embrace and hold her tightly to him. Yet, at the moment, she reminded him of a beautiful creature of the wild who had been restricted much too long in captivity. To touch her would be to inhibit her free spirit, to speak would only shatter the entrancing spell that seemed to hover about her. What was she thinking, he mused pensively. Was she anticipating the unfamiliar world that awaited her or was she only seeking the freedom that he had promised her? Would she immediately plan to return to England or would she stay in Virginia until the *Mesmer* sailed back to Bristol?

Without uttering a word, Brianna slowly raised her golden eyes to Seth and held his steady gaze, searching the rugged lines of his face, as if memorizing the sight of his dark features. As her black lashes fluttered softly against her cheek, she ducked her head and strolled across the deck and disappeared down the ladder. A perplexed frown creased Seth's handsome face before he glanced back to see Derrick walking up behind him.

"Will we weigh anchor tonight and dock at first light?" he questioned stiffly as he cast the captain a quick glance.

"Aye," Seth replied with a slight nod. "It will serve no purpose to maneuver among the other schooners in darkness." He paused momentarily to study Derrick's expressionless face. "You're in love with her, aren't you?" he asked bluntly.

Sayer's sun-bleached brows furrowed as he eyed the captain levelly. "She's your wife, and you and I have always been close friends."

Seth chuckled at Derrick's evasive reply. "I didn't ask whose wife she was. And since we are friends I expect an honest answer."

A sly smile touched Derrick's lips as he peered into the captain's eyes that glistened with mild amusement. "Is there a man on board this ship besides Grant Talbert who is not taken with the sea witch?" he quipped. "That's what they call her, you know. The whole damned lot of those superstitious sailors honestly believe that the reason we suffered no storms at sea on this voyage was because of that golden-eyed sorceress. They think she has charmed the *Mesmer*."

Seth laughed heartily at Derrick's words. "And do you believe Brianna is capable of murmuring incantations and casting spells over the schooner and those who sail upon her decks?" he mocked as he crossed his arms on his chest and regarded his first mate suspiciously.

Arching a taunting brow, Derrick lifted the gold medallion that lay on the captain's neck and brushed his fingers lightly across it. "You wear this good luck charm. You have married Brianna after I have heard

257

you swear time and time again that you would never wed for love or money. And you have just returned from a journey at sea on which we have met with not even one day of bad weather. Tell me, Captain, how is it that we have never crossed the Atlantic without being swept off course by turbulent winds, except for this one time? Why do you wear this talisman and, better yet, why did you wed the woman that you yourself claimed to be a witch?" Derrick produced a wicked grin as he let the coin slip through his fingers. "When you can sufficiently answer my questions then I will answer yours, Captain."

As Derrick sauntered away, a dark scowl furrowed the lines of Seth's rugged face. Surely Derrick didn't believe all that superstitious nonsense, he muttered under his breath. Lifting the chain over his head, Seth clasped it in his hand and quickly tossed it into the sea. "I need no golden talisman," he mused aloud. "Brianna is but a woman. She possesses no magic spell. Any man who claims such foolishness is demented. I don't believe in witches!"

Brianna had just stepped up on the main deck. Seth's words seemed to float down upon her as she watched him hurl the chain through the air and saw it disappear in the murky water. Spinning away, she hastened down the steps to the captain's cabin and gathered her belongings. A fitting end, she thought discouragingly as she folded her gowns and tucked them in her pouch. Seth had returned to his homeland and he no longer had any use for her. No doubt there was a limitless supply of willing wenches who awaited the captain's arrival with open arms. She would quickly be forgotten when he stepped ashore.

After leaving Seth a note to say that she would be joining Grant and Sabrina for supper, Brianna grabbed her leather pouch, stepped outside the cabin, and moved down the companionway to the steps that led to the lower level. As she turned the corner, a firm hand covered her mouth, silencing her scream of alarm. She was whisked into the storeroom by two men whose faces were dark and forbidding. In silence they stuffed a gag in her mouth and hastily bound her hands and feet.

"Did ye retrieve the loot?" Jed questioned in a hushed voice as he tossed Brianna over his shoulder like a sack of feed.

"Aye, but I don't know why you are so dead set on taking the wench along with us," Lucas grumbled disgustedly as he opened the door and checked to ensure that the way was clear.

"Because she's a good luck charm and a beauty to boot. When I'm through with 'er, we can sell 'er back to the cap'n," Jed explained with a sinister gleam in his gray eyes.

A sly smile spread across Patton's stubbled face as he glanced back at Catlin. "I think for once you've come up with a decent idea."

"I'm full of 'em," Jed assured him arrogantly, "but ye never think anyone but yerself 'as any brains."

Brianna's eyes narrowed as she listened to the two men and their plans for her. The thought of where she had heard the two familiar voices seemed to spark a new fear. These were the men she had confronted while she was fleeing to the schooner, and one of them would have thrashed her for merely bumping into him.

As the sailors cautiously made their escape, Seth was just returning to his quarters to find Brianna's note. 'Tis just as well, Donnovan thought to himself as he lit his cigar and leaned back to relax in his chair. The time had come for him and Brianna to discuss what was to be done about their arrangement, and he was apprehensive about bringing up the subject. They had never talked about the agreement since he had used her so brutally. It was a bitter memory which was best forgotten.

Seth had invited Grant and Sabrina to stay at his plantation until they sailed for England, and Talbert had quickly accepted the invitation. Perhaps Brianna would decide to remain in the colonies since her brother was staying a little over a month at the plantation. As the white smoke curled about his raven head like a wispy halo, Seth heaved a disheartened sigh. What the hell was he to do about Brianna? Should he ask her to stay with him at least for a time? Did he really want her to remain with him? She was such a temptation, but what if she yearned for society instead of the simple life of his colonial plantation?

After Seth had taken his evening meal alone, bathed, and paced the floor, waiting for Grant to bring Brianna back to his cabin, he finally decided to retrieve her himself. The hour was late and he and Brianna must talk before they docked in Petersburg.

When Seth rapped on the Talberts' door, Sabrina answered it and quickly glanced back at Grant.

"What is it, Captain?" Grant questioned as he arched a curious brow and motioned for Donnovan to enter.

His emerald eyes swept the small room and a look of concern gathered on his face. "Where is Brianna?"

"Brianna? I haven't seen her since this morning," Grant replied.

"She left me a note saying that she was joining the two of you for supper," Seth explained anxiously.

"But where could she be if she's not in your cabin or here?" Sabrina questioned as a perplexed frown crossed her features.

Seth shrugged leisurely, attempting to hide his own concern. "She may have changed her mind and decided to visit Derrick before leaving the ship tomorrow. I'll go see if she and Sayer are roaming the deck."

When Seth moved down the dark companionway and started up the steps, his boot hit against Brianna's pouch. As he reached down to pick it up, his heart skipped a beat when he recognized the bag. Damn! he muttered under his breath as he squinted in the darkness and listened for some sound that would alert him to her presence. But nothing but silence surrounded him. Seth checked the storeroom and then the hold where the cargo was stored. As Captain Donnovan held the lantern above his head and scanned the musty quarters he noticed that several of the crates had been moved aside and rearranged, but there was no sign of Brianna.

After dashing down the companionway and taking the steps two at a time, Seth went to Derrick's room to find that he hadn't seen Brianna since that afternoon. A sickening dread settled about his shoulders as he imagined the worst. The unidentified sailor might have kidnapped her and he could visualize what the seaman had in mind for her. His clenched fist slammed into the palm of his left hand in rage. Who would dare to take the captain's wife? When he got his hands on the black-guard, he would choke the life out of the man who dared to touch Brianna.

"Get five men and check every damn niche on this ship," Seth ordered sharply as he pulled Derrick along the deck with him. "If I find the bastard who took Brianna, I'll hang him from the mast!"

"Not unless you find him before I do," Derrick muttered angrily.

After an hour's searching the captain and his first mate came up empty-handed, but it was discovered that Lucas Patton and Jed Catlin were also missing. When Seth checked the life boats to find one of them gone, an enraged growl echoed across the decks. Derrick retrieved his pistol while the captain had the other skiff lowered into the water.

Seth squinted toward the dim lights on shore while his mind raced with vengeful thoughts. When he caught up to those men they would be begging for mercy and he would show them none! If they had touched Brianna, their lives wouldn't be worth a shilling!

Brianna sat motionless while Jed and Lucas rowed toward the docks. While the two men had loaded their belongings Brianna had discreetly lifted her dagger from the side of her boot and cut away the ropes that bound her feet. The men were preoccupied with their chore and the anticipation of receiving a large sum for the jewels they had stolen in Bristol. Brianna cautiously loosened the ropes from her arms, waiting tensely for the men to row close enough to shore for her to swim away. She squinted at the lights that lined the wharf, her heart beating frantically, knowing she had only one chance to save herself.

While Jed and Lucas were bragging about past conquests and future plans, Brianna bolted from her seat and stepped up on the edge of the skiff, startling both men who had paid her little mind since they had left the *Mesmer*. As they reached for Brianna the skiff tilted with the uneven weight, capsizing as they grabbed her legs. She dived into the cold water that took her breath away. Brianna gasped and choked as an ocean of water swallowed her up. Dead weight seemed to be tied to her ankles and she fought in panic to make her way back to the surface.

As Seth and Derrick rowed toward the shore they caught sight of the skiff. Seth's spirits plunged as he moved alongside the capsized boat and silently cursed his luck. If he hadn't thrown that damned talisman into the sea, none of this would have happened. Donnovan shook his head, forcing such ridiculous thoughts from his mind. This was madness! The charm had nothing to do with Brianna. It couldn't . . . could it? Her fate had been the same as the charm's, but— Nay, it was only coincidence. . . . Wasn't it? Seth groaned at the course his thoughts were taking. He was as superstitious as the rest of his crew when it came to Brianna, and he of all people should have known better.

"Now what, Captain?" Derrick breathed disheartenedly.

"We go ashore and see if anyone knows if the wench made it to the docks," Seth replied determinedly as he took up the oars.

"Do you honestly believe that she could have made that swim to shore in this cold water? How could she have the strength to—"

"Damn it, Derrick!" Seth snapped harshly. "I'm not giving up hope yet and I don't want to hear any more of your pessimistic remarks." The hint of finality in his sharp tone made Derrick swallow the rest of his words, but he could not share the captain's confidence that Brianna could have possibly survived such a long swim in that icy water.

When they reached the wharf, Seth hastily tied the skiff and climbed to the dock to begin his search. After an hour of inquiring about Brianna and checking the beach for any sign of the woman whose face kept rising above Seth, urging him to continue looking for her, he was ready to call off the search for the night. Her golden eyes silently called him from the darkness and he could not bring himself to believe that she had perished. Yet, she was nowhere to be found.

"Come on, Captain," Derrick insisted as he grabbed Seth by the arm and pulled him back toward the skiff.

"The Talberts will be waiting for us. You'll have to tell them what has happened. I'm sorry," he murmured quietly.

Donnovan nodded reluctantly as he allowed Sayer to pull him along. What would he tell Grant? Talbert would probably blame him for not keeping an eye on Brianna, and Sabrina had never been too fond of him in the first place. She would most likely accuse him of neglecting his duty where Brianna was concerned.

When the skiff came alongside the *Mesmer*, the entire crew was waiting as the captain climbed aboard. The only face that captured his attention was Grant's and he walked solemnly toward the anxious young man.

"The boat capsized and there was no sign of any of them," he stated quietly. "We checked the docks, but we didn't find a trace. Maybe tomorrow we will be able to continue our search."

Sabrina sobbed hysterically as she huddled against Grant. "Oh God!" she wailed. "Not Brianna!"

Seth stiffened when Sabrina looked up at him through tear-filled eyes that flared in condemnation. He knew what she was thinking and the fact that she was right did nothing to console him.

Grant wrapped a comforting arm about his wife. "Don't give up hope, Sabrina. You know Brianna is an excellent swimmer. Perhaps she managed to make it to shore and was hiding or maybe—"

"But what if she was tied? What if she were unconscious?" Sabrina choked out. "She may never have had the chance to save herself."

"You better take her below," Seth suggested. He did not need to hear Sabrina's opinions voiced since he had already considered them himself. "There is nothing more we can do tonight. Tomorrow every man on board will help us search."

Grant heaved a heavy sigh and glanced at Donnovan. Talbert's eyes mirrored his grief and Seth felt his heart sinking, knowing that he was looking at his own reflection. He had been so preoccupied with his duties of maneuvering the schooner through the canal that led to Petersburg that he had not spent much time with Brianna that day. It might have been the only opportunity he would have had. God, how he ached for the sight of those golden eyes and mischievous smile. He would never be able to forgive himself if he had lost her.

The crew slowly dispersed and finally Seth stood alone, gazing out over the bay that glistened in the moonlight. The sound of the water slapping against the hull was all that kept him company. His emerald eyes continued to search the darkness as he leaned his elbows against the railing, expecting at any moment to see Brianna saunter toward him with that impish grin playing on her tempting lips and that radiant sparkle in her eyes.

When he returned to his cabin, he pulled one of Brianna's gowns from her leather pouch, gently smoothing the blue silk that had been wrinkled by its confinement. The feminine fragrance that always clung to her began to fill his senses and he dropped his head with a hopeless sigh. "If I had only married you as Grandfather requested, you would have been safely tucked away in Bristol. But nay, I was too stubborn to let the old man have his way with me. And now only God knows where you are or if you even managed to survive."

As he stretched out on the bunk, a great emptiness gnawed at his belly. He quickly recalled the feel of Brianna's yielding body against his, responding to his caresses, urging him to fulfill the passionate need that equally matched his own, and returning his embrace with an ardent fervor that sent him soaring to rapturous heights. Seth rolled to his side and without thinking, he reached out to pull Brianna against him as he had done so often in the past. Pulling the quilts tightly about him, he attempted to smother the void of loneliness and despair that tugged at his heart and tortured his sanity.

Brianna shivered while her teeth rattled in her head. No matter how hard she tried, she simply could not quit shaking. Finally she decided to venture to the captain's cabin on a schooner and plead for assistance if there was anyone about. If she didn't get out of her cold, wet clothes, she would certainly catch her death. As she knocked lightly on the door a low grumble came from within the cabin.

Finally the door opened and Brianna peered anxiously at the tall seaman who attempted to look at her through groggy eyes. At the sight of Brianna's wet clothes that clung to her shapely form, revealing each tempting swell and curve that lay beneath the damp fabric, his eyes widened and slowly drank in the alluring sight.

"Sir, I need assistance," she managed through her chattering teeth.

Captain Barton grabbed her arm and pulled her inside his quarters. Quickly yanking the quilt from the bunk, he turned back to Brianna. "Take off your clothes," he ordered hastily.

Brianna's amber eyes widened in alarm, but Lance grinned down at her, amused by her modesty when she was in such dire need of help.

"Do you wish to take pneumonia, my dear?" he quested mockingly.

"Nay," she answered hoarsely as she grabbed the quilt from his hand. "Nor do I wish to undress in front of a total stranger. Turn your back!" Brianna glared at him as she raised a stubborn chin. She had enough of men for one night and if this rogue thought he had just met some simple twit, he was sorely mistaken.

With a light chuckle, Lance spun around and crossed his arms on his chest. "Since I am a gentleman, I will obey your request, but with a good deal of reluctance. 'Tis not every night that a mermaid comes ashore and raps on my door."

Brianna eyed him warily as she wrapped the quilt about her and shed her soggy breeches and shirt. When she was huddled beneath the dry blanket, she allowed the captain to face her once again.

Urging Brianna into a chair, Lance rested a hip on the edge of his desk and peered curiously at her. "What is your name, my dear?"

"Brianna," she replied between shivers. "And yours?"

"Captain Lance Barton at your service, m'lady," he answered, bowing slightly from his half-sitting position. "How is it you were swimming in the ocean on such a cool night?"

Brianna pulled the blanket tightly about her and eyed him levelly. "I will be all too happy to explain if you would be so kind as to fetch me some tea to ward off the chill. Otherwise, I may not live long enough to relate the incident, Captain Barton," she retorted impatiently, watching his brown eyes roam over her like a circling vulture that waited to devour his prey.

As Lance hopped to his feet he produced a charming smile. "'Twas terribly inconsiderate of me not to offer you something. I'll go to the galley and see what I can find," he replied.

When the door closed behind him, Brianna hastily searched in his trunk at the foot of the bed and shrugged on his clothes. After tucking the hem of the dark breeches in her wet boots, Brianna opened the door and peered outside. Finding an empty deck, she dashed toward the plank and hurried along the dock. She found a small fishing boat that would serve as her bed for the night. She was too exhausted to row out to the *Mesmer* and decided to wait until the schooner docked before she returned. Curling in a tight ball, Brianna fell asleep, thankful that she had managed to escape, but rueful that she would not be particularly welcome when she went aboard the schooner. Seth was more than happy to see her gone and would probably be disappointed when she returned.

Chapter Seventeen

Priscilla Weatherby watched anxiously as the gang-plank bridged the gap between the dock and the deck of the *Mesmer*. When those who had awaited the schooner's return made their way on board, she shrieked gaily at the sight of the dashing Captain Don-novan. Rushing toward him, oblivious to all those about her, Priscilla threw her arms about the captain's neck and showered him with joyful kisses. Although Seth was numb to any emotion since the disappearance of Brianna, he accepted Priscilla's blatant display of affection without returning her zealousness.

Brianna's quicksilver temper made fast work of reaching a boiling point as she moved up the plank with the crowd and watched the shapely redhead devour the captain. It seemed to her that Seth was not the least bit concerned about her disappearance and had intended to waste no time replacing his unwanted wife. Damn him! Brianna cursed under her breath as she wrapped the quilt closely about her and moved toward Grant and Sabrina.

Captain Barton was on hand to welcome Seth home and had caught sight of the bedraggled beauty who had escaped him the previous evening. As he pushed his way through the crowd he called out the woman's name, attempting to gain her attention. He brought the entire crew and its captain to a startled halt, all eyes searching for the bewitching features they never

269

expected to see again.

Seth inwardly cringed as scorching sparks of gold drilled into his chest. If looks could kill he would have been pushing up daisies, not that he didn't appreciate them. He just didn't relish the idea of staring at them from the roots up.

"I take it that you know Brianna," Lance commented as he extended his hand to Seth, his eyes still searching for the woman who had been swallowed up by the crew who were bombarding her with questions.

"Aye, but how do *you* know her?" Seth questioned, his eyes sliding over Lance's shoulder.

Lightly snickering, Lance's smile broadened to show even white teeth. "I was visited by a mermaid late last night and I . . ." His voice trailed off as Seth walked across the deck, rudely leaving Lance, in the middle of his sentence, and Priscilla with her jaw sagging.

Seth had seen Brianna make her way toward the steps and he hastily pursued her. Priscilla's blue eyes narrowed angrily as she watched Seth follow the bedraggled chit who had captured the attention of everyone on the *Mesmer*. Who the devil was she? What was her connection to Seth?

After entering the captain's cabin, Brianna found her pouch and quickly yanked one of her gowns from it. Before she could begin to dress, the door opened and Seth's massive form filled the entrance. Brianna glowered at him, still smoldering over the scene she had witnessed when she came aboard.

"Brianna," he breathed, his eyes roaming over her loose-fitting garments.

He was met by another murderous glare as she wheeled to face him. "I didn't expect you to be overly concerned about my disappearance, dear Captain," she hissed, her tone dripping with venom. "But I did expect you to play the bereaved husband for more than a day.

Instead, I find you in another woman's arms so quickly that it even made *my* head spin. Tell me, did you plan to search for me at all?" Her brow arched as a tight smile thinned her lips. When Barton came up behind Seth, Brianna addressed him with a wider smile, assuring Seth that the one he had received was void of affection. "Captain Barton, I will return your garb as soon as I am allowed to change. I did not have the opportunity to properly thank you for your help last night. I am *most* appreciative." *Let Donnovan think the worst,* she thought spitefully.

Seth glanced over his shoulder, casting Lance a suspicious glare, wondering what had happened between the two of them. Lance ignored Seth's black look, his hungry gaze roaming over Brianna.

"Think nothing of it, my dear," he began as he stepped around Seth and swaggered toward Brianna. "Under the circumstances, there was no time for long good-byes. Perhaps we can take up where we left off after you have had time to change." He winked slyly as he reached for her hand, placing a light kiss upon it. Lance intended to make his interest in Brianna known before Seth had the opportunity to console her.

After a sleepless night of worry, Seth was in no mood to find that Brianna had spent the evening with another man, especially Lance. He was a close friend as well as a neighbor and had a reputation with the ladies that equaled his own.

"Just what the hell are you two talking about?" Donnovan snapped in an impatient tone, his emerald eyes narrowing accusingly, first on Brianna and then Lance.

Brianna shrugged nonchalantly, and Lance only grinned wickedly.

"You owe me an explanation!" Seth insisted in an agitated growl. "You left me a note saying that you were dining with Grant, who knew nothing about your plans. When I went to inquire about you, I found your leather pouch in the companionway." With an accusing glare at Brianna, his thoughts began to twist illogically as his anger distorted his rationality. "Did you talk Lucas and Jed into taking you ashore? What did you offer those two scoundrels to do your bidding? Money—or something more to their liking?" he questioned caustically, his heavy brow arching as his mouth twisted in a menacing smile. "And what of Lance? What else did he have to gain besides your clothes?"

Brianna gasped indignantly at his degrading insinuations. "How dare you suggest such a ludicrous notion! I saw you toss the good luck charm into the sea and heard you vow that you wanted nothing more to do with me," she ground out in an enraged snarl. "I was going to dine with my brother and I intended to stay the night with him and Sabrina. It seemed to be the easiest way of ending it between us. Jed and Lucas grabbed me and tied me up. They had planned to take me with them and I can well imagine what my duty was to be after they delivered the jewels that they had stolen in Bristol," she added bitterly as her delicate face reddened in anger and painful recollection.

Seth's eyes shot open wide as he listened to Brianna's account of what had happened and watched the rising color slowly ebb.

A chalky white film seemed to hover over her features, giving them a ghostlike appearance as she spoke again.

"I was carrying my knife in my boot and I cut away the ropes while they rowed toward shore. When I started to dive into the water, they both reached for me and the boat capsized. I don't know if either of them made it to the beach and I certainly didn't wait around long enough to find out. When I went aboard Captain Barton's ship I took some of his dry clothes while he was fetching some tea. I slept in a small fishing boat with nothing more than this blanket to warm me." Brianna paused a moment, attempting to catch her breath. She was cold, exhausted, and the room was beginning to spin furiously about her. It had taken all of her will and determination to endure her experience, and her strength was dwindling all too quickly. Her legs seemed to be turning to jelly, but she intended to finish what she had to say before she crumpled to the floor. "If I had planned to escape from the ship last night I certainly would not have taken anyone with me, as you well know," she added jeeringly. "And when I came back here this morning, expecting you to be at least *slightly* concerned about my welfare, I find you embracing some red-haired wench. You were probably thrilled to think that I had drowned or had been kidnapped." Brianna chuckled bitterly once again as she grabbed the back of the nearby chair for support. "Those blackguards even intended to hold me for ransom, but I can see now that you would not have paid them a farthing for my safe return. You didn't give a damn about what had happened to me. I am left to wonder if perhaps it was you who arranged for them to carry me off!" she accused as she shot Seth a look of contempt.

Brianna saw Priscilla dash up behind Seth and her eyes narrowed to hard, angry slits as she focused on the attractive wench. "You can have this miserable cad, m'lady. I want nothing more to do with him. He has served his purpose and the matter is over and done!" She weaved unsteadily against the chair as her last words came out in a forced whisper: "The agreement stands as it was made."

As blackness covered her eyes, Brianna crumpled

lifelessly and Lance quickly swept her up in his arms before she collapsed on the floor. He had been standing beside Brianna, listening to both Seth and the shapely lass, thoroughly confused and completely amazed by her account. Who was this woman? he mused silently as he carried her to the cot and carefully laid her beneath the quilts. What agreement was she talking about?

"She's burning up with fever," Lance stated as Seth knelt beside him.

Seth brushed his palm across her forehead, smoothing the tangled tresses of ebony away from her white face. "Damn," he muttered.

"Who is this woman?" Priscilla asked in annoyance as she stalked up behind the two men who bent over the unconscious wench.

"Now now, Priscilla," Seth snapped rudely as he tucked the quilts closely about Brianna's trim form.

"I demand an answer!" she persisted as she stamped her foot impatiently. "What is she doing on your schooner?"

Seth glanced back over his shoulder at the pert beauty, wondering what he had even seen in her to begin with. She was spoiled, demanding, and insistent and he was in no mood for one of her tantrums. "Brianna is my wife," he replied matter-of-factly.

"Your wife?" Priscilla choked out as she stepped back, her blue eyes widening in bewilderment. It was as if Seth had slapped her across the face, and Priscilla did not want to believe her ears. How could he do this to her!

Lance peered curiously at Seth, not daring to believe what he had heard either. Seth married? The very idea was ridiculous. Donnovan had vowed never to take a wife.

After Priscilla had picked up the front of her pink

silk skirts and stomped from the room, Lance stared curiously at Seth. "Were you telling the truth? Are you really married to this woman or were you just in a rush to be rid of Priscilla?"

Seth focused his attention on the lifeless form on his bunk and wrapped his fingers in the cascade of coal black curls that sprayed across his pillow. Lance frowned bemusedly at the tender smile that softened the rugged lines of Seth's face, wondering what emotion had been captured for an instant.

"We are married for a time," Seth replied softly.

Lance arched a dubious brow as he regarded Donnovan. "And just what the hell is that supposed to mean? I didn't know you could rent them out at your convenience," he mocked dryly.

"Only if you wed a witch," Seth teased, his emerald eyes roaming over Brianna's pallid face. "You are allowed to keep her only as long as she allows it."

Lance's brows gathered in another frown. "Witches," he scoffed. "Surely you don't belive in such idiocy."

With a leisurely shrug, Seth allowed his gaze to slide to Lance for a moment before it returned to Brianna. "Brianna is like a she-cat—quick-witted, clever, and as agile and graceful as a black panther. Her fiery temper is matched by her devastating beauty. And no matter which way you toss this incorrigible wench, she always manages to land on her feet like a cat that has been blessed with nine lives."

Seth chuckled lightly as he traced his fingers across Brianna's pale lips. "Aye, at first I had my doubts, but no more. The lady is a witch. No one else could have hoped to survive what she has come through, but Brianna managed to escape. She is weak and exhausted, just like the black panther that returns to her den to lick her wounds. Brianna will come back to life, stalking the night, after she has had time to heal." Seth met Lance's bewildered gaze and then he smiled wryly. "I can see that you are skeptical now, but when you come to know Brianna as I do, you will curse yourself for not taking heed to my warning. She is a witch who is as indestructible as Satan himself." His gaze swung back to the deathly looking form on his bed. "Aye, my friend, heed my words. Brianna has the Devil's luck."

Lance rolled his eyes skyward. What in the sweet loving hell had come over Seth? Why was he acting so strangely? Lance had known Seth for over ten years and had fought alongside him against the British. Never once had Donnovan taken leave of his senses even though many situations could have effected such a response. But at the moment Lance was skeptical of the man's sanity. The odd expression on Seth's face was one that Lance had never seen, and his words were difficult to swallow. The entire day had him baffled. Seth had claimed that he had married this fascinating young wench who had managed to escape her captors. He had spoken of witches and charms, black cats, and had even sent Priscilla packing. That in itself was enough to cause Barton concern.

With a hopeless shake of his head, he glanced at Brianna who was beginning to rouse. When her golden eyes fluttered open, he caught his breath as he gazed into the bewitching amber pools that seemed to draw him into a hypnotic spell. Her eyes were rimmed with dark, sooty lashes and within the vast depths of glittering gold it seemed as though sun rays were sparkling in them. Lance sat entranced as he appraised the soft, tanned features of her lovely face. Although he had recognized her to be a stunning beauty even as she stood before him in soggy clothes the previous evening, only now did he fully realize her true loveliness. There was something mysteriously majestic about her—so gentle yet strong, so delicate yet powerful. To gaze at her now would deny her miraculous feat. And yet, there was that mischievous sparkle in those golden eyes that warned him never to doubt her resourcefulness.

Had Brianna broken the bond between Seth and Priscilla? Seth had always adored the ground Priscilla had walked upon and had even professed to love her at one time, but Priscilla had married Kyle Weatherby because of his prestigious rank and wealth. After Kyle died at the battle of Yorktown, she had come to Seth, offering to become his wife after being his mistress during her marriage to Kyle. Seth had laughed in her face and told her that she would never claim the name of Donnovan, but that he would enjoy her passions until he tired of her, intent on punishing her for what she had done to him in the beginning. Priscilla had been persistent. She even allowed Seth to take other women as lovers, hoping to convince him that she was truly devoted to him and would continue to love him no matter how cruelly he treated her at times. But Seth had never trusted her, although he could never seem to get the wench out of his blood. Somehow it seemed that Donnovan's need for revenge had calmed in the wake of this mystifying young woman who lay before him. Perhaps Seth was right. Maybe Brianna was a witch. Lance was slowly brought from his pensive musings as Brianna spoke in a raspy whisper.

"You didn't think I could survive did you, Captain?" she questioned Seth as a weary smile bordered her quivering lips.

Brushing his knuckles against her soft cheek, Seth returned the faint smile. "I knew you would, vixen," he assured her huskily. "I have finally come to the conclusion that you are indestructible."

Brianna had been furious with him earlier, but the gentleness in his emerald eyes had melted her anger and her weakened condition mellowed her urge to continue to fight with him. "I only returned to haunt you, you know," she teased, her voice barely above a whisper.

Seth nodded slightly as his smile broadened. "I might have guessed as much. Some men are fortunate enough to be blessed with a guardian angel to watch over them, but it seems that I have been plagued with a witch—lovely and enchanting, but a witch nonetheless."

"For a time," she breathed weakly, a hint of remorse touching her quiet reply.

As Brianna's silky lashes fluttered against her cheek, she sank into an exhausted sleep. Seth slowly rose to his feet and strolled over to pour Lance and himself a stiff drink. Leaning casually against the edge of the desk, Seth sipped his brandy while he continued to stare at Brianna.

Lance eased down in the chair across from Donnovan and raised a quizzical gaze to his friend. "Where did you meet Brianna?"

A reckless smile played on his lips as he swung his attention to Lance. "She climbed into my carriage late one night in an attempt to escape from her escort. I aided her in much the same way you did—I was only present. She was managing quite nicely on her own, as is always the case with Brianna," he added with a light chuckle. "With you, she left quietly while you were fetching tea, but she punched *me* squarely in the jaw, greatly annoyed with a remark I had made, and fled into the darkness without giving me her name."

"I gather you made it a point to seek her out," Lance surmised before taking a sip of liquor and easing back in his seat.

"Nay, as a matter of fact, I did my damnedest to stay away from her when I found out who she was," Seth replied blandly. "'Twas a long, perplexing story, Lance, but to be brief, my grandfather initially arranged a marriage contract between Brianna and myself. He was convinced that I deserved to be saddled with this little bundle of spirit." Seth grinned slyly as he allowed his eyes to rest on Brianna for a moment. "If Grandfather knew of all the hell this wench has put me through during the past two months, he would be quite pleased with himself."

"So you married her only because of an obligation to Lord Donnovan." Lance snorted in disbelief. "Somehow I cannot imagine you submitting to the contract, even for Andrew."

Seth shrugged noncommittally and continued with his explanation. "Brianna was not in favor of the wedding and stowed away on the *Mesmer* unaware that I would be there. She was following after her brother, and it seemed under the circumstances we had little choice but to wed. We struck up an agreement that would suit our own purposes and satisfy both the Donnovans and the Talberts. We are free to come and go as we please with whomever we please. 'Tis a marriage of convenience," he finished in a glib tone.

"That name sounds familiar," Lance mused aloud. "I have often heard of Brianna Talbert and her escapades while I was in Bristol. I took in all those stories with a grain of salt, thinking that those dandies of the English aristocracy were merely deluding themselves by devising stories of some legendary goddess." Lance gazed at the sleeping form on the bed and chuckled in amusement. "It seems I was a bit cynical of those English dandies. It appears that they spoke the truth and I am left to wonder if perhaps I should believe all that I have heard about this vixen."

"Believe it," Seth insisted as a hint of pride laced his deep voice. "The wench defies all that you have ever known or would have believed in. There is not another like her."

Lance frowned at Seth's sudden praise of Brianna and he thought of what Seth had said earlier about a marriage of convenience. Perhaps Seth intended to keep Priscilla as his mistress and this high-spirited wench as his wife. Maybe he intended to make the most of the situation. Lance was confused. He had seen the gentle expression in Seth's eyes when he had gazed down at Brianna. Could he have been mistaken? Lance wondered curiously. Perhaps it had only been a look of relief that Brianna was alive and well. There was one way to find out for certain.

"Your agreement sounds quite satisfying," Lance remarked nonchalantly. "I was quite taken with Brianna, and it seems since the two of you only share your name that I need not limit my attention with the lively wench to a merely friendly acquaintance."

Seth arched a skeptical brow as he shot Barton a quick glance. "You would pursue the wife of your most trusted friend?"

"Why not?" Lance countered with an indifferent shrug. "As I recall, you were guilty of just that at one time."

Lance's comment did not set well with Seth. Donnovan did not need to be reminded of his friendship with Kyle Weatherby. "I believe this conversation has gone far enough," Seth stated abruptly. "Brianna can do as she pleases, and I have business to attend on deck."

After Lance had finished his brandy, he followed Seth out of the cabin but paused to glance back at Brianna. Donnovan was a fool, he thought to himself. Seth may have married Brianna only to appease his grandfather, but only an idiot would keep the terms of such an agreement with one as lovely and spirited as Brianna.

Seth had suggested a comfortable hotel in Petersburg where Grant and Sabrina could stay until they traveled to the Donnovan plantation. After overseeing the unloading of part of the cargo he returned to check on Brianna. Just as he started down the steps, Priscilla's voice reached his ears. He turned toward her with a bland, impersonal expression etching his bronzed face that brought Priscilla's annoyed disposition to a state of fury.

"Why did you marry that bedraggled bitch?" she quipped in a tone that could only be described as a venomous hiss.

A rueful smile parted Seth's lips as he appraised the shapely redhead. He had spent the better part of seven years lusting after another man's wife. What had been so fascinating about Priscilla? he wondered. Was it because he could not have her as his own when he wanted her? And when she came to propose to him, claiming that she had cared for no one but him, he had scoffed cynically and vowed to take her to his bed when the mood suited him. Never would he take her as his wife. He had sought out other women on many occasions to satisfy his needs, but he had always come back to Priscilla. Odd, he mused thoughtfully, as lovely and desirable as she was, he had no urge to touch her at the moment. Perhaps when Brianna was back on her feet and the agony of believing that she had perished had faded, he would again yearn for the feel of Priscilla's soft flesh against his. But not now. He was not ready to see if that weakness was still there and he would only know when he touched her.

"Well?" she snapped impatiently. "Was it just for spite, Seth? You always said you would never marry me, but I never dreamed you would snatch some bedraggled child from her cradle and drag her home with you."

Seth was unaffected by Priscilla's hateful words and proceeded to explain in a placid tone, "I married

281

Brianna for the same reason I do all else—because it suited my purpose."

"And just what am I supposed to do?" Priscilla queried as she arched a haughty brow. "Am I to remain your mistress while you parade that little tramp all over Petersburg so all of my friends can laugh in my face? I even sent out the invitations for the ball we planned to give at the end of the month. Now what am I to do?"

"The party will be my wedding celebration," Seth retorted as a satanic smile curved the corners of his mouth upward. "I'll tell Brianna that you handled all of the necessary arrangements. I'm sure she will be most grateful for the effort you have made in her behalf. And by the way, Priscilla," he added as he turned back toward the steps, "my wife is no tramp. She is from a well-respected family in Bristol and I want to hear no more derogatory references from you. Even if it were true, it would never do for the pot to call the kettle black."

As Seth disappeared into the dark companionway, Priscilla gasped at his stinging insult and stamped her foot disgustedly. If Seth Donnovan thought she would bow out gracefully he had better think again! She was not about to let that wench take her place. As Priscilla spun on her heels she bumped into Derrick. The sly grin on his face only enraged her further.

"I suppose you are delighted about this ridiculous marriage," she snarled as she shot Derrick a reproachful glare. "You probably held Seth at gunpoint to ensure that he wed that wench."

"Nay, Mrs. Weatherby," Derrick corrected while the undaunted smile remained on his sun-bronzed features. "I would have married her myself if I had had the chance, but Seth beat me to it."

Priscilla's creamy white face turned crimson red with fury. "Next I suppose you intend to tell me that none can resist that dark-haired bitch who has claimed the Donnovan wealth."

Derrick tucked the package that he was carrying under his arm and casually appraised the infuriated wench before he cocked a mocking brow and replied to her remark, "Did you happen to notice how many pairs of eyes were on Brianna when she came aboard this morning? I think the attention she received was proof enough, madam. I rest my case." As he bowed before her, Priscilla muttered angrily and stomped away while Derrick's amused chuckle nipped at her heels.

"Good riddance, Priscilla," he said when she was out of earshot. "If we never chance to meet again, that will be soon enough."

When Seth stepped inside his cabin, Brianna was struggling to sit up on the edge of the bed. As she raised her weary eyes, Seth's brows knitted in concern. Her face was pale, and the golden pools that usually rippled with a sunny sparkle were as lifeless as a stagnant pond.

"Brianna, I suggest you stay in bed. You don't have your strength back," he insisted as he hastened toward her, pulling a chair along with him. As he straddled the chair he casually rested his arms on its back and surveyed Brianna's pallid complexion. "If you want something, I'll fetch it for you," he offered blandly, his tone disguising his concern.

"'Tis very kind of you, sir," Brianna replied, forcing a slightly sarcastic smile. "I am fine, really. All I need is a little nourishment. I haven't eaten or drunk anything except an ocean of salt water since noon yesterday."

"What would you like, my dear? Name it and I shall see that you have it." Seth's eyes twinkled in amusement. If she was fine, he would eat his own hat. She could hardly sit up. How the hell did she expect to stand up?

If Brianna could have mustered one ounce of

strength she would have defied him and insisted that she go to the galley to prepare her own meal, but it seemed she was too weak to raise her arm in protest. With a reluctant nod she accepted his gracious offer. "I'll take whatever the cook has to eat. I'm too famished to be particular."

As Seth came to his feet, he pressed Brianna back to the pillow and lowered his head, intending to kiss her pale lips, but the knock at the door halted him. "Come in," he called over his shoulder as he tucked Brianna back into bed.

Derrick sauntered into the cabin with his package tucked behind his back. "How's my favorite witch?" he teased as he came up beside the captain and gazed at Brianna's chalky white face.

Brianna managed a shallow smile. "Alive, but not so well, I fear."

As Derrick bent down to place the package beside her, he sent her a quick wink that spoke of his fondness. "I brought you a wedding gift," he explained in a gentle tone.

"Will you open it for me? I can barely raise my head without sending the world spinning about me."

Derrick unwrapped the package, lifted a sheer nightgown of pale gold from the box, and held it up for Brianna's approval. Then he laid it against Seth's chest. "He'll look lovely in it, don't you agree?" he questioned with a devilish grin.

Brianna chuckled at his foolishness and she sputtered and coughed in attempt to catch her breath. Both men glanced at each other with worried frowns. "'Tis very pretty and quite thoughtful of you, Derrick. I hope you won't mind if I don't model it for you right now."

"Would that you could, madam," he breathed forlornly. There was a trace of truth in his jest and Seth was quick to catch it.

"Derrick, if you will keep an eye on Brianna for a moment, I'll see what we can find for her to eat."

Derrick nodded as he straddled the chair that Seth had vacated earlier, all too happy with his task. When they were alone, Sayer gazed tenderly at Brianna's weary face. "I don't know how you survived the ordeal, Brianna. I was ready to believe the worst, but Seth would not accept the fact that you had perished. How did you manage to escape?" he questioned curiously.

Her delicate brows furrowed slightly at his admission. She would have guessed that Seth would have given her up for lost without a search. "I cut myself from the ropes and swam ashore," she explained simply.

Clasping Brianna's hand he pressed a lingering kiss to her wrist. "Forgive me for ever doubting you. I will never again believe that you have met with defeat."

"Thank you, Derrick. You're a dear friend," she replied, warmed by the tender expression in his sea blue eyes.

"I wanted more," he admitted as he held her steady gaze, "but I guess I'll have to learn to be content with that."

As Derrick scooted from his chair and placed a longing kiss to her lips, Seth opened the door to see the fond display of affection. With a disapproving frown, he cleared his throat to make his presence known and strolled up beside the chummy twosome, masking his irritation with a bland statement.

"The cook managed to find something edible. It may not be too appetizing, but 'tis nourishment." Seth sent Derrick a silent command to leave and Sayer reluctantly rose to his feet.

"I'll come by to check on you this evening," he murmured quietly.

Brianna nodded and produced a wan smile, wishing that it had been Derrick who had stolen her heart instead of the raven-haired rogue who towered above her. As she struggled to prop herself up on her elbow to eat her meal, Seth tucked another pillow behind her head and dipped up a spoonful of stew to hand-feed her.

"You don't have to pamper me, Captain," Brianna grumbled before begrudgingly accepting the tasteless broth. "I'm not completely helpless."

Seth grinned mischievously as he forced more broth into her mouth. "I had always heard it said that the noble ladies of British society were born with silver spoons in their mouths. I was only attempting to treat you in the manner to which you have grown accustomed, madam."

Brianna scoffed at his cutting remark. "If you are insinuating that I have been coddled and spoiled, I shall take offense and might even resort to biting the hand that feeds me," she warned with a challenging smile brimming her lips.

Playfully pulling the spoon away, Seth peered at Brianna in feigned alarm. "Have I not suffered enough at your hands already? I've been battered, stabbed, clubbed, and threatened more times than I care to count. Surely you would not turn on me again, especially while I am playing your humble and devoted servant," he mocked with a rakish smile.

As she arched a dubious brow, she squirmed to settle herself in a more comfortable position. "And just why is that? Isn't it slightly out of character for you to portray the meek attendant? The very thought makes me a mite suspicious."

Seth's rugged face sobered a moment, but another smile quickly surfaced as he lifted the spoon to Brianna's lips. "'Tis the least I could do since you were whisked away by two of my men. 'Tis my moral obligation to nurse you back to health." His tone was heavily laden with sarcasm and his emerald eyes twinkled with amusement, drawing another skeptical glance from Brianna.

She pulled a face at him and reluctantly accepted a little more soup. A tide of weariness seemed to wash over her and she felt herself sinking into exhaustion. Her senses were not alert enough to continue bantering words with Seth. Raising a weak arm to protest the flow of broth, Brianna shook her head. "No more, kind sir," she said weakly. "I just want to sleep."

After Seth pulled the extra pillow from behind her head, he felt her feverish brow and frowned in concern. Brianna cocked her head and glanced up at him as a half-smile tugged at the corner of her mouth.

"Why, Captain, you look worried. Could it be that you actually care what happens to me, or is it that you just feel a bit guilty because those two scoundrels from your crew are responsible for my weakened condition?" she taunted in a raspy voice.

Seth propped his elbows on his knees and studied her for a long, silent moment as his emerald eyes focused on her soft, tempting lips. "Perhaps a little of both, my lovely witch," he conceded quietly, surprising Brianna with the hint of tenderness that laced his hushed voice. "And if I only had the recipe for the brew that you sorceresses can concoct, I would quickly stir up a pot of it and get you back on your feet," he added, carefully avoiding her pointed question.

"I fear that I must struggle along without the potion, sir. We witches have taken a solemn oath never to reveal our secrets to mortals." The light chuckle that ended her remark brought on another seizure of spasmodic coughs which she attempted to muffle. "Now run along and leave me be. I'm much too tired to match wits with you," she commanded with a weak flick of her wrist to shoo him on his way.

Seth nodded as he rose from his chair and watched Brianna squirm down in the quilts, turning her back to him. After he strolled across the room, he paused at the door and glanced over his shoulder at the petite form that was nestled in his bed. He had promised to meet Lance and two of their business associates for supper, but Brianna seemed so weak and helpless that he was afraid to leave her alone for any length of time. The meeting was important, but he felt a responsibility to Brianna. As Seth closed the door behind him, he heaved a troubled sigh. Where was the simple life he had known before his last voyage to England? Now Priscilla was raging like a mad hornet and Brianna had managed to embroil herself in another mishap, drawing every man she met under her mystical spell. Derrick was in love with her. That was obvious. Lance was fascinated by her and had made it clear that he did not intend to be a stranger to Brianna. And the whole damned crew idolized the witch who brought them good fortune and smooth sailing. And just what did he feel for Brianna? he questioned himself as he made his way to the deck. This odd, protective feeling that swept over him when he saw her so vulnerable and weak was playing havoc with his thoughts. He would save himself many headaches if he would make arrangements to send her back to Bristol and wash his hands of the high-spirited bundle of trouble. But Grant wanted to wait at least a month before disembarking and Seth would not dare to ship Brianna off without her brother for protection.

"Ah, Brianna," Seth muttered as he raked his fingers through his raven hair and hopelessly shook his head. "What am I to do with you? One minute I don't want to see you go and the next instant I regret even allowing such a thought to cross my mind."

From the dark shadows of the forest stepped a cloaked man with a stooped frame. His gaze swept the area with close inspection. When he saw the crumpled body lying face down, he swore under his breath. With a booted foot he rolled the unconscious man to his back to see the cold, pallid face of Lucas Patton. With considerable effort he dragged the body to the shack that lay hidden among the trees. When he managed to haul Patton onto the cot, he quickly searched his clothes, looking for a leather pouch, but he came up empty-handed.

Gibbons waited a few minutes, but when Patton didn't open his eyes, Gibbons became impatient. Since he hadn't been blessed with the ability to show compassion, he grabbed a bucket of water and doused the unconscious man.

Patton sputtered and slowly opened his eyes to see the grim, forbidding face that glowed in the dim lantern light. Gibbons's piercing gaze drained him of what little strength he had mustered to rouse.

"Where have you stashed the loot?" Gibbons growled, his graveled tone showing no sign of sympathy for Patton's weakened condition.

Patton's breath came out in a rush, forcing the words from his lips. "The pouch lies on the bottom of the ocean." He winced at the menacing sneer that curled Gibbons's lips.

"You bungling fool!"

"'Twas not my fault," Patton protested weakly, trying to draw himself up on an elbow. The task proved so difficult that he decided to remain where he was.

Gibbons scoffed at the excuse. "I've heard that before . . . from *ex*-smugglers. I have little patience for foolish mistakes," he assured Patton, his voice carrying a threatening hiss.

"But it was Lady Donnovan who caused us to lose the jewels," he hastened to explain.

Gibbons's graying brows formed a hard line across his wrinkled forehead. "There is no Lady Donnovan," he snorted. "Your fever has gotten the best of you." Another thought crossed his mind and a cynical frown settled deeper in his features. "Or have you devised this little charade, intending to keep the jewels for yourself? I warn you, Patton. Don't cross me. I have dealt with your kind before."

"There is no scheme," Patton fiercely insisted. "'Tis as I have said! Catlin and I rowed ashore, just as planned, but we thought to hold the captain's wife for ransom." When Gibbons's brow furrowed skeptically, Patton rushed on, "Donnovan married the wench during the voyage. And she's a witch with hair as black as the night. I swear I saw her fly from the mast of the *Mesmer*. She should have fallen to her death from high above the sails, but she escaped unscathed. And she even cast a spell on the schooner to bring her safely to port."

Gibbons eased back in his chair, staring thoughtfully at Patton. Donnovan had married? Lady Weatherby was the only one who was to claim that title. This new marriage would put a strain on the operation, he mused bitterly. He had long relied on Priscilla Weatherby to provide him with reason to make connections with the smugglers and buyers of the stolen goods.

Since Gibbons was sitting quietly, Patton took the opportunity to descibe the incident in detail. He had hoped that Gibbons would spare him once he had heard the whole of it, but the man became even more enraged.

"You were duped by a woman?" Gibbons's bitter laugh sent a cold chill sailing down Patton's spine. And then his breath froze in his throat when the darkly clad man reached for his whip.

"Perhaps this will remind you not to tamper with my orders—or with treacherous women. You will receive your just punishment now and I will deal with Lady Donnovan later," he assured Patton.

Fear gripped Patton as Gibbons rose and raised the whip above his head. The cry of agony that escaped his lips barely reached his ears before he lost touch with consciousness.

Patton couldn't be certain how much time had passed before he lifted heavy eyelids and then winced when he felt the raw, stinging gashes on his back. His face twisted in pain and hatred. He would find a way to repay Lady Donnovan for all that she had done, he vowed as he gritted his teeth to keep from screaming at the vision that was hovering above him. He would long bear the scars of dealing with that witch, but he would have his revenge if Gibbons didn't find her first.

Chapter Eighteen

Seth stopped short when he walked from his meeting with the merchants who intended to buy his cargo. Priscilla rose gracefully to her feet and walked across the lobby, pausing directly in front of him.

His brow arched mockingly. "I'm surprised to see you, my dear. I thought perhaps your last fit of temper would keep you a safe distance away from me."

Her hand slid up to the lapel of his coat, and she toyed with the rich fabric beneath her fingertips. "Nothing can keep me away from you, Seth. I have loved you as long as I can remember and I know you feel the same way." A sly smile pursed her moist lips as she lifted them in open invitation. "The times we shared . . . They are not easy for me to forget."

Seth clasped her hand in his and brought it up to his lips, brushing over it lightly. "Dear Priscilla, you always did have a way with men . . . all of them."

Her lip jutted out in an exaggerated pout, but then she transcended her irritation and smiled once more. "You always love to taunt me, don't you?" Before he could reply, Priscilla curled her hand around his elbow and urged him toward the steps. "I have something for you in my room. When I saw it, I knew it should belong to you."

As they ascended the stairs, Seth stared down at the perfect complexion that was framed with red-gold curls. A wave of memories chose that moment to converge on him and he smiled to himself.

As the door of Priscilla's room closed behind them, she hurried over to retrieve the gift she had selected for his homecoming. She turned back to the handsome sea captain, her eyes aglow with pleasure.

"For you, my love," she purred as she placed the small box in his hand.

Seth opened the package and lifted the gold time-piece that dangled from a chain. The back of the watch was engraved with a schooner sailing on a calm sea. "Thank you, Priscilla," he murmured appreciatively.

She came deliberately toward him, her gaze locked with his, searching their green depths for some sign that she still held the key to his heart. But with Seth it was difficult to tell. He could expertly guard his thoughts, allowing nothing to show in his gaze. As she wedged her way into his arms, she raised parted lips to him, her fingertips lightly tracing the sensuous curve of his mouth.

"It seems an eternity since we have been alone together. No words can begin to express the loneliness that has plagued me since I watched your ship depart so many months ago." She laid her head against the hard wall of his chest and heaved a longing sigh. "I came to Petersburg a week early, just in case you returned before expected. Each day I went to the dock and gazed out to sea, hoping to catch sight of that schooner on the horizon. You have been in my dreams each night and on my mind through the endless days that we have been apart." Priscilla drew away only far enough to study the handsome lines of his face. "And now you're home and all those days of worry and wanting are behind me. We are together again and nothing or no one can keep us apart. We were meant for each other." She reached up on tiptoe to place a feathery kiss on his lips. "Love me, Seth. I have dreamed of this night for months on end."

A mellow smile grazed Seth's lips as he gazed down at Priscilla. She had tempted and taunted him for years, playing on his desire for her. He had never been able to resist her charms, not from the minute he had first laid eyes on her. And now she was offering herself to him as she always did. Seth closed his eyes as her lips melted on his, his senses filled with the sweet perfume that she always wore. And when he withdrew, he could read the passion in her eyes, a passion that he had savored even through the bitterness that plagued him. It was the moment of truth. Now he would know if she still held that strange power over him.

Brianna's eyes fluttered open and she turned her head to the side, gazing up at the shadowed silhouette who had just poured himself a drink of brandy.

"Seth?" Brianna squinted at the dark form across the room.

"Nay, I'm afraid 'tis only me," Derrick replied as he glanced over at her. "Feeling better?" He strolled toward her and seated himself beside the bed. With a concerned frown knitting his brow, he reached out to brush his hand over her forehead, assuring himself that her fever hadn't skyrocketed.

"I suppose." She struggled up on one elbow and groaned miserably. Every muscle in her body seemed to rebel against any movement. "I feel as though every ounce of strength has deserted me," she breathed wearily.

"I would imagine it took all you had to make the long swim to shore. I am still amazed that you survived being exposed to that cold water," he remarked, his quiet voice laced with admiration for Brianna's feat. He could name no other that could have endured what Brianna had been through.

Brianna shrugged and then turned questioning eyes to the first mate who continued to watch her every move. "Where is the captain?"

"He had to go into town," Derrick replied absently. His thoughts were far too entangled with Brianna to pay much attention to the reason for her question.

Her brow furrowed suspiciously. "Why?"

Finally, Derrick concentrated on the conversation. "Seth had to meet with some of his associates, merchants who might be interested in buying part of the cargo. It might take them awhile to agree upon a price. But I can assure you that he would be by your side if not for his meeting."

She eyed Derrick skeptically. "More likely a rendezvous with that red-haired wench."

"You mean Priscilla Weatherby? Nay," he replied with a light chuckle. "I doubt that Seth planned to see her although Priscilla may throw another of her tantrums if he attempts to avoid her."

Brianna's brow arched quizzically but then she decided not to inquire about the woman. She was in no mood for the subject of Priscilla to be discussed at length. "I want to go up on deck," she announced determinedly.

"I don't think you're up to that yet. You just said you were weak," Derrick reminded her as he watched her struggle to her feet.

"I'm going if I have to crawl part of the way." Her chin tilted defiantly as she pulled on a robe and began to weave her way across the dark room.

Derrick hopelessly shook his head and drank the last of his brandy. "I swear you are by far the stubbornest woman I have ever come across."

Brianna opened the door and leaned unsteadily against the casing while she forced a shallow smile. "Then I hope you will not waste your time and mine by

295

arguing. My temper has a short fuse tonight."

Quickly grabbing a quilt and crossing the room in hurried strides, Derrick swept her up in his arms and carried her up the steps. When they passed one of the sailors, Derrick requested that he bring Brianna's supper tray to the deck. After finding a comfortable chair and wrapping the quilt closely about her, Derrick leaned back against the railing and crossed his arms over his broad chest.

"And now, madam, are you planning to take another cold dip tonight or will you be content to sit on deck and view the ocean from afar?"

Brianna chuckled as she glanced up at Derrick's handsome face, watching the moonlight glisten on his flaxen hair. "I am satisfied to stay where I am," she assured him. "And I promise not to cause you any more trouble."

"If I don't cross you, that is," he finished for her, flashing her a wry smile. "All I have to do is give you your way and you will be compatible."

Her eyes twinkled merrily as she displayed an impish grin. "You seem to know me well, Derrick. Perhaps I should have married you instead of Seth. I think you learn more quickly than he does."

A rueful smile hovered on his lips as he regarded the enchanting goddess who sat on her throne, nestled in quilts. "Aye, perhaps you should have, Brianna," he murmured softly.

When McGowan swaggered toward them Brianna raised her gaze to meet the salty old seaman.

"Here, lass, I brought your supper tray." After he had placed it on her lap he leaned back against the rail and studied her carefully. "Are you feeling up to snuff yet?"

Brianna nodded slightly as she lifted the lid on the tray. The aroma of the food made her realize that she was starving. Eagerly, she picked up her fork and tasted her hash.

"I've been wondering about your swim to shore," McGowan began as he lit his pipe and drew lightly upon it.

"I suppose you're going to ask her if a merman came along and offered her a lift," Derrick snorted caustically.

McGowan offered the first mate an indulgent smile. "Nay, lad, sea witches manage by their own devices." His gaze slid to Brianna and he gave her a wink. "The rest of the crew was ready to give you up for lost, but I knew you would find your way. I came to the conclusion a few weeks ago that you had some unusual powers. It came as no surprise to me that you survived the mishap."

Suddenly, he turned his attention to Derrick and raised a bushy brow. "Have you ever seen a merman, lad?"

"Nay, I can't claim that I have." Derrick suppressed a smile, knowing Brianna would ask the inevitable, which she did. He would have preferred to have Brianna all to himself, but McGowan had baited her into hearing another of his stories.

"Have you?" Brianna glanced up from her plate, her gaze quizzical.

"Aye, twice," he affirmed with a nod. "But a mermaid, only once. I was sailing on the *Lady Sarah*. We had been at sea two months. Two long months," he recalled as he sent a smoke ring curling about his gray head. "We had been besieged with storms. One night at dusk, a mermaid swam alongside our schooner, singing a chant that would lull a wailing baby to sleep. The likes of her song you've never heard, the tune so soft and sweet. . . ." He breathed a sigh and then hummed the serene melody. "There was among us a

297

young lad who became enamored with her lovely face, unconcerned that scales covered her lower half. The lady of the sea kept calling out to him, pleading with him to come live with her. We tried to tell him that she was only searching for a soul and that the only way a mermaid could possess one was to marry a mortal. But the lad could not see her deceit. He could not look past her bewitching face." McGowan eased back and crossed his feet in front of him, taking a long draw on his pipe, holding Brianna in suspense.

"Well, did he follow her?" she questioned impatiently.

A wry grin lifted the corners of his mouth upward. "Aye. He paid no attention to the rest of us and dived into the sea to follow her. And then the winds began to blow, the waves pitching and tossing about, taking us off course, and we never saw him again."

Derrick sent the sailor a dubious frown. "The boy must not have had both of his oars in the water if he wouldn't heed your advice," he smirked, not swallowing a word of the tale.

"Nay," McGowan disagreed. "He was a bright lad, but mermaids, like sea sirens, can cast a spell over a man with her song and the lad fell in love at first sight."

As McGowan ambled away, Derrick's attention focused on Brianna's every movement, bewitched by all she did. He frowned thoughtfully, wondering if perhaps the old storyteller was right. Brianna had the gift of attracting a man with little more than one of her smiles. Although her face was drawn, her ebony hair in a tangled cascade that fell like a cape about her shoulders, she was still one of the loveliest women he had yet to meet. Her amber eyes glowed with that mystical charm that could captivate all who looked upon her.

Derrick found himself remembering the feel of her trim body against his, the gentle fragrance of jasmine that often filled his senses when she was near, and the sweetness of her lips when he had dared to kiss her. Aye, he would have dived overboard if that gorgeous face had surfaced from the black depths of the sea . . . and without regret. He wouldn't even put up a fight if she requested his soul as well.

Heaving a despairing sigh, Derrick turned away to lean his elbows on the rail and gaze out at the lights of Petersburg. He would never know Brianna's passions or claim her as his own. He would have to be content to share only her friendship, the brotherly type, he mused sullenly. And that was no easy task. The more time he spent with her, the more difficult it was to control the desire to take her in his arms.

Seth never hesitated to ask Derrick to keep an eye on Brianna, knowing how he savored her nearness. But the sweet torture of it was enough to chip at his sanity. How Seth could even think of dividing his time between Brianna and Priscilla was beyond him. There was no comparison. As attractive as Priscilla was, she could not hold a candle to the dark-haired beauty with those mischievous golden eyes.

"Derrick?" Brianna arched a quizzical brow. "What are you pondering so seriously?" She set the tray on the deck and peered at his broad back. He had been extremely quiet that evening, remote and pensive. She could not fathom the cause, but each time he smiled at her there was a hint of remorse, as if something weighed heavily on his thoughts, preoccupying him.

When he made no reply, she demanded his attention by reaching out to tug at the hem of his peacoat. "Derrick? What are you thinking about?" she persisted.

Her question finally cut its way into his musings and his shoulder lifted in a nonchalant shrug. He allowed himself a quick glance in her direction and gave her a feeble smile. "I'm afraid 'twas nothing that would make for interesting conversation, Brianna. I was just day-dreaming."

A phaeton rumbled along Dock Street and then came to a halt. Brianna and Derrick glanced up when the sound of hooves on the cobbled street broke the silence of the night. A woman's reckless laughter floated up to them. Brianna's eyes narrowed angrily when Seth stepped from the coach. Damn him!

"I thought you said the good captain had a business meeting," she said dryly, casting the first mate an annoyed glare.

"He did, but it appears that Priscilla managed to find him," Derrick replied. "That wench doesn't give up easily. She has been after Donnovan for the last two years. I think it has become old habit with her."

"What are you doing out of bed?" Seth questioned as he ambled up the plank to find the couple sitting on deck.

"I'm doing as I damn well please and obviously you have adopted the same policy," she snapped, sarcasm dripping from every word. Brianna turned a dazzling smile to Derrick. "Would you help me back to my cabin and see that my tub is readied, sir? Since you have frowned on an evening swim in the sea, I should like a warm bath."

As Brianna rose unsteadily to her feet, Derrick bit back a grin. Brianna wrapped herself in his embrace as he swept her into his arms. Derrick inwardly chuckled at the envious glaze in Seth's eyes. Seth was getting exactly what he deserved, Derrick mused as he carried Brianna to the captain's quarters. If Seth would trade an evening with Brianna for Priscilla's company then he was every kind of fool.

As Derrick sat her on the edge of the bunk, she placed a light kiss on his lips. "Thank you, Derrick. I truly enjoyed our evening together. I had abandoned

300

the hope of finding my knight in shining armor, but it seems that chivalry is not dead after all."

Sayer chuckled aloud and returned her kiss, unconcerned that Seth was standing in the open door. "Madam, I will carry you off on my stallion as soon as you give your consent. We shall find King Arthur's castle together." With an exaggerated bow and a subtle wink, Derrick backed away and spun on his heels while Brianna giggled in merriment.

Seth seemed disinterested in the intentional display of affection as he moved out of Derrick's way. "Thank you for entertaining Brianna while I was in town," he commented blandly.

"The pleasure was all mine, Captain," Derrick assured him with a rakish smile and then closed the door behind him.

"Are Grant and Sabrina still on board?" Brianna questioned tightly, attempting to mask her irritation.

Seth strolled over to the desk and eased back against the edge to light his cheroot. "Nay, they decided to stay at the hotel. I saw them this evening. They said to wish you well," he replied glibly as he pulled the cravat from his neck and carelessly tossed it over the back of the chair. "They seemed to be enjoying their stay in Petersburg and the comforts offered at the inn."

"I think I'll join them tomorrow. I'm tired of having the bowels of this ship for scenery," Brianna sniffed disgustedly. "I should hate to think that I have traveled all the way across the ocean and never had the opportunity to view the colonies."

"I don't think that would be a wise idea, madam." A slight frown gathered on his heavy brows. "We have found no sign of Catlin and Patton. Until we do, I want you to remain on this ship at night where I can keep an eye on you. If you feel well enough to venture out in the morning, you can tour Petersburg to your heart's con-

301

tent," he offered graciously.

"I intend to be back on my feet," she assured him determinedly. "And I shall see Petersburg on the back of a horse. I have waited an eternity to ride again."

"I don't think you should plan on riding until you have regained your strength," he insisted as he sent Brianna a quick glance.

Her brow arched tauntingly as a mischievous smile curved the corners of her mouth upward. "Are you thinking of my welfare, dear husband, or is it your reputation that you are afraid may be tainted if I ride through town in the same fashion that I galloped through the park in Bristol?"

Seth chuckled heartily. It seemed that Brianna was well on her way to recovery. She was in true form once again—ornery, challenging, and rebellious. "Do you plan to race through the streets, mumbling incantations and cackling like a demented witch, or was a quiet, sightseeing tour what you had in mind, my dear wife?" The endearment dripped heavily with mockery and Brianna bristled in annoyance.

"It all depends on my mood," she retorted flippantly.

"Then perhaps I should come along with you. If perchance you make a fool of yourself, I should hate to miss the scene." Seth strolled to the cabinet to pour himself a brandy, chuckling quietly while Brianna pulled a face at his shaking shoulders.

"You may continue to do as you wish, Captain. I will neither request nor deny your company. As a matter of fact, it makes little difference to me what you do," she informed him icily.

"How very generous you are, my dear." Seth bowed and then raised his glass in toast to the bedraggled beauty. "This marriage of ours was most certainly made in heaven."

"Made in heaven, perhaps," Brianna agreed with a

caustic smirk, "but unfortunately, it has taken up residence in hell."

"Come now, Brianna," Seth mocked dryly. "It has not been all fire and torture."

"Nor has it been a haven that angels would envy," she countered. "Despite your high opinion of yourself, I don't think you are the perfect spouse!"

"And I suppose you think you are?" Seth asked haughtily as he sent a lazy smoke ring floating above his dark head. "Name one instance in which you have enriched my life with your praise and devotion to only me. Well," he snorted impatiently, shooting Brianna an accusing glance. "You cannot name even one because—"

"Captain?" came a voice from outside the door.

Seth had begun to detest doors; it seemed someone was forever interrupting them by rapping incessantly. He would be thankful when they were off of the *Mesmer* so he would not be hassled with that constant tapping on his cabin door!

"Come in, for God's sake. What is it?" he snapped rudely while Brianna giggled at his sour temper and said a silent prayer that she was not forced to answer Seth's challenge.

A steady line of sailors filed into the chamber, nodding a greeting to Brianna as they poured their buckets of warm water into the tub. Seth cursed under his breath. Brianna was always supplied with whatever she needed. She never had to ask twice. Damn that wench! If she had suggested mutiny, Seth would have undoubtedly found himself tossed overboard before she had time to finish making her dastardly request. If he had known Catlin and Patton were planning to kidnap her, he should have paid them for their efforts and assisted them so they wouldn't have fouled it up!

Brianna produced a blinding smile and graciously

thanked all those who had become her devoted servants. Seth turned his back and downed his brandy and promptly refilled his empty glass. When the crowd left the room, Brianna sauntered toward the tub, removed her robe, letting it fall to the floor at her ankles, leaving only Captain Barton's shirt, which she was still wearing, extending past her hips. When her long, shapely legs were revealed so temptingly, Seth's hawkish gaze devoured every inch of bare flesh. She was deliberately taunting him again and they both knew it. Seth reached for the bottle to pour yet another drink, spilling its contents over the rim because his eyes were not tending to his task, but rather to the wench who was about to shed the last of her garments.

"You may leave now, Captain," Brianna commanded as she unbuttoned the linen shirt and left it hanging loosely about her, revealing the gentle curve of her breasts. *Let him gawk,* she mused wickedly. That was what he deserved after spending the evening with that other wench. He could devour Brianna with his hungry eyes, but he would have none of her, she thought spitefully.

"I have been gone all evening, madam. I have no intention of being ousted from my own cabin, not even by you," Seth assured her as he wiped up the brandy he had spilled on the desk, his gaze never wavering from her shapely form.

"Suit yourself," she replied glibly as she shrugged off the shirt and stepped into the warm bath. A pleasureful moan escaped her lips as the soothing liquid melted away her aches and pains. She had intended to taunt him mercilessly, but she put aside her vengeful thoughts as she sank into the tub.

Seth was aware of her ploy, but the effect Brianna had on him was nonetheless devastating. And then suddenly it seemed that she no longer cared that he was in

304

the room at all. He eased back in his chair and slowly sipped his brandy while he watched her splashing playfully like a small child who could find enjoyment in whatever she was doing.

Pouring himself another brandy, Seth eased down in his chair and drew the papers from his desk drawer to complete the bookwork. As Brianna held the sponge over her head and allowed the water to trickle down her arm and shoulder, her golden eyes sparkled delightedly. Seth had to force himself to look down at the parchment in front of him. The sight of her full breasts glistening with beads of water was branded on his mind and the numbers of the ledger that lay before him seemed to disappear as the image of the bewitching temptress materialized on the paper. Seth shook his head, attempting to break the spell, but it was hopeless. Finally he lifted the ledger onto his lap and turned to face the wall. If he was to keep his mind on business he had to divert his eyes from the delicious witch who was steaming in her kettle.

After Brianna washed her hair, she glanced about her through blurry eyes. "Seth, could I have a towel please?" she asked as she twisted the mass of wet curls up on top of her head.

Seth glanced over his shoulder and rolled his eyes. She sat with her arms folded over the edge of the tub and her head resting on her hands, looking much too lovely as she waited patiently for him to obey her request. All she thought she had to do was to produce one of those blinding smiles and he would kneel at her feet, Seth mused resentfully. Well, he was not her pawn nor her slave. She had a whole damned ship full of eager servants. And, by God, he was *not* one of them!

He smiled tightly. There was nothing pleasant about his expression and Brianna frowned curiously at him as she wiped the water from her eyes. "Retrieve it yourself, my dear. I have better things to do than fetch and heel."

"I thought you were going to play the meek servant," she mocked. "So much for promises. Apparently you make them as easily as you break them."

"You seem to have enough servants without adding my name to the list. Why don't you call in one of your houseboys to do your bidding?" he suggested sarcastically. "I'm sure any of them would delight in obeying your request."

Brianna's chin tilted defiantly. She sent Seth a blatant go-to-hell look that was armed with fire. By damned, she would show that scoundrel! A deliciously wicked grin parted her lips as she rose from the tub. Seth cocked a wondering brow as she sauntered toward him. She curled up on his lap and shivered uncontrollably, purposely soaking his clothes.

Seth had not expected such a reaction from the unpredictable vixen. A derogatory comment meant to prick his pride would not have surprised him, but for Brianna to come to him, seeking warmth, caught him off guard. She cuddled against his hard chest like a contented kitten and his arms instinctively came about her.

The cold shiver that flew down Brianna's spine instantly reminded her of the chilling swim she had made in the darkness. Climbing from Seth's lap she hurried to the bed to wrap herself in a tight cocoon of quilts while Seth peered at her with quizzical green eyes. One moment she was nestling in his arms and the next instant she was cowering on the bed like a frightened child.

"What's the matter, Brianna?" he questioned as he eased down beside her on the bed and cupped her chin in his hand.

"I'm so cold that I cannot stop shaking," she managed hoarsely.

Gently wrapping his arms about her, Seth pulled her onto his lap, nuzzling his face against the top of her head. They sat in silence for a few minutes, both strangely content. Brianna slowly raised her gaze and rested her head against Seth's sturdy shoulder, studying his rugged features.

"It seems that I cause you constant distress, Captain," she murmured quietly, lightly tracing her fingertips across his lips. "First I show up on the *Mesmer* after you thought you were rid of me and now I have returned to disrupt your affair with Priscilla. I hope you were able to explain the arrangement to her."

Seth chuckled lightly and then shrugged. Brianna was unable to read the expression in his emerald eyes. Was Priscilla the woman that Seth could not forget, the one who claimed his heart?

"Priscilla understands the situation explicitly," he assured her.

Brianna attempted to squirm from his lap, but Seth's arms clamped tightly about her, preventing any further movement. "I'm fine now, Captain. You may let me go."

A mellow smile crept to Seth's lips. "You have tempted and taunted me this evening and you will pay for your mischievousness. I do not intend to let you go. Not yet anyway."

Seth pulled Brianna down beside him and reached over to snuff out the lantern before removing the quilts from her velvety flesh. As Seth's mouth covered hers in an unusually gentle kiss, Brianna closed her eyes. All thoughts fled her mind. It made no difference that Priscilla was his mistress, or that she might have had some claim on his heart. Right now she needed what protection and tenderness Seth could offer. When his skillful hands moved across her flesh, a warm, delicious tremor skitted across her skin. She brushed her fingers

307

across the dark hair of his chest, parting the linen shirt that gapped open to his waist. A blazing flame of desire set their pulses racing. Both Brianna and Seth were swept up in the breathless urgency that consumed them. Seth came to her with an unquenchable need to become a part of her, tasting her passions, giving of himself to the lovely witch who could bring him unbound rapture. As the world about him exploded in a myriad of colors, he groaned and clutched her close, wondering what strange power this witch-angel had over him. And then they were one, soaring to passion's lofty pinnacle, viewing that boundless horizon that they had seen so many times before. But each time was like the first as they remained suspended in timeless ecstasy.

A steady flow of tears burst from Brianna's eyes as the wild sensation sent a continuous wave of pleasure rushing through her veins. Seth brushed away the tears from her flushed cheeks while a satisfied smile curved his lips. He could not claim her free spirit or control her feisty temperament, but he had learned to master her desires. It was always good with Brianna. Teaching her the ways of passion had become his coveted fantasy. He had made her his own, and no others had accomplished that feat with this uninhibited temptress. She was his alone.

"Brianna," Seth whispered huskily. "Do you love me?" A ghost of a smile hovered on his lips, haunting Brianna with its presence.

Pride turned the key that locked the tender words that might have flowed from her heart and she answered evasively. "I just did, Captain." Her raspy voice was laced with mischief. "Do you love me?" Brianna's amber eyes glowed with a mysterious sparkle as she toyed with the raven hair that laid against the nape of his neck.

Seth chuckled and hopelessly shook his head. "I knew better than to expect an honest response from a ruthless witch."

"And I knew better than to expect any answer at all from a frivolous rogue," she countered. She paused a long moment, and then sighed weakly as Seth rolled beside her. Glancing up into the darkness, Brianna continued in a quiet voice. "If I loved you, I would never allow our agreement to stand. I could not share you with another woman, knowing that she had experienced the same passion that I have found in your arms. You would be the only man whom I would yearn to touch. I wouldn't wish to know the pain of sharing you with another and the torture of giving my love to a man who could not return it and value it within his heart. Perhaps it is part of a childish dream, but if I gave my soul to the man I loved, I would expect him to do the same without regret."

"It sounds as though your love would be extremely demanding, madam," Seth teased with a mocking smile. "Is there anything you do not require of the man who earns this binding love?"

Brianna squirmed away so that she could gaze up at Seth's dark face. "Nay, Captain," she assured him. "If he truly loved me, he would not be intimidated by my requests. Perhaps that is why I have been so particular in the past. I was looking for a man who could be both a friend and lover. And what of you, Seth?" she questioned curiously. "Do you expect the woman you love to be devoted to only you?"

Seth pressed a light kiss to Brianna's honeyed lips. "You are much too inquisitive, my lovely witch. If I shared my innermost thoughts with you, I fear the results would be disastrous. I would probably regret it later."

Brianna pulled a face at his response. "You must

think that I'm incredibly wicked," she pouted as her bottom lip jutted out. "What have I ever done to merit your total distrust?"

"Punched me squarely in the jaw, used another's name instead of your own, knocked me over the head and escaped while I—"

"That's enough," Brianna breathed in exasperation as she turned her back to him. "I suppose I cannot condemn you for being so cynical. I have given you very little reason for you to consider me a friend."

"Nay, you haven't, Brianna," Seth agreed as he pulled the quilts about them and settled himself in a more comfortable position. "I would trust you with my life and any responsibility that I could name because of your cunning, but not with my heart." Seth scoffed bitterly. "I have seen too many men brought to their knees by affairs of the heart. I have no desire to be played for a fool. Before I would admit to love, I would be absolutely certain that the wench was sincere."

Brianna chuckled at his remark. "I am positive now that you have been in love at least once. No man could be so skeptical unless he had suffered an unpleasant experience. You sound just like Grant before he found Sabrina." Propping up on her elbow, Brianna stared down at Seth's shadowed face. "One day you will fall in love again, Seth Donnovan," she assured him confidently. "You will fight against it, but nevertheless it will happen. Would you like to know the maiden's name who is destined to claim your heart, who will take your soul even when you would wish to protect it?"

"Lord, don't tell me this witch also has the gift of prophecy along with all of her other unusual talents," he groaned as he shot Brianna a quick sidelong glance. Somehow he could almost believe it.

"But, of course," she replied saucily. "Now are you interested in knowing the lady's name or do you prefer to stumble blindly ahead?"

Brianna's light, playful mood was becoming contagious. Seth found himself unwillingly smiling up at the enchanting lass. "All right, madam. Since I doubt that you will grant me peace until you have completed your little game, out with it. Who is this irresistible wench who will have me groveling at her feet like some obedient pup?"

Her amber eyes glowed in the dim moonlight that sprayed across the room. Brianna leaned close to press a light, taunting kiss on his full lips. "Me," she whispered seductively. "Ironically, one day you will find that no matter how much trouble I have caused you, it was worth the suffering. It was not coincidence that we continued to meet in Bristol. 'Twas fate," Brianna assured him as she traced gentle kisses across his rugged cheek to his lips. "Mark my words, Captain. You will come to love me, but in the meantime, you will love me now."

Her arousing caresses kindled a flame of desire. If he were to be cursed by this temptress, then so be it. The feel of her satiny flesh molded to his was enough to spur his passions into wild abandon. When Brianna offered herself to him, he could never seem to deny himself the pleasures that awaited him. She was like an intoxicating brew to which he had become addicted. Although he knew he should beware of her, he could not resist the heady sensation that consumed him when he took her in his arms and sailed on rapture's gentle sea.

Again they tasted passion's sweet nectar and floated on the rippling waves that cradled them far from reality's shore. Contentment faded into pleasant dreams that knew no beginning and no end.

Chapter Nineteen

When Brianna was dressed in her best gown, Seth appraised her with a dubious frown. "Is that what you intend to wear to town?"

Brianna rested her hands on her hips and squared her shoulders, meeting his gaze with fiery golden eyes. "'Tis the best I have, sir. If you are too humiliated to be seen with me, then I will go alone. I certainly have no wish to embarrass you," she mocked dryly.

An amused chortle floated from his lips as he strolled around the hot-tempered wench and thoughtfully touched his finger to his chin, critically regarding her apparel. "I suppose I could lower myself to be seen with you since my reputation has already been tainted."

Brianna shot him a disdainful glare. "I had originally planned to spend my time in the hull of this ship and I did not bring along my most fashionable dresses for the voyage," she grumbled in irritation.

Seth chuckled again as he pulled Brianna into his arms and placed a fleeting kiss to her unresponsive lips. "Come along, witch. We have much to do."

As Seth grasped her elbow, Brianna reluctantly followed, wishing that her gowns had not suffered so miserably from the trip and from her lack of care. Once they were in the phaeton that rumbled through the streets of Petersburg, Brianna forgot all except the bustle of activity around her. She was caught up in her new surroundings.

"Why are we stopping here?" she asked as she raised her eyes to Seth. "You promised to take me riding."

Seth stepped from the coach and quickly pulled her down beside him. "We will ride after we pick up a few necessary supplies," he assured her with a sly smile.

Brianna's brows furrowed in confusion as she glanced up at the sign that hung over the shop. Although she adamantly protested Seth's intentions of purchasing her some new gowns, Seth ignored her and selected several dresses and two riding habits that suited his expensive taste. As they walked from the boutique, heavily laden with packages, Brianna dropped her head and heaved a sigh.

"That really wasn't necessary, Captain. I have more gowns in Bristol than I can ever wear. I don't wish for you to spend your money on me when I—"

"Brianna," Seth snapped brusquely. "If I choose to purchase you some decent clothes, then I will do it. And in the future I would greatly appreciate it if you would cease from chastising me. You have grown accustomed to pursuing that annoying talent."

Brianna gasped irately as Seth whisked her into the coach and securely slammed the door. "If you think just because we have set foot on *your* stomping ground that I am going to charade as some mealy-mouthed twit, then you are gravely mistaken, sir!" she informed him in a harsh tone. "I am not some empty-headed doll that you can dress in some fashionable gown that *you* have selected and then display me to your friends. If you think my behavior has been scandalous in the past, then you better hold on to your hat, Captain, because you haven't seen anything yet!" Brianna's voice seemed to thunder about them as her full breasts heaved against the tight bodice of blue silk with each angry breath she took.

Seth's retort was made in the same crisp, explosive

tone that Brianna had used. She bristled in annoyance when he glared down at her. "You are my wife and I expect you to act like the genteel lady that your noble breeding dictates. If I purchase you a gift, the very *least* you could do is show a little appreciation," he sneered hatefully.

Brianna leaned back in the cushioned seat and displayed a mischievous grin, delighting in agitating him. "We made a bargain, Captain," she taunted. "The terms will be kept as they were made. If I choose to act like an uncivilized heathen, then I shall. If you provoke me, I will even stoop to making a spectacle of myself, just to spite you. You were the one who said I could even ride through the streets like Lady Godiva if it met my whim."

The anger in Seth's emerald eyes dwindled to mild amusement as he crossed his arms on his broad chest and studied the stubborn chit for a long, quiet moment. "She had a cause, madam," he reminded Brianna. "Lady Godiva wanted her husband to lift the taxes from the people of the community. For you to make such a ride would serve no other purpose than to astound the good citizens of Petersburg."

"Nay, Captain, I would have a cause. I would be protesting my dear husband's attempt to dominate me," Brianna assured him saucily.

"All right, madam," Seth conceded. "We did make a bargain and my grandfather's curse has finally come to haunt me. I probably deserve to be saddled with such an insolent misfit." He swept his top hat from his head and bowed mockingly from his sitting position. "I have been corrected. You are free to do as you wish."

Brianna nodded haughtily, acknowledging his caustic apology. "Thank you, Captain, but I wonder how long your fiery temper will allow you to keep your word."

"*My* fiery temper?" he repeated incredulously. How

314

could that little spitfire accuse him of being quick to anger when she could explode over little or nothing? Seth hopelessly shook his head and rolled his eyes in disbelief. Andrew had indeed found him a wench who could prick him with her sharp tongue. The witch could transform herself into a serpent by merely blinking an eye. She could easily sink her poisonous fangs into his controlled patience, attempting to see just how immune her victim might be. "Perhaps now is the time to ask how long you plan to remain in the colonies, madam. If I am aware of how long I will be required to endure your companionship, maybe I can pace myself and manage to salvage my sanity."

Brianna always delighted in getting under his skin. His snide remark did nothing to dampen her feisty spirit. "I will leave when Grant and Sabrina set sail. I have not yet discussed the matter with him," she replied with a careless shrug and then playfully patted his clean-shaven cheek. "Cheer up, my dear devoted husband. You will not be plagued with me for an eternity."

Seth muttered under his breath. One moment he could not wait to be rid of her and the next instant he didn't want her to leave. Never in his life had he been so indecisive. "Just don't cross me too often, Brianna," he warned in a tight voice. "I can be a tyrant, as you well know. The bargain stands as it was made. If you attempt to annoy me to the limit of my patience, you will have hell to pay."

Turning steady amber eyes to him, Brianna appraised the dashing rogue who was dressed in tailor-made brown velvet. "I can also be a tyrant, Captain," she assured him flippantly. "Perhaps we should both take heed and beware of each other."

Seth released a derisive snort. "I rather doubt that precaution is one of your well-developed qualities, madam."

315

This bantering had gone far enough and Brianna chose to put an end to it. She was anticipating her ride through Petersburg and would not allow their arguments to spoil it. Leaning slowly toward Seth, she placed light, provocative kisses on his lips. "I fear you are right," she whispered against his sensuous mouth while her breasts pressed wantonly against the muscled wall of his chest. "I have always been a bit impulsive. I often react without giving thought to my behavior."

Here was yet another moment when Seth had no intention of allowing Brianna to return to Bristol. When she displayed such affection he was reluctant to stay a safe distance away. When the carriage came to a halt in front of the hotel, Seth lifted Brianna out beside him and handed her one of the packages.

"Go change into your riding habit. I have a matter to attend to and then I will come back for you."

A blinding smile radiated from her face as she gazed into the fathomless emerald pools. Brianna reached up on tiptoe to place a fleeting kiss on his parted lips before spinning away to dash into the lobby. As Brianna started up the steps to Grant's room, her gaze narrowed at the disturbing sight of Priscilla who stood on the landing above her. Priscilla looked as fresh and dainty as a spring flower in her pale yellow gown of silk and lace. Brianna felt like a wilted weed in her wrinkled dress that was worse for wear. The reddish-gold curls were neatly arranged on top of Priscilla's head and a delicate string of pearls lay against the creamy skin of her neck. Brianna inwardly cringed when she finished comparing herself with the woman. It was little wonder that Seth found this wench so desirable. She was graceful, attractive, and very shapely.

When Priscilla looked down her nose at Lady Donnovan, Brianna raised her proud chin, forced a faint smile, and continued up the stairs. A strained moment passed between them as they carefully surveyed each other, neither liking what they saw.

"Hello, Priscilla." It was the best she could manage without being impolite.

Priscilla smirked haughtily. "You really don't think that you can keep your husband very long, do you?" she inquired rudely.

Brianna bristled at the woman's audacity. If Priscilla thought she could intimidate Brianna, she had sorely misjudged her competition. Brianna had spoken in anger the previous day when she had told Priscilla that she did not want Seth. If Priscilla thought Lady Donnovan would bow out gracefully, she would be in for one hell of a surprise. "I can keep Seth at my beck and call for as long as it suits my whim. You, Priscilla, are not his wife, I am," she reminded her with a smug grin. "You would do well to keep that in mind."

"You may be his wife, but I am the one he loves and he always has," Priscilla taunted cruelly. "You may claim his name, but I possess his heart. Each time he wants me I will go to him. Don't be too disappointed if Seth only wishes to sleep when he comes home to his *own* bed."

Brianna was tempted to slap the arrogant expression off of Priscilla's face, but she squelched the urge. "And don't be surprised if Seth has no time to spend with you, Priscilla. I will be keeping him much too busy at home for him to have the strength to rap on your door." Although she spoke quietly her voice was laced with determination.

"I don't give up easily, Brianna, especially when it comes to getting what I want. He only married you to punish me for something that I did many years ago. He has never forgiven me. He always comes back to me no matter how far he roams. He will quickly tire of you and I will be waiting with open arms, just as I always have."

"I'm afraid that I can't share your confidence and I

317

do hope you can accept the pain of losing Seth permanently." Brianna picked up the front of her skirt and started up the stairs, but Priscilla's words brought her to an abrupt halt.

"My room is the first door on the left, Lady Donnovan. Your husband was there just last night. If you would care to use my chamber to change into something more presentable, I won't mind."

Brianna's face turned red with rage, but she didn't allow Priscilla to see that she was infuriated. Without glancing back, Brianna clenched her fist, crushing the edge of the package that she carried in her hand, squared her shoulders, and ascended the stairs to find Grant's room. When her brother questioned her on her black mood, Brianna snapped at him and refused to explain what had upset her. She quickly changed into her riding habit and exited before she took her frustrations out on him. There were many things she wished to discuss with Grant and Sabrina, but the confrontation with Priscilla had ruined her morning. All she wanted to do was to ride into the wind.

Standing at the top of the staircase, Brianna watched Priscilla saunter toward Seth who had just appeared at the door.

"Are you coming to my room tonight?" she questioned provocatively.

"I don't know what I'll be doing this evening," Seth answered blandly, his expression revealing nothing of his thoughts.

Priscilla curled a dainty finger under his chin and smiled sweetly. "I'll be waiting for you."

The nerve of that woman! And Seth! He was no better! Perhaps Priscilla was right. Maybe Seth could never turn her away. Brianna was at odds with herself. Part of her wanted to fight for Seth's love and part of her wanted to run. Mustering her courage she started down the steps and brushed past Seth on her way out onto the street.

Seth started to speak but when he saw the murderous gleam in Brianna's flaming gold eyes, his breath caught in his throat. And then he smiled wryly. Brianna must have seen Priscilla talking to him. Was it jealousy that he had seen in her burning gaze? With Brianna he could never be certain, for the slightest incident could cause her to breathe fire. Priscilla may have nothing to do with her anger. Perhaps Grant had informed her that they were traveling to the Donnovan plantation and she was furious about it.

When Brianna stepped outside she spied the magnificent black stallion that was tethered in front of the inn. She moved toward him to rub his soft muzzle, but the steed jerked his head startledly. As Brianna spoke quietly to him, he accepted her gentle caress.

"He's yours, Brianna," Seth murmured as he stepped up behind her.

Brianna's brow arched quizzically as she glanced back at Seth. Why had he given her this beautiful steed? He cared nothing for her. The stallion looked so much like Thor that a sudden pang of homesickness dampened her mood. Those carefree days were gone forever, she mused sullenly. She quickly pulled up onto the steed's back, straddled the sidesaddle, and urged the stallion into a gallop with a cloud of dust at her heels. Seth swung up on his big chestnut to pursue her.

As Lance Barton strolled down the boardwalk, he paused when he saw Brianna, dressed in her green velvet riding habit, perched on the muscular steed. A wry smile surfaced on his face as he watched Seth trailing along behind her. A reckless chuckle escaped his lips as he watched them disappear at the corner. Donnovan would have his hands full attempting to keep a tight rein on that little vixen, he thought to himself. Brianna was as spirited as the stallion she rode. Why had Seth allowed her to take such an animal for a mount? He had been with Donnovan the previous day when he purchased that fancy piece of horseflesh at a high price, but Lance had never expected Seth to allow his wife to ride such a steed.

When Petersburg was behind her and there was open road ahead, Brianna reached up with her free hand to pull the pins from her hair, releasing the ebony strands to fly out behind her. With the wind in her face, she urged the stallion to a faster clip, thrilling to the sound of his powerful hooves pounding the hardened earth. All of her troubled thoughts seemed to take flight and she reveled in the exhilarating emotion that raised her sinking spirits. It had been an eternity since she had been able to ride. The strange new land that surrounded her did much to add to her enjoyment.

Suddenly, a firm hand grabbed at her reins, pulling the steed to an abrupt halt. Brianna glared at Seth in annoyance. He had invaded her private world and she was not ready to let the moment end.

"Let me go!" she ordered gruffly. "I've waited far too long to enjoy riding and I have no intention of settling for a short jaunt."

Seth's emerald eyes twinkled in amusement. It was as if Brianna had come to life once again. Here was the wicked witch with the blazing amber eyes in her own natural habitat. "Couldn't you enjoy your ride at a slower pace? 'Tis difficult to sightsee when the world is flying past you so quickly."

Brianna's long, sultry lashes brushed against her cheeks as she toyed with the reins. "I've done it again, haven't I?" she muttered.

With a lighthearted chuckle Seth quickly agreed, "Aye, Brianna. You have again proven that conformity is not one of your characteristics."

"And you are not annoyed with me?" She almost hated to ask, but the words seemed to rush from her lips before she could bite them back.

"I have learned to accept what I cannot change. That is one of my noble qualities," he teased with a subtle wink.

It was impossible to suppress the smile that parted her lips when she gazed at the handsome rogue. "I wasn't aware that scoundrels possessed noble qualities, Captain," she remarked dryly as she swung her right leg into the proper position to ride sidesaddle.

Seth cocked a wondering brow as he observed her graceful movement. "Shall we tour Petersburg, m'lady?" he queried, reining his chestnut gelding toward town.

"Aye, Captain. It will be difficult for me to run away if I don't know exactly where I'm going. I should hate to meet with trouble."

Gazing back over his shoulder, Seth studied Brianna curiously. He could never be certain when she was jesting or stating fact. Escaping from unwanted situations had become a habit with the wench. "Then I shall take great care in acquainting you with Virginia. I should hate for you to meet with disaster as you have done in the past."

After an hour's ride, Seth halted in front of the hotel and lifted Brianna from the saddle. When she spied Priscilla coming down the boardwalk, her eyes twinkled with devilment. She planted a passionate kiss on Seth's lips, wrapping her arms about his shoulders. Seth was taken by surprise, but his hands involuntarily encircled her trim waist. It was a long moment before he raised his head.

"Thank you for the stallion, Seth," she murmured softly. "I can think of nothing that would have pleased me more."

Priscilla silently fumed as she witnessed the scene, and she spun on her heel to hurry away. Since Seth had his back to the shapely widow, he did not realize that her appearance was the cause of Brianna's amorous gesture. But he was well aware that those who were near them were startled by Brianna's brazen behavior.

When Priscilla was out of sight, Brianna squirmed from his arms and fondly patted the stallion's neck. "I think I'll call him Tyr," she stated with a fond smile.

Seth's brow arched curiously as he glanced down at her.

Seeing his quizzical expression, she explained, "In Norse mythology Thor and Tyr were brothers, the gods of strength. My stallion in Bristol was named Thor and he looks exactly like this beautiful beast. They could easily pass as brothers, don't you think?"

"Aye, m'lady," Seth agreed with a light chuckle. "Two devil stallions whose mistress is a witch." Seth laid his hand on the small of her back and urged her toward the inn, but Brianna stepped away.

"I have something to purchase. I'll join you in a few minutes," she informed him hurriedly as she started down the street.

Seth frowned bemusedly. She had been acting strangely since he had left her at the hotel that morning. First she was playfully taunting him, then she was as mad as a hornet, and then she was overly affectionate. Now she was rushing off to attend to some mysterious business. Seth shrugged hopelessly as he entered the inn. Who could know what game Brianna was playing, except perhaps the devil himself.

Finding Grant and Sabrina waiting at a table, Seth joined them explaining that Brianna would be a few minutes late. Grant studied Donnovan curiously and finally decided to ask the prying question that had been on his mind.

"Did you and Brianna have words before she came to change clothes?"

Seth cocked his head to the side and peered curiously at Talbert before he replied, "No more than usual. Why do you ask?"

"When Brianna came upstairs she was fuming, but she wouldn't tell us what had happened."

The dawn of understanding brought an amused sparkle to Seth's green eyes. Brianna must have run into Priscilla since they were both in the hotel at the same time. He would have dearly loved to hear that conversation. For once Priscilla was on the opposite side of the fence, he mused spitefully. After all these years, she would finally know how Seth had felt when she had married Kyle. What had Priscilla told Brianna? There was much she could say to infuriate Brianna, but just how much she would dare to say, he didn't know.

With a casual shrug, Seth lit his cheroot. "I don't have the faintest idea what annoyed Brianna," he lied as he met Grant's gaze. "You know how she is. It only takes a small spark to set her temper blazing."

Talbert chuckled and nodded in agreement. "Aye, she's a little spitfire. And you are probably right. It may have been nothing."

"Captain Donnovan," the waiter began as he strolled up to the threesome and bowed slightly. "Someone wishes to see you in the lobby."

After Seth excused himself from the Talberts, he ambled outside the dining room to find Priscilla smiling broadly.

"Lance offered to take me to dinner and the theater tonight," she explained. "I hesitated to give him my answer until I found out what time to expect you."

Seth eyed her levelly and allowed a hint of a smile to play on his lips. "I told you that I'm not making definite plans for the evening."

"I won't go with him if you don't wish me to," she replied as she edged a step closer to Seth. "You know that I love only you. Lance only helps to while away the lonely hours."

"You have always done exactly as you pleased, Priscilla. I do not intend to dictate to you. Do as you wish," he suggested indifferently.

"I wish to have you," Priscilla replied boldly as she pressed her full breasts against his arm. "You know that we were meant for each other. Marriage never stood in our way in the past, nor will it now. Nothing has changed between us."

"I want you to gather your belongings from my plantation. My wife will be occupying your room," Seth stated abruptly.

Priscilla was furious with his command, but she masked her outrage and produced a shallow smile. "If that is what you wish, Seth. I will have Gibbons take me to your plantation tomorrow."

Seth nodded slightly. "And now if you will excuse me, Priscilla."

Brianna seemed to have the misfortune of appearing at the most inopportune moments that day. When she stepped into the lobby with a package under her arm, her temper reached the end of its short fuse. *Damn that woman!* she muttered under her breath. Forcing a faint smile she walked past the couple and entered the dining room to take a seat with Grant and Sabrina.

When Seth eased into the chair beside her, Brianna completely ignored him, attempting to talk with her brother and sister-in-law. But the vision of Seth and Priscilla kept forming in her mind's eye and she was having difficulty thinking of anything else. The mocking smile that crept to Seth's lips each time she glanced at him only enraged her further. He was delighting in flaunting his mistress right under her nose, but she was determined to act as if she wasn't the slightest bit concerned.

"When are we leaving for your plantation, Captain?"

Grant inquired anxiously.

"It will be at least four days before I have finished my business in Petersburg," Seth explained, noting the look of surprise on Brianna's face. Apparently she did not know that the Talberts were planning to stay at his home for the next month. "If you wish to go on ahead without me, I will see to the arrangements."

"I'm anxious to see more of the colonies. I think we will take your offer. Are you coming with us, Brianna?" Grant questioned as he narrowed his attention to his sister.

Brianna was speechless. She had expected the Talberts to return to Bristol as quickly as possible. She knew nothing of their intentions. "Aren't you and Sabrina sailing soon?"

"Captain Barton has consented to let us travel with him, but his ship doesn't disembark for over a month. Since Seth has graciously offered for us to stay at his plantation, Sabrina and I thought it would be more enjoyable than remaining at the hotel," he replied with a leisurely shrug. "And what about you? Are you coming with us?"

"I haven't made up my mind," she replied, averting her gaze from her brother's quizzical brown eyes.

"I would prefer that you wait and travel with me," Seth requested with a sly smile.

Brianna was uncertain of his reasons for making that comment. Did he wish to have her view more scenes between him and Priscilla? Most likely! If she traveled with Grant and Sabrina, she could spare herself the humiliation. Intentionally avoiding the subject, Brianna began to tell Sabrina about the stallion Seth had purchased for her and their morning ride.

Sabrina's eyes lit up as she listened to Brianna and quickly pleaded with Grant to take her on a similar excursion that afternoon. When Grant agreed, Sabrina hurriedly finished her meal. She requested that

Brianna return to the room with her to change, which Brianna did, much relieved to escape from Seth.

"I'll make all of the arrangements to have my home prepared," Seth offered as he casually glanced at Grant. "You and Sabrina may travel to the plantation day after tomorrow."

An appreciative smile touched Talbert's lips. "Thank you, Captain. You have been more than generous. I'm afraid my family has caused you nothing but trouble and yet you have responded most graciously."

Seth chuckled as he rose from his chair. "Think nothing of it. After all, we are family now. My home is yours."

"Will you be joining us this afternoon?" Grant questioned.

"I'm afraid I have business to attend, but Captain Barton could go with you, if you wish to have a guide," Seth offered.

Grant hesitated a moment and then touched the sleeve of Seth's coat to detain him. "I think the two of us need to talk." His voice was quiet, but there was a hint of urgency in it.

Talbert's tone and his solemn expression drew a muddled frown from Seth. "About what?"

"Whom," Grant corrected, a faint smile creeping to one corner of his mouth. "About Brianna."

"Do you think there are enough hours left in the day to sufficiently discuss her?" he smirked caustically.

"Nay, Captain, but I will be candid and brief so that you will not be late for your meeting," Grant assured him with a subtle wink.

Seth nodded slightly. "Very well. What about her?" He eased back into his chair and lit his cigar, patiently waiting for Grant to delve into the one subject that continued to baffle him.

Chapter Twenty

After Lance had shown Brianna and the Talberts the sights of Petersburg, he acquainted them with the history of the three settlements that were combined to form the community. He told them how the British had seized the settlement during the Revolution. Lance pointed out the areas that had been rebuilt after they had been burned during the war. Brianna detected a hint of bitterness in his voice, but did not question him. When they headed south, intending to see the country-side, Brianna dug her heels into her stallion's flanks and galloped away. Sabrina giggled excitedly and pursued her friend, loving the feel of her muscular steed beneath her and the wind in her face. When Brianna slowed her pace, Sabrina reined up beside her, her blue eyes beaming with pleasure.

"This reminds me of our races at your country estate," she breathed happily. "But so much has happened since the days when we used to trail along behind Grant and his friends."

Brianna nodded in agreement, a rueful smile parting her lips. Sabrina was deliriously carefree and content. Her emotions showed on her face. No doubt she preferred the present to the past, but Brianna did not share her pleasure. If only she could be as satisfied as Sabrina, she mused pensively. But she was not to enjoy the fate that had brought Grant and Sabrina together in blissful matrimony.

The Talberts' marriage sailed on peaceful waters, but the Donnovans had met with nothing but stormy seas. She sighed weakly at the thought of the worst tidal wave that could completely sink their leaky skiff— Priscilla. She had seized every opportunity to make her intentions for Seth plain. The fact that Seth and Brianna were husband and wife did nothing to affect that pernicious wench.

Brianna swung out of her saddle and allowed her stallion to graze as she leaned back against a sturdy tree, expecting Sabrina to join her. But Sabrina reined back toward Grant and left Brianna to her troubled thoughts.

When the Talberts disappeared in the thicket, Brianna glanced up to see Lance dismounting.

"Do you mind a little company? I think perhaps Grant and Sabrina wanted to be alone." He chuckled as he peered at Brianna. "It seems the newlyweds are still on their honeymoon."

Although Brianna forced a faint smile, she found no amusement in Lance's remark. She envied Grant and Sabrina's perfect relationship.

Lance cocked a curious brow as he appraised the bewitching lass. He was tempted to take her in his arms, but caution won out over his impulse. If he wanted to feel those inviting lips against his, he would have to proceed carefully. Brianna was not the type of woman who could be taken by force and she was far too clever to be trapped. He had discovered that the first night he had met her.

"Well, what do you think of Virginia?" he asked as he strolled up beside her and propped his arm against the tree where Brianna was leaning.

"'Tis very lovely, at least what little I've seen of it," she replied as she glanced up into Lance's warm brown eyes. "'Tis not at all what I had expected. I have yet to meet the red savages and heathens that were rumored to inhabit these backward colonies."

Lance chuckled heartily at her somewhat distorted impression. "They only appear at night when the moon is full and the wind wails," he teased.

Brianna shot him a reproachful glance. He was mocking her and she had enough of that for one day. "I suppose the colonists are the ones who spread those terrifying stories to keep from having their precious land invaded by the British."

"Your assumption is correct, m'lady," he snickered. "The British are a bit stuffy and pompous. The fewer there are around, the better I like it."

Brianna's blue mood eased slightly as she gazed up at Lance. She was acting rather boorish and it was little wonder why Lance had no use for the English. It wasn't his fault that she was miserable. She had no reason to take her frustrations out on him. An honest smile parted her lips. Her amber eyes filled with renewed sparkles of tiny sunbeams, causing Lance to swallow his breath when he saw the lustrous radiance in those lovely pools of gold.

"I suppose you think I'm one of those stuffy aristocrats," she retorted with a sheepish grin.

"You are breathtaking, Brianna," he murmured. "If I could hand-pick a few Tories whom I would allow to remain in the colonies, you would be among them."

"I'm very flattered, Lance. Obviously you are not very impressed with my fellow countrymen."

"Nay, I'm afraid not. The Revolution has left a few bitter memories that are not quickly forgotten." His thoughtful tone made Brianna's brows furrow slightly.

"I'm sure the tragedies of war never are," she agreed. A long quiet moment passed between them before

329

Brianna spoke again. "Do you live in Petersburg?" she asked, hoping to bring Lance out of his pensive musings.

"I own a tobacco plantation southwest of here. My land adjoins Seth's," he explained.

"Have you known him long?" she asked as she strolled along the creek bank.

"Long and well." A smile finally began to invade his sober expression. "We have been through the jaws of hell together and just about everywhere else for that matter."

Brianna chuckled at his remark. Lance was a very likable sort—charming, handsome, and interesting. Although her first impression of him was that he was a rogue of whom she should be cautious, she found him to be enjoyable company.

When Brianna looked up, Lance took her in his arms and gave her a gentle kiss, startling her with his forwardness. He knew that she and Seth were married, but it seemed to make little difference, even if he and Seth were close friends. To the Americans, marriages did not appear to be of much importance, Brianna mused as she pulled away from his embrace. Both Lance and Priscilla had a tendency to overlook the bonds of matrimony.

"I've been wanting to do that since the night you came on board my ship," he confessed in a raspy whisper, his eyes roaming over her delicate features.

"Oh?" Brianna arched a dubious brow.

"I have a weakness for beautiful women," Lance continued as he pulled Brianna back into his arms. "And you are one of the loveliest that I have chanced to meet."

Dodging his intended kiss, Brianna cocked her head to the side and pressed her hands to his chest, holding him at bay. "I think perhaps we should search for my brother." Her emphasis on the last word halted Lance's amorous assault.

Reluctantly, he released his grasp on Brianna. "Perhaps you're right, m'lady. I seem to have forgotten my place." A guilty smile surfaced on his lips, but it did not seem sincere enough to suit Brianna.

Brianna had guessed that the eerie sensation that had trickled down her spine was due to Lance and his over-zealous pursuit. Had she known they were being watched, she would have attributed her anxiety to the red savages who crept from the brush when she and Lance had gone in search of her brother.

The chief's black eyes followed the dark-haired woman until she disappeared from sight. Then he spoke to the three braves beside him. In silence they retreated to the thicket by the creek. The vision of the woman lingered in White Hawk's mind, taunting and calling to him. She was the goddess with hair the color of midnight and eyes as radiant as the sun. She was the spirit of both day and night and he knew they must meet again. And when their paths crossed, he would follow her. The dark-haired woman was an omen, a sign of fortune to the Tuscaroras. When she was among them, his people would again walk with the sun.

Seth had just walked out of one of the shops where they had unloaded cargo when he saw Lance lift Brianna from her steed.

"Did you keep an eye on my wife and see to it that she stayed out of mischief?" he inquired with a lazy smile.

"I took excellent care of her. I took up your role since you were unable to keep her company," he assured Seth, winking subtly.

The underlying sarcasm in Barton's voice caused Seth to arch a dubious brow. Lance was implying something intimate. A simple yes was what Seth had

331

expected and, indeed, all that he wanted to hear. When he peered at Brianna, she quickly averted her eyes, making Seth believe that his suspicions were correct. What could have happened? Hell, he knew damned well what might have happened. Lance had already made it clear that he would pursue Brianna if the opportunity presented itself. And Seth had foolishly allowed it to happen. Sending Lance with Brianna was as ridiculous as expecting a wolf to protect a lamb.

Seth's eyes narrowed accusingly as he glared at Lance and roughly pulled Brianna with him to the phaeton. "Have the horses stabled, *friend*," he snorted caustically. "We're going back to the *Mesmer*."

Brianna bristled at Seth's abrupt actions. "What do you think you're doing?" she snapped as Seth forced her into the coach. "I don't appreciate being whisked away before being allowed to say whether or not I wish to go with you!"

"You're my wife and you will do as I tell you, when I tell you!" Seth assured her in a razor-sharp tone. "And you will go where I say!"

"Everywhere?" she quipped harshly. "Even to your lover's room—the first door on the left at the top of the stairs where you were last night?" Brianna had not intended to bring up the subject of Priscilla, but it seemed her anger had loosened her tongue.

Seth's jaw sagged slightly as he glanced into Brianna's stormy, amber eyes. "How did you know that?"

"Priscilla offered to let me use the room to change clothes. Of course, she couldn't wait to inform me that my frivolous husband knew his way to her chamber," she hissed venomously.

Suddenly Seth was chuckling out loud. It seemed Priscilla had dared to say a mouthful. "What else did she tell you, my dear?"

His nonchalant acceptance of the situation brought Brianna's temper to a rolling boil. "Plenty, and I do not wish to discuss it," she informed him curtly as she folded her arms beneath her breasts and stared out the opposite window, ignoring her companion. She was aggravated at Seth, but also with herself for allowing her tongue to outdistance her brain.

"Would you prefer to discuss Lance?" he taunted as he pulled a cheroot from his pocket and lit it. His dark brow arched slightly as a trace of a smile skitted across his lips and then disappeared.

"I would prefer silence!" Brianna ground out harshly. She stared at the packages that filled the carriage seat across from her, noting that the gown she had purchased was on the top of the stack. A devilish gleam filled her eyes. She would show that red-haired wench!

Seth laid his arm on the back of the seat and gently wrapped his lean fingers around Brianna's neck, drawing her to him. The warm flame in those golden pools held him entranced. For a moment he could only stare into the lovely face that was framed in lustrous ebony. A wry smile parted her soft lips as she came to him. He had known from the beginning how devastating Brianna could be, but until that instant he was not fully aware of how powerful her mysterious spell was. Lance could not have resisted her. Oddly enough, he could not blame Barton or any other man who had been attracted to this golden-eyed witch.

As their lips touched, Brianna slid her arms over his shoulders. Her fingers brushed over the raven hair that lay against the back of his neck. As Seth pulled her close, he tossed his cigar out of the window, along with his hope of ever being able to resist the vixen whom he held in his arms. Another smile crept to Brianna's lips, knowing that Seth still desired her. She would give him no opportunity to seek out Priscilla, she vowed to herself. The wench would sleep alone tonight and every other night.

When Seth reluctantly withdrew, he gazed into her golden eyes. "Do you respond to Lance in the same manner?"

A deliciously wicked grin curved the corners of her mouth upward. "Are you certain that you want an answer, Captain?" Brianna moved slowly toward him, placing a taunting kiss on his lips before he could reply. With all of the knowledge she had gained from Seth's skillfulness, her kiss deepened, exploring his mouth with her tongue while she molded herself to his muscular frame.

Nay, he didn't really wish to know. They had made an agreement and he was the one who had set the terms. The last time he had lost his temper over the arrangement he had cruelly abused Brianna. He had sworn never to make that mistake again no matter how she taunted him. Seth wasn't sure how long the carriage had been stopped on the wharf because the world was still spinning from Brianna's arousing kiss. She could make him forget that life existed outside the quiet realm of her intoxicating embrace. A lopsided smile tugged at the corner of his mouth as he wrapped his hands in the silky hair that lay across her shoulder.

"You're a witch," he murmured huskily.

"Aye," she agreed as she traced the lines around his eyes with her index finger. "'Tis a pity that you tossed your talisman into the sea. You could have been rid of me. But because of your folly, you have been cursed."

"I'm aware of that." His smile quickly faded as his emerald eyes took on a frosty glaze. "I have an appointment this evening. Derrick will remain on the schooner. Have him bring your supper tray."

His placid tone made Brianna bristle angrily. But for once she held her tongue and stepped from the carriage. When Seth handed her the packages, she nodded stiffly and started up the plank, attempting to peer around her armload of gifts to ensure that she did not fall headlong into the water.

"Brianna?"

She glanced back and raised a quizzical brow to Seth.

"Take care of yourself."

"I usually do, don't I?" she said as a hint of bitterness laced her tone.

Seth gave directions to the driver and leaned back inside the window, forcing the thought of Brianna from his mind. She could indeed take care of herself and had proven her capabilities on numerous occasions.

When Derrick saw Brianna coming across the deck he quickly lifted the packages from her arms. "Where's the captain?" he questioned.

Brianna produced a relieved smile and shrugged leisurely. "He said he had some unfinished business in town."

Derrick cocked a dubious brow, but did not allow Brianna to see his concern. Donnovan had told him before he left the schooner that morning that he would spend the evening on the ship. What could have come up? If it had something to do with Priscilla, Derrick would make certain that Seth knew exactly what he thought of the way the captain was treating his wife!

When Derrick left Brianna alone in her cabin, she was ready to climb the walls. She had the feeling that Seth was going to Priscilla, just as Derrick had. She was wasting her time trying to win the love of a scoundrel whose heart was as cold as ice. He must love Priscilla, she decided with a hopeless sigh. Seth was obviously devoted to that red-haired wench. Brianna impulsively grabbed the pitcher and hurled it against the door, watching it shatter to pieces like all of her hopes of winning Seth's love. Derrick slowly opened the door and cautiously stuck his head inside. When he saw the slivers of porcelain scattered on the floor a wry smile creased his lips.

"Did that just accidentally slip out of your hand?" he questioned. With a light chuckle he stepped over the broken pitcher.

Brianna grinned sheepishly. "'Twas clumsy of me, wasn't it?"

As Derrick eased down on the edge of the desk, he drew Brianna's trim body close. He lifted her chin to gaze into her amber eyes, seeing the hint of tears that lingered just beneath the surface. "You still have me, Brianna."

Brianna wrapped her arms about his neck and laid her head against his sturdy shoulder. "I wish it could have been you, Derrick. You know that, don't you?"

Derrick heaved a sigh. "I wish it could have been that way too, but I suppose it just wasn't meant to be."

"Seth will never know the truth and I'm fighting a losing battle. Priscilla must have some mysterious power over him."

Derrick frowned thoughtfully. "Nay, I think not. At one time I believe she did. She married one of Donnovan's closest friends because of his title and wealth. Although Seth hated her for that, he could never seem to let her go. But now I have noticed a cool indifference in his reactions to Priscilla. I think the captain's problem right now is the captain." Quickly hopping to his feet, Derrick clicked his heels together and bowed before Brianna. "Will you join me for dinner, m'lady? If I can't have your love, at least allow me the pleasure of your company."

An easy smile played on Brianna's lips as she gazed up at the handsome first mate. She curtsied and batted her lashes coyly. "I would be very happy to accept your invitation, sir."

When Derrick returned with the tray, Brianna had set two places at the table and lit a small candle to place between them. As she turned to smile at him, Derrick's heart wrenched in behalf of his own self-pity. If he were the one Brianna yearned for, he would never treat her as Donnovan had. Damn, but Seth was a blind fool!

Brianna's delicate brow arched as she noted Derrick's rueful smile. "Is something wrong?"

Forcing a broader smile, Derrick winked at her. "Nay, Brianna," he assured her as he ambled toward the table and set the tray upon it. "There is not much to be had in the galley, and I fear the food cannot equal what we could have had in Petersburg."

Shrugging nonchalantly, Brianna lifted the lid from the stew. "'Tis no matter what we eat as long as it is taken in good company."

With an exaggerated bow, Derrick placed a light kiss to her wrist and then pulled out a chair for Brianna. "Thank you, madam. I intend to swallow that flattery. It will, no doubt, make our meager stew taste more like steak."

Brianna's reckless laughter filled the shadowed cabin and her mood became carefree once again. Derrick had become like a brother to her since Grant was preoccupied with Sabrina. She could talk to him. She was always at ease with him although she knew that he felt more for her than just friendship. It made her wish that she could return the deep affection.

"Why is it that you have never married, Derrick?" Brianna asked as she peered at him over the rim of her teacup.

"Because it seemed the timing was all wrong. Love never came at a point in my life when I could wed," he replied casually.

"Have you been in love more than once?"

"A thousand times," he chuckled as he touched the napkin to his lips and grinned at the inquisitive beauty.

"Will you be serious?" She sent him a disapproving frown. "Tell me yea or nay."

Derrick sighed weakly as he leaned his elbows on the edge of the table and met the quizzical eyes of glowing amber that reminded him of a warm, cozy hearth. "Aye, a time or two," he confessed soberly. "Once, during the war, I was in the militia in New York. I met a lovely lass. But our troops were relocated and I lost track of her. After the Revolution had ended and I went back to find her, she was gone."

Brianna thoughtfully chewed on her bottom lip, wishing she had not pried into his private affairs, but she was unable to be content until she knew more of the woman. "What was her name?"

A sad smile crept to his lips as he eased back in his chair. "Barbara. . . . She had warm brown eyes and brown hair. She was gentle and lovely. She was a nurse, and we spent a great deal of time together while I was recovering from an arm injury I received in battle."

"She must have been a very special lady for you to have fallen in love with her," Brianna said quietly. "I'm sorry you could never find her." Remembering Derrick's earlier remark, she continued, "And was there someone else?"

Derrick chuckled as he picked up his spoon and regarded her warily. "Dear Brianna, you are the most inquisitive little witch I have yet to meet." He sipped his stew and then winked fondly at her. "My timing was even worse the second time around. The lady already has a husband."

Brianna averted her gaze, knowing full well that he was referring to her. At least one colonial recognized the bonds of matrimony and regarded it seriously, unlike Lance and Priscilla.

When they finished their meal, Derrick returned the dishes to the tray and rose from his chair. "I'll take these back to the galley and then we'll take a stroll," he suggested. "'Tis far too lovely a night to spend in this confining cabin."

With a grateful smile, she nodded in agreement. "I'll change clothes and will be waiting for you to return."

When Derrick left the cabin, Brianna strolled over to lay out one of the gowns that Seth had purchased for her. As the door eased open, Brianna chuckled lightly. "That was quick, Derrick. What did you do, toss the tray and dishes overboard?"

When Derrick made no reply, Brianna glanced over her shoulder and gasped just before a callused hand clamped over her mouth, muffling the cry of alarm that waited on her lips.

Chapter Twenty-One

Derrick felt himself pulled up against strong, supporting arms and he slowly opened his eyes to see Seth's concerned face peering down at him. His skull throbbed in a torturing rhythm with his heartbeat and he found no way to hold his head that didn't hurt. Slumping forward once again he groaned in agony, yielding to the blackness that seemed to beckon to him. The cold dampness on the back of his neck brought him around. Then he sputtered and coughed when he was mercilessly drenched with a bucket of water.

"Damn it, Derrick, can you hear me?" Seth bellowed impatiently. "What the hell happened?"

"I don't know. I was walking down the steps with the supper tray and someone must have hit me from behind. That's all I remember," he choked out.

Seth hated to ask, but he had to know. "Could it have been Brianna?"

Derrick shook his aching head and shot Seth a disgruntled frown. "Nay, I had just left her alone in your cabin." His eyes widened frantically. "Where is she? Did somebody—"

"I have found no trace of her. The candle on the table was to the end of its wick and one of her gowns was lying on the bed, but nothing is missing except Brianna."

"God, maybe Jed and Lucas came back for her." Derrick attempted to rise, but his legs were unsteady and he swayed toward Seth. "We've got to find her."

"I'll get Lance and Grant to help me. You're going to lie down. You're too dazed to be of help," Seth muttered as he pulled Derrick along with him.

"I'm sorry, Captain," he apologized dismally. "I should have been paying more attention instead of daydreaming."

"It wasn't your fault," Seth insisted with a disgusted sigh. "There is always trouble when Brianna is involved. There is nothing anyone can do about it."

When Seth had Sayer bedded down, he went back to Petersburg to have the horses saddled and then went in search of Barton, who was right where Seth expected him to be—with Priscilla.

As Seth burst through the door, Priscilla gasped in alarm, pulled the sheet about her, and glanced over at Lance.

"Brianna's been kidnapped again," Seth ground out as he tossed Lance his breeches and stalked toward the door. "I'll be downstairs waiting for you. Hurry up!"

With that he slammed the door and went to Grant's room to give him the distressing news. Grant hurriedly dressed and met Donnovan and Barton outside of the hotel.

After searching all of the taverns and inns in the area where Patton and Catlin might have taken Brianna, Seth had come to the conclusion that they had disappeared into thin air. No one had seen the woman they described or either of the two men. The threesome returned to the hotel at the break of dawn. Seth was at his wit's end. There was no way of knowing what direction the men could have taken if they had decided to flee from town.

"Do you suppose they are planning to hold her for ransom?" Lance questioned wearily.

Seth's shoulder lifted in a shrug. "They will save us a great deal of time and effort if they send a note. I can think of nowhere else to search."

Grant forced a feeble smile as he stepped up on the boardwalk. "If there is a way to escape, Brianna will find it. I have confidence in her resourcefulness."

It was an encouraging thought, but he knew as well as Seth that these men had been tricked once and they would be leery of Brianna now.

Brianna squirmed as the ropes bit into her wrists and ankles. Heaving a sigh, she glanced up at the dark scowl on Patton's stubbled face. "What do you intend to do with me?" Her voice showed no sign of fear, only an impatience to know her fate.

Lucas's craggy features twisted in a satanic smile. "Punish you, witch," he sneered cruelly.

Brianna defiantly met his menacing grin. "What did I do besides save myself from you the last time we met?"

As Lucas squatted down beside the tree to which he had securely tied Brianna, he glowered at her again. "You don't know, do you?" When she shook her head negatively, he explained, "You tipped the skiff and we lost the jewels. The man who expected to receive a goodly sum for the gems had me whipped." Lucas's eyes narrowed, remembering the pain he had suffered. "And you killed Jed. He couldn't swim a lick. He nearly drowned me trying to save himself."

Brianna ducked her head from his accusing glare. "I'm sorry. I didn't know."

Lucas smirked scornfully. "You wouldn't have cared. You were always too good for the likes of us, you and your high-and-mighty brother. I tried to tell Jed that you were trouble, but he thought you were his good luck charm. You cost him his life. Witches carry curses not good fortune." The contempt in his eyes made Brianna shiver uncomfortably.

As she averted her gaze, the moonlight glistened on

the body of the snake that slithered toward them. She did not dare move a muscle and it took a moment to find her tongue. "There's a snake behind you," she murmured.

Patton had expected another of Brianna's tricks and he only chuckled haughtily. "I suppose you've called upon the other demons of the night to come to your aid this time. But you won't escape me. I learned better than to trust you." Lucas checked the ropes, assuring himself that she hadn't loosened them and was waiting until he turned his head so she could attack.

"I'm telling the truth," she insisted in a hushed voice as the snake coiled at the sound of Patton's harsh tone.

When Lucas heard the timber rattler's warning he glanced behind him and then screeched in pain as the viper struck him in the leg. Brianna bit back a cry of alarm and watched wide-eyed as Patton, in demented rage, lunged for the snake, only to be struck in the neck. With a maddened growl that sent the birds to their wings in the tree above them, Patton glared at Brianna as if she were to blame. Grabbing the wound on his neck, he dashed through the trees to his horse.

The beady eyes of the rattler were on Brianna, sending her the silent warning that she was to be the next victim. She watched in terror as the rattler slid toward her, at last knowing her fate.

A rustling in the bushes on the opposite side of the creek drew her attention. The bare-chested savage raised his tomahawk and hurled it. The snake twisted and curled about the blade until its lifeless form came to rest beside her.

When she looked up, the savage was towering over her with his feet apart and his hands resting on his hips. The buckskin breeches he wore clung tightly to his muscular legs. Brianna stared in awe at the virile savage who had saved her from an agonizing death. White

Hawk spoke quietly and three braves appeared from the underbrush while he grabbed his tomahawk and cut the rattle from the snake's tail.

Brianna had been frightened within an inch of her life. She knew that she should fear the bronze-skinned man who moved silently beside her, but she was too numb to be afraid. When one of the braves untied her arms and legs, White Hawk pulled her to her feet and effortlessly swept her up into his strong arms. A hint of a smile touched his lips as he gazed down into the mystical golden eyes that had captivated him earlier that day.

Moving quietly along the edge of the creek, White Hawk made his way to the birchbark canoe waiting in the tall reeds.

After Grant and Lance had gone back to the hotel, Seth was on his way to the stable to tend the horses when he heard Patton's steed thundering down the street with its rider slumped on its back. The gelding halted in front of the blacksmith's barn and Seth grabbed a handful of Patton's hair to yank his head up. An icy glaze covered Patton's eyes as he met Seth's deadly scowl.

"Rattler," he whispered, forcing a single word from his lips.

"Where's Brianna?" Seth growled harshly. "What have you done with her?"

"Creek," Patton's voice was so quiet that Seth had to strain his ears to hear his reply.

As Patton's lifeless body tumbled to the ground, Seth leaped to his mount and spurred him into a gallop. Patton got what he deserved trying to capture Brianna, Seth thought spitefully. If the rattler hadn't killed him, Seth would have.

Seth drew the winded steed to an abrupt halt and

darted through the brush, searching for some sign of Brianna. When he found the ropes and the snake by the tree where she had been tied, his eyes narrowed thoughtfully. As he squatted down on his haunches to see that the rattler's tail had been severed, he spied the moccasin prints in the mud and quickly followed the path that led along the bank of the stream. When the tracks ended Seth continued to walk at the water's edge until he found two canoes hidden in the thick weeds. Following the tracks up the high bank, Seth spied four bucks leaning over Brianna.

A slow smile crept to his lips as he walked into the small clearing. "White Hawk has become reckless in his old age. His ears no longer alert him to the sound of a man's footsteps," he said in the Indians' tongue.

Brianna gasped when she heard Seth's deep voice. He had moved as silently as the savages and she could only stare at him in awe as he boldly faced her captors. Had he lost his mind? How could be confront these Indians alone and unarmed?

White Hawk rose and appraised the raven-haired man who stood before him. "It has been two summers since our paths have crossed, my brother. And time has not dulled your sharp tongue," he countered as he crossed his arms on his muscular chest and returned Donnovan's sly grin.

Although both men spoke in the Indian language, she did not miss the hint of mockery in their tones. She watched in amazement as Seth and the savage embraced.

Seth lifted the two snake tails that hung on a leather strap around White Hawk's neck. "You have added another rattler."

White Hawk nodded slightly. "The snake first brought us together as strangers and now as friends. How have you come to be here?"

"You have something that belongs to me and I came to collect my possession."

White Hawk peered curiously at his blood brother.

"The woman you have saved belongs to me," Seth explained as he glanced at Brianna for the first time since he had walked into camp.

A trace of a smile touched White Hawk's bronzed features. "The woman has special powers and is a good omen for my people. What if I don't want to give her up?"

Seth released a derisive snort as he met the savage's coal black eyes. "Among your people she might be blessed by the gods, but in the white man's world she walks with the demons."

White Hawk chuckled heartily as he bent his gaze to Brianna. "If she consorts with the spirits of darkness why do you wish to keep her?"

"She is still my woman and I am responsible for her."

"What will you trade for her?"

Spite could have tempted Seth to barter for Brianna after the constant trouble she had caused him, but he replied soberly. "The woman cannot be bought for any price. I choose to keep her."

White Hawk frowned disappointedly. If Seth had not been his blood brother and if he did not owe Donnovan a debt, he would have taken the woman, even if by force.

After White Hawk offered them food, they sat down together to eat. Seth took his place by Brianna, but did not speak to her.

"I have a proposition for you, White Hawk. I will buy all of the furs your people can hunt and trap and give you a fair price for your goods."

The chief nodded affirmatively and smiled to himself. Perhaps this was the good fortune that the

346

woman was meant to bring to him. His people could obtain needed supplies from the trade with Donnovan. When the arrangements were made, Seth pulled Brianna up beside him and said good-bye to White Hawk, but Brianna would not budge from her spot.

"What now?" he muttered disgustedly.

"How do I say 'thank you' in his language?" she questioned as she looked back to the Indian.

When Seth had slowly pronounced the unfamiliar syllables, Brianna repeated them to herself, and then walked back to White Hawk to show her gratitude.

White Hawk produced a lazy smile. "You walk with the sun in your eyes. The shadows of darkness fall behind you. You have brought my people good fortune, Golden Eyes. For that I thank you," he replied in broken English.

As the Donnovans walked back to Seth's horse, Brianna demanded a complete explanation of all that had been said and how he had come to know the Tuscarora chief.

"When the tribal elders sent White Hawk out to test his manhood, he was bitten by a rattler," he began wearily. "It was the second year I had been in the colonies. I was trapping and hunting in the wilderness. I heard him cry out and found him in time to save him. We spent many days together until he regained his strength. When he was well enough to travel, he took me back to his village and I spent the summer with the Tuscaroras, learning to hunt and trap like an Indian. Before I left them, White Hawk and I became blood brothers in one of their tribal ceremonies.

"White Hawk is now the chieftain. Although the other Tuscarora chiefs joined forces with the British during the Revolution, White Hawk and I remained friends. He did not agree with the other leaders, but he

347

had to obey the wishes of the majority." Seth heaved a tired sigh as he stepped up into the saddle and pulled Brianna up behind him.

"And now tell me about you and Patton."

Brianna related her adventure as they rode back to Petersburg. When she finished, she rested her head against Seth's broad back. "How did you find me?"

"Patton told me where you were."

"Were you able to save him?" she asked quietly.

"It was too late." There was no hint of remorse in his voice. It was only a cold statement of fact.

After stopping at the hotel to inform Grant that Brianna was safe, the Donnovans returned to the *Mesmer*. Seth bathed and changed clothes and returned to town to meet with one of the merchants. Brianna crawled into bed, completely exhausted from her sleepless night and was not aware what time it was when Seth came back to the room to lie down beside her.

With the carriage loaded, Grant and Sabrina bid farewell and rumbled away. Brianna wished that she could have traveled to the plantation with them. Seth had completely ignored her since they had returned from White Hawk's camp. When Brianna had commented that she might go with her brother, Seth had refused, saying that she could find enough trouble in which to embroil herself while she was right under his nose. He had no time to journey to the plantation to rescue her from one of her near catastrophes. A heated argument had ensued and Seth had vowed to lock her in the cabin if she did not agree to remain in Petersburg with him for two more days. They had hardly uttered a word to each other since their quarrel the previous afternoon and there was always a strained silence between.

Brianna was much relieved when Seth left her in Captain Barton's company while he met with one of his associates. After Lance escorted her back to the schooner, Brianna paced the floor. Lance had offered to take her riding, but after what had happened between them earlier, Brianna thought it best to avoid any situation that allowed the two of them to be alone together. She was more at ease with Derrick and preferred to remain on the *Mesmer* with him. There was always the chance that if she stayed in Petersburg, she would confront Priscilla and Brianna wanted nothing more to do with that annoying wench.

Derrick and Brianna spent the better part of the afternoon playing cards. Brianna was having a perfectly enjoyable time until Seth entered the cabin, bringing a stilted silence into the room. Seth informed Derrick that he could go ashore if he wished and then silently dismissed him with a nod. Derrick excused himself. When Brianna and Seth were alone, Seth sat down in the chair that Derrick had vacated and picked up the cards. Tossing the bad hand back on the table, Seth insisted that he be dealt fresh cards. Brianna complied with his gruff request and then pulled a face at him when he glanced down at his new hand.

"I saw that," Seth assured her dryly.

Brianna shrugged carelessly and played one of her cards.

The afternoon passed in silence. When Derrick returned shortly after dark, Seth left again, ordering Brianna to lock the door and remain in the cabin. It was the early hours of the morning before Seth returned. Brianna refused to allow him inside, knowing exactly where he had been and with whom.

"Open this damned door!" Seth bellowed angrily.

"Go sleep in Derrick's room!" Brianna's tone was just as loud and sharp as Seth's.

"Damn it, woman, this is my cabin!" he hollered as he glared at the locked door.

"Go to hell!" she stormed back.

When Seth stomped away, Brianna climbed back into bed and slammed her fist into her pillow. Damn him! If he thought he could lay with Priscilla and then come sleep beside his wife, he was demented. *Damn that scoundrel!* For a long moment Brianna almost wished the rattler had put her out of her misery. Seth was punishing her for all of the trouble she had caused him, spitefully torturing her each time the opportunity presented itself. She wouldn't have been the least bit surprised if he had dragged her to the hotel with him and ordered her to wait until he returned from Priscilla's room. *Damn that man!*

Seth rapped impatiently on Derrick's door until the first mate let him in. He scowled at the crooked smile on Sayer's face.

"So you're back to swords and daggers again," Derrick concluded with a taunting chuckle.

Seth shot him an irritated glower. "Mind your own business."

"I have made Brianna my business. One of these days you're going to push her too far and she will turn to me completely," he warned. "When the time comes, I'll welcome her with open arms and this odd marriage of yours will end. Excuse my forwardness, Captain, but you are a damned fool."

After tossing his shirt aside, Seth hopped into the hammock and shot Derrick a cold glance. "If you're finished criticizing me, I'd like to get some rest," he grumbled harshly.

Derrick threw up his hands and muttered under his breath as he crawled back onto his cot. "You're as stubborn as she is. I never thought I'd see the day that—"

"Enough!" Seth bellowed angrily. "I don't need you to play the mother hen! I can manage my own affairs and I don't need your advice. Now go to sleep and let me rest in peace!"

"Damned fool," Derrick mumbled to the wall, not allowing Seth to hear his final comment.

Chapter Twenty-Two

Brianna had all of her belongings packed when Seth tapped on the door the following morning. As soon as he stepped inside, Brianna brushed past him and stalked from the cabin to tell Derrick good-bye. When the coach was loaded, Brianna slapped away the helping hand Seth extended to her and stepped up into the coach. Brianna did not utter a word to him until they had left Petersburg behind.

"Stop the carriage," Brianna ordered as she leaned out of the window to call to the driver.

Seth cocked a curious brow as Brianna hopped from the coach. "What's wrong?"

"I'm riding Tyr," she snapped as she picked up the saddle and tossed it on the stallion's back. Tyr side-stepped at her abrupt manner, but she calmed him with gentle words that were meant only for the horse and never again for the horse's ass who was her husband.

Seth leaned back against the wheel of the coach, never offering to assist her, and watched Brianna saddle and bridle her mount. "Would you care for some company?"

"Nay, why do you think I chose to ride instead of sitting in the carriage with you?" Her golden eyes raked him with a look of disgust.

Seth shrugged indifferently and climbed back inside to stretch out on the cushioned seats. He had had little sleep the previous night and welcomed the opportunity of dozing during the journey.

When the Donnovan plantation appeared in the
distance, a shiver of anticipation and delight trickled
down Brianna's spine. She gazed wide-eyed at the huge
home that stood before her. The massive brick struc-
ture was a symbol of civilization in this untamed land
with its stately pillars marking the entrance to the
grand home. Brianna instantly recalled what Seth had
said about having his own fortune and never living long
enough to spend it. A faint smile touched her lips as she
viewed the mansion. It did indeed appear that Seth had
made his own way in the colonies. It was little wonder
that Priscilla was so determined to keep Seth. Priscilla
was probably as greedy as Caroline who sought the
wealth of the Duke of Bourdoin instead of Grant.

As Seth's voice slowly filtered through her pensive
musings, Brianna bent her gaze to meet his expressionless green eyes.

"Are you going to climb down from your perch and
come inside or do you wish to sit atop that steed for the
rest of the day?"

Brianna swung down from her saddle, brushing
Seth's hands away as they came around her waist to
assist her. "I have been climbing off and on horses since
I was old enough to walk. I do not need your assistance," she informed him icily.

Brianna was met at the door by Sabrina and Grant
who had nothing but praise and compliments for the
master of the plantation. Seth accepted their greeting
with a slight nod and called to the servants to bring in
their belongings. When Seth touched the small of
Brianna's back to urge her forward, she cast him an
irritated glance which he chose to ignore.

"Let me acquaint you with the house," he suggested.

"'Tis no house, sir. It can only be described as a

353

palace in the wilderness," she corrected flippantly.

"And you do not approve?" His dark brow arched curiously.

"'Tis not my place to criticize *your* home, m'lord. 'Tis just that it is not at all what I had expected."

"I suppose you thought I lived in a shabby lean-to shack similar to the one that stands beside the barn," he concluded with a mocking smile. When Brianna made no comment, he continued tauntingly, "I should have suspected that from you, being from a snobbish British social circle. You probably thought that we colonials had none of the class and luxuries that are so common among the British."

His biting words made her bristle indignantly. Perhaps because she suddenly felt as though she had indeed been too skeptical of this new country. "Are you going to acquaint me with the house or do you intend to spend the rest of the day insulting me?"

Seth chuckled lightly and gestured toward the large study before drawing Brianna with him. "This is my personal library, madam. Although it isn't as finely stocked as your father's, perhaps you will be able to find a few books that interest you during your stay."

The walls of the huge room were lined with books and by the window sat a large marble-topped desk. Along the east wall was a fireplace around which several chairs and a sofa were arranged. Brianna stared in amazement at the elaborately furnished study. There were twice as many books here as could be found at both Talbert estates. The room was larger than either of her father's libraries.

"This is where I come to sit alone and think. Of all of the rooms in this house, this is my favorite," Seth mused aloud, but immediately regretted speaking at all.

"'Tis a pity that you only come in here to contemplate," she smirked as a mischievous gleam flickered in her golden eyes. "Your study would, no doubt, be inhabited more frequently if it served some other purpose."

Seth clamped down on her arm and whisked her back into the tiled entryway. "Come along, witch. I'll show you the rest of the house if you can control that sharp tongue of yours."

"Will I be allowed to enter *your* study, m'lord?" she questioned sarcastically. "Or is it off limits to all except the master?"

Casting the chit a quick, sidelong glance, Seth nodded affirmatively. "If you find that you would like to make a feeble attempt to meditate instead of speaking and acting impulsively, you are welcomed to it. But deliberated forethought has never been one of your notable qualities."

Brianna instantly regretted making her remark. It seemed that they were destined to engage in a war of words, she thought to herself as she and Seth entered the sitting room, which was no less elaborate than the study. It was most fortunate for both of them that the house was monstrous; otherwise, they would be at each other's throats for the next month. Brianna was certain that she could spend an entire day in this mansion and never bump into her annoying husband at all.

When Seth had taken Brianna through the rooms on the ground floor, he urged her toward the stairs. As they approached the master bedroom, Brianna's eyes widened in awe when she spied the intricately carved bed and matching dressers, wardrobe closets, and chairs. The drapes, carpet, and bedspread were a rich gold, drawing the elegance of the fine wood and velvet into unity. Never had she seen such a magnificent room!

"And now let me show you to your room," Seth

suggested dryly.

Brianna stiffened at his complacent tone. So he had no intention of sharing a bed with her, she mused. Well, that was just as she would have wanted it. He could travel to Petersburg to see Priscilla if he wanted a woman to keep him warm at night! She had intended to lock him out of his own bedchamber again tonight and every other night, but instead he had made it clear that it suited him fine.

As Brianna stepped into the adjoining room, she strolled around, carefully examining the furniture that was just as elegant as that of the master bedroom, but not as massive. The room was decorated in pale blue and was obviously intended for a woman. Brianna brushed her hand over the top of the dressing table and then casually opened the wardrobe closet, thinking it was much too large since she had not brought many of her gowns with her on the voyage. A curious frown furrowed her brows when she spied the dresses inside. She pulled one of them from the closet to inspect it carefully.

Seth's face darkened in a scowl when she held up the dress. It only took Brianna an instant to realize that Seth had not purchased them for her since they were too big. They were Priscilla's! Brianna tossed the pink velvet gown on the bed as if it had singed her hands and quickly opened the dresser to find several undergarments and nightgowns inside.

Turning back to Seth, her face red with rage and humiliation, Brianna shot him a contemptuous glower. How dare he flaunt that wench in front of her nose and then expect his wife to sleep in the same room where Priscilla had stayed! An enraged growl escaped her lips as she stalked toward Seth.

"I hate you!" she hissed, her golden eyes blazing like a forest fire. Her hand found its intended mark and the sound of flesh meeting flesh cracked like the thunder.

As Brianna dashed from the room, Seth rubbed his stinging cheek and muttered under his breath. When he had seen Priscilla the previous evening, she had sworn that she had collected all of her belongings from the plantation. Damn that deceiving wench! He should have had one of the servants toss Priscilla's clothes into the creek instead of relying on her to tend to the task. Suddenly a wry smile crept to Seth's lips as he recalled something that Grant had said. Perhaps it was for the best that Brianna had found the gowns. He chuckled to himself and strolled back to his own room to change clothes.

As Brianna flew down the steps, fighting back the tears, Grant gazed up at her with a bemused frown. "What the devil is wrong with you?" he questioned as he watched Brianna brush past him and storm toward the front door.

"Everything! And it's all your fault!" she snapped in raw fury, turning flaming amber eyes on her bewildered brother.

When the door slammed behind her like the clapping of thunder, Grant continued to frown in confusion. What the hell had he done to upset her? She had not been in the house over an hour. He had hardly had the opportunity to do more than greet her. With a hopeless shrug, Grant stuffed his hands in his pockets and started up the steps. His wife was waiting in their room and *she* had no complaints about him. A demure smile tugged at the corners of his mouth, knowing what awaited him at the top of the stairs. Sabrina was all that he ever wanted. Let Seth handle Brianna. Grant had paid his dues for twenty-one years as that ornery little misfit's brother and he had only made matters worse. Now it was up to Donnovan to corral that wild spirit of hers. As Grant entered his room, all thoughts of

Brianna fled. Sabrina lay on the bed with a provocative smile curving her lips. Grant returned her willing grin as he closed and locked the door.

Brianna gathered her stallion's reins and leaped to his back in her haste to escape from Seth and the image of the dainty blue room that matched Priscilla's taunting eyes. Digging her heels into Tyr's flanks, she urged him to a gallop and reined toward the pasture. The devil stallion leaped the fence and bounded into his fastest gait. Brianna leaned against Tyr's neck, allowing the tears she had so carefully held in check to burst from her eyes in a steady stream.

Seth was cruel and heartless. How could he have tortured her so spitefully? She would only have played such a ruthless trick on her worst enemy. And that was exactly what Seth had become—the challenger who sought to destroy her. Well, he would not see her simpering and whining. Nor would he defeat her, Brianna vowed determinedly. She pulled Tyr to an abrupt halt and slid from his back, allowing the laboring stallion to catch his breath after his wild run. She had never backed down from a fight and was not about to start now. If Seth wanted a war then, by damned, he would have it! She would tempt him, taunt him, even pretend to seduce him at times, and then cast him aside. He could go to Priscilla for comfort, but only after Brianna refused to allow him to touch her. She would make him desire her. Priscilla would become his consolation. Seth would yearn for the woman he could not possess, just as he had longed for Weatherby's wife. *Damn him!* Brianna cursed in a gritted growl. She would make that scoundrel rue the day they ever laid eyes on each other, she vowed spitefully. And when she returned to Bristol, Seth would know that there was one woman who had not succumbed to his powers. *The devil take him!* He had often accused her of being a witch, but at that moment, Brianna could have sworn that Seth was the devil himself! She could just imagine the wicked smile that had curled his lips when she had stormed from that room.

Brianna clenched her fist at her side and stalked toward the clump of trees to kneel down beside the stream. After she had washed her face and dried it on her skirt, she peered curiously about her, suddenly finding interest in the countryside that she had failed to notice in her fit of temper. Wandering along the footpath, she explored the area by the creek, carefully watching for any snakes or other dangerous creatures that she might come across.

When the sun began to fade on the blue horizon, Brianna decided it was time to return to the plantation. As she turned back to follow her footprints along the muddy path, she gasped startledly as a long shadow fell across the stream.

White Hawk stood on the high bank above her with his arms crossed on his bare chest. He arched a dark brow as Brianna glanced up at him.

"What are you doing here?" she breathed as her heart slowed its frightened pace. "You nearly scared my wits from me."

As Brianna lifted her skirt and climbed the rocks toward him, White Hawk squatted down and extended his sinewy arm to assist her to the top of the bluff. His strong hand clamped about her elbow as he drew her up by his side.

"We go to our village. I saw you in the meadow," the chief explained as his black eyes slowly appraised Brianna's torn gown. "Why have you come here?"

Brianna shrugged leisurely as she gazed down at the path that led back to the pasture. "I was just exploring."

White Hawk caught his breath as he peered into her golden eyes, carefully observing Brianna while she was unaware of his intense inspection. The sun seemed to sparkle in those vivid pools. They radiated with an inner strength that White Hawk was quick to admire. She was a rare woman, he mused thoughtfully.

"Will you come to my village with me?" he questioned abruptly.

Her delicate brow arched at his sudden request and she gazed deeply into his dark eyes. Brianna knew why the British had referred to Indians as savages. There was something wild and uncivilized about their virile, partially clothed bodies. And yet they were a noble and proud people whom she found fascinating. White Hawk was like a beast of the wilderness who could move with the swiftness of a panther and the soundlessness of the wind. She could not fear this man. He had earned her respect and his mere presence could warm her soul.

"No one but you knows where I am. They might come searching for me if I do not return," Brianna replied quietly. "If not for the others I would go with you."

"When the sun wakes again to warm the earth, I will be here waiting for you," White Hawk murmured as he lifted a necklace over his head and placed it around Brianna's neck. "When my brother sees this, he will know where you are going."

As White Hawk turned away and disappeared into the brush, Brianna stood mesmerized by the peacefulness of her surroundings and the silence with which the chief had vanished. A thoughtful frown creased her forehead as she edged down the rock slope to follow the footpath. Why did White Hawk want her to see his village? What had he meant when he said Seth would know where she was going?

It was after dark when Brianna returned to the house. As she stepped inside, the warmth of the fire that blazed in the study drew her like a moth to the flames. Brianna shivered as the dampness of the evening settled on her shoulders, and she knelt by the fire to ward off the chill. Thoughtfully staring at the crackling embers, she sighed wearily. She could have been happy here if Seth could only forget about Priscilla and offer his love to his wife. Brianna's temper had mellowed after meeting White Hawk. The events of the afternoon faded. She had survived Seth's cruel treachery. The tears of humiliation had dried, yet a sense of hopelessness pierced her heart. Brianna had fallen in love with the man she had married, and his only concern was torturing her. A rueful smile parted her lips as the vision of her father appeared in the glowing fire. His curse had followed her across the ocean to this new land. Maybe she deserved to be married to a man like Seth and suffer this strained existence after all the misery she had caused her father. Gerald would be delighted if he knew that the man he had chosen for her had stolen her heart and handled it carelessly.

Brianna felt a presence in the room. Her eyes strayed back over her shoulder to see Seth standing behind her, his arms folded on his chest. His gaze carefully swept her disheveled appearance, but he made no comment about the condition of her clothes.

"I had your room prepared. All of the excess garments have been removed," he informed her in a bland tone.

Brianna needed no reminder of the incident that had sent her fleeing in outrage. The mere sight of Seth brought the scene to mind.

"You wasted your time," she replied crisply. "I do not intend to stay in that room while I remain on this plantation."

Seth strolled up behind her and then squatted down on his haunches, lifting a tangled ebony curl from her shoulder. A faint smile grazed his lips as he toyed with the lustrous strands. "Would you prefer to sleep in the master bedroom?"

A mischievous grin threatened the corners of her mouth as she glanced at Seth. Perhaps he thought his gentle tone and his light caress could erase the hurt and bring her to his bed. "Aye, I would prefer it, m'lord," she murmured as she raised parted lips to him, intending to lead him to the edge of the cliff before shoving him off.

A flame of desire shot through him when he kissed her. His arms enfolded her as he pulled her to him. She accepted his embrace although she was silently cursing him for what he had done. A long moment passed before Seth could force himself to draw away.

"I'll have the tub prepared for you, Brianna," he whispered as he helped her to her feet. When he noticed the necklace she was wearing, his brows knitted into a thoughtful frown. "You are going with White Hawk."

It was not a question, only a simple statement of fact. Brianna returned his frown. How did he know that she was going with White Hawk just because she wore the necklace? When Seth made no further comment, her frown deepened. Perhaps Seth had asked the savage to dispose of her. That scoundrel would stop at nothing to have her out of the way once and for all, she thought bitterly. Maybe the necklace was a sign that she was to meet with the same fate as the snakes that had their tails severed. Brianna shrugged away the thought. White Hawk could have disposed of her earlier if that had been his intention.

Seth sat in the chair in his bedroom, casually puffing his cigar, watching Brianna bathe. His eyes burned hungrily over her flesh, touching every inch of exposed skin. He had been pleasantly surprised when Brianna had not ordered him out of the room. Since he was permitted to feast upon the tempting sight, he made no attempt to disguise the lust in his gaze.

Brianna was aware of the effect she had on the loathsome cad. She inwardly chuckled as she eased back against the rim of the tub, relaxing in the soothing water. Let him think she would accept his caresses without protest, she mused spitefully.

It was childish vengeance that spurred her, wanting to hurt him as he had hurt her earlier that day. Brianna stood up in the tub, water droplets glistening on her skin. Her expression was masked in a willing smile that reached out to Seth from across the room.

He bit into the end of his cigar and swallowed with a gulp. She appeared to be some immortal goddess who was bathed in beads of sunlight, so pure and serene that Seth swore all over again that she was indeed a witch. She was calling to him with those captivating eyes, taunting him, pushing him to the limits of restraint. His gaze boldly touched her as she slipped the white gossamer gown over her head and carefully smoothed it into place.

When he finally dragged his eyes from her alluring figure and focused them on her face, he held his breath, wondering if she had forgiven him and was prepared to offer herself to him.

Brianna came to him and bent over him, allowing him to seduce her with his gaze. If she had not been so intent on revenge she would have wilted beneath his rakish smile.

"Do you like my gown?" she murmured, her finger tracing the sensuous curve of his mouth.

"I like it very much," he breathed appreciatively as he snuffed out his cheroot and pulled her down on his lap.

His hands roamed over her breasts as she curled up like a contented kitten, purring softly. "Do you wish to make love to me?" she asked brazenly.

His searing kisses trailed down the hollow of her neck to her bare shoulder, bringing an unwilling response of goose pimples skitting across her skin. "What do you think?"

Her reckless chuckle floated about him. "Perhaps."

Seth wrapped his hand around her neck, bringing her head to his. His kiss began gently as he parted her lips, but as his tongue explored her mouth, his embrace became more passionate and demanding. Despite her attempt to remain unaffected, Brianna felt her heart doing flip-flops beneath her breasts. He had a strange power over her, even when she was doing her damnedest to feel nothing for him.

"And then again, perhaps *not*," he said with a devilish grin as he lifted her to her feet and stood up himself.

Brianna shot him a contemptuous glare that would have left a lesser man cowering in the corner. When he laughed at her, her temper came to the end of its short fuse. Brianna grabbed the figurine that sat on the stand by the chair, intent on hurling it at him.

"Careful, my dear," Seth chided mockingly. "That is a valuable work of art. If you break it, I promise you'll pay for it—one way or another. And I shall decide how to extract its worth from you."

"Get out of here!" she spat furiously, her golden eyes spewing fire as she cocked her arm to throw the statue.

"With pleasure, madam," he replied, chuckling at the angry red that had made fast work of staining her cheeks.

Brianna's temper exploded. Before she realized what she had done, the figurine crashed against the door and shattered on the floor. Seth strolled back inside the bedchamber and crossed his arms on his chest, staring at the broken statue that lay at his feet.

"Madam, you really must learn to control your temper. You will have this entire house laying in a shambles at our feet," he said dryly. "'Tis time that you and I come to an understanding."

Brianna's chin tilted defiantly as he stalked toward her. "I think we understand each other perfectly."

"Nay, Brianna. You seem to forget that I am your husband and the master of this house. When I give a command, I expect it to be followed without argument." His voice was low, but Brianna did not mistake the thread of anger that laced his tone.

"And *you* seem to forget that I am not your slave. I do not take orders from you. Only when you have earned my respect will I follow your *requests,* but never without question," she assured him as her voice rose testily.

"Madam, you have respect for no one."

"That's not true," she defended as her golden eyes locked with the icy green pools. "I respect White Hawk. He is a man among men. He saved *my* life and yet he treats me with dignity and honor."

"And do you love him?" His tone was softer. The hatefulness had vanished.

What kind of question was that? Brianna thought to herself as she cocked her head to the side. "Love? Aye, in a special way," she conceded quietly.

"'Tis good that you do, my dear," Seth assured her as he lifted the necklace into his hand. "If you are to be his squaw, you will be much happier if you can be content with him and your life among the Indians. However, it will be most difficult for me to explain to your father that you chose to become one of the barbaric savages. The British have difficulty accepting the proud heathens as well as you do."

"Squaw?" she repeated as her eyes widened in bewilderment. "I have no intention of becoming a squaw. What are you talking about?"

A lopsided grin curved one side of his mouth upward as he gazed into her delicate face. She didn't know. But, of course not. White Hawk would have naturally assumed that she had understood. "White Hawk gave you his necklace as a symbol that he wants you as his woman. If you go to the village with him, he does not intend that you return."

"*What?*" Brianna gasped. "But you and I are married. How can he think that I would wed him when I already have a husband? A rather lame excuse for one, but a husband nonetheless," she added flippantly.

Seth chuckled at her biting remark. "The white man's customs are of little importance to the Indians, Brianna. If you become one of them, it will make no difference to the chief that you were once wed, or that you have slept with another man. Do you remember that I told you that life begins for the Indian when he and his squaw are as one?" he queried as he hooked his arm about her trim waist and held her face in his hand, searching the vibrant pools of gold for some hint of emotion. "If you wish to go with him, I will not stand in your way. I will allow you to make your own decision."

If he cared for her at all, he would have insisted that she stay and obviously he didn't. But Brianna could not live with the Indians, nor could she accept White Hawk when she loved Seth. "You don't care, do you?" she questioned as her thick lashes brushed lightly against her cheeks, shielding her eyes from his unwavering gaze.

"I did not say that, Brianna. I said I would not stand in your way," he corrected as his hand caressed her

366

cheek. He lowered his raven head to seek her tempting lips.

His tender kiss seemed to melt the anger that had coursed her veins a few minutes earlier. Brianna gingerly wrapped her arms about his neck, yielding to his warm embrace. A soft moan escaped her lips as his strong arms encircled her and lifted her from the floor. All of her solemn vows to keep Seth at a safe distance and to refuse his caresses vanished among the shadows as he carried her to his bed. She wanted him, but more than that, she wanted him to desire her, to possess her if only for this night. As his skillful hands roamed across her pliant flesh, she shivered uncontrollably and sought his lips in passionate response.

A wildfire seemed to ignite in Seth as Brianna silently urged him to take her. It was in her eyes. Those fiery pools of amber were alive with flames of desire. Seth could not deny himself the pleasure that awaited him. Venturing through the fires of hell would be worth the cost if he could have this vixen. The gentleness was gone from his touch as urgency encompassed him. He was driven by the winds of desire that fanned passion's tempest into a wild eagerness that sent his heart racing. It had been an eternity since he had held her in his arms, kissing those tempting lips, and caressing her magnificent body. He could not get enough of this woman. She could drive him insane with the want of her, and yet he hated his weakness.

The raging blaze consumed their flesh as Seth moved above her. She opened her thighs to him, shamelessly offering herself to him. And then, as she eagerly accepted his hard thrusts, Seth knew that she had taken him. He was her possession, holding him within her, drawing from his strengths. As he clutched her close, striving for unattainable depths, their souls were forged by the fire of desire and they were one, gliding on rapturous clouds, unaware of all else. Time was held suspended in ecstasy as they clung together. There was only the moment—no past to tear them apart, no future to separate them.

Seth shuddered above her and held Brianna so tightly that she could barely breathe beneath his heavy body. But she had been to heaven. No price was too great to pay for the rapture that she had found in his arms. As Seth lifted himself from her and gathered her in his arms, a contented smile parted Brianna's lips. She laid her head back against his sturdy shoulder and gazed into his emerald eyes. Seth returned her grin. He carefully removed the leather band from her neck and then laid it on the table by the bed. When he turned back to Brianna, he searched her face with his probing gaze before he touched her lips in a light, feathery kiss.

"You have repaid me for the figurine—far more than its original cost," he teased as his kisses trailed across her bare shoulder.

Brianna arched a delicate brow as she glanced sideways at him. A hint of mischief radiated from her amber eyes. "Shall I break another one?"

"Nay, madam," Seth chuckled as he rolled to his back and lifted Brianna above him. "We have yet to pick up the pieces of the first one."

As Brianna's silky hair tumbled over her shoulders to surround them, she pressed a taunting kiss to his lips. "I had no intention of allowing you to sleep in your own bed tonight," she confessed. "But now that you are here, I don't think I will allow you to leave."

Seth's arms came about her and his hands traced a weaving path to her shapely hips. "I don't plan to sleep in my bed if you intend to remain in it," he retorted with a sober glance. When Brianna attempted to pull away, annoyed with his remark, he pressed her to her back.

He leaned over her as he laid his leg across her thighs to hold her securely in place. A mocking smile curved the corners of his mouth upward as Brianna glared up at him. "Not yet anyway," he finished with a wicked chuckle. "And then again, maybe not at all. Even when I think I've had my fill of you, I find myself wanting more. You may not sleep at all tonight, my tempting witch," he warned in a raspy voice as he lowered his head.

"Witches do not survive on sleep," Brianna assured him in a provocative whisper.

As she wrapped her arms around his neck, Seth touched her lips that tasted like wine. He instantly lost himself to the intoxicating brew and the subtle fragrance that clung to her. His senses reeled in delight as she boldly caressed him, arousing a passion that was unquenchable when she was warm and willing in his arms. Again they drank from the fountain of desire and found themselves drifting on an endless sea, cradled on the rocking waves that lulled them to sleep. And each time Brianna moved beside him, Seth came from the depths of drowsiness and took her in his embrace, sending them from dreams to ecstasy. He made love to her as if there would be no tomorrow. And yet, he found forever in her limitless passions.

Chapter Twenty-Three

As the first light of dawn sprayed sunbeams across the room, Brianna stirred slightly and slowly opened her eyes. Carefully slipping from the cozy quilts she grabbed the necklace and hurriedly donned her breeches and shirt. She could not leave White Hawk to wonder what had become of her, not after all he had done for her. She owed him an explanation.

After saddling Tyr herself, she led the stallion outside the stables and climbed onto his back. Without command the dark steed lunged forward, seemingly knowing his destination. Brianna made no attempt to rein him. With the crisp, cool air billowing through her hair, she smiled to herself, listening to the mighty steed's powerful hooves thundering across the meadow. As she pulled him to a halt, she slid from his back and followed the path to the bluff where she had met White Hawk the previous evening. When she looked up to the rocks above her, she sighed despairingly. Perhaps he had left and she would have no opportunity to say farewell. While Brianna stood staring at the ground, kicking at the pebbles by her feet, a long shadow fell across her. She glanced back up to see the magnificent savage who was clothed in buckskin and a headdress of colorful feathers that streamed from his raven hair to his broad back.

"So you have come." His dark eyes slowly swept her shapely form.

Brianna nodded slightly. "Aye, but . . ." her words trailed off as White Hawk looked past her and frowned.

When Brianna gazed over her shoulder, she saw Seth standing behind her. He moved quietly, never making a sound to alert her to his presence. A new respect for Donnovan grew as she appraised the fringed buckskin garments that Seth wore. With his bronzed skin and dark hair he did indeed appear to be White Hawk's blood brother. Her jaw sagged slightly as she continued to study his virile form.

"What kind of man takes his brother's woman when he knows that his brother does not wish to give her up?" Seth questioned in the red man's own language.

"What kind of man would allow his woman to roam this land like a creature of the wilderness if he had truly claimed her as his own?" White Hawk countered as he crossed his arms on his chest and gazed down at Seth.

"Would you attempt to hold the hawk captive and chain it to the ground? This is no ordinary woman. You yourself have said those very words, White Hawk. I do not keep her at my heels like an obedient squaw. Her spirit is untamed. She cannot walk. She must fly," Seth defended as he met the chief's unwavering gaze.

"Will you two speak in English? I have a right to know what you are saying," Brianna interrupted as she sent both men an irritated frown.

"I saw your woman with two other white men. One wanted her and the other would have killed her. If she is your woman then why do you not watch over her with the eyes of the eagle?" The Indian turned dark, steady eyes to his brother and waited his reply.

"Many men have wanted this woman," he answered as he moved a step closer to Brianna. "I have spent many sleepless nights trying to find a way to protect her

371

without tying her down. Could you find a way to hobble this one without turning her against you?" he challenged as a mocking smile curved his lips. "You say that she walks with the sun in her eyes and darkness on her shoulders. If White Hawk seeks to make her his squaw she will then be just a woman, no longer the strong spirit whose powers match the sun and moon."

White Hawk considered his brother's words as a thoughtful frown gathered on his brows. "And you will allow her to remain free in the white man's world after the danger she has faced?"

"She has survived much trouble and only once has she been forced to rely on a man to rescue her. Only you have come to her aid. But tell me, White Hawk, was the rattler you killed protecting this woman or attacking her?"

The Indian glanced away to gaze out over the land, again contemplating his brother's comment. Then he nodded reluctantly. "She stays in your world. But when you come to collect the furs that my people have gathered to trade, you will bring Golden Eyes with you to my village." A rueful smile touched his bronzed lips as his eyes rested fondly on Brianna.

As Brianna started up the rocks, she reached up to White Hawk and he squatted down to pull her up beside him on the bluff. Brianna lifted the necklace from her head and gently took his hand to return his gift. "I will come with Seth. I am honored that you would want me," she murmured softly before reaching up on tiptoe to place a kiss on his rugged cheek.

White Hawk placed his hands on either side of her face, gazing deeply into the golden pools that had first captured his interest. He had never seen eyes so bright and colorful, and he stood mesmerized for a long moment before turning his attention to Seth.

"Watch over this one, my brother, or the gods of my

people will no longer smile fondly on you," he warned in his own native tongue.

"You ask a great deal," Seth replied as a hint of a smile brushed across his lips.

Both men exchanged knowing glances. The chief dropped his hands from Brianna's face, spun on his heels, and quickly disappeared among the dense trees.

Brianna edged down the slope toward Seth and raised quizzical eyes to him. "What did he say?"

Seth laid his hand on the small of her back, urging her along the narrow footpath. "He told me to keep an eye on you or I would not be welcome by the Tuscaroras. I only hope he realizes how difficult that task is."

A mischievous grin spread across her lips. "Perhaps it was meant as a curse," she retorted with a chuckle.

"No doubt." His expression sobered quickly. "To whom was White Hawk referring when he said he had seen you in another man's arms?"

Brianna shrugged leisurely. "Perhaps it was Captain Barton. When we were walking by the creek after our ride, he became rather friendly," she replied glibly.

Seth snorted disgustedly. "No wonder White Hawk thought you were not really my woman."

As Brianna arched her brow, she sent Seth a quick glance. "I am not really. I have your name, but our agreement did not demand fidelity. Since you have chosen to wander elsewhere I saw no reason why I should not do the same." There was a hint of bitterness in her voice although she had attempted to sound indifferent.

"That agreement has become an annoying thorn in my side," Seth mused aloud.

Brianna quickly slapped his hand from her waist and turned to face him, squaring her shoulders and tilting her chin defiantly. "Do you think I haven't wished that

I had not bargained with you?" she asked caustically. "All that has come from this arrangement is misery. I should have dived overboard and ended the torture before I even set foot on shore!"

"You would have had to push me out of the way if you wanted to be first in line, madam," he smirked, slightly amused that she had misinterpreted his previous remark. "I considered feeding myself to the sharks on more than one occasion."

"Then why didn't you allow me to go with White Hawk? I would have never known that he had not planned to return me. You would have been rid of me once and for all."

"Because somehow you would have managed to escape from the Tuscaroras and would have returned, intent on slitting my throat. No doubt, you would have accused me of not telling you what White Hawk had in mind," he explained as a wry smile played on his lips.

Seth knew her well. She would have been so infuriated that she would have found a way to get even with him. Returning his smile, she shrugged noncommittally and strolled up the bank to where Tyr had been tethered.

Seth quickened his pace to catch up to her. "You would have come back with revenge in your heart, wouldn't you, Brianna?" he persisted as he grabbed her arm, detaining her attempt to swing into the saddle.

A deliciously wicked grin parted her lips as she met his inquisitive gaze. "Aye," she assured him as she removed his hand from her arm. "Revenge and something more."

"What?" he questioned as he cocked a curious brow.

Brianna stepped into her stirrup and settled herself in the saddle before looking down to him. "You may never know, my *dear* husband. You may never know."

"Why not?"

With a reckless shrug she reined Tyr away from Seth. "Because I may never have cause to tell you."

A muddled frown creased his forehead as he watched the black stallion canter across the pasture. Seth hurried to his mount and quickly pursued the dark-haired vixen. When he caught up with Brianna, he pulled on Tyr's reins, bringing the steed to a halt.

"Would you like to see the plantation, madam? I have an hour before I have to leave." Seth's chestnut sidestepped nervously after coming in contact with the stallion. Neither steed seemed particularly fond of the other and Seth spurred the chestnut. "Stand still, nag," he barked gruffly.

Brianna giggled as both horses pranced tight circles, protesting their closeness until Seth was forced to release Tyr's reins. It was that or have his arm yanked from its socket. "Where are you going?" she questioned as she patted Tyr, soothing his agitation with her gentle caress.

"I have to ride to the settlement. Patton's family lives there and I must give them the news of his unfortunate death," he explained as he watched the demon stallion calm beneath Brianna's mere touch.

"What will you tell them?"

Seth shrugged as his gaze wandered across the tall grass that swayed in the breeze. "That he died of a snakebite."

Brianna hung her head and toyed with Tyr's long mane. "And what about Jed Catlin? Lucas said he had drowned when he fell from the skiff. He couldn't swim."

"I don't know where Catlin called home. Perhaps Mrs. Patton knows."

"May I ride with you?"

"If you like, Brianna. Now, how about a short tour?" he questioned as a hint of a smile traced his lips.

After Seth had shown Brianna the tobacco fields, the sheds where the leaves were stacked to dry, and explained the procedure to her, they returned to the house for lunch. Brianna's mood was light and carefree once again and she was content to be with Seth. If they could keep from fencing with words, she would never wish to leave the plantation and return to England. But she knew that wars were made of many skirmishes. Although they had ceased fighting for a time, eventually they would be at odds, just as they had been in the past.

Seth requested that Brianna remain outside while he talked with Patton's widow. Brianna walked through the small settlement and stepped inside the dry goods store to browse while waiting for Seth. As another woman entered the store, she glanced up and listened curiously to the conversation between the woman and the merchant.

"How is the good doctor feeling today?" the store-keeper asked.

"Much better," the woman replied with a warm smile. "He insists that doctors have no time to become their own patients, but I have ordered him to stay in bed for another day or two."

"'Tis most fortunate for him that you are capable of seeing to the sick," the merchant remarked as he strolled to the counter. "Is this all for today, Miss Watkins?"

Brianna studied the young woman thoughtfully. A faint smile creased her lips and she followed the lady outside the store.

Seth heaved a heavy sigh after bidding farewell to Patton's widow. He had given her the pay her husband had earned and had slipped extra funds in the pouch, hoping it would see her through the winter. She knew nothing about Catlin or where he called home, but she had mentioned Gibbons. Seth frowned thoughtfully, wondering how Priscilla's henchman fit into the scheme. He was a frightful little man with a foul disposition. Why Priscilla kept him around was beyond Seth, but after talking to Mrs. Patton, Seth couldn't help but wonder if Priscilla had an ulterior motive. He would have to do some checking on Gibbons.

All thoughts fled him as Brianna sauntered toward him, a self-satisfied smile brimming her lips. Seth cocked a curious brow, eyeing her warily.

"Well?"

"Well what?" Brianna smiled innocently as Seth effortlessly lifted her onto the saddle.

"You look terribly pleased with yourself. It worries me."

Brianna's reckless laughter settled about him, drawing another skeptical glance from Seth. "You will find out soon enough, m'lord."

"I swear you are up to no good, witch," he accused as he swung onto his mount.

"For once you are mistaken," she assured him as she nudged Tyr into a trot, leaving Seth frowning bemusedly.

It made him uneasy, knowing Brianna had something mysterious brewing. Lord, what was that woman up to now? A reluctant smile pursed his lips as he followed behind Brianna. At least she was a pleasant diversion to the calm life at his plantation. He never knew what the next moment would hold when Brianna was around. Sometimes it was heaven and sometimes it was hell. Seth let his breath out in a rush and hastened his pace to catch up with her, wondering how long it would take for him to forget her when she returned to England, leaving a hole the size of the Atlantic Ocean in his heart.

*   *   *

When Lance Barton strolled into the entryway, Brianna was descending the stairs. His gaze remained fixed on the form-fitting breeches and shirt Brianna wore. As Seth strolled out of the study he frowned at Lance's deliberate appraisal of Brianna. After clearing his throat to make his presence known, he ambled into the hall.

"It appears that you left Petersburg and the flock of convenient women to seek out those closer to your plantation, however unavailable they might be." His eyes silently rebuked Lance's lusty stare.

Undaunted, Lance shrugged carelessly as he dragged his gaze to Seth, only to have it immediately swing back to Brianna. He sauntered over, bowing slightly from the waist as he pressed a kiss to her wrist. "There are no beauties in the city to match this wild but stunning rose that flourishes in the country," Lance breathed as his eyes made yet another all-consuming sweep of Brianna.

"Why, Captain, such flattery will have me blushing with embarrassment," Brianna chided playfully. When her eyes came to rest on Seth's condemning scowl, she pulled her hand from Lance's grasp, her expression sobering. "Tell Sabrina that I'll be waiting in the stables for her."

Barton's lusty eyes followed Brianna and rested on her shapely hips that swayed gracefully in her tight garb. "The mere sight of that woman sets my mind racing with ravishing thoughts," he mused aloud, unconcerned that Seth had overheard him.

Seth snorted disgustedly as he turned back to the study to pour them both a drink. "That is *my* wife you are discussing with your loose tongue, *friend.*"

"'Twas not so long ago that you were guilty of the same accusations, *friend,*" Lance taunted. "How can you condemn me when you thought nothing of making

378

candid remarks about Priscilla?"

Whirling to face Barton, the muscles of Seth's jaw twitched angrily. "Envy and damaged pride spurred me to say many foolish things about Priscilla. Now which of those reasons brings such words from *your* lips? And keep in mind," Seth added, gaining control of his composure, "I did not favor Kyle with my remarks. They were spoken to you in confidence. Only a fool flatters a man's wife as blatantly as you do."

"Each time in the past, when I have commented on that delicious wife of yours, you have shrugged it off, seemingly unconcerned about whom and what she did with her time. Could it be that you have actually fallen in love with that tempting wench?" Lance accepted the brandy from Seth and eased down in his chair as he arched a curious brow.

Seth seated himself across from Barton and drew two cigars from the box that sat on the table. "'Tis none of your damned business," he replied with a mocking smile as he offered Lance a cigar.

"And what of this arrangement that you made with Brianna?" Barton persisted. "Do you still allow her to go her own way?"

"I have no intention of making her decisions. She is much too stubborn and independent for me to lay down the laws for her. She would step right over them just to spite me."

"Then there will be no hard feelings on your part if I pursue her as enthusiastically as I have in the past," Lance concluded as he puffed on his cheroot.

Seth made no attempt to respond to Barton's last remark and quickly questioned, "What brings you here? Business or pleasure?"

"Both," Lance replied, allowing the matter of Brianna to drop. "I am sending my wagons of tobacco to Petersburg day after tomorrow. I thought perhaps you might be interested in taking yours along to have them loaded."

When Seth nodded affirmatively Lance continued, "I also have a message from Priscilla. She would like to see you as soon as possible. She has not been feeling well and has been in the sourest mood since you left Petersburg."

Seth shrugged nonchalantly. "She has always been plagued with a foul disposition, especially when she is not getting her way. What does she want to see me about?"

"I think she is considering the sale of her estate so that she can remain in Petersburg permanently. No doubt she expects you to see to the arrangements for her since you have managed her affairs in the past." There was a gibe in that remark and Seth was quick to catch it.

He muttered under his breath. "I'll be ready to leave Thursday morning. How long do you intend to remain in town?"

"Two or three days at the least and a week at the most," Lance replied before sipping his brandy. "I must load the cargo and check with a few merchants. We sail for England in less than two weeks," he reminded Seth. "Are the Talberts still planning to return to Bristol?"

"Aye. And you might want to talk with Grant while you're here," Seth suggested.

When Lance nodded affirmatively, Seth strolled to the door of the study to request that Grant be summoned. Sabrina had just descended the stairs and Seth gave her Brianna's message. As always, Sabrina regarded him with apprehension. Seth was well aware that she had little use for him after their first confrontation aboard the *Mesmer*. Seth had treated Sabrina roughly, and she had never forgiven him for prying information from her. She was much like Brianna, he mused thoughtfully. He watched her stroll to the front door, pause to glance back at him, and then exit with nothing more than a forced smile touching her lips.

When Sabrina walked down the stone path to the barn, Brianna was waiting with their mounts. "What are you up to?" she questioned as she observed Brianna's mischievous smile.

"What makes you think I'm up to anything?" Brianna queried as her expression became the picture of innocence.

Sabrina shot her an accusing glare. "I have seen that devilish sparkle in your eyes far too often not to recognize it at first glance."

"I'm taking you to meet a friend of mine," she explained as she swung into her saddle.

Sabrina frowned bemusedly as she stepped into her stirrup. "Who?"

"White Hawk. I saw him at a distance last night while I was riding. I thought you might want to meet him."

Sabrina gulped hard as her eyes widened in concern. "Do you think it safe to search him out? After all, he is a savage, Brianna. I'm not at all sure I would enjoy being captured by those redskins."

Brianna waved her hands for silence. "Don't be ridiculous. You have a misconception of the Indians, just as I did. When you see White Hawk, you'll quickly change your opinion. Indians are just like white men. There are some honorable ones and they have their scoundrels. I can name more than a handful of white men whom I consider worse heathens than any Indian I have yet to meet."

"Your husband for one," Sabrina scoffed as she wrinkled her nose.

Brianna shot her a reproachful glare and Sabrina quickly defended her comment. "Well, he hasn't treated you very well. You will be much better off when you return to Bristol with Grant and me. Leave him here where he belongs—with the heathens and savages."

Brianna gave her ebony hair a denying shake as she rode along beside Sabrina. "Seth is not as bad as that, Sabrina. 'Tis just that he is his own man and chooses to do things his own way. How could I ever condemn him for that?"

"Because he has treated you unfairly," Sabrina insisted in a harsh tone. "He flaunted that woman right in front of you. I saw him several times at the hotel when you were stashed away on the schooner. Honestly, Brianna, I don't know how you could remain with him after what he has done, unless you were hopelessly in love with the blackguard. And surely you could not be so foolish as to give your heart to that miserable cad. Not after all the respectable men you have turned away from your door in Bristol."

When Brianna ducked her head to consider Sabrina's words, Sabrina groaned disappointedly. "Don't tell me you are actually in love with him?"

Brianna nodded slightly. "I'm afraid I am, Sabrina. I know the very idea borders on insanity, but I do love him. Perhaps part of the reason is because I could never maneuver him as I could the others. He does not grovel at my feet like those bungling fops in Bristol who were always all too eager to offer flattery. More than once I have envied your relationship with Grant. I know that Seth and I will never share such a peaceful existence. But I am more miserable when I'm away from him. We have had less arguments since we left Petersburg and . . ." Her voice trailed off quietly.

"Priscilla," Sabrina finished for her. "You may as well learn to say her name, Brianna. You cannot ignore the fact that she is his mistress. I saw her exquisite gowns being carried from your room and it was not too difficult to see what type of arrangement they had." Although Sabrina knew she was being cruel, she hoped to bring Brianna to her senses. Seth was not good enough for her.

"Enough!" Brianna snapped angrily. "You have made your point."

"Very well," Sabrina said with a reckless shrug. "I have had my say and obviously you chose to accept him as he is—a frivolous rogue who has a heart of solid rock. At least I tried to open your eyes to your folly. I will say no more."

"Thank you, Sabrina. I greatly appreciate your silence in this matter," Brianna retorted caustically.

"Now where is this savage?" Sabrina questioned as she stood up in the stirrups and squinted her eyes as she scanned the area.

"I don't know exactly. He will find us."

"What kind of man is he? The way you describe him it would seem that he has eyes in the back of his head and the alert ears of some wild beast," she taunted with a smirk.

As they made their way along a dry gully, Sabrina gasped in alarm as she glanced up to see the bare-chested savage standing above them on the cliff. A broad smile lightened Brianna's face as she met White Hawk's coal black eyes. When they had ridden along the winding path, White Hawk stepped from the brush and lifted Brianna from her stallion.

"Did you not think that your brother was capable of keeping track of me?" Brianna teased as his strong arms swept her from the saddle and held her a long moment before releasing her.

A sly smile touched White Hawk's lips as he gazed into the amber eyes that danced with sunrays. "You have spent too much time with my sharp-tongued brother, Golden Eyes."

Brianna chuckled lightly as she turned in front of him. She looked up at Sabrina who sat on her bay gelding, her jaw sagging, her pale blue eyes wide in amazement. It was obvious that she was impressed with the Tuscarora chief whose bronzed body rippled with strength. "This is Sabrina," she managed between chortles. "I did not want her to return to England with the wrong impression of the red man. At least one of my fellow countrymen will be able to speak the truth about your people."

White Hawk stepped around Brianna and lifted Sabrina down beside him. "I saw this one too, the day I first saw you, Golden Eyes."

Sabrina still had not found her voice and could only stare at the magnificent savage in awe.

"Does she have no tongue?" White Hawk questioned as he glanced back at Brianna.

"Aye, and she had the most difficult time controlling it only a few minutes earlier. Perhaps my brother's wife said too much before and now there are no words left for her to speak," Brianna teased wickedly as she peered around White Hawk's broad shoulders to grin at Sabrina.

Sabrina was jolted to her senses by Brianna's taunting remark and she blushed with embarrassment. "Forgive me, White Hawk." Extending her hand in a gesture of friendship, she displayed a cautious smile.

White Hawk grasped her small hand in the white man's fashion and placed a kiss on her wrist, surprising Sabrina with his chivalry.

Brianna burst out laughing at Sabrina's odd expression and then turned radiant golden eyes to White Hawk. "What brings you back? I thought you had returned to your village."

"We have come in search of game and furs. I bring many braves to hunt. When my brother comes for the pelts we will be prepared to fill his wagons," he explained as he gazed to the west. "This land is rich in game since the white man has planted many crops. The beasts use the fields as their food supply and take cover in the hills. We have been fortunate in our hunt."

As Brianna and White Hawk walked together along the shallow stream, Sabrina hastened after them. No longer was she afraid of the red savage who carried himself so proudly.

When White Hawk had bid them farewell, Brianna and Sabrina returned to their mounts. Brianna questioned curiously. "What do you think of the red savages now?"

Sabrina displayed a wide smile. "The Tuscarora chief is a remarkable man. He was nothing like I expected."

"I thought you might change your mind once you had met him," Brianna replied with an I-told-you-so grin. "He is one of very few men whose proud nobility has given him an air of confidence without arrogance."

"And it is obvious that he is enamored of you. You should have married him instead of Captain Donnovan. At least White Hawk treats you with the respect you deserve," she assured Brianna.

"You promised not to harp on that subject," she chided with a disapproving frown.

Sabrina shrugged off the rebuke and tilted her chin defiantly. "I was speaking of White Hawk and his affection for you. I cannot help it if that scoundrel's name happened to slip into the conversation. Do you prefer that I never talk of him at all?"

Brianna chuckled to herself. It was as if she were looking at her own reflection as she glanced at Sabrina's stubborn expression. "After I cleverly managed to bring you and Grant together, I should think you could best show your appreciation by dispensing with your lectures on what I should do and with whom," she mocked dryly.

"All right," Sabrina replied as she heaved a hopeless sigh. "I will hold my tongue until we depart for Bristol. Maybe by then you will be able to talk of Captain Donnovan and see him as he really is—an infamous rake."

Brianna reluctantly allowed Sabrina to have the last word without raising her voice again in Seth's defense. After all, Sabrina was right.

Chapter Twenty-Four

Seth had not mentioned his plans to Brianna until the night before he intended to leave, purposely avoiding any argument that might arise. He lay in bed with his arms folded behind his head, carefully studying Brianna who sat at the dressing table brushing her hair.

"I'm traveling to Petersburg tomorrow to take the wagons of tobacco. Lance is anxious to have the goods loaded on his schooner, and I've agreed to help him," he announced.

Brianna arched a wondering brow as she leisurely bent her gaze in his direction. Would he ask her to go along or did he think she would be in his way? Was he going to Priscilla?

"Oh," she said lamely as she rose from the table and eased down on the edge of the bed. "How long will you be gone?" Brianna leaned over to snuff out the lantern and then glanced at Seth.

As the room filled with shadows, Seth's rich voice sent a tingle down her spine. "Three or four days. A week perhaps. It depends. . . ."

Brianna lay back on her pillow and pulled the light quilt over her breasts. "On what?" she queried curiously.

Seth's chuckle floated lazily about them as he reached over to slip his hand beneath the quilt that covered her full breasts, gently caressing their peaks to tautness. "On what awaits me when I return. Will it be heaven or hell, my lovely witch?"

Brushing his hand away, Brianna presented her back to him. "That depends, m'lord."

"On what?"

Brianna glanced back, resting her chin on her shoulder as she met his curious regard. "What you do while you're in Petersburg and how long you're gone."

"And if I hurry home will I be met with open arms?"

"Perhaps," she replied with a casual shrug before looking away.

Seth reached around to pull Brianna back against his muscular chest. His breath was warm against the hollow of her neck as his skillful hands began to make her body kindle with desire. "Would it matter to you if I said that I didn't really wish to go at all?"

A pleasureful moan escaped her lips as she was pressed to her back. Seth's mouth captured hers in a passionate kiss. Brianna was never allowed to answer as he continued to kiss her. When his lips traced a searing path to her breasts, the scorching fire that coursed through her body was all that concerned her. She found herself wanting to please him as she had never before. Their last night together before he left must be a tender memory that he could not put aside.

Her hands boldly caressed him, filling him with raging fires of passion that she alone controlled. He was her pawn, moving on command, responding to her touch as his heart raced wildly against his ribs. Brianna had learned much from him and used her skills to weave him in her spell. He was like a helpless fly caught in the black widow's web. No longer was he in command. Brianna carried him on turbulent waves that cast him from reality's shore. Suddenly he moved above her, unable to deny the breathless urgency that demanded that he take her. Brianna gasped as he pulled her to him. But then as he moved within her she was overcome by a wild, budding pleasure that took her breath away. As Seth wrapped his sinewy arms about her, lost to the rapturous ecstasy that spurred him, his ragged breaths caressed her neck. He murmured quiet words of desire before he was caught up in the height of swirling passion.

As he shuddered above her, Brianna was encompassed by an uncontrollable pleasure that sent a stream of tears trickling down her cheek. Her love for this man could bring happiness and sorrow all in the same instant.

"This bed will seem lonely tomorrow. I wonder if yours will be," she mused aloud as Seth rolled beside her.

Seth leaned over to place a lingering kiss to her lips. "Good night, Brianna," he murmured quietly.

Brianna whispered a muffled reply and closed her eyes, only to have Priscilla's face form above her. She was in Seth's arms, loving him just as Brianna had, only with far more experience, knowing how to please him in ways that Brianna had not discovered. The picture was too vivid and Brianna quickly slid from the covers and donned her robe.

As she strolled into the study, the dim coals drew her to the hearth and she knelt to stir the fire. Brianna was in an odd mood. Suddenly she was restless, discontent, and troubled. After fixing herself a drink she curled up in Seth's favorite chair and forced down the first swallow of brandy, choking on the burning brew that sent a strange sensation pulsing through her limbs. Glancing at the table beside her, she lifted the lid of the box and drew a cigar from it as a mischievous smile curved her lips. When she lit the cigar, she choked on its bitter taste and took another sip of brandy to smother the taste of the cigar. Then she drew slightly on the cheroot to drown the liquor's biting flavor. And so it became a vicious circle that Brianna found amusing. She chuckled to herself as she attempted to make a smoke ring as she had often seen Seth do when he was casually puffing on his cheroot. If her father could have seen her, it would have driven him mad. Brianna snickered again and sipped freely on the brandy that no longer left a repulsive taste in her mouth.

When she rose from her chair to refill her glass for the third time, the room was swimming about her. She grabbed for the mantel to steady herself before venturing to the corner to fetch the brandy. Brianna quickly turned her head, waited for her eyes to catch up with her, and giggled giddily as she lifted her empty glass to toast the vision of her father whose condemning eyes bore down at her.

"Here's to you, Papa," she muttered in a slurred tone. "You arranged this marriage of mine and see what it has done for me? I have tainted the soiled name of Donnovan, and the Talberts are rid of this misfit." Brianna puffed on the cigar, sending a smoky halo about her tangled ebony tresses before weaving toward the bar to fill her glass. Returning to the hearth she stared into the fire, mesmerized by the flickering blaze that reached up like curling fingers, drawing her into its magic spell. She began to copy the entrancing movements of the crackling fire and then chuckled at her silliness as she sent another smoke ring floating about her head.

"Madam, what in the sweet loving hell do you think you're doing?" Seth's tone carried no condemnation, only a hint of amusement. He had been watching Brianna for several minutes and had to strangle the chuckles that had almost burst from his lips so that Brianna would not know that she had an audience.

As Brianna abruptly turned to face him, her loosely

tied robe parted to her waist, exposing the fullness of her breasts. Seth nearly choked on his breath. With the glowing fire behind her, a rich golden hue settled on her creamy flesh, mesmerizing him as he strolled toward her. His eyes raked her seductive appearance like sharp claws that touched every inch of exposed skin, drawing a deliciously wicked smile from Brianna.

"'Tis the witching hour, my handsome rogue." Her raspy voice tickled his senses as he approached. "'Tis the time when restless spirits are about. You tread on dangerous ground. Have you no fear for your safety?"

"Strangely enough, I am prone to believe you," he replied as his emerald eyes flickered in amusement.

Brianna untied the belt of the robe, allowing the royal blue velvet to fall to the floor. Her inhibitions had taken flight and she sauntered toward Seth while another wicked grin played on her lips. As she looped her arms about his bare shoulders, she pressed the peaks of her breasts against his chest. She cocked her head to the side as she arched a delicate brow, half questioning, half answering the need that smoldered just beneath the flesh.

Seth was ablaze with desire the moment her silky skin touched his. He lowered his head to capture her lips, but a throaty chuckle shattered the silence. "I have never kissed a woman who smoked cigars. 'Tis a new experience, madam," he managed between chortles.

Brianna giggled giddily as she tossed back her head, sending the lustrous ebony strands cascading down her back. "And have you ever made love to one?" she questioned as she traced her fingertips across the dark furring on his chest.

"Not until now," Seth assured her as he drew her to the soft rug in front of the fire.

"I thought this study was where you came to meditate, m'lord," she murmured tauntingly. "I always thought it to be a waste."

Seth laughed softly as he ran his fingers through the dark tresses that lay at the nape of her neck. "In the future when I come here to think, there will be one memory that captures my thoughts, my enticing witch. It will be this night and I'm certain I will have one hell of a time routing the picture of you from my mind," he mused aloud as his all-consuming gaze roamed over her satiny flesh.

Suddenly, all playfulness vanished when their eyes locked. An electrifying spark bridged the gap between them, spurring a breathless desire. Seth's skillful hands caressed her pliant flesh and she eagerly responded to his touch. Words of want and need escaped her lips, stirring his passions like a churning whirlwind that spun out of control. His scalding kisses traced a path from her neck to the peaks of her breasts and she arched to meet his wandering caresses, moaning softly as she yielded to the arousing sensations that flooded her veins. Brianna gasped as his kisses continued to move to her abdomen, leaving each inch of skin that he touched burning with desire. He was teasing her to breathless heights of ecstasy, driving her mad with the want of him.

Brianna twisted away and pressed him to his back, her hands roaming boldly over his muscled flesh, wanting to arouse him to delirious rapture, making him want her as much as she ached for him. Her caresses rediscovered the feel of his finely toned body, taunting and teasing until it tore at his thoughts, stripping them completely.

Seth crushed her to him, his sinewy arms like bands of steel that held her so tightly that she could barely draw a breath. But it didn't matter because Brianna no longer recognized that she was suffocating in a passion that overruled the body and flesh. She was in Seth's arms, loving him so completely that nothing mattered.

Her name was on his lips as he lifted her from him and moved above her, no longer able to deny his need to be a part of her, spiraling to passion's pinnacle. Seth came to her with an urgency that drove him to the brink of his sanity and he pressed against her womanly softness, groaning in tortured ecstasy as he possessed her. Thrusting deeply, striving for unattainable depths of intimacy, he moved within her, oblivious to all except the rapturous sensation that demanded fulfillment. She could make him forget another world existed when he was consumed by blazing desire.

Brianna dug her nails into the hard muscles of his back as he took her to the heights and depths of pleasure. As he shuddered above her, clutching her to him, a breathless moan escaped her lips. She surrendered to the overwhelming emotion that held her suspended, unable to move, barely able to breathe, unsure whether it was reality or fantasy that had drained every ounce of strength and left her helpless.

An endless moment held them together as they nuzzled in their contented embrace. Heaving an exhausted sigh, Seth forced himself to roll away and then gathered Brianna into his arms. When she laid her head against his sturdy shoulder and smiled drowsily, Seth chuckled and placed a fleeting kiss on her tempting lips.

"Do you plan to spend the rest of the night here, madam?" he questioned hoarsely as he propped himself up on an elbow to gaze down into her perfect face.

"I suppose we would have the servants' tongues wagging if they found us like this, but I'm not sure that I have the strength to move," she whispered, her golden eyes glowing with the pleasure of contentment.

As Seth slowly rose to his feet, he pulled Brianna

up with him and grabbed his breeches and her robe. "You're right. We would be found out and we wouldn't wish to taint the soiled name of Donnovan," he managed between chortles.

If Brianna had been in full command of her senses she would have blushed, knowing that Seth had seen and heard all of her outrageous performance while thinking that she had been her only audience. But as it was, she merely shrugged and returned his mocking smile. "Nay, m'lord. It would be unforgivable to tarnish such a noble name."

Seth wrapped a supporting arm about her waist and urged her forward. When they reached the stairs, Brianna halted and gazed up the mountain of steps that she must scale to reach her room.

"'Tis a long way to our bed. Perhaps we should chance the rumors and sleep in the study," she suggested sluggishly. "I'm not sure . . ."

When Seth swept her up in his arms, Brianna's words trailed off and she nestled against his muscular shoulder. Seth heaved a relieved sigh when he reached the top of the steps and quickly set her to her feet.

"You'll have to walk the rest of the way, madam," he breathed wearily, his emerald eyes slowly sweeping the disheveled beauty.

"Shall I carry you the last mile?" she questioned as she arched a delicate brow.

"If I thought you could, I would readily accept your offer." Seth clutched her arm and led her to bed while a fond smile played on his lips. After watching his bewitching wife that evening, Seth was certain that there was nothing she couldn't or wouldn't do, except that which was physically impossible for such a petite lass.

Brianna nestled in his protective embrace and squirmed beneath the light quilt like a contented kitten seeking comfort. Seth pressed a light kiss to her forehead before surrendering to drowsiness. But he was awakened again in the early hours before dawn as Brianna's hands roamed boldly over his naked flesh, bringing him from the depths of sleep to the heights of rapture. He smiled to himself, wondering how this lively vixen could entangle him so hopelessly in her mysterious web. Her passions were as fiery as her temper, her kisses were as intoxicating as wine, and her caresses could set his thoughts spinning in rapturous chaos. She was unpredictable, impulsive, irresistible, and Seth could only shake his head in wonder before sinking back into dream-filled slumber while the memory of that night became a mélange of fact and fantasy.

When Seth stirred beside Brianna the following morning, she could not seem to lift her aching head from her pillow. He carefully eased from her side to dress and collect his belongings. Before leaving, he strolled back to the bed to place a kiss to her lips. His light touch made her unconsciously cuddle beneath the quilts.

Seth paused at the door and glanced back at Brianna. Her long ebony hair streamed about her in thick tangles. The exquisite features of her face were soft and serene in repose. He had seen the many faces of this witch-angel, and here was yet another to stir his thoughts. Brianna was like the wind that could be calm and gentle, bringing a slight caress to the tall grasses of a meadow or a light rustling to the leaves of trees. And at other times she was as violent and devastating as a whirlwind from which man and beast would seek shelter to prevent being caught up in the whipping gales of anger and fury. She was ever changing, constantly moving, tireless. And at moments like these, when he saw her so quiet and delicate, Seth was left to wonder if a man could ever capture the spirit of such a remarkable woman who could take him to heaven or hell without his ever knowing for certain where he was going until he was there.

Hopelessly shaking his head, Seth closed the bedroom door and descended the stairs. Even if he lived to be one hundred, he would never be able to predict that witch's moods. One look in those fathomless depths of gold that were rimmed with black lashes could quickly convince him that it was impossible to read her mind. She was such a strange concoction of devastating beauty, cleverness, and boundless imagination. Brianna had an uncanny knack for brewing mischief. If she could find no trouble stewing, she merely used her own well-seasoned recipe. In no time at all the world about her was steaming with a heady aroma that no man could ignore.

When Seth approached Lance who waited in the entryway, he was still chuckling to himself as the vision of Brianna rose above him again. She was scrambling into his carriage, thundering across the park on her demon stallion, strolling seductively toward him while a provocative smile played on her lips; she was standing before the glowing hearth with a smoky halo encircling her ebony hair. And then she was moving toward him with no restraints, urging him to make love to her, boldly caressing him, sending him soaring to limitless heights of passion until—

"What are you grinning so wickedly about so early in the morning?" Lance questioned as he cocked a curious brow.

Seth chortled again as he met Barton's quizzical regard. "If I told you, I doubt that you would believe me."

A bemused frown creased Lance's handsome face as

396

he followed Donnovan through the door. "Where's Brianna? Isn't she coming down to bid us farewell? I had hoped to see her before we left."

With another hearty chuckle Seth held open the door for Barton and met his confused gaze while his emerald eyes danced with pleasure. "Brianna bid me farewell last night," he explained with a rakish grin. "All night. . . . That witch has more spells to cast upon a man and 'tis a wonder that I survived."

The implication of Donnovan's words made Lance roll his eyes in disbelief. "You expect me to swallow such nonsense?"

Seth shrugged nonchalantly. "I told you that you probably wouldn't believe it."

The lazy smile that played on Seth's lips on the long ride to Petersburg did much to arouse Barton's curiosity, but Seth would not reveal anything that had happened. He just sat there with that silly, damned grin that was driving Barton mad with inquisitiveness.

Brianna barged into Grant and Sabrina's room without bothering to knock, her carefree tune floating about like a songbird chirping on a spring morning.

"What do you think you're doing?" Grant muttered and then squinted his sleep-drugged eyes as Brianna drew back the drapes, allowing the bright sunlight to invade their room.

"'Tis too beautiful to sleep the day away. I've planned an outing for the three of us," she announced as she tossed an old pair of Grant's breeches to Sabrina.

Grant sent his sister a suspicious frown. "What deviltry are you up to now that Seth has left you to your own devices? I promised him I would try to restrain you if you began showing signs of returning to your old tricks."

Brianna rested her hands on her hips and shot him an annoyed glance. "Do you consider a picnic harmless enough?" Her delicate brow had a mocking tilt as she continued to peer at her brother. "I had planned for us to do some fishing with nothing more dangerous than a line and hook."

Sabrina bounded from bed and grabbed the garb Brianna had brought for her. "That does sound like fun. I haven't been fishing in ages."

Grant resigned himself to the fact that he would have to accompany them, but then he had nothing better to do, especially if Sabrina was going out.

"Are you coming?" Brianna questioned impatiently.

"Aye, I suppose," Grant breathed, his tone lacking enthusiasm.

"Well?" She stood at the foot of the bed, staring at Grant. He was just lying there with his hands folded behind his head, studying the ceiling, as if something there held his undivided attention.

His brows furrowed bemusedly as he bent his gaze to Brianna. "Well what?"

"If you're going, why are you still lying there?" she queried, her expression surprisingly innocent.

His breath came out in a rush and he rolled his eyes at the ridiculousness of her inquiry. "Because you are still here."

Brianna stared at him in astonishment. "Since when did you develop the quality of modesty?"

"Since I married," Grant grumbled and then gestured toward the door. "Now will you please leave so I may dress?"

A taunting smile hovered on her lips as she sauntered toward the door. "I've seen you in your unmentionables for the last twenty years. I cannot understand why you're suddenly shooing me out and Sabrina has the right to remain just because she signed her name on a marriage license."

Beet red made fast work of staining Sabrina's cheeks. "Brianna . . ." Her glare was a warning signal that she did not approve of the direction the conversation had taken.

Brianna's shoulder lifted carelessly. "Well? It does sound a bit preposterous doesn't it?"

"Get out!" Grant ordered sharply, feigning his irritation, but it was difficult to hide his smile when Brianna's eyes were sparkling mischievously.

"I'm gone," Brianna assured him as the door closed behind her.

As Grant started to rise, the door creaked and Brianna poked her head inside, sending Grant beneath the quilts. "I'll be downstairs waiting for you."

"Fine . . . wonderful," Grant grumbled as he flicked his wrist, waving her away. "Just shut the damned door."

"'Tis done!" The door slammed with such force that the picture hanging on the wall crashed to the floor.

Sabrina giggled in spite of herself as she walked over to replace the picture, her eyes dancing in amusement. "That's the Brianna I remember."

Grant swung out of bed and donned his breeches. "Aye, so do I," he agreed. "That ornery little hellion. She always did love to antagonize me."

As Sabrina drew the gown from her shoulders and tossed it aside, Grant's eyes made a sharp turn and halted on his attractive wife. When he strolled up behind her, his arms slid about her waist, drawing her trim body back against his. There was a familiar question in his gaze as he turned her in his arms. When his lips descended upon hers, Sabrina had to drag herself away from his intoxicating kiss.

"Brianna is waiting for us," she reminded him in ragged breaths.

His hands dropped to his side as he heaved a frustrated sigh. "Ah, yes, the picnic. Personally, I would prefer to picnic right here in our room," he added, his eyes taking on a suggestive gleam that Sabrina had no trouble detecting.

She reached for her breeches and shirt and hastily shrugged them on, casting Grant a coy smile. "That can be arranged . . . later."

A rakish grin curved the corners of his mouth upward. "Then I suppose I can endure fishing in the great out-of-doors. . . ."

Brianna impatiently tapped her foot until her brother and sister-in-law finally appeared at the top of the stairs. "I was about to give up on you," she muttered as she grabbed the lunch basket and headed for the front door. "If you don't quicken your pace, the fish will have already taken their dinner and will turn up their noses at the bait!"

Grant smiled secretively. That was Brianna—always in such a rush to go and too impatient to remain anywhere for long intervals. He was willing to bet that she would grow restless with fishing before an hour had elapsed.

As they rode along the path that led to the creek, Sabrina glanced up at the low-hanging branches that shadowed the road, a fond memory coming to mind. "Brianna, do you remember the time we were staying at your country estate?"

"You'll have to be more specific. We spent many childhood days there." She was too engrossed in thoughts of Seth and their last encounter to guess what incident Sabrina had in mind. She had chastised herself over and over again for the way she had behaved. It wasn't difficult to imagine that Seth had laughed all the way to Petersburg. She had made a fool of herself occasionally, but that last shenanigan took the cake!

"Remember the time we climbed up the tree to wait for Grant and Robert to ride down the road. We straddled that rough, uncomfortable branch the better part of the afternoon."

Grant chortled lightly. "And we heard someone giggling. Two little imps were perched above us with braided pigtails hanging over their shoulders, wearing the clothes I had outgrown and had thought were discarded." A thoughtful frown creased his brow as he glanced at his sister. "I wonder if that was the moment Robert fell in love with you."

Brianna's shoulder lifted indifferently. "I rather doubt it. Robert didn't approve of such attire. He preferred to see ladies in dresses, not breeches. I always thought he was a bit stuffy."

"If that was the way you felt about him, why did you consent to be his wife?" Grant questioned curiously.

Brianna frowned at his prying question and gave it a moment's thought. "I suppose I just wanted to hear a marriage proposal." A smile worked its way to her lips when she noticed Grant and Sabrina's muddled expressions. "If I was to be an old spinster, I wanted to be able to say that I had at least been asked and that I chose not to accept."

Grant returned the smile. He could picture Brianna with graying hair, sitting in front of the fire, spectacles propped on her nose. She would be repeating some of her adventures. And he could hear her saying that she had tried almost everything once and that she had lived her life *her* way. Aye, she would be an interesting old woman, and yet Grant wondered if she would ever give up that adventurous spirit and resign herself to rocking in a chair beside the hearth. He doubted it.

"I will agree that Robert was not your type, but he was still very much the gentleman," Grant said blandly.

"Unlike your present husband," Sabrina interjected, the words flying from her lips before she could bite them back. She had a strong opinion of Seth and it was difficult for her to contain it. When Grant and Brianna shot her reproachful glares, she tilted a stubborn chin. "It *is* true even though neither of you want to admit it. No man with any sense of decency would treat Brianna the way Seth Donnovan does. And what baffles me the most is that you endure it, Brianna. It is out of character. One day I'm going to tell him exactly what I think of him, even if you won't."

Grant's hand snaked out to rein Sabrina's mare to a halt. "You seem to forget that Donnovan owns the horse upon which you sit and the house where we are staying. He has been very generous to us and I happen to like him," he reminded her in a clipped tone.

"And you also have a fondness for stray dogs and old women," she countered, her voice heavily laden with sarcasm. "Not that I disapprove, but befriending that unscrupulous rogue is carrying things a bit far."

"Sabrina, I think you have said quite enough," Grant snapped gruffly.

"Here is the fishing spot I told you about," Brianna interrupted, bringing their bickering to a speedy halt. She was having enough difficulty keeping Seth out of her thoughts without having Grant and Sabrina arguing about what she should do.

"How do you know the fishing is grand here?" Grant inquired, thankful for the change of subject.

A wry smile grazed her lips as she swung from the saddle. "A friend of mine told me so."

"Who?" he prodded as he stepped from the stirrup and untied the picnic basket from behind his saddle.

"Just a friend," she replied vaguely.

As Grant had predicted, Brianna had grown tired of the simple outing within the hour. She walked restlessly along the bank of the creek while Grant and Sabrina dragged in fish as fast as they could re-bait their hooks.

A movement in the brush caught Brianna's attention and she ambled away from the couple who were engrossed in their fishing.

"Where are you off to?" Grant questioned, casting her a quick glance before his gaze returned to his line.

"I'm going for a walk," she called over her shoulder. "If I'm not back by the time you decide to leave, just go on without me."

"What the devil is she up to now?" Grant mused aloud.

"White Hawk," Sabrina said quietly as she watched Brianna disappear in the brush. "He's never far away when she is about."

Grant scrambled to his feet, but Sabrina grabbed his arm to detain him. "Let her go. White Hawk would never hurt Brianna. She's far safer with him than she is with that two-timing husband of hers."

He regarded her for a long moment and then squatted down on his haunches beside her. "What has turned you against Donnovan?" he questioned point blank.

"Don't ask." Her chin tilted stubbornly as she stared off into space.

"Don't ask," Grant mimicked. "That is exactly what Brianna said when I asked what incident sent them their separate ways on board the *Mesmer.*"

The dawn of understanding hit Sabrina like a slap in the face and she despised Seth even more. She could well imagine that Seth had insisted that they consummate the marriage which was to be nothing more than a convenience, allowing both of them the freedom they desired. Sabrina would never forget how rough the captain had been with her. He had kissed her so

403

demandingly that Sabrina could barely draw a breath beneath his devouring assault. Brianna had probably put up a good fight, but she was no match for his male strength.

Sabrina squeezed her eyes shut, blocking out the picture that formed in her mind, knowing that Brianna had most likely suffered a worse fate than she had the night Donnovan had interrogated her. One day she would tell Seth Donnovan what she thought of him, and in no uncertain terms. That scoundrel deserved to be hanged from the mast of his own ship!

Her vengeful thoughts melted when Grant's playful kisses trailed a path along the back of her neck. She would worry about what she wanted to say to Captain Donnovan later, but for now . . .

"I believe 'tis time for our own private picnic," Grant murmured as he nibbled at the corner of her mouth.

Sabrina was given no time to reply. His lips captured hers and she was hopelessly lost to the man who had stolen her heart.

White Hawk crept from the bushes, following in Brianna's shadow. When she glanced back at him, his dark eyes were carefully scrutinizing her. There was a hint of puzzlement in those fathomless depths and Brianna frowned curiously.

"Is something wrong?"

He gestured to her attire. "Do all the women from your country dress in this manner? I noticed that Sabrina was wearing breeches."

Brianna chuckled slightly. "Nay, and I'm afraid most of them would be appalled at the sight of some other woman wearing them, but personally, I find them more practical than cumbersome gowns."

His eyes made a deliberate sweep of her shapely figure and then he gave her a smile. "I do not think other women could wear them as well as you do, Golden Eyes."

Brianna was flattered. White Hawk's compliment was open and honest. If only she and Seth could share such intimacy, perhaps their marriage wouldn't have been a disaster. Instead, they talked in circles, avoiding the important matters that plagued them.

"Where is Donnovan?" White Hawk questioned, bringing her from her silent reverie.

"He has gone to Petersburg on a business matter," she explained, wishing that was the real reason for his journey. But she knew better. It was because of Priscilla.

White Hawk's bronzed hand slipped beneath her chin, raising her reluctant gaze to his. "And do you miss him?" he queried frankly.

"I have been keeping myself occupied."

A hint of a smile made its way to his lips. This golden-eyed goddess intended to reveal nothing of her feelings for his blood brother.

Brianna removed his hand from her face and turned away. "I suppose I had better go back."

"If you do, you will be interrupting," he informed her, his smile widening to encompass every feature of his face.

It wasn't difficult to imagine what White Hawk was suggesting. Of late, Grant had nothing but Sabrina on his mind. She was well aware that he had consented to go fishing only because Sabrina anticipated the outing; otherwise, he would have never made it past his bedroom door.

White Hawk clasped his large hand around hers, leading her through the brush. "Come, Golden Eyes."

When they had weaved their way to a clearing that was tightly encircled with trees, Brianna watched as the handsome savage walked over to retrieve his bow and knife. Her brows furrowed bemusedly as White Hawk strolled back to her, extending the bow.

"I taught my brother to use our weapons, just as he taught me to use those of the white man. Now you will learn the skills of the bow and knife."

A mischievous twinkle filled her eyes as she accepted the knife. White Hawk regarded her skeptically as she pointed to her target, but astonishment covered his face when Brianna hurled the blade and found her mark with ease.

Her reckless laughter filled the air as she glanced back to see his frozen expression. "But I have no experience with the bow," she admitted.

White Hawk withdrew an arrow from its sling and drew back his bow, aiming at the target Brianna had hit with the knife. The arrow sailed past her and quivered in the bark, only an inch from the knife. Brianna turned back to him, anxious to learn the technique. She listened carefully as White Hawk told her how to assure the accuracy of the bow and arrow. With practice and White Hawk's instruction, Brianna drew the bowstring back to her cheek, peered down the arrow, and released the string as the savage had explained.

When the arrow notched on the other side of the knife, White Hawk swallowed hard. He had expected her to become proficient, but not so quickly.

"Beginner's luck," she assured him with an impish grin. "I doubt that I could repeat the feat."

White Hawk withdrew another arrow and handed it to her. He had the strange feeling that luck had little to do with her accuracy. Brianna's next effort proved him correct. The arrow lodged directly below the knife. Humbly, he took the bow from her hand and hung it over his shoulder.

"You need no practice," he said flatly.

Brianna realized that she had managed to embarrass

him and that had not been her intent. "'Twas only a stroke of luck," she insisted. "Let me try again."

As she reached for the bow, White Hawk grasped her hand, holding it in his own. "I have seen enough. Many times I have taught young braves to use this weapon, but none have learned so quickly. You are blessed by the gods, Golden Eyes."

"I have no special powers," she protested.

White Hawk cupped her face in both of his hands, studying the exquisite features that continued to fascinate him. "They are visible in your eyes," he said solemnly. "You have been granted the power of strength and determination. Do not take them lightly. There are many who would give all they own to possess those qualities."

His face came slowly toward hers and she knew he was about to kiss her. But then suddenly, he wheeled away, protecting her with his body as Grant stepped out of the brush.

Both men eyed each other suspiciously until Brianna stepped between them. "White Hawk, this is my brother, Grant."

Grant's expression remained sober, offering no pleasant greeting to the bare-chested savage who towered behind Brianna.

"Sabrina and I are riding back to the house. Are you coming?"

As Brianna started to walk toward her brother, White Hawk clutched her elbow, his gaze fixed on Grant. "I will see that she is safely returned to my blood brother's home."

A stilted silence hovered between them. Finally, Brianna forced a smile for her brother. "I'll return later. Go on without me," she urged.

"Don't be long." It wasn't a request. It was a command.

As Grant marched off into the brush, White Hawk crossed his arms on his chest and stared thoughtfully after Talbert. "He does not approve of me," he mused aloud.

"Grant just hasn't given himself the chance to know you," she explained, carefully selecting her words. "He has heard too many stories about the colonists dealing with your people. I know that by the time they reach England that they have been blown out of proportion." Her chin tilted to meet White Hawk's gaze. "As for me, I know no other man whom I can confess to respect as much as I respect you, White Hawk."

A faint smile appeared as his thumb leisurely caressed her cheek. "Respect? And what of your husband?"

Brianna thoughtfully chewed on her lip a moment. "I respect him," she admonished.

"Nothing more?" he pressed.

Brianna ambled away. "I think I better return to the house."

White Hawk followed silently behind her until she reached her stallion. Before she could pull up into the saddle, he cupped her face in his hands, gazing deeply into her amber eyes. "I will be watching for you from afar. Come to me when your spirit yearns for freedom." A rueful smile hovered on his lips as he continued to study her bewitching face. "If our spirits had not been confined to this mortal flesh, perhaps we . . ." His voice evaporated in the warm breeze.

A strange sadness overcame Brianna, knowing what he had intended to say. She greatly admired the noble savage, but Seth had taken her heart and Brianna was afraid she would never be the same again. Even White Hawk could not break the spell Seth had cast over her. Her love belonged to Seth, even if he had no desire to return her affection.

"Good-bye, White Hawk," she murmured as she stepped into the stirrup and reined Tyr toward the house.

As she galloped away, White Hawk stared after her, wishing he had never laid eyes on the enchantress, but knowing his life was far richer because he had. When she had disappeared from sight, White Hawk retraced his footsteps through the brush to find his braves, but his thoughts lingered on Brianna. He had never envied the white man or his ways, but he was beginning to wish he could exchange places with his blood brother, if only for one night. Each time White Hawk drew his bow, he pictured Brianna, alert and poised, concentrating on her target. A secretive smile played on his lips as his dark eyes swung to the east, wondering what she was doing at that moment, wondering if she would come to him again.

Brianna strolled in the front door and halted abruptly when she met Grant's angry glare. It was a look that he rarely bestowed on her. He had always been good natured and patient until he was pushed to his limit. It took a great deal to annoy him, but when he reached his breaking point, Brianna always preferred to be a safe distance away.

Her brow furrowed puzzledly. What had she done to deserve that irritated expression. "Is something wrong, Grant?"

"Where the hell have you been? I expected you to be only a few minutes behind us. We arrived forty-five minutes ago," he snapped sharply.

Her chin tilted defensively. "You have paid very little attention to me these past few months. Why have you suddenly decided to keep such close tabs on me?"

"Because you seem to have forgotten yourself, Brianna," he shot back at her. "You are a married woman and I do not enjoy watching my sister with a savage!"

His voice was so harsh that Brianna did a double-take, wondering if it truly was her own brother who was raving at her.

"How can you criticize me when my husband is probably parading around Petersburg with another woman at this very moment?" she countered, her voice rising testily.

"'Tis *your* morals that concern me most," Grant insisted as he stalked toward her, brown eyes clashing with gold ones. "You've always been as ornery as the devil, but you always maintained your sense of decency . . . until now!"

Brianna gasped at his biting insult. "How dare you suggest that White Hawk and I . . ." She couldn't finish the sentence. As she glared at her brother, her chin tilted a notch higher. "I have done nothing to be ashamed of. Seth is the one who deserves your criticism, not I. You and I are flesh and blood. I expected you to come to my defense, not his!"

"I caught you embracing that savage, but I have yet to see your husband with another woman in his arms," Grant retorted, gritting his teeth to keep from bellowing at his sister.

"Only because you have not been at the right place at the wrong time, as I have. He is by no means perfect," she sniffed caustically.

"Nor are you," he mocked, his tone as sarcastic as hers.

Brianna brushed past him, giving him the cold shoulder. "I'm going to my room. I do not wish to discuss the matter."

Grant grabbed her arm, his lean fingers cutting into her flesh. "I am not yet finished, Brianna," he assured her, his eyes narrowing into hard slits.

"Then you may talk to the walls if you wish, but I will hear no more of this!" Brianna yanked her arm from his grasp and marched toward the stairs, but Grant followed at her heels.

"Do you love him? Tell me yea or nay," he demanded.

"To whom are you referring? The so-called savage who possesses every quality of a gentleman or my unfaithful husband whose description fits that of a savage?" she taunted as she leveled a gaze to Grant.

"Donnovan, of course," he snorted impatiently.

Brianna turned to squarely face her brother, a mischievous smile brimming her lips. "Perhaps if you hadn't been so gruff with me, I would have answered that question. You have behaved so rudely that I feel no obligation to respond to you, brother or not."

"Why are you so damned stubborn?" His breath came out in a rush as he rolled his eyes toward the ceiling.

"'Tis just luck, I suppose," she replied saucily.

Grant's temper mellowed and an unwilling smile caught one corner of his mouth. "Brianna, I care a great deal about you. If I didn't I wouldn't—"

"Meddle?" She cut him short. "That *is* what you're doing."

His head dropped and he shrugged slightly. "Call it what you wish, but the fact remains that I want the best for you. I don't want you to destroy your chance for happiness."

Happiness? Brianna was beginning to wonder if she had forgotten the meaning of the word. Her brother's sympathetic expression touched her heart and she reached out to clasp his hand. "Please don't worry about me, Grant."

"But I do," he breathed in exasperation.

Brianna curled her index finger beneath his chin,

raising his gaze to hers. "Thank you for caring," she murmured softly.

When Brianna had closed the door behind her she heaved a frustrated sigh. There was a time that she confided everything to Grant, but it seemed they had drifted apart. Admitting her innermost thoughts was difficult now, especially when Grant was so determined to see her marriage work, apparently at any cost. Brianna could not forfeit her pride and that was what she had to lose if she admitted to loving Seth. For some reason, Grant considered himself to be her guardian and he couldn't be satisfied until her life was arranged. But how could she confess to love a man who didn't return her affection? How could she admit that her fickle heart had at last been tamed by a man who had no desire to claim it?

Brianna felt tears scalding her eyes, but determinedly, she wiped them away. Why hadn't she returned to her father instead of sailing to the colonies? Being at Seth's plantation, waiting for him to return was torturous. Why had fate thrown them together? Brianna sank down on her bed and yielded to the tears that threatened to wash her away. She was so lonely and miserable. Never in her life had she known such agony.

The master of the Donnovan plantation was gone a full week and each day that he did not return caused Brianna more distress. She had made a complete fool of herself by behaving so outrageously the night before he left. She had probably driven Seth back to Priscilla who would never dream of acting so shamelessly. Seth was undoubtedly relieved to be away from his wife and was in no hurry to return, Brianna mused despairingly.

When Seth finally arrived at the plantation, Brianna was riding Tyr and did not come to the house until late afternoon. Seth was leaning casually against the door of the study when she entered the house.

"You're back," she stated cooly, quickly masking the pleasure of seeing him again.

"So it appears," Seth replied before sipping his brandy. "Would you care to join me in a drink, madam?" His heavy brow arched mockingly and Brianna bristled at his remark.

That lopsided grin that brimmed his full lips brought a disgruntled frown to her features. "Nay, I've decided to avoid brandy."

"You once told me you would never touch another glass of champagne. Now 'tis brandy. Perhaps you would like to try some wine," he suggested as he sent her a quick sidelong glance.

"Nay, sir, I have come to the conclusion that all types of liquor have a tendency to play havoc with my sanity. I think perhaps I should partake of nothing stronger than tea if I am to keep my wits about me."

"Do I detect a hint of bitterness in your voice, madam?" Seth mocked, his dark brow arching even higher.

Brianna shot him a disdainful glare and stalked upstairs to her room without bothering to reply. He would probably never allow her to forget what a fool she had made of herself. *Damn that rogue!*

Seth frowned thoughtfully as he stared into his glass and swished the liquor around the rim. He had hoped for a cheerful reception when he returned from Petersburg, but Brianna did not seem overjoyed to see him. As a matter of fact, it appeared that his presence had caused her distress. With a casual shrug he ambled back to his desk to finish the bookwork that awaited him. There was no way of knowing what thoughts flowed in that woman's mind and he was wasting his time attempting to analyze her.

*　　*　　*

When Seth walked into the bedroom later that night, Brianna appeared to be sleeping. Although he was tempted to wake her, his own stubborn pride bade him to leave the wench alone. If she could ignore him as if his return was as inconsequential as another bee reappearing in a crowded hive, then he could damned well play that game too. He was not about to beg for affection. *Damn that wench!*

Chapter Twenty-Five

A strained silence became a barrier between husband and wife after Seth returned from his journey. Seth would be damned if he would play the simpering fool to receive her attentions. Brianna was too proud to bend to the passions that pleaded to be fulfilled when darkness crept into their bedchamber and she heard the slight creaking of the bed when Seth eased down beside her.

Only on the day of the party which was being held in honor of their marriage did Brianna put aside her bitter thoughts and prepare for the ball with renewed enthusiasm. She was gay and carefree again and Seth quickly noted that the devilish gleam had returned to her golden eyes. A curious frown gathered on his brows as he watched Brianna dress in a pale blue gown that displayed her shapely form and the fullness of her creamy breasts. The torture of observing her as she flounced about the room, arranging her hair and completing her toiletry was even more agonizing to Seth. Brianna seemed so preoccupied with some delicious thought that she refused to share with him.

"You're certain that Derrick will be here?" Brianna questioned for the third time in less than an hour.

Seth heaved a frustrated sigh and turned away from the tempting witch. "Aye, madam, but why do you keep questioning me about him? Your secretiveness is most distressing. I cannot imagine why you are so interested in seeing Derrick unless he is planning to sweep you up onto his white horse and whisk you away," he remarked glibly.

"You'll find out when the time comes," she retorted as another deliciously wicked grin set her eyes sparkling like priceless gold nuggets.

After she hurriedly exited from the room, leaving Seth with his muddled thoughts, Brianna checked with the cooks to ensure that the refreshments were prepared and that all was in its proper place.

When Seth joined her in the entryway to greet the guests, he introduced Brianna to his friends and neighbors, noting that every man's eyes were prone to linger on the low bodice of velvet and lace. It seemed that he was destined to spend the evening watching his friends and associates gawk at the bewitching wench that he had claimed as his wife. When Derrick arrived, Brianna shrieked delightedly and hugged him close, startling both Seth and Derrick with her over-zealous show of affection. Tugging impatiently on his arm, she led Derrick into the ballroom and promptly instructed him to dance with her. Seth strolled to the door and watched enviously as Brianna smiled up at Sayer, her amber eyes flicking with unmistakable happiness, her cheeks blushing with excitement. Perhaps it was Sayer who had truly won the vixen's heart, Seth mused sullenly as his intense gaze followed the couple across the dance floor. Maybe he had left Derrick in Brianna's company much too often, thinking that his trusted friend would keep her out of trouble. Seth had always been aware of Derrick's devotion to Brianna, but now he was left to wonder if she returned Derrick's obvious affection.

"Do you know what you are to do?" Priscilla questioned as she glanced quickly at the small, disfigured man who sat beside her in the carriage.

"Aye, Mrs. Weatherby. I will tend to this with pleasure." His wicked chuckle lingered in the stillness of the night, sending a cold shiver down Priscilla's spine.

She was repulsed by the sight of the henchman's scarred face, but she knew that she could depend on Gibbons to see to this business. "After I give her the news, she will undoubtedly flee from the house. Just make certain that she does not escape from you. Do with her what you will. Keep her for yourself, sell her to the savages, whatever you wish, but never allow her to return," she demanded firmly as she placed a sack of coins in his gnarled hands.

"If I did not hold a grudge for this wench, I might consider taking her, but it will give me greater pleasure to dispose of her," he replied in a raspy voice that was laced with revenge.

Priscilla arched a wondering brow, but did not question the man's remark. With a reckless shrug she stepped from the carriage and walked gracefully toward the front door of the Donnovan mansion, her thoughts spinning in excitement. Before the evening ended Seth would be hers again. Nothing and no one would come between them.

Brianna urged Derrick out onto the terrace and glanced around his broad shoulder, making certain that the other woman waited in the swaying shadows.

"I have someone I want you to meet Derrick," Brianna began, attempting to muffle the joyous laughter that fought to be released.

Derrick cocked a curious brow and regarded the lovely lass with a great deal of wariness. He had seen that mischievous sparkle in her amber eyes on too many occasions not to know that something was brewing.

"Hello, Derrick," came the soft voice from behind him.

The color immediately drained from his face as he gazed down at Brianna's blinding smile and recalled the voice that he had come to hear only in dreams. He turned slowly to see the small, dark-haired woman whom he had known in another lifetime.

"Barbara," he breathed in awe and disbelief.

As they embraced, Brianna leaned back against the railing, watching the scene that melted her heart and brought a sentimental tear to her eye.

"How . . ." Derrick had difficulty finding his voice as he turned a questioning gaze to Brianna who hastily wiped away the tears with the back of her hand.

"When I was in the settlement south of here, I over-heard Barbara and the storekeeper talking. After you had described Barbara to me, I was almost certain that she was the same woman you met during the war."

Derrick stared at Brianna for a long, quiet moment, still holding Barbara close. Only this lovely witch could have found a needle in a field of haystacks or searched out one very special woman when he himself had failed, he mused before focusing his attention on the delicate lass in his arms.

"My father and I were held captive by one of the British regiments," Barbara explained, seeing the questions in Derrick's eyes. "They forced us to travel with them and care for their injured soldiers. We escaped from them after the battle at Yorktown. Father took up his medical practice in the settlement. We did not attempt to return to New York after the Revolution. My father was content to remain where we were and I could not leave him."

They had much to discuss and Brianna decided that she was no longer needed. As she stepped inside the terrace doors, her happy smile vanished when she spied Priscilla hanging on Seth's arm like a clinging vine. But it was Brianna who was as envy green as the ivy to which she had just compared that disgusting wench. Seth was grinning down into Priscilla's face and Brianna was inwardly fuming. The nerve of that woman! How could she show her face at their wedding party? After Seth had escaped from Priscilla's possessive clutches and disappeared into the entryway, Brianna walked toward the redhead, her golden eyes narrowing to cold, angry slits.

Sabrina had stepped forward to speak to Brianna, but when she realized what her sister-in-law had in mind, she paused to watch Priscilla display her sticky-sweet smile.

"What are you doing here?" Brianna questioned icily, clenching her fists at her side to keep from clawing that pretentious grin from Priscilla's pink lips.

"I am the one who arranged the ball and saw to the invitations," she replied flippantly. "I saw no reason why I shouldn't come since Seth and I are such *close* friends."

"You never quit, do you, Priscilla?" Brianna arched a mocking brow. "You have even put aside your pride in your attempt to make an utter fool of yourself."

Priscilla laughed recklessly and toyed with the white lace that trimmed the sleeve of her pink silk gown. "I am not the fool, Brianna. 'Tis you, my dear. Your husband comes to me to seek his pleasure and chooses to remain by my side. I am the woman that he desires."

"'Tis often difficult for a man to recover from a dreadful illness," Brianna began as a spiteful flicker flashed in her amber eyes. "But given time he will recuperate from the disease. And you, *dear Priscilla,* are the sickening disease for which there *is* a cure."

Priscilla was undaunted by the younger woman's biting words because she was certain that her next remark would send Brianna into a fit of rage. When she stalked away, Gibbons would be there to dispose of this annoying wench once and for all. "I am the one with the illness. At least some women consider it to be." Priscilla shrugged casually. "However, I do not consider pregnancy to be a dreadful sickness. To me, 'tis a welcomed pleasure since your husband is the father of the child I carry."

Brianna's eyes widened in shock and she stilled the urge to strangle the vicious wench. Priscilla had expected Brianna to burst into tears and flee from the room, but Brianna was too proud to allow the crafty bitch to outwit her. Quickly summoning her composure she met Priscilla's self-satisfied grin. "Then 'tis your misfortune, Mrs. Weatherby, because your child will never claim the name of Donnovan or the fortune that you desire. You have made me all the more determined to keep my married name. And do enjoy the party," she added as she forced a shallow smile.

As Brianna disappeared among the guests, Priscilla frowned worriedly. What would it take to rout that troublesome wench from Donnovan's bed? Priscilla had to get Brianna out of the house or her plan would never meet with success.

Sabrina had edged close enough to eavesdrop on the conversation and had nearly choked on her drink when Priscilla made her announcement. By the time Sabrina had gathered her wits and sought to find Brianna, she was nowhere to be seen. Seth Donnovan was a scoundrel, Sabrina muttered under her breath. He had treated Brianna shamefully. Having his mistress at his wedding celebration to break such humiliating news to Brianna was unforgivable! The man was heartless, vicious, cruel, ruthless . . . Sabrina gritted her teeth and silently fumed at this despicable situation in which Seth had embroiled Brianna. If she did not agree to return to Bristol, then Sabrina would make certain that Grant forced her to come with them! Damn that Donnovan! He was the devil incarnate!

As Seth confronted one and then another of his guests, inquiring about Brianna, it seemed to be an invitation for a conversation about his wife's beauty and charm. But that was not what concerned him at the moment. Her whereabouts had him baffled. Derrick had told him that she had been on the terrace and had disappeared from sight. Seth had sent a maid upstairs to search her out, but she was nowhere to be found. The only place he had not considered was the study where many of the men had gathered to play cards and heavily partake of his good stock of liquor. *Lord, she wouldn't dare,* Seth muttered under his breath. Women did not intrude on a gambling table. Surely Brianna had not joined them.

Making his way through the crowded ballroom, Seth marched to the study door to find what he had hoped he wouldn't see—Brianna sitting at the crowded table with many of his friends, shuffling the deck as agilely as a card sharp. About her hovered the gentlemen who had lost their stakes and chose only to watch the finale. Their eyes roamed over her creamy breasts that were temptingly displayed in the gown that he had specifically selected for the occasion. The leering gazes of those whom he had named as friends were boldly touching his wife. Seth was instantly reminded of a sky full of circling vultures that eyed their prey, waiting for the right moment to swoop down and devour their feast. And Brianna . . . If he could have plucked her from the hungry-eyed group at that moment he would have strangled her! She had a stack of coins beside her elbow that would have paid a king's ransom. Damn that witch! If she had cheated his friends out of their money, he would indeed choke the life from her!

Seth ambled into the room and casually poured himself a drink, attempting to control the rage that had him boiling like a volcano that was about to erupt. When he appeared in the study, guilt seemed to appear on the faces of those who had been gawking at Brianna instead of watching the cards. The men repositioned themselves as Seth came up behind his wife. Brianna glanced over her shoulder to see Seth's jaw twitching angrily, but she returned her attention to her hand, her expression masked behind a carefully blank stare.

"Well, Mrs. Donnovan?" Lance cocked a curious brow. "Do you stay or fold?"

"I'll stay." Brianna pushed her entire stack of winnings to the center of the table.

Lance chewed on the end of his cigar and eased back in his chair to reconsider his cards while estimating the amount Brianna had raised his bet. After a long moment, he heaved a sigh of defeat, tossed in his cards, and collected what little funds he had left. "I think I'll go seek my pleasure on the dance floor. Brianna is unbeatable tonight. It seems she has the devil's luck."

All of the cards dropped on the table as the other men nodded in agreement. Brianna had only lost two or three hands and there was naught else to do but admit defeat to the lovely lady.

As Brianna scooped the money from the table, Seth's hand clamped on her arm. "I wish to have a word with you, madam," he ordered quietly but sternly.

Brianna's face twisted as his painful grasp dug into her flesh. She strangled the cry that waited to be voiced as she turned flashing eyes on him. "You're hurting me."

"Not as much as I intend to if you don't come with me this instant," Seth threatened, his voice cracking with impatience.

He escorted her from the room and led her down the dark hall before he turned on her. "You cheated them, didn't you?" he accused in a harsh tone. He shook her soundly, fighting the urge to clamp his fingers around her lovely neck.

"You're damned right I did!" she snapped hatefully, loathing the sight of the man she thought she loved.

The vengeful spark in her golden eyes made Seth's brows furrow bemusedly. She was trembling in rage and he could not imagine that his rebuke could have spurred such a vicious reaction, not even from Brianna.

"As you once told me, if your opponent is too good and you do not intend to lose, then cheat," she continued curtly. "I plan to use the money to pay my passage back home."

"What the devil has gotten into you?" Seth was ready to swear that she had been bitten by a rabid dog and had contracted the disease after watching her snarl at him.

As he eased his grasp, Brianna jerked away from him as if she had been scorched by his touch. "The devil himself," she sneered, her eyes spewing fire. "I have overlooked his pernicious faults like a fool, but no more! 'Tis done! Finished! Do you understand me? I will take no more of this torture, but our bargain stands as it was made. I don't want to see you unless absolutely necessary."

He didn't understand. What was she ranting about? Lord, the wench was crazed! The real witch had finally possessed her and she was ready to scratch out his eyes.

Brianna wheeled away and flew up the steps, taking them two at a time in her haste to seek refuge in her room. But it wasn't her room. It was Seth's. And in it was the bed where he had made love to Priscilla. She could never again sleep in that bed, knowing that Priscilla carried Seth's child—the one that she had hoped to give him when he finally came to love her.

Angry tears stung her eyes as she choked on sobs of humiliation. She had never been one to cry over little or nothing, but since she had met Seth, tears came all too frequently. Love was agony and she wanted no more of the pain that tore at her heart and twisted at her insides. She could forgive him for having a mistress, but she could not accept another woman bearing his child, especially Priscilla, who flaunted, taunted, and tortured Brianna unmercifully. She hated them, both of them. They deserved each other.

Brianna yanked off her gown and grabbed her breeches before the hard rap at the door halted her.

"Open this door this instant!" Seth barked impatiently.

"Nay. I never want to lay eyes on you again! Stay away from me!" she stormed back at him.

There was only silence. When she remembered the door to the adjoining room, she dashed over to lock it. She had just secured the door when Seth reached the entrance.

"Damn it, Brianna, let me in!" he bellowed furiously.

"Never!" she thundered back at him. "We have nothing left to say to each other. Go find that red-haired bitch of yours and leave me be!"

She hurried back to the main door and dashed down the stairs in her haste to escape from the torture that twisted like a knife in her back. She could have forgiven him almost anything, except this. He had destroyed her love for him.

With tears clouding her eyes she hurried around the corner of the house to dart to the stables. From the looming shadows, a dark figure appeared, grabbing her and wrestling her to the ground. Before she could scream, the man's fist put quick death to her attempt to cry out for help. And then the fear was gone. She welcomed the dark silence that shut out Seth and his treachery. Her limp body was scooped up and carried away while a wicked chuckle shattered the night.

"I'll count to three, Brianna, and if you don't open this door I'll break it down!" Seth growled angrily, but he was met with silence.

Not bothering to count, he raised the heel of his boot. He kicked the door with one powerful blow, splintering the casing where the lock had been attached a moment before. As he stormed into the room his eyes swept the empty chamber and came to rest on the open door. "Damn," he muttered under his breath. What had happened to upset her? What the hell had he done that she found unforgivable?

As Seth rushed down the stairs to follow after Brianna, Sabrina met him on the landing. "Where is Brianna?" she questioned as she cast Seth a heated glower.

"She ran outside," Seth mumbled as he brushed past Sabrina in his haste to pursue Brianna.

"I wouldn't blame her if she never returns," Sabrina called after him. "What you did was deplorable!"

Seth turned on the stairs and gazed up into Sabrina's smoldering blue eyes. "Everyone else seems to know what I've done except me."

"You know exactly what has upset Brianna, but you don't even care. I told her she was foolish to put up with you," Sabrina spat hatefully. She had attempted to be courteous to her host, but no more! He had hurt Brianna and if she would not stand up to this cruel scoundrel then Sabrina would tell him what a miserable cad he was! "You have continued to

425

humiliate her by keeping your mistress around for your convenience. But Brianna claimed that she loved you and that she could live with your infidelity if it meant being near you. She has taken leave of her senses!"

Seth's dark brows shot up in surprise. "She admitted that she loved me?" he questioned as a hint of a smile touched his lips.

"Aye, she told me so and how do you think she felt when Priscilla informed her that she carried your child? How could you—"

"*What?* Priscilla told her that tonight?" Seth snorted.

"Aye," Sabrina hissed as she started down the stairs to continue her verbal attack, face to face. "You are the only man Brianna has ever loved and you have treated her abominably. I told her you were a worthless cad, but she wouldn't listen to me. Now you have finally driven her away. The least you could have done was give her the news yourself instead of letting Priscilla delight in having her revenge in a crowded ballroom. You are a heartless, ruthless scoundrel! A deceitful brute!"

Seth had heard all that he needed to know and hastened down the steps. As he dashed out of the door, Sabrina gasped in outrage. She was not finished with her name-calling, and it infuriated her that she was unable to complete her tirade of insults. She was just gathering steam and she stomped her foot and spun on her heels while muffling a long string of curses to that damned rogue. She hurried up the stairs to gain control of her temper. It was several minutes before she was able to rejoin the party without breathing fire on the first person who confronted her.

Gibbons had managed to prop Brianna's unconscious body in front of him on his horse and reined his mount toward the creek. He would take no chances by traveling the road. As he spurred the steed into a gallop, his wicked chuckle again floated in the darkness of the night.

"You cost me a fortune, wench," he growled at Brianna. "But I will extract your worth from you and receive double for the loot that you lost."

Gibbons fully intended to take a ransom note to Donnovan and collect yet another purse before he traded Brianna to the savages. He had often traded liquor to the Indians and he was certain that they would give a high price for this wench. He would be a rich man when he had gathered all of the coins and furs that he would receive for one night's work.

As Gibbons thundered across the meadow and veered south along the creek, Brianna roused slightly and he tightened his grasp on her waist. When Brianna began twisting frantically, he pulled the steed to a halt and yanked her from the saddle as a vicious sneer curled his lips.

Brianna screamed at the top of her lungs, but he held her firmly and sent her senses reeling with another hard blow to the jaw. As Brianna crumpled to the ground Gibbons grabbed for his horse, attempting to keep the steed from galloping away in alarm. Grumbling under his breath, Gibbons clutched at Brianna and dragged her closer to his flighty mount. As he attempted to hold both the horse and Brianna, the gelding reared and pawed the air with his powerful hooves, striking Gibbons on the side of the head. His agonizing scream pierced the air, frightening the horse. Another hoof struck Gibbons on the back of the neck. As he fell face down in the grass, the steed lunged forward and galloped away, leaving Brianna and Gibbons alone in the dense trees that grew along the creek.

Brianna was picked up in two strong arms and

carried back to the stream. White Hawk laid her against the gentle slope and dipped a cloth in the water and carefully washed her face. His ebony eyes roamed over her shapely form. He reached out to trace the delicate lines of her face while a fond smile curved the corners of his mouth upward. As the moonlight caressed her creamy skin, White Hawk shook his head in wonder.

"For one so small you have found your share of trouble, Golden Eyes," he mused aloud.

"Aye, White Hawk, this woman does not know the meaning of serenity," Seth assured him as he moved toward Brianna's still form. "Only when she sleeps is the rest of the world at peace."

White Hawk's smile faded as Seth squatted down beside him. "You have allowed another man to capture your woman," he accused, turning steady eyes to his brother.

Seth nodded slightly. "I knew nothing of this deceitful trick until I saw Gibbons's body. He's dead and will no longer harm her, nor will the words of another woman send her fleeing."

Arching a quizzical brow, White Hawk surveyed Seth's stern expression. "Why did Gibbons take her from you?"

Seth heaved a sigh and sat down cross-legged before facing White Hawk's curious regard. "You already know that Gibbons traded whiskey to your people, but he also worked for a woman who owned a plantation to the east. She sent this man to dispose of Brianna for her own selfish reasons. The woman didn't know that Gibbons was part of a theft ring. The man that kidnapped Brianna when you rescued her the first time worked for Gibbons. He stole jewels when we were in England. Gibbons would pawn the loot to merchants and probably used part of it to trade with your people."

White Hawk shook his head affirmatively. "I have

seen some of his trinkets. Many of my own people have traded with this viper, even when I have forbidden it."

"I don't know what he planned to do with Brianna, but I'm sure he intended to collect a healthy sum. His greed has driven him to his grave. I just found out about his business a few weeks ago when I talked to the woman whose husband was bitten by the rattler. It seems that all of those who wished to harm Brianna have met with disaster."

"And what of you, my brother?" White Hawk questioned as a faint smile creased his dark features. "Do you also meet with disaster?"

Seth nodded thoughtfully, his gaze sliding to Brianna. "There has been a war of wills between us since we first met and now I'm not certain that she will ever come back with me again. She has been hurt deeply and she is too stubborn to listen to reason."

"There has been no harmony between you. Each time you look to each other, you do not search deeply into the other's soul. If you cannot find peace together, why do you not release her?"

Turning his attention to White Hawk, Seth displayed a knowing smile. "For the same reason you chose to hunt near this plantation. I know there is plentiful game closer to your village."

White Hawk returned Seth's sly grin. "Do you no longer wish to call me brother when you know what I feel for this woman, that I would keep her with me as my squaw?"

Seth's expression quickly sobered. "I will always call you friend and brother, just as I did when your Tuscarora warriors took arms against us to aid the British. The strong bond cannot be broken by war or women."

"Even if I took this woman from you?" White Hawk queried.

"If she wanted to go with you, I would not stand in

her way. I have been selfish with her, but because of me she has suffered. Now 'tis only her happiness that concerns me. She must make her own decision," Seth murmured as he reached out to touch Brianna's cheek. "I'm afraid after what has happened tonight that I have destroyed any chance of taking her with me."

Brianna stirred slightly and a soft moan escaped her lips. Both men turned their full attention to her.

"Go now," White Hawk requested quietly. "Wait for me at the creek where the waters part."

Seth hesitated a moment, watching Brianna's head roll from side to side, and then he moved along the stream to disappear in the shadows.

As her amber eyes fluttered open, she saw White Hawk hovering over her. "Where is the man who—"

"He is dead, Golden Eyes," he quickly assured her as his arms came about her shoulder to steady her when she struggled to sit up.

"I didn't even know him. Why did he wish to harm me?" she asked in confusion.

"My brother will answer all of your questions. He knows. . . ."

"I never want to see him again!" Brianna interrupted. He had probably sent that scoundrel to dispose of her. "I want to go to your village with you and never return to the white man's world." She could never go back to Seth now. She was too humiliated and ashamed to face him or her father. A steady stream of tears flowed down her bruised cheeks as she gazed up at White Hawk. "Please take me with you," she choked out.

"You would give up your life with your own people with no regrets?" he queried, his dark eyes searching deeply into the golden pools that glistened with tears.

"Aye, and I would never go back," she assured him all too quickly.

"Because you run *away* from my brother or because you run *to* me?" he persisted as he clasped her chin in his hand, forcing her to meet his unwavering gaze.

"Both. There is nothing left for me in the white man's world."

White Hawk dipped the cloth in the water and carefully washed away the tears. "Can you leave my brother and never think of him when I hold you in my arms?"

His questions were much too personal. Painful memories flooded her thoughts. Why couldn't White Hawk just sweep her up and carry her away? Why must he know what haunted her soul?

Her hesitation brought a slight frown to his rugged face. "Do you love him, Golden Eyes?"

When Brianna turned her head away from him, White Hawk cupped her chin again, raising her face to his. "Look at me and tell me that you do not love this man who has made you weep, the one you run away from only to return to him each night."

Brianna peered into the pools of glistening ebony, wanting to say that she hated Seth for the pain he had brought to her heart. But after all that he had done to hurt her, she could not speak of contempt. She could not lie to White Hawk and she could never make the proud Tuscarora chief happy. Another tear formed in the corner of her eye and slowly trickled down her cheek.

"You cannot say the words, Golden Eyes, because there would be no truth in them. You have not told my brother of this love you keep in your heart. You must always walk in truth or you will walk alone."

His quiet words shattered her composure and Brianna suddenly threw her arms about his neck. She sobbed against his chest while White Hawk gathered her close and tenderly brushed the long strands of

431

ebony away from her face. "I cannot go back to him now. He loves another and I am too ashamed to face him or my father again."

"Has he told you this?" White Hawk questioned softly.

"Nay, but I know it just the same," she managed between sobs.

White Hawk held Brianna at arm's length, staring into her clouded eyes. His brother and this beautiful woman were too much alike to ever find peaceful harmony, he mused thoughtfully. But the bond between them was too strong to be severed. If White Hawk allowed her to go with him, she would never be truly happy, nor could he, knowing that when he made love to her that she would treasure another man in her heart. Perhaps if someone besides his blood brother had taken her, he could make her love him. But that was not the case. White Hawk's guilt would continue to plague him.

"Come, Golden Eyes," he commanded as he wrapped a protective arm about her waist and urged her along the narrow footpath.

As they walked past the high banks that rose on either side of them, Brianna glanced up to see the dark figure standing above them. She halted abruptly when she realized it was Seth. When she attempted to squirm from White Hawk's grasp, he held her firmly in place and she turned an accusing glare to the Indian.

"Brianna, I want to talk to you," Seth called down to her.

"I don't want to see you," Brianna muttered, twisting frantically in White Hawk's strong arms that held her captive.

"I have not touched Priscilla since we returned from England," Seth assured her as he edged along the bluff.

"Lies," she screeched, her amber eyes blazing fury.

"Why don't you admit the truth for once in your life!"
A hint of tears lurked near the surface and Brianna
determinedly fought them back.

"Damn it, woman. I am not lying," he insisted, his
voice rising testily. "You were always ready to believe
the worst about me. Priscilla told you she carried my
child, knowing that you would flee from me. She seems
to be much better at predicting your actions than I am.
She had Gibbons waiting for you when you ran away
tonight. I'm willing to bet she paid him a small fortune
to whisk you away. Gibbons is the man who sold the
jewels that Catlin and Patton stole in Bristol. He had
another motive for following Priscilla's orders—
revenge. You probably cost him another fortune and
two thieves that he had to replace in his ring of smugglers."

"I believe what you say about Gibbons, but not Priscilla," she hissed venomously. "She told me that you
had always loved her. If you didn't, you wouldn't have
continued to see her. You can never forget that wench
and she is welcome to you. Both of you can burn in hell
together for all I care!" The tears burst from her eyes,
scalding her cheeks as she glowered at Seth.

"I saw her only to make you jealous, to force some
commitment from your lips, but you wouldn't give in.
You're too damned stubborn!" he scoffed as he crossed
his arms on his broad chest and eyed her levelly. "I even
took your brother's advice, hoping that he had gained
some insight after living with you and learning your
moods. Grant told me that what you thought you
couldn't have was what you were determined not to do
without. He suggested that I have patience with you
and wait until you admitted that our arrangement was
ridiculous. 'Let Brianna be the one to speak of love
first,' he said. 'Don't grovel at her feet as her other
foolish suitors have done,' he said." Seth released a

derisive snort and hopelessly shook his head as he shot Brianna an angry glare. "Even your brother did not realize that you were far more obstinate than a damned jackass!"

Seth quickly closed the distance between them and roughly grabbed a handful of ebony hair, twisting it tightly around his fist. "You want the truth, madam? Then by damned for once you shall have it!" His eyes lost their angry spark and mellowed to a softer hue of green as he met her steady gaze. "I love you, you little witch," he assured her, his voice laced with affection. "I have not been able to rout you from my mind since you scrambled into my carriage late one night in Bristol. I don't even know how or when the fascination ended and love replaced it. You have threaded yourself so tightly into my thoughts that I can never be free of you. I have been to hell and back trying to tame you, but I have come to the conclusion that the task is impossible. I can't seem to live with you and I have no desire to live without you. You, madam, are an unmanageable misfit. Now I have become like every other bungling fop who had unsuccessfully tried to master your wild spirit." His grasp on her hair loosened, becoming a caress as his eyes adoringly followed the path of his hand. "I wanted to be your champion, saving you from disaster each time someone tried to take you from me." A bitter laugh escaped his lips as he hung his head. "But you have the devil's luck, m'lady, and I cannot compete with him. I would have fought your battles for you, risked my life against any odds, but you always managed by your devices. Never once can I claim to have whisked you away from the path of oncoming disaster. You always saunter away from foul situations smelling like a rose. I wish you could have needed me even once, but you haven't and I'm afraid you never will."

Seth heaved a disheartened sigh. His eyes roamed over her exquisite face, memorizing the gentle curve of her lips and the delicate lines that could harden in determination or soften in one of her tender moods. "Perhaps White Hawk can find a way to tame you, to earn your respect where I have failed. I am at my wit's end with you and I cannot ask you to remain by my side if that is not your wish."

When White Hawk felt Brianna relax in his arms, he backed away, knowing in his heart that he had lost the golden-eyed enchantress to his blood brother. The darkness of her shadow swallowed him and in the silence of the night he moved away, leaving a part of his soul behind.

A hint of a smile found its way to her lips as she looked up at the man who had long been a part of her dreams. "You, Seth Quentin Donnovan are a rogue and a scoundrel." When pain flashed in his eyes, her grin broadened and she laughed recklessly. "It took me awhile to admit to myself that I loved you, despite my better judgment. I was miserable because I was too proud to defy the bargain we had made."

Seth returned her grin as he wrapped his arms about her waist and pulled her full length against him. "And I told you not too long ago that our agreement had become a thorn in my side. You misinterpreted my meaning, my lovely witch. You were always prepared to judge and hang me before I was even allowed a trial."

Brianna looped her arms around his neck and leaned back in his encircling embrace. "I thought you were ready to be rid of me and I loved you too much to leave, even if I had to endure our quarrels and my jealousy of Priscilla."

Releasing a throaty chuckle, Seth shook his head in denial. "Nay, Brianna, I have no wish to let you go. I must admit there were times that I wanted to be rid of you because I found myself becoming dependent on the sight of those golden eyes. I didn't want to find myself hopelessly entangled in your bewitching spell."

Brianna reached up on tiptoe to place a fleeting kiss on his lips. "I love you, Seth Quentin Donnovan. If you ever so much as look at another woman, I will cut your heart from your chest and leave you as a feast for the hungry vultures."

Seth cocked a dark brow, a lopsided grin curving one side of his mouth upward. "And if you ever let another man know you as I have, I'll feed both of you to the wolves," he warned playfully.

"There could have been only one other man who might have tempted me, but I met him after I was too much in love with you. He would not have me because he knew my heart and soul belonged to you." Brianna glanced over her shoulder, her eyes sweeping the swaying shadows. "White Hawk?"

Seth reached beneath her chin and lifted her eyes to him. "He is the only one I would have allowed to take you from me if I thought he could have made you happy." Seth's countenance became serious. "He cares a great deal for you, Brianna. I have never seen him so protective of a woman."

When they heard a soft whinny, Seth and Brianna turned toward the sound to find White Hawk holding the reins of the chestnut gelding. White Hawk extended his hand and dropped the reins in Seth's hand.

"Now you ride as one," he said quietly, his gaze sliding to Brianna to linger a long moment. He slowly returned his eyes to his blood brother.

Seth smiled knowingly. "This golden-eyed witch has found her way into both of our hearts. I only wish—"

"Say no more," White Hawk commanded. "It is better for her to remain with you and her own people." He brushed his hand across Brianna's bruised cheek and smiled tenderly at her before glancing at Seth. "You must love her for both of us, my brother."

When Seth had pulled up into the saddle, White Hawk swept Brianna up into his strong arms. She pressed an affectionate kiss to his rugged cheek before he placed her on the steed's back.

White Hawk stepped away and eyed them levelly. "The bond between you and your woman will not be broken. It is as strong as our friendship, my brother. Time and trials cannot sever what your souls have forged together." A rueful smile grazed his lips. "Go in peace, as one."

Seth reined the gelding toward the plantation and tightened his arm about Brianna when she nestled against him. When they arrived at the house, most of the guests had left, but Grant and Sabrina were there to greet them.

Sabrina quickly stepped forward and then ducked her head apologetically. "I'm sorry, Captain Donnovan. I behaved shamefully. After what Grant has told me about your feelings for Brianna, I feel like a fool for speaking to you the way I did."

"I'm afraid Sabrina has been breathing the fire of dragons tonight," Grant chuckled as he glanced at Seth, who could not take his eyes off of Brianna. "Not only did she lash out at you, but she had several choice comments to make to Priscilla. When Sabrina was finished with her, the woman was in tears. Captain Barton offered to take her to his plantation for the night."

Seth nodded slightly. "'Tis good that he has agreed to comfort Priscilla. No doubt the child she claims to carry is his."

Brianna's eyes widened as she looked up at Seth, stunned by his words. Then she turned her attention to Sabrina and grinned. "You better learn to curb your tongue. Grant will declare that you are as impossible to manage as he has often claimed me to be."

"He already has," she assured Brianna with a subtle wink. "I almost had him convinced that I was perfect. Tonight I fear that I have spoiled my charade."

Grant pulled Sabrina close and pressed a light kiss to her forehead. "Nay, Sabrina, you only made me realize that I have married well. I only hope your father will be pleased with the match when we return to Bristol with the news." He glanced quickly at Brianna. "And speaking of Bristol"—Grant cocked a curious brow—"just what are your plans, dear sister?"

"I am not returning to England until my husband sails on the *Mesmer*," she replied as she looked up at Seth, lost to the depths of green that could twinkle with amusement or glow with passion.

"You are leaving me alone to face Father and Lord Rutledge? You're positively wicked, Brianna," Grant teased.

"Aye, that she is," Seth agreed, "but I'm not letting her out of my sight until I can place her in my grandfather's hands. Then I will listen to him tell me that he had arranged the perfect match and that I should have obeyed him in the first place." He cast Talbert a hasty glance. "And now if you will excuse us, I think we will retire. It has been a long evening."

When they entered the master bedroom, Brianna noticed that the door to the adjoining room was standing ajar and the lock was dangling from the splintered wood. "I see you managed to gain entrance."

"But I was met with an empty room," he chuckled as he tossed his shirt over the back of a chair. "The witch I sought had been spirited off into the night as she had been once before."

As Brianna unfastened her linen shirt and stepped from her breeches, a devilish smile curved her lips. "I have no reason to leave you again, my handsome rogue." Her voice was hushed, her tone seductive as she strolled toward him. "You should have kept your good luck charm to ward away the demons. Now you have nothing to protect yourself from me."

Seth's lusty gaze burned hungrily over her flesh. The flame of passion in those sea green pools held Brianna entranced as he spoke. "You are my golden talisman, Brianna. I married the lady who has the devil's luck and I have no need of charms on chains. I love you," he murmured huskily. "I intend to remind you of it until you tire of hearing those words."

Brianna looped her arms about his neck, smiling adoringly at him. "I will never tire of hearing them. At last my childhood dream has come true and it was worth the wait. I have never admitted to loving a man until I met you. Now I freely confess it from my heart." Her fingertips trailed over his cheek, her eyes glowing with that mysterious sparkle that Seth could never forget. "And you were very wrong," she assured him softly. "I *do* need you. You are my reason for being. Tonight I was prepared to leave you, because I thought you didn't need me, but I knew I would be leaving part of my soul behind. I need you, just as I need air to breath and nourishment to survive. I can't live without your love."

Seth crushed her to him, feeling the urgency in her own response. In breathless anticipation, they scaled rapture's mountain, finding love's heady pleasure growing more abundant at each crest. As Seth hovered above her, his eyes were alive with tender emotion. Brianna moaned softly as her heart filled with pride for the man who was bold enough to tame her wild spirit, gentle enough to spur her passions, and daring enough to earn her respect. She pulled his head to hers and opened her lips to him, wanting to be totally possessed by the man who had claimed her soul.

"I love you," he murmured hoarsely, his breath caressing her neck. "I want only to make you happy, to bask in the warmth of your love. We will live wherever you wish. Just ask for what you want and it will be yours, my lovely witch."

She propped herself above him and rearranged the tousled raven hair on his forehead. "I want our home to be here. I think this misfit will readily adjust in this young country where heathens and red savages stalk the night like packs of hungry wolves. I will miss my father and brother, but you are essential to my happiness," she assured him, her amber eyes glowing lovingly at him.

Seth's hands brushed across her shoulder in a lazy caress. "I was hoping you felt that way. Each time I travel to Bristol and walk those cobbled streets it makes me realize how much I thrive on the way of life the colonies offer."

"There is only one other place I would go," Brianna replied, a thoughtful frown gathering on her exquisite features.

Seth cocked a curious brow and glanced sideways at her. "Where is that?" he questioned, completely baffled by her remark.

The frown transformed itself into a provocative smile, her golden eyes radiating with that devilishness that Seth loved to see in them. He could lose himself in those amber pools that took his breath away with their mystique. He quickly understood what she meant. His arms came about her, an agreeable smile curving the corners of his mouth.

They sought that quiet world of paradise where time ceased to exist, where peaceful clouds touched the azure sky like a gentle kiss and the sun's warmth was like a tender caress.

"Send the world away," she murmured breathlessly as she clung to his muscular frame, loving the security she found in his arms.

Across the borders of reality, they set sail on a sea of contentment, knowing that they would find love's distant shore. For another timeless moment they lingered in their haven of ecstasy, seeking nothing more than each other's loving arms.

Epilogue

Andrew Donnovan sat at his desk, attempting to keep his mind on the papers that were spread before him. But it was useless. His thoughts were on Quentin and Brianna. When Grant had returned with the news of Quentin's marriage and a letter of explanation, he was elated. His grandson assured him that the *Mesmer* would reach port in late September. Andrew had faithfully driven to the wharf each day to find that the schooner had not yet docked. He had finally given up and remained at home. Perhaps the *Mesmer* had met with bad weather that had swept them off course, delaying their return. In any event, he was forced to wait and wonder.

Bascom strolled into Andrew's study and stood waiting until he was noticed. "Sir, there is someone here to see you."

"Show him in," Andrew requested disinterestedly.

As Quentin appeared in the door, Andrew's wrinkled face came alive with pleasure. "So at last you have arrived. I had begun to doubt that you would return at all." He pushed away from his desk and hurried to greet his grandson.

Quentin chuckled, his emerald eyes sparkling radiantly at the old man. "Not return? And miss my usual rebuke for being a frivolous rogue, or whatever subject you chose to harp upon? Nay, Grandfather, I would not think of robbing you of your pleasures." He quickly closed the distance between them and shook the old man's extended hand.

Andrew was in no mood for taunting and promptly came to the point. "Well, where is she?" he questioned impatiently.

Quentin arched a mocking brow. "I thought you would be overjoyed to see me again, but it seems I was mistaken. To you, I am merely the servant who is to deliver your valued possession."

"Damn it, Quentin!" Andrew snorted disdainfully. "I have waited over ten years to see you standing beside your bride. I do not intend to wait a moment longer. Is she staying with the Talberts?" Andrew grabbed his coat from the nearby chair and shrugged it on his shoulders, prepared to venture out to see his grand-daughter-in-law. But Quentin grabbed his arm to detain him.

"I haven't seen you move so fast in years," Quentin teased wickedly. "Brianna, you better come in here before Grandfather completely loses his patience with me," he called over his shoulder.

Brianna stepped into the doorway and smiled coyly at the old gentleman whose blue eyes made fast work of appraising her. She had dressed carefully that morning, hoping that Lord Donnovan would not be disappointed. Her hair was neatly arranged in loose curls on the top of her head and her gold velvet gown had been purchased specifically for her formal introduction to Andrew.

Lord Donnovan's brows furrowed thoughtfully as his gaze settled on Brianna's bewitching face and then lingered on the empire waist of her gown. She was even more enchanting than he had remembered, but . . .

"Really, Grandfather," Quentin chided as he walked back to Brianna and wrapped a possessive arm about her. "It is all too obvious where your eyes have strayed.

You are indeed correct. Brianna and I are expecting a child this winter."

As Andrew hastened forward to clasp Brianna's hands in his own, a proud smile alighted his face. "You have made me a very happy man, my dear. When you finally agreed to marry this irascible grandson of mine, you answered a long awaited prayer. The news that there will be a great-grandchild for me to pamper and spoil has brought me even greater elation."

With a light chuckle, Brianna turned mischievous, golden eyes to her husband. "I must admit it has been a torturous sacrifice. Only to please you, I have married Quentin." It sounded odd to refer to her husband as Quentin since she had only known him as Seth.

"I'm sure it was," Andrew agreed with a subtle wink to his grandson. "But I was certain that no other woman could hobble this rascal as well as you could."

Andrew and Brianna stared at each other for a long moment, exchanging knowing smiles.

Quentin heaved a weak sigh. "It has been a long voyage, Grandfather. I know that you would prefer to spend the next few hours insulting me, as usual, but I think Brianna should rest now. You can finish telling her of all my faults later this afternoon. I seriously doubt that she has overlooked any of my flaws," he added glibly, "but if she has, I'm sure you will have ample opportunity to bring them to her attention." He nodded slightly and urged Brianna toward the door.

"Quentin," Andrew said quietly, halting his grandson's hasty retreat. As Brianna and Quentin glanced back at him, he smiled warmly. "I only hope the two of you are as happy as I am."

Quentin nodded affirmatively before his loving gaze met the golden pools that could always take his breath away with their unmatched sparkle of devilment. "Even more so, Grandfather," he admitted. "Your clever scheme has brought me more happiness than I could ever imagine existed."

When Quentin and Brianna exited from the room, Andrew poured himself a brandy and raised his arm in toast to the lingering image of pleasure and devotion he had seen in Quentin's green eyes. "I never thought I would see the day that love was written on your face, but it was there today, Quentin. You will never be able to forget Brianna," he mused aloud. "That bewitching lass has your heart and all of my respect." A broad grin spread across Andrew's wrinkled face as he ambled back to his desk. He had lived to see his dream come true.

When the bedroom door was securely locked behind them, Seth unfastened Brianna's gown, a rakish smile parting his lips. "I'll go back downstairs to visit with my grandparents while you rest, love. I'm sure Grandfather would like to gloat over the success of his arrangement."

Brianna turned to face him, a provocative smile curving the corners of her mouth upward. "Not yet, my handsome rogue. I still have need of your services." She looped her arms about his neck and raised inviting lips to him as she whispered, "Your grandfather has waited many years. He will survive a few more minutes. But I am impatient and impulsive. You are well aware of how frightful my temperament becomes when I am not allowed to have my way."

Seth released a husky chortle as he lowered his raven head to press a kiss on her parted lips. "I know of your faults, my love, and in your condition, I would not dare annoy you."

The world about them vanished in a hazy mist as they tenderly embraced, breathing words of love and affection. They were quickly taken to rapture's haven, reveling in the blissful existence they had found together.

Andrew paced the floor of his study, knowing full well what had detained his grandson. He finally eased back into his chair and took his quill in hand. If he was expected to wait until Quentin had eased his unquenchable desires for that high-spirited wife of his, Andrew decided to give some serious thought to naming his great-grandson. And it would be a boy. Of that he was certain. He thoughtfully touched his chin as several appropriate names came to mind. He hastily jotted them down on the parchment, a satisfied smile brimming his lips. Andrew Donnovan was at last a contented man.

MORE SEARING ROMANCE
by Elaine Barbieri

AMBER FIRE   (0848, $3.50)

AMBER PASSION   (1501, $3.95)

AMBER TREASURE   (1201, $3.50)

CAPTIVE ECSTASY   (1398, $3.50)

DEFIANT MISTRESS   (1839, $3.95)

LOVE'S FIERY JEWEL   (1128, $3.75)

PASSION'S DAWN   (1655, $3.95)

SWEET TORMENT   (1385, $3.75)

Available wherever paperbacks are sold, or order direct from the Publisher. Send cover price plus 50¢ per copy for mailing and handling to Zebra Books, Dept. 0105, 475 Park Avenue South, New York, N.Y. 10016. DO NOT SEND CASH.